EUMERALLA

Secrets, Tragedy and Love

Joanna Stephen-Ward

Popham Gardens Publishing

Popham Gardens Publishing

January 2011

This edition December 2012

Copyright © Joanna Stephen-Ward 2012

The right of Joanna Stephen-Ward to be identified as the author of this work has been asserted in accordance with sections 77 and 78 of the Copyright Designs and Patents Act 1988.

The characters in this work are fictitious and any resemblance to actual persons, living or dead, is coincidental.

All rights reserved. No part of this publication may be reproduced, stored in a retrieval system, or transmitted in any form or by any means: electronic, mechanical, photocopying, recording, or otherwise, without written permission from the publisher.

Popham Gardens Publishing
www.publishingforyou.com
e-mail: enquiries@publishingforyou.com

Please visit the author's web site at:
www.joannaauthor.co.uk
for more details of this book and other books by the same author.

In loving memory of my father

Carlyle Stephen

For my husband

Peter

who encourages me to fulfil my dreams.

BY THE SAME AUTHOR

VISSI D'ARTE
A Story of Love and Music

THE DOLL COLLECTION
A crime novel

ACKNOWLEDGEMENTS

I am indebted to the members of the *Richmond Writers' Circle* for their support and constructive criticism, especially, **Gerry Ball**, **Rebecca Billings**, **Suzanne Bugler**, **Feola Choat**, **Jennie Christian**, **Peter Clark**, **Alan Franks**, **Harry Garlick**, **Michael Lee**, **Vera Lustig**, **Peter Main**, **Vesna Main**, **Annie Morris**, **Malcolm Peltu**, **Charles Pither**, **Richard Rickford**, **Mike Riley**, **Anna Sanders**, **Miranda L Taylor** and **Susan Wallbank.**

Special thanks to **Nancy Godwin**, **Laurelei Moore** and **Jenny Webb** for reading the manuscript and giving me valuable feedback.

For their encouragement I thank my colleagues at *The National Archives* especially, **Francois Belholm**, **Lucy Brain**, **Hannah Griffiths**, **Olive Hogan**, **Kelly Kimpton**, **Diana Nutley** and **Karen Perry.**

Sheena Klapper provided me with agricultural and social information about the Darling Downs, and pointed out where I had gone wrong. Any mistakes are mine.

The poem *Deserts* is by **Owen Wheatley** who kindly gave me permission to use it.

(First published in ROOM 14 AT 8 O'CLOCK, the anthology of the Richmond Writers' Circle 2001. © Owen Wheatley).

CHARACTERS

THE OLDER GENERATION

The Mitchells

Eleanor Mitchell – born 1918 (Owner of Eumeralla)
Greg Mitchell – born 1916 (Eleanor's husband)

The Clarksons

William – *born* 1885 *died* 1947
(Owner of Acacia) Married his first wife in 1912
She died in 1930.

Their Children

Laurence – *born* 1915 *died* 1965
Jonathan – *born* 1916 *died* 1946
Virginia – *born* 1918

The Lancasters

Margot – *born* 1900
David – *born* 1908
Alex – *born* 1911
Francesca – *born* 1917 *died* 1945
Ruth – *born* 1919

THE YOUNGER GENERATION

The Mitchells

June – *born* 1946
Tom – *born* 1947
Hazel – *born* 1948
Neil – *born* 1950

The Clarksons

Keith – *born* 1949 (Laurence's son)
Gabriella – *born* 1950 (Laurence's daughter)

The Lancasters

Fiona – *born* 1946 (adopted daughter of Virginia & Alex)
Catriona – *born* 1947 (David's daughter)
Kim – *born* 1948 (David's daughter)

Other Characters

Stefan Jovanovics

Marriages between the Clarksons and Lancasters

1933 William Clarkson and Margot Lancaster

1935 Laurence Clarkson and Francesca Lancaster

1938 Virginia Clarkson and Alex Lancaster

Deserts

How much of our lives we spend in deserts,
Leaving the fertile uplands – shades
Of green and the sensuous roll of raindrop
Down the central vein of a leaf from root
To tip, where, in slow motion it swells and drops,
shattering glass-like on stone,
Soaking leaf-mould with wet earth smells
Of urgent growth you can almost see.

But somehow we're here. Bone dry and bone white
The hiss of windblown sand and white light
Like a fist in the face, and swollen tongues
Scrape cracked lips in hopeless pain
While hot grit sears burning lungs
And we fall, despairing, but crawl on again,
Empty, just this side of death.

Owen Wheatley

Part One

THE SECRET

1972

January to April

CHAPTER 1

Queensland ~ Australia

January 1972

There was a snake on Jonathan's grave. Deadly venomous, it basked on the white marble slab, its tan coils gleaming in the dawn sun. Shocked out of her daydream, Eleanor froze. She was about to back away, when a kookaburra laughed. The Tiapan woke and slithered into the brown grass.

Expelling her breath, she looked up into the trees. "You beauty," she whispered. Aware that kookaburras preyed on dangerous snakes, she paused in case there was a battle. When nothing happened, she placed a posy of wattle and gum leaves near the headstone.

"I had the most shameful thought on my way here," she said, pulling up the weeds that had grown since her last visit. "If I could go back twenty-five years and change things I'd wish away my children. Not have them killed, just never born. It's because the hope that things would get better died this morning when I was driving past *Acacia*."

She traced his name with her finger: **Jonathan Clarkson 1916 – 1946**. Whenever she saw the brevity of the inscription, she regretted that she had been too devastated to take charge of his funeral arrangements. Not a day passed without her feeling responsible for his death. Wrenching her thoughts away from the image of his decayed body in the coffin, she made herself remember the day he had asked her to marry him. They had come to plant a eucalyptus tree in memory of his mother, and had wandered through the monuments and crosses, stopping every few moments to kiss.

On their wedding day, she and Jonathan and his sister and brother had come straight from the church to the cemetery. At their mother's grave Jonathan and Laurence had put the carnations from their buttonholes with Eleanor's and Virginia's bouquets. The solemnity of the moment lasted until they arrived at the gates of *Acacia* where the silence had been broken by the cheers of the wedding guests waiting to welcome them. Virginia had leapt out of the second bridal car and, hitching up the long skirts of her yellow silk dress, joined in the one-mile race to the homestead. Greg had picked up her discarded shoes. Years later he had told her that her wedding day had been torture for him. He had disguised it well. Eleanor remembered him laughing at Virginia's exuberance and congratulating Jonathan.

Shaking herself out of her reverie, Eleanor looked at the carefully tended grave next to Jonathan's. Interspersed with the names of Laurence's wife and children were words she wished had been engraved on Jonathan's headstone. 'Beloved', 'devoted', 'husband' and 'father'.

As she walked down the path to the section where her parents were buried, she hoped Greg did not suspect that visiting Jonathan's grave was the real reason she came to the cemetery. Not wanting to upset him, she never came on any of the dates associated with Jonathan. Instead she came on her parents' birthdays, wedding anniversary and the dates of their death, even though the memories of her mother, who had died when Eleanor was four, were hazy. Today would have been her father's eightieth birthday.

Her unhappiness was not Greg's fault. He had given her the opportunity to break their engagement, when Jonathan had returned. "He's your husband, Eleanor. I'll understand." But she had seen his sadness. She didn't want to cause him the same anguish Jonathan had inflicted on her.

'I was conceited,' she thought, as she hurried back to the car. 'Greg would have found another girl and Johnny – ' She reached the car and yanked the door open. "Stop it," she told herself. But the knowledge that she had delayed telling Greg she couldn't marry him tortured her soul. She had worked out the kindest way to tell him. But when he arrived to take her to the country fair, he was so loving and excited about their future, her resolve failed. A week later Jonathan was dead.

The car started on the third attempt. Before it could cut out she thrust it into gear and stuck her foot on the accelerator. The roar of the engine frightened a flock of birds and they flew out of a nearby tree. She drove down the dusty track onto the smooth surface of the road. As she passed the prosperous farms of the Darling Downs with their fields of wheat and cotton, she thought with distaste of the chores that lay ahead. "Every day's the same. We all work from sunrise to sunset," she muttered. "And what have we got to show for it? Nothing. The car's falling to bits and we can't afford the spare parts. There are too many vet bills, leaking water tanks and tractor repairs."

When their children had left school and started working full-time on *Eumeralla*, she had thought they would be able to buy a few luxuries. What she most wanted was an inside flushing toilet instead of the stinking one that was eighty yards away from the house, but Greg insisted that the money was saved in case of floods or bush fires, a failed wheat crop or a drastic fall in the price of wool. Only once had he let them break into their savings and that was to buy paint for the peeling exterior of the house.

Of all their children, only Hazel was like Eleanor. She wanted something more than *Eumeralla* and had gone to live in Brisbane as soon as she left school. Greg had been disappointed, but Eleanor understood her desire to live in a comfortable flat that had electricity and modern facilities. Tom, Neil and June were like Greg. To them the land was all that mattered. The house was nothing more than a place to eat and sleep.

Five years ago when she had been in the middle of a difficult menopause, Eleanor decided to sell some of the land. Tom, Neil and June had shared Greg's horror.

She tried to explain about the toilet. "It's disgusting."

"Eleanor, it'll cost a fortune," Greg said. "Miles of pipes have to be laid."

"And we don't spend much time in it, do we?" said Neil.

"It's not just that," she said, frustrated by their refusal to consider her feelings. "We look like tramps. How long is it since any of us had new clothes? Look at Juju's trousers – if they had any more holes they'd fall off."

June shrugged. "Who cares?"

"How much do you want to sell?" asked Tom.

"Two thousand acres."

"Almost half?" said June. "You're joking."

"My God, you can't," said Greg. "The scummy lot on *Acacia* will buy it. They'll chop down all the trees we've planted. Is that what you want? Do you want them to ruin *Eumeralla* like they've ruined *Acacia*? Your dad left *Eumeralla* to you. How would he feel about you selling his grandchildren's inheritance."

Tom looked stupefied. "Hang on, Dad – *Eumeralla*'s yours too, isn't it?"

"Your mother's name is the only one on the deeds."

"So she could sell without your agreement?" asked Neil.

"Yes."

"Stop talking as if I wasn't here," snapped Eleanor. "I won't sell anything without your agreement. For goodness sake, I only want to sell a bit of land."

"Half. That's not just a bit, Mum," said Neil furiously. "What about me? I might as well go and get another job now. By the time you've finished hacking it up it'll be too small for Tom and me to share. Do you want me to go to Brisbane and get a boring clerical job like Hazel?"

"It's a fair question, Eleanor," said Greg.

She felt herself losing. "We'll have less land, but we won't have to slave all day. We can get electricity, a television – "

Tom looked baffled. "Why do we want a television?"

"To keep us in touch with what's going on in the world."

"We've got a radio and we get the newspapers," said Tom.

"I've lived here all my life and nothing's changed," Eleanor said despondently. "We've never improved anything– "

Neil looked exasperated. "Look at what we have got and stop

whining about what we haven't."

"Don't speak to your mum like that," said Greg. "Eleanor, I know some things need doing, but we can't afford anything just now."

"That's why I want to sell some of the land. Everything's primitive!" she shouted. "They had more luxuries on *Acacia* forty years ago than we've got now."

"How do you know?" asked Tom.

Too late, Eleanor remembered that she and Greg had told them that the previous owners were reclusive. "I – they once – "

Greg looked at her warningly. "She had to ask them for help when her dad was ill."

Eleanor had an impulse to tell the truth. She imagined their incredulous expressions if she did. 'They'd think I was insane,' she thought. 'Maybe I should tell them now and if they ever find out I can say that I'd told them, but they didn't believe me.'

"Eleanor, we'll get electricity and a new toilet soon," Greg promised.

But five years had passed and they were still using oil lamps, a wood burning stove and the toilet was the same. She could defy them all and sell. Hazel would understand. Greg would eventually forgive her, but Tom, Neil and June would never understand or forgive.

As she drove past *Acacia*, Eleanor saw a Rolls Royce driving down the driveway. The sun glinting on its shining chrome dazzled her. Greg and Eleanor, like other long-established families in the district, still referred to the present owners of *Acacia* as the new owners even though they had lived there for twenty-five years. Brash and avaricious, they had never fitted in. Everyone had been outraged as the trees, which generations of Clarksons had planted, were felled to make room for extensive wheat fields and luxuries more fitting to a mansion in the city.

She stopped the car at the entrance to *Eumeralla*. In stark contrast to *Acacia*'s smart gates, *Eumeralla*'s was rusty and squeaked when she opened it. She tried to blot out her discontent. But as she drove up the winding, tree-lined track towards the house, she envied the family in the property over the creek who had recently had electricity installed. She looked at the mixture of evergreen and deciduous trees they had planted over the years. All over *Eumeralla* were small areas of woodland, teaming with wildlife and providing shade for the sheep. They had sacrificed wheat fields to plant the trees and as a result *Eumeralla* was one of the most beautiful properties in the Darling Downs. It was also the poorest.

As she rounded the bend she saw a new car parked in the shade of the enormous white magnolia tree. "Blast!" she muttered as she parked next to it. "The reporter. I didn't realize how late it was." When she opened the gate their border collie ran to greet her. "Hi, Toddles," she said, giving her a quick pat. Red, their new kelpie, whined and strained at the long rope tethering him to the tree. As he was not yet properly trained, they tied him up when visitors came. He would not bite, but his growls and barks frightened people who did not know him.

After checking to make sure his water bowl was full, she ran up the steps leading to the back verandah. The family and the reporter, who was from Queensland's top agricultural magazine, were sitting round the table.

"Sorry, I'm late," said Eleanor. She noticed that June, her sons and Greg were wearing their newest jeans and shirts. Compared to the fawn linen trousers and crisp white shirt worn by the reporter, they looked scruffy. Not even his visit had made any of them abandon the habit of going barefoot in the house.

He stood up and pulled out a chair for her. "You're not late, Mrs Mitchell. I'm early. I had an appointment at *Acacia*, but they didn't like my questions about greed and told me to scoot. I'd heard they were loathed around here, but I wanted to see for myself." He looked at June, who was scowling. "But I've annoyed your beautiful daughter by suggesting she's the cook."

"We all do our share in the kitchen," said Eleanor. "My sons make better bread than I do."

June smirked. "Neil's the best cook."

Neil glared at her. "Shut up, Juju."

Eleanor kept her expression serious. "We have a rota system – two weeks in the house doing the cooking, housework, gardening and laundry, two weeks on the animal rota – going round on horseback checking the sheep, making sure the horses and chickens are okay. And two weeks – "

"Sure, that's all very interesting, Mrs Mitchell, but I want to know how you rotate the crops, not how you rotate your family." He laughed.

Eleanor smiled rigidly. June looked at him in disgust.

Undaunted, he winked at her and turned to Greg. "Right, you were telling me about the water tanks."

"Yes," said Greg. "It's vital the livestock have water all year round even if there's a drought, so we erected water tanks all over the property." He drew a sketch. "Groups of tanks are set together and joined by a hose that's buried in a shallow trench. If it hasn't rained for a few weeks we ride to all the tanks and turn on a valve so the water seeps out through the holes in the hose. It's left on for an hour and then turned off."

"It sure works," said the reporter. "The first thing that struck me about *Eumeralla* was all the patches of green. You're respected round here. The people over the creek said that you do things the right way, but it takes courage and comes at a cost."

"We're lucky with our children," said Greg. "All theirs live in Brisbane."

Eleanor wondered what he thought of the house with its worn linoleum and shabby furniture. The blue check tablecloth hid the broken leg of the table that was held together with fencing wire.

"Did you know the people who used to own *Acacia*?" he asked.

She looked down to hide her unease. "Slightly."

"Is it true that their father cut them out of his will?"

Greg jumped up and pointed into the garden. "Snake! Brown one!"

June, Neil and Tom shoved back their chairs, ran to the verandah rail stamping their feet and yelling. Knowing there was no snake and that Greg was getting the conversation away from *Acacia*, Eleanor shook with laughter at the reporter's expression. Greg picked up a broom and hurled it into the bushes. In the back garden Red started barking. Toddles raced through the house.

June grabbed her collar. "Stay!"

"Well spotted, Dad," said Tom.

"I just saw it disappearing into the bushes."

"Has it gone?" asked the reporter.

Eleanor tried to speak, but was laughing too much.

"Yes," said June.

"Is that all you do? You don't kill them?"

"No," said Greg. "Most people who get bitten by snakes are trying to kill them."

"And they control rats and mice," said Tom.

"What about shooting them and getting a couple of cats?"

Greg shook his head. "We don't have a gun. The last owner of the property over the creek was climbing over a fence when he fell. His gun went off and he was killed."

Eleanor wiped her eyes. "Cats ... " She started laughing again and couldn't continue.

"I'm sure pleased I've entertained you, Mrs Mitchell," he said with a grin.

"Cats scare the birds away and birds eat aphids. Our garden is pest free," said Tom.

"Come and have a look," said Greg, leading him down the steps.

"Don't birds eat your fruit?"

"No." June uncoiled the hose and began to fill the bird baths. They're too busy eating the grubs and aphids."

Greg picked an apple. "Have one."

The reporter looked into the laden tree and grinned. "Sure you can spare it? The people over the creek said something about a barter system ... is that right?"

"Yes," said Eleanor. "In return for vegetables, fruit and eggs, they give us milk, butter and cream. They've got a few dairy cows and when they got electricity they began making butter – just for the locals. We all barter round here. The people at the property to our west keep bees and give us honey."

"The *Acacia* lot really miss out, don't they?"

Greg nodded. "I hate talking about them."

The reporter chewed the apple. "Well if it's any consolation I'm going to attack them in my article. Before I started on about greed I took plenty of photos." He laughed. "They thought I was impressed."

Tom smiled. "I'm looking forward to reading it."

Greg picked a bunch of grapes and gave them to him.

"Gosh, thanks."

"Do you like passion fruit?" asked Neil.

"Sure do."

Greg found a cardboard box and filled it with fruit and vegetables. "Just so you can sample our stuff."

They showed him the flowers that they planted among the vegetables to attract bees.

"I've got a heading for my article: 'Natural Snake Deterrents, Natural Everything' – how does that sound?"

To Eleanor's relief, when they returned to the verandah, the reporter went back to the discussion about water tanks. He looked into the distance. "Where are they? I didn't see any on my way in."

"You wouldn't," said Tom. "They're ugly things so we surrounded them with trees."

"Cheap and effective," said the reporter.

"Not cheap," objected Eleanor.

He gestured dismissively. "In the end it must have saved you money. No dead animals during a drought." He looked at Tom when he asked his next question about crop rotation.

Eleanor resisted the temptation to tell him that she was the owner of *Eumeralla*. Greg didn't deserve to have his pride hurt. Resignedly she gestured to June and they went into the kitchen.

"Bloody man," said June. "Flash car, flash clothes. Thinks – "

"Sh, Juju," she said, searching the cupboards for plates that were not chipped.

June sliced the loaf of bread Neil had made that morning. "I don't care if he hears."

Eleanor took the lemonade out of the icebox. "I do. We want him to write a good article about us." She was disappointed that yet another affluent man had failed to impress June. 'Damn it, Juju, why couldn't you be interested in him?' she thought, as she put the glasses on a tray. 'He'd pour money into *Eumeralla*.'

Their arrival back on the verandah was ignored. June dumped the slices of bread, butter and a jar of apricot jam on the table.

Eleanor handed the reporter a glass of lemonade. "We made this with our own lemons," she said, interrupting Tom's explanation about how the compost heaps worked.

He drank half the glass in thirsty gulps. "Best lemonade I've ever tasted."

"Ask Neil for the recipe," said June, ignoring his glower. "We water the compost heaps with our urine – much better than using chemical fertilizers. It all goes into a bucket – "

"I've just told him all that," said Tom impatiently.

"When the bucket's full we pour it on the compost heaps and we work the compost into the soil in the fallow sections," continued June. "Neil did it this morning, but I bet he forgot to wash his hands before he made the bread."

The reporter clicked his fingers. "That must be why it's got such a great flavour. The jam's good too. Did you make that?"

"Yes," said Eleanor. "From our own apricots."

"You'll miss your children when they leave home."

"We're never leaving," said Tom.

"What about when you get married?" asked the reporter.

"Our wives will come and live here."

"What if they don't want to?"

"The girl I marry will have to want to live here."

"What about you, June?"

"I'd only leave here for another property in the Darling Downs."

"Have you got a boyfriend?"

"Sort of. He's doing a grand tour of the world. He wanted to travel before he settled down."

"Will you get married when he comes back?"

"I doubt it. He doesn't like *Eumeralla* much," said June.

"And we don't like him," said Tom. "He kept telling us how we could make more money. He's like the *Acacia* – "

"He's right about a lot of things," Eleanor interrupted. "He'd be happy to live here. I hope June does marry him when he gets back."

Tom looked angry. "He'll want us to make vast profits!"

Seeing the reporter was worried about a row breaking out, Eleanor stopped herself from saying 'good.' Adopting a conciliatory tone, she said, "Things can't stay the same for ever. If they did we'd still be cutting wheat by hand."

The reporter reached down and picked up a camera from the floor. "Let's have some photos of you all."

Eleanor controlled her impulse to shriek. She saw Greg looking at the camera as if it was a death adder. "Shall we … " she began, trying to think of the best way to stop him photographing June.

"Let's take you round the property first – we'll get you a horse. Save the photos till then," said Greg.

Eleanor, conscious that her face was bright red, was puzzled that the reporter, instead of being suspicious, looked guarded.

"It would be better if we went by car. I'd get to see more," he said. "I've got to be back in Dalby soon."

"Can't you ride?" asked June bluntly.

"No," he admitted.

"Right, come on, Neil, Tom, get the truck out," said Greg.

As June walked towards the back steps, Eleanor grabbed her arm. "Stay here with me."

"No. Why?"

"We must get these things washed up."

"Neil's on home rota, not us."

Greg turned on her. "You're staying here, June!"

Eleanor saw June's bewilderment as she watched them walk to the sheds to get the truck. Greg rarely snapped at her. That he'd called her June and not Juju indicated how angry he was. "What's up with him?" she asked.

"You were antagonizing the reporter. If you'd needled him any more he might have labelled us as cranks."

June tipped the bread crumbs into a bowl for the chickens. "He thinks women are stupid."

"He would – he's a man."

"Dad's not like that – neither are Neil and Tom."

"Of course, Juju. They flew to our defence today, didn't they?"

"They thought they might look unmanly, I suppose."

Eleanor sighed. While June collected the glasses and plates and took them into the kitchen, she leant on the verandah rail as the men disappeared into the shed. Minutes later they drove off towards the wheat fields in the open truck, a trail of dust billowing behind them.

June joined her. "You're always strange after you've been to the cemetery."

"Am I? How?"

"Far away. Like now. Where are you?"

"Nowhere, Juju," she said, thinking how cathartic it would be to be able to talk about Jonathan, Laurence and Virginia. How they had all played as children and grown up together. She wished she could describe her joy when the boys returned from their boarding school in Sydney for the holidays. 'What a release to be able to tell someone,' she thought.

When she and Jonathan were married *Eumeralla* and *Acacia* had shared their domestic help and Eleanor only cooked when she felt like it. She and Virginia preferred riding round the properties with the men. Only when there was a possibility that she might be pregnant did she stay in the house. Then Jonathan would come home early. The image of him running up the steps and kissing her before picking her up and carrying her into their bedroom was strong.

"Mum?"

"What?"

"What are you thinking about?"

Imagining June's reaction if she said, 'sex,' she smiled.

"Tell me, Mum."

"For heavens sake, Juju, stop nagging. Get those things washed up."

"Can't they wait till Neil gets back?"

"No! Do you want us to be invaded by ants?"

"You're so crabby these days, Mum."

Eleanor, seeing June's dejection, sighed. "I'm fed up with scrimping and worrying about money."

"It's Hazel's fault," said June, filling the kettle with water. "Continually going on about her flat. She criticizes *Eumeralla* every time she visits. I'm fed up with her moaning about how uncivilized we are."

"She's right."

"Come on, Mum. Her friends are enchanted when they come."

Eleanor grunted. "It's the novelty. They don't have to live here."

"Why didn't you sell it when your dad died?"

"I loved it then." She knew she sounded wistful.

"Did you? What's changed you?"

"It's my age," she said wearily.

June squeezed a tiny amount of washing-up liquid into the sink. "You haven't forgotten it's Neil's birthday on Sunday, have you?"

Eleanor had forgotten. "Do you think I'm senile?"

"No, just vague and forgetful. Funny to think he's twenty-three."

"You can't catch me out that easily," said Eleanor, who had seen June's sly smile. "He'll be twenty-two." She laughed to cover her guilt. 'I didn't really forget,' she thought. 'I bought him a present and card last time I went to Brisbane to see Hazel.' She tried to remember where she had put them.

The men were away so long that June began to worry. "They might have had an accident. Let's go and look for them."

"No," said Eleanor. "You know how they are when they start talking about crops and water and fire breaks."

She knew Greg was spinning out the tour so the reporter would have to leave straight away and not return to the house. 'Stupid of us not to realize he'd want photographs of us all,' she thought.

"He wanted to come back and take photos of you and Juju," Greg told Eleanor later. "But I delayed him so long at the water tanks he had to rush off."

"Well done," said Eleanor. "The last thing we want are photos of Juju circulating round the Darling Downs for Keith and Gabriella to see."

CHAPTER 2

Keith stood in the doorway of his sister's bedroom. Making sure Gabriella hadn't committed suicide while he was asleep was the first thing he did every morning. When he saw the sheet moving with the rhythm of her breathing, he went into the kitchen and put on the kettle. While he waited for his mother to arrive, he read the farming magazine, debating whether to cancel his subscription and give up his dream of buying land and becoming a grazier. He hated being a postman, but his father had not been insured and after his death his mother had become a cleaner for the council so she could buy food and clothes and pay the rent. Having to look after his sister was delaying his plans. He wanted to finish his education at night school. With his Matriculation he could apply for jobs with promotional prospects and save up to buy a block of land. His ultimate dream was to buy *Acacia*.

The headline, **A Tale of Two Properties**, captured his attention. The first part of the article was about *Acacia*. Without using the word, the acquisitiveness of the owners was implied by the description of their lifestyle. There was a photo of the new homestead and one of the old one. Deprived of the trees and bushes that had surrounded it when Keith's father had lived there, it looked exposed. There were photos of the swimming pool, tennis courts, garages, the Rolls Royce, Ferrari and Porsche.

The piece about *Eumeralla* was different. The photos were of Greg Mitchell and his two sons, and the reporter wrote generously about their farming methods. 'Did Dad know them?' he thought. 'Greg looks about the same age as Dad would have been now.'

He heard his mother's car arrive as he was making the tea.

"Did Dad know the family on *Eumeralla*?" Keith asked as they had their breakfast.

Her agitation, although quickly checked, was unmistakable.

"Mum?"

"He didn't mention them to me ... or if he did ... I've forgotten. It could have been called something different then."

Keith gave her the magazine. "They've been written up in this. And *Acacia* too."

Her eyes flicked over the photos and when she turned the page he saw her hand was shaking. Her sigh of relief was spontaneous.

"What is it, Mum?"

"Nothing. Now you'd better get off to work."

Keith went to the dresser. "I forgot to give you Fiona's letter yesterday," he said.

Ω Ω Ω

Longing to get under a cold shower, Fiona Lancaster waited for a tram outside the *Ansett Airline* office where she worked in Melbourne. During the half-hour journey to Hawthorn she read the first chapter of the biography of Anne Boleyn that she had bought. She was so engrossed she almost missed her stop. Scrambling off the tram at the last minute, she walked to her unit. The flowers she had brought for her aunt were wilting in the heat.

In her letter box were two bills, a letter from her parents and another from her cousin Keith. As soon as she got inside she put the flowers in a bucket of water. Anxious for news about Gabriella she delayed her shower and opened Keith's letter.

3rd February 1972

Dear Fiona,

Mum and I are petrified that Gabby will kill herself.

"Oh, God," said Fiona. She bit her lip as she looked at Gabriella's wedding photograph on the bookcase. Tears blurred the picture of the radiant bride, dressed in white chiffon with a pearl headdress holding her veil in place. She read the rest of Keith's letter, trying to think of something to write that would not sound clichéd. She put his letter back in the envelope and went into the bathroom. 'I could go to Queensland for a week,' she thought, as she stepped under the shower. She turned on the cold tap, gasping as the icy water hit her. Gradually she adjusted the temperature to warm. Suddenly she remembered something. Rinsing the herbal-scented conditioner out of her hair and finishing her shower with another icy blast, she dried herself and wrapped her hair in a towel. In the lounge she went to the desk and filled her fountain pen with black ink.

Dear Keith,

This is just a hurried note, because I'm going out. Remind Gabby of the time I saved her when those louts threw her off the pier in Sydney. She couldn't swim, you couldn't swim and no one else was about. I saved her life. Tell her there must have been a reason. I didn't save her to have her killing herself ten years later.

After addressing the envelope she looked in her diary to see when she could conveniently go to Queensland. The tennis club was having a travelling dinner on Saturday and she was hosting the dessert course. There was a competition match the following weekend, but she was free the next week. She pencilled the date in her diary and put it back in her handbag.

She unwrapped the towel from around her head and her platinum blonde hair fell to her waist. While she waited for it to dry she watered her window boxes and cut off the dead flowers from the geraniums. In spite of its length and thickness, her hair dried quickly. Unable to bear it hanging down her back in the heat, she twisted it in a knot on top of her head. Pleased to see that the flowers were recovering, she went into her bedroom and dressed in a white linen sundress and sandals. She walked the long way to her aunt's house so she could post her letter to Keith.

Ruth put the plates of smoked salmon and lemon wedges in the fridge while she buttered the bread. When the doorbell rang she covered them with a glass dome and hurried down the hall. Through the fly-screen door she saw Fiona.

"Hello, Aunty Ruth," she called.

Ruth pushed up the latch and let her in. "Hello, Fiona," she said, careful not to sound too eager. Virginia had told her that Fiona hated being hugged or kissed, but Ruth suspected that this was more to do with their turbulent mother-and-daughter relationship than coldness on Fiona's part. However, wary of rejection, she always let Fiona kiss her first. With a dart of pleasure she saw that she was wearing the amber necklace and silver and amber earrings she had given her for Christmas.

Fiona handed her a bunch of red chrysanthemums and kissed her cheek.

"They're glorious. You can put them in a vase while I get the starter."

While Fiona arranged the flowers, Ruth went into the kitchen to get the starter and the bottle of white Burgundy.

"Smoked salmon – yum," said Fiona.

Ruth put the wine in an ice bucket. "I didn't cook anything – it's too hot. It's egg salad, then oranges soaked in Cointreau for dessert."

During dinner Fiona told her about Gabriella. "So, I'm going to Queensland in a few weeks – that's if I can get time off."

Ruth coughed to cover her alarm. "Sorry, something caught in my throat. That's a good idea," she managed to say. 'She can't have told Alex and Virginia – they would have rung me,' she thought. 'We've got to stop her.'

They finished their salads and Ruth collected the plates. "No stay there, it won't take a minute, it's all ready."

In the kitchen she stood dazed by panic. She was tempted to go into the lounge and phone Alex and Virginia, but knew that Fiona might overhear. By the time she came back to the dining room with the oranges and a jug of cream she had an idea. She prayed Fiona would agree.

As soon as she thought she could sound normal, she said, "Gabby needs a holiday. Why don't you and Keith take her on a cruise?"

"That's a fabulous idea." Fiona poured cream over her oranges. "I'll get some brochures tomorrow."

Ω Ω Ω

Gabriella knew she was being selfish and cowardly. When rays of light shone through the blackness of her despair she pushed them away. Afraid that the happiness she had once taken for granted would return only to be snatched away again, she spurned her mother, her brother Keith and her friends. Ignoring their comfort and advice, she submerged herself in mourning.

When she and Brett had married she was at teachers' college and he was in his final year at university. Barely able to afford the rent, they lived in a cramped flat with one bedroom. The first year of their marriage had been bliss. The last six months had been hell. Despite the grim warnings from the doctors about the inevitability of Brett's death from leukaemia, she had refused to give up hope. He would get better. He was young.

When he had died, Gabriella had been too exhausted and disbelieving to exhibit signs of grief. Keith, her mother and friends, thinking she was coping well and being brave, helped her search for a block of land she wanted to buy with Brett's insurance money. As soon as she had found the three-acre, heavily-wooded plot just outside Dalby, she wrote to her uncle Alex asking if he had time to design her house.

I want it to disappear among the trees as if the logs had fallen and formed themselves into a house, she wrote.

He replied immediately.

Designing a house to your unusual specification stimulates me. I've started the plans already.

Alex and Virginia, able to get discounted plane fares because Fiona worked for Ansett Airlines, had frequently come up to Dalby. Gabriella was astonished by how soon the house was completed. Built in natural timber that blended in with the landscape, it was surrounded by a wide verandah and shaded from the sun by giant eucalyptus, wattle and jacaranda trees. She planted exotic shrubs and fruit trees in the garden. Virginia helped her choose furniture and Gabriella enjoyed the luxury of having plenty of money. The day before Virginia and Alex flew back to Sydney she held a party.

After the weekend she was alone in the quiet house. She had wandered through the rooms. But, instead of appreciating the new furniture and grey slate floors that, along with the pale walls, made it look cool and spacious, she longed for the tiny flat that she and Brett had rented. Reality swamped her. She would never share this house with Brett. She would never have his children. She would never see him again. Depression descended like a curtain.

That night she lay awake. When she should have been getting up she fell asleep and did not wake till late that afternoon. When she explained her absence to the headmaster he had been sympathetic. He tried to support her, but when Gabriella repeatedly came to school late, dirty and untidy, he had to ask her to resign. She did not care. Brett's insurance money had enabled her to pay cash for the land and house and have plenty left over.

Unable to sleep, Gabriella's mind had been tortured. When she began talking about killing herself, Keith had left the house he shared with his friends and moved in with her. He had swapped his carefree life for one that was almost that of a warder. She knew he had done it willingly, but she did not thank him or respond to his company.

In the background she heard her mother's voice. Instead of allowing it to comfort her, she resented it. She would suggest that Gabriella ring this friend or that friend. Now they had got to the job saga. Gabriella must look for a job and find something to occupy herself to help her get over her grief.

'As if Brett was a pet dog that I can replace with another pet dog,' she thought as she pulled the last cigarette out of the packet. She did not notice how pale her mother looked, she just wished she would go. 'Why can't anyone understand how I feel? They think that because I'm young I'll recover and find another husband. But I expected fifty years of marriage and children and I've been deprived of that.'

"Fiona rang me last night, Gabby. She thought it would be fun if you and Keith and her went on a cruise – she's got some brochures. There's a sixteen day cruise to Fiji – "

"A cruise, a job – anyone got any more ideas as to how I can recover?" Gabriella threw the cigarette packet on the coffee table. "Why don't you all hold a competition? No I don't want to go on a cruise." She tore the skin from the reddened area round her thumb nail and watched the blood seep out.

"Gabby, don't bite your nails. You used to have beautiful nails."

"I used to have a lot of things, Mum. Go home. I'm okay." But she knew her mother would stay until Keith arrived home. Gabriella wanted to kill herself, but was too frightened. Once she had read a novel about a woman who had gone to hell, where she was condemned to suffer the punishment of strangulation for eternity. The graphic descriptions had stuck in her memory. She was not religious. She had attended Sunday School and she and Brett had been married in the local Methodist church, but phrases from the Bible that portrayed God as unforgiving frightened her. If there was divine retribution she might be punished for committing suicide. Her body rotting in a coffin or being consumed by the fires of cremation was one thing – suffering for eternity in a gruesome way was another.

"Fiona's right, Gabby," she heard her mother say. "It must have been meant."

"What?" she asked irritably.

"Fiona saving your life."

"Nothing's meant, Mum. I wish I had drowned." But as she said it, she remembered the salt water stinging her eyes and going up her nose, her terror, and frenzied struggles for air.

"Darling, that's a terrible thing to say."

Rage exploded in Gabriella's brain. "You don't understand how it feels!" she screamed. "No one does. I'm sick of your inane chattering. Every day you arrive falsely cheerful with a silly smile on your face. Leave me alone – I don't want you here. There's only one thing I want and that's Brett."

Her mother covered her face with her hands. Gabriella had rarely seen her cry, but when she had, her tears had been controlled and nothing like the sobs that racked her now. Overcome with remorse, she jumped off the sofa. "Oh, Mum. Mum." She flung her arms around her.

"Gabby," her mother gasped. "When your father died I had to put on a brave act for you and Keith. I didn't have the luxury of a quiet time to grieve. What would you have done if I'd fallen apart?" Her voice was shaking.

"Mum, I didn't mean it."

Her mother pulled herself out of Gabriella's arms. "You did, Gabby. You're so wrapped up in yourself you can't see what's happening around you." She rummaged through her handbag looking for a hanky. "Keith's girlfriend dumped him because he spends too much time with you. She told him to let you wallow in melancholy if that's what you want. He rarely sees his friends now. It's a dreary life for a young man. You've been struck by tragedy but it's time you were brave and considered other people." She walked to the door, hoping Gabriella would stop her from leaving, but she didn't. Feeling defeated, she drove back to the small rented house in Cecil Plains, the country town where she and Laurence had begun their married life. He had been full of dreams in those days.

"I won't be a gardener all my life. I'll save up and buy *Acacia* back one day."

Futile dreams that had come to nothing and ended with his death seven years ago. He had been fifty. She hadn't known he had an ulcer. She hadn't known he was seriously ill until he collapsed when the ulcer perforated. It wounded her that he had never told her how ill he felt. "Just a bit tired," was all he had said when she had expressed concern about his colour.

The short walk from the car to her front door left her breathless. She had a pain in her chest. It had been there all day and was getting worse. 'Damn indigestion,' she thought. Engulfed by a sensation of doom, she went into the lounge and sat on the sofa, trying to get her breath. She wondered if, like their father, Gabriella and Keith were cursed.

A photo of Laurence in uniform when he was twenty-four stood on the desk. Virginia had taken it just after he'd joined the army and before he had left for the training camp. He was smiling in the photo. Smiling in a way she had never seen. Confident, relaxed and supremely happy. Content in his marriage to Francesca, and as yet untouched by war, he looked at ease and optimistic.

How different from the haunted man she had first met in 1948 at a tennis party. His expression then had been the same as Gabriella's was now. All the girls had tried to attract his attention. With his thick blonde hair, turquoise eyes and well-shaped limbs, he was exceptionally handsome. The aura of tragedy surrounding him had added to the fascination. Between matches he had sat on the grass pretending to watch the other games, but she realized he was immersed in his own thoughts and unaware of the eager girls. She was new to the district and knew nothing about him, not even his name, and felt disadvantaged. Too shy to ask questions, she had listened to snippets of conversation.

"*His wife died at the end of the war.*"
"*He's still devastated.*"
"*He was supposed to inherit* **Acacia**, *but he and his brother were cut*

out of the will and their stepmother got everything."

"He works as a gardener for the council now."

When they were introduced Laurence had spoken kindly to her and she was grateful. Not many men bothered with plain women. During the day he resisted the attempts of other girls to engage his attention and asked her to be his doubles partner for the next match. She went home that night in a haze of joy that lasted until she looked in the mirror. "You dill," she told her reflection. "As if a man like him would be interested in a plain thing like you. He was just being kind because you're new and didn't know anyone."

She often wondered if he had married her because she was robust and energetic: the opposite to Francesca whose fragile beauty had underlined her fragile health.

The pain in her chest intensified. When it shot down her left arm she knew it was not indigestion. She was having a heart attack. She was going to die. It was too late to destroy the photos and letters in her bedroom. Keith would find them when he was clearing out the house.

'Burn all the letters and photos,' was the last thing Laurence had said to her.

The last word he had said was 'Cheska.' It was his first wife who occupied his thoughts as he lay dying, not his second who sat by his hospital bed, holding his hand.

'Virginia,' she thought. 'I'll ring Virginia and tell her about the photos and letters.' She tried to calm herself. 'No. I'll phone for an ambulance and then I'll ring her.'

Cautiously she stood up and took two steps towards the telephone. A crushing pain exploded in her chest and she collapsed.

A neighbour, worried when she failed to arrive for the committee meeting of the Country Woman's Association, found her at nine o'clock that night. She was dead.

Ω   Ω   Ω

Eleanor woke from the dream about Jonathan at six o'clock on Tuesday morning. Her happiness dissolved as the image of her and Jonathan riding round *Eumeralla* was replaced by the reality. She heard Greg chopping wood. 'It's waking from the dream that is the nightmare,' she thought, staring at the battered chest of drawers. She had recurring dreams about Jonathan, but this one had been different. Instead of being in the past this dream had been in the present. *Acacia* and *Eumeralla* were one property as they were meant to be. Laurence and Francesca were alive. They were all wealthy, with a station manager and his assistant, stockmen, gardeners and staff.

Things in her dream were as they would have been if Jonathan had not left. If he had not died. The two facts were linked in Eleanor's mind because if he had not left her he would not have died in the way he had. She told herself she had been right to send him away instead of allowing him to come back to *Eumeralla*. Even Jonathan's father had agreed with her decision and blessed her marriage to Greg. She sighed. Nothing she did to justify her actions eased the guilt. The knowledge that her existing life was based on the timing of Greg's return from the war added to her desolation. One month later and the outcome would have been different. She would have taken Jonathan back and Greg would have returned to his old job as the assistant station manager of *Acacia*. She knew that such thoughts were irrational.

'All my yearning can't alter things,' she thought. 'And Johnny might still have died violently. Men like him don't die peacefully in their beds.' She grunted. 'Who am I fooling? If I'd let him come back he'd be alive. There's no peril here that he couldn't have managed. We've had no serious bushfires. He wouldn't have got bitten by a snake, he was too strict about bush law. And no horse would ever have thrown him. It's safe here. He would have been alive if he hadn't gone back to Brisbane. If I hadn't forced him to go.' She threw back the mosquito net and sat on the edge of the bed, staring at the cream wall that needed a fresh coat of paint. "Johnny," she murmured.

She went over to the window and watched Greg raise the axe and split a log in two blows. 'Where does he get the energy?' A thunderstorm had woken them at midnight. Rain had drummed on the corrugated iron roof for two hours, keeping them awake. The two acre garden surrounding the house was a riot of purple bougainvillea, scarlet hibiscus and yellow wattle. During the night apricots had fallen and the ground under the tree was a patchwork of golden fruit and white petals from the magnolia tree.

'Greg's a good husband and father – he deserves better than me with my mind stuck in the past,' she thought, knowing that she would be unsettled all day. She always was after these dreams. She recalled the drawings of the new homestead for *Eumeralla* that Virginia's husband Alex had made. Excitedly she and Jonathan had studied the plans. They had discussed the large kitchen with the cook, taking her requirements into account. The plans had never left the paper on which they had been drawn.

Putting on her dressing gown, she went down the hall hoping a shower would revive her. As she passed the kitchen the smell of baking bread wafted out. Neil was pushing more wood into the stove. He shut the door and glanced up. The kitchen was hot and his tanned face was flushed from the heat of the fire.

"Hi, Mum," he said with a grin.

His cheerfulness made her feel more alienated. Everyone was happy except her. She stood in front of the mottled mirror in the bathroom and trimmed her hair. Dark brown curls streaked with grey fell into the cracked white basin. When she finished she threw them into the waste basket and stepped under the tepid water of the shower. Three minutes later she turned off the taps and dried herself, momentarily comforted by the thickness of the new towel Hazel had bought her. As soon as she had started working in Brisbane, Hazel had given her mother presents whenever she visited *Eumeralla*. Except for birthdays and Christmas she had stopped buying things for her siblings and father. June had been indifferent to the fragrant herbal shampoo and conditioner. Greg, Neil and Tom had sniffed the bottles of aftershaves suspiciously, then told her they didn't want to smell like queers. Only Eleanor had been grateful for the violet-scented talcum powder and soap. Her precious gifts from Hazel included a tube of hand cream, a tub of moisturizer and a bottle of perfume. But it hurt her pride and increased her frustration that she had to depend on her daughter for things that most people these days regarded as necessities.

After dressing in clean jeans, a shirt and sandals, she cut her nails short and rubbed lotion into her tanned hands that were mottled with brown blotches. Fifty-four years of exposure to the harsh sun had left its mark. The parched skin on her face soaked up the moisturizer. Seeking comfort, she took the bottle of perfume out of her drawer and sprayed a small amount on her neck. Its scent evoked memories of Jonathan and their eight-year marriage when money had been plentiful and she wore perfume every day.

Taking a bucket from the verandah, she went down the steps into the garden. Greg was stacking the wood in the shed. With a stab of guilt for sleeping in, she saw that he had already packed fruit and vegetables in the box for the family in the property over the creek. She began picking up the apricots, throwing any that were bruised or split onto the compost heap.

Greg came out of the shed as she was pulling lemons, oranges and grapefruit off the trees. "Stewed apricots for breakfast, lunch and dinner for the next two weeks," he said. "And we can make some more jam."

Tom and June were walking towards the house, carrying a pail of milk and a basket of new-laid eggs. Tom said something and June threw back her head and laughed.

"I bet he's telling Juju his smutty jokes," said Greg.

They finished picking up the apricots and went up the steps to the house. The table on the back verandah was set for breakfast. Three flies buzzed lazily round, waiting for the food to be put on the table. June picked up a fly-swat, killed them and tossed them into a spider's web in the corner of the verandah. The spider darted forward, eager to devour its prey. Greg took a jar of stewed apricots out of the ice-box and filled each bowl.

When the phone rang, Eleanor went into the lounge to answer it because she was nearest to the door. "Hello?" she said, expecting it to be one of their neighbours.

"Eleanor?"

She recognized Virginia's voice at once. "Yes," she whispered.

"Keith and Gabriella's mother died last night. Fiona's coming up. She's arriving tomorrow afternoon. I'm not sure how long she's staying. It won't be long – she's got to get back to work. Alex and I are arriving the next day."

She saw Tom come into the room and said in a stilted voice. "Thanks for letting me know," and hung up the receiver.

"Who was that, Mum?" asked Tom.

She ran her sweating hands down her jeans. "Not one of your girlfriends."

"You okay?"

Her cheeks flamed with agitation. "Yes. Go back to the table."

Twenty-three years ago it had seemed so simple. They thought it was just a matter of Alex and Virginia staying away from Queensland. Then in December 1949 Laurence Clarkson's son Keith was born and his daughter Gabriella followed two years later. The two families had gone to inordinate lengths to keep their children apart. Laurence sent Keith and Gabriella to a different school, and went to Sydney on holidays. Then Fiona had grown up and her parents could no longer control her.

The first panic had taken place seven years ago when Laurence had died. Fiona, then aged eighteen, had insisted on accompanying Alex and Virginia to his funeral. Two years ago Fiona was one of Gabriella's bridesmaids. For the duration of her stay in Queensland Eleanor and Greg had been tense. Fiona's two year holiday in England and Europe had been a welcome respite. But now she was back in Australia and coming up to the Darling Downs for another funeral.

Eleanor went back to the verandah and sat at the table. She ate her apricots in silence, ignoring the inquisitive looks from her children. She knew Greg would guess by her manner that Virginia or Alex had rung. Neil began to collect their empty plates, but Eleanor interrupted him. "I'll do it." She went into the kitchen and Greg followed.

"Keith and Gabriella's mother died last night," she whispered. "Fiona's coming up."

"What are you two plotting?" asked Neil from the doorway.

Eleanor jumped. "Nothing," she snapped. "Go back to the table."

Neil shrugged and turned away.

Greg broke eight eggs into a bowl and whisked them. "Act normal or they'll get suspicious," he said quietly.

She began chopping a handful of parsley. "I dread them finding out," she whispered.

Watching the doorway, he said softly, "You know, the only time I feel that you're with me, really with me and not on walkabout, is when there's a crisis about Fiona."

"I'm sorry, Greg. I can't help it."

He poured the eggs into the pan and stirred them. "I know. That makes it worse."

She sprinkled the parsley over the mixture. "Are you sorry you married me?"

He shook his head. "I'm sorry about a lot of things, but not that. Never that. But I haven't made you happy, have I?"

"It's not you, Greg."

"What do you want? Tell me."

"Nothing," she said. 'Nothing you can give me anyway,' she thought.

After breakfast Eleanor went to tidy the tack room. Neil, who was on home rota, made sandwiches for June's, Tom's and Greg's lunches. He packed them in the saddlebags with oranges, apples and thermos flasks of water.

"Is Mum okay?" Tom asked as they saddled their horses.

Greg tried to look puzzled. "Yes." He took his horse's reins.

June opened the paddock gate. "She's jittery, Dad. So are you."

Greg wanted to relieve their worry and wished he could concoct a plausible reason for his and Eleanor's behaviour. Now that Fiona's visits were becoming more frequent it must only be a matter of time before their luck ran out. He felt the burden of foreboding.

"Dad?" asked June.

"It's nothing, Juju. We're both getting old and a bit grumpy." He turned his horse in the opposite direction. "See you tonight." He didn't hear their horses and knew they were watching his retreating figure. 'We've got to tell them,' he thought, as he rode over to the wheat fields to supervise the harvest. 'Before they find out themselves. The silly thing is that none of us expected Laurence to get married again. Not even Laurence. We never thought this through properly. If we had, Laurence would have moved out of Queensland when Keith was born. After he lost *Acacia* there was nothing to keep him here. I'm sick of worrying. All I ever wanted was to live on *Eumeralla*. To experience the joy of waking up with Eleanor. Just peace, and the pleasure of my children and the land.'

Eumeralla was his life. He did not own it. Eleanor had never suggested putting his name on the deeds as joint owner, and he, worried that she would misinterpret his motives, had never mentioned it. One day his children would own it and that was enough for him.

His father had been a drover and by the time Greg was five he had travelled over most of the Queensland outback. When his mother, fed up with the impermanence and craving for a settled life, had left them and taken the job of a cook on a cattle station, Greg stayed with his father. He missed his mother, but not the arguments that erupted every time she tired of life on the road. Six years later arthritis had slowed his father down, and, when they arrived at *Eumeralla* they stayed. His father had found a companion in the widowed owner and Greg had made friends with his daughter Eleanor Osborne and the Clarkson children on *Acacia*. Eleanor's black hair, brown eyes and olive skin had been a foil for the blondness of Virginia, Jonathan and Laurence.

Although Eleanor and Virginia had looked very feminine, their dispositions had made them androgynous. They had climbed trees, vaulted fences and ridden horses and bicycles as well as Laurence, Jonathan and Greg did. It had been impossible to impress them with feats of male superiority. Greg knew that, compared to the Clarkson boys, he had looked insignificant. He was stocky and only five feet six inches tall with coarse brown hair and hazel eyes. Jonathan and Laurence had been over six feet with thick silver-blonde hair that shone in the sun. Unlike many very blonde people, they had black lashes and brows that added definition to their handsome faces. They had confidence and charisma. Greg was awkward and had lacked the social graces that had come naturally to the Clarksons.

'In those days Eleanor was as passionate about *Eumeralla* as Johnny, Laurence and Virginia were about *Acacia*,' he thought.

When Eleanor had married Jonathan in 1936, he would have left the district, but he was the assistant manager of *Acacia* and William Clarkson depended on him. The outbreak of war in 1939 gave him the excuse he needed.

Greg had never been able to understand why Eleanor had been intending to divorce Jonathan. 'Did she use me to get back at Johnny for leaving her? If he hadn't been killed would she have taken him back?'

His thoughts returned to the present and he tried to gauge their reactions to the truth. 'June? I hate to think. Can't imagine Tom and Neil getting angry. As long as it didn't interfere with her life in Brisbane, Hazel wouldn't care. What if we'd told them that Eleanor was a widow before I married her? Would they have wanted to know who he was and all about him? Or would they have just accepted it? Neil and Tom might have, but Juju and Hazel would have been curious. They would have asked questions and we would have forgotten what lies we'd told and contradicted ourselves. That would have got them interested.' He remembered Hazel's enthusiasm for detective stories. 'She would have been beside herself with excitement if she'd found out that her mother had been married to the heir to *Acacia*.'

When he heard the noise from the harvesters, Greg urged his

horse into a canter. Pushing his thoughts away, he dismounted when he reached the wheat fields and smiled at the men, hoping his apprehension was hidden.

After June and Tom finished checking the sheep and water tanks on the northern section, they rode to a coppice of gum trees by the widest part of the creek. When they dismounted they let the horses wander to the water to drink.

Tom spread out a rug. "What do you reckon is wrong with Mum?"

"Her age." June pulled a face. "I'll go like that one day," she said, unscrewing the top of the thermos flask and pouring out a cup of water.

"No, Juju, it was the phone call. She might be having an affair."

June almost dropped the cup. "Tom!"

"Well, she might be."

June shook her head. "She's too old."

"But she looked so guilty. Why?"

June shrugged and unpacked their saddlebags.

"Hell, Juju. I've just thought of something."

"What?"

"She could be planning to sell some of *Eumeralla* behind our backs. What if it was someone from *Acacia* on the phone?"

She stared at him. "I'd rather she was having an affair."

"So would I."

CHAPTER 3

Gabriella tried to escape into sleep, but Keith's voice was insistent.

"Gabby." He shook her. "Gabby, wake up!"

She heard the alarm in his voice. 'He thinks I've overdosed,' she thought. 'If only I had the guts.' She was too conscience-stricken to tell him she had upset their mother the day she had died. He thought it was grief that kept her in bed all day. It was grief. And guilt. She opened her eyes and stared at him. His tanned face was too thin and his green eyes were troubled. There was blood on his chin where he had cut himself with his razor. His blonde hair was wet from the shower. He smelt of soap, deodorant and toothpaste. She knew she stank of body odour and cigarettes.

"Gabby, have a shower."

She frowned. "Why?"

"Because I'm going to the airport to get Fiona. We'll be back in five or six hours."

"So?" She yawned and he recoiled from the smell of her breath.

"Please, Gabby. Don't let her see you like this. Have a shower – it'll do you good. You'll feel better."

She sat up. "You reckon?"

"Yes."

She noticed that he looked at her less gently than usual.

"You reckon? Gabby has a shower and feels better? Gabby goes and sees her friends and feels better. Gabby does this and Gabby does that and it will make her feel better?"

"Yes," said Keith. "Better than lying in bed all day. What are you achieving? You've lost a husband, but I've lost a brother-in-law. He was a great bloke and I miss him. Not the same as you do, but I miss him. Like I miss Dad and like I'll miss Mum. And I miss you too."

For the first time since Brett's death he was challenging her. He was no longer terrified she would kill herself. A new sorrow had blunted the old.

"Will you have a shower?" he persisted.

She took her cigarettes off the bedside table and lit one. "I might."

He left her and went outside. She heard him drive away in her car. When she had finished the cigarette she stubbed it out and went back to sleep.

Keith drove through the bush towards Brisbane, wishing he was on his motorbike. He wanted to feel the wind on his face and hated being cooped up in Gabriella's car with the air-conditioning. Imagining his sophisticated cousin on the back of a bike made him smile briefly. He had not seen Fiona since her return from overseas. The letters and postcards she had sent them when she had travelled through Europe were absorbing with observations about the differences between Australia and whatever country she was in. His mother remarked that the letters were unlike her. Keith agreed. Fiona was an uncomfortable person to be around. On the rare occasions that she stepped out of the shadows into the light, she was fun. Then, as suddenly as her sunny self emerged, it vanished, leaving him bereft and confused. 'How,' he often wondered, 'can someone slip from one mood to another without warning?'

As the towering gums of the bush gave way to the suburbs, his sensation of claustrophobia increased. He glanced at the neat front gardens. "There's no wildness. It's as if people in cities are frightened of nature. Clipped lawns and hedges that look as if they've been cut with a scalpel. Do people go round with a spirit level?"

As he parked the car at Brisbane Airport he hoped that Fiona's flight was on time. When he walked into the terminal and looked at the board, he was relieved to see the plane from Melbourne had landed.

Fiona was waiting for her luggage. She was wearing an ice-blue sundress in fine cotton, and white sandals. The dress showed off her long suntanned legs. Her shining platinum- blonde hair was twisted into a loose knot on top of her head. Several men were looking at her admiringly, but she was oblivious. As he walked towards her, Keith compared her freshness and vitality with the wreck that was Gabriella. She had just grabbed her cases from the carousel when she saw him.

Abandoning her luggage, she dodged the crowds and threw herself into his arms. "Keith."

The intensity of her embrace surprised him. She usually avoided kissing and hugging. He held her, relishing the smell of her clean hair. "I'm so glad you're here. Let's rescue your cases before someone takes them."

They walked out of the airport into the dazzling sun.

Fiona put on her sunglasses. "How's Gabby?"

"Worse." He opened the passenger door and she slid into the seat. After putting her cases in the boot, he got into the car and turned on the air conditioning.

When they were out in the bush he sighed gratefully. "That's better."

"I'm dreading seeing Gabby," Fiona admitted. "I'm hopeless with grief – I never know what to do."

"You wrote her a comforting letter when Brett died."

"Writing's different – I wasn't there. I didn't have to do anything."

"How's Melbourne?"

She fiddled with her delicate silver necklace. "All right. I miss Sydney."

"Why do you live there then?"

"To get away from my mother."

Wanting to avoid a catalogue of Virginia's shortcomings, Keith did not respond. He slowed down as two kangaroos hopped across the road.

"Oh, look!" she exclaimed.

"Townie. Have you got a boyfriend at the moment?"

"No."

"What about the airline pilot?"

"We broke up. He bored me." She sighed. "Am I incapable of loving anyone? I've never been in love. Have you?"

He nodded. "A couple of times. At least I thought I was. You will one day. You love your dad."

The bush gave way to farmland and the road stretched ahead straight and deserted. Half an hour later Keith pulled the car off the road. "Guess where we are."

Fiona looked at the fields of wheat. "Not *Acacia*?"

He nodded. When she opened the door hot air rushed into the car. She got out and stood at the wire fence.

Keith joined her. "The gates are just up there – the homestead's a mile away."

"Have you ever seen it?"

"Only in photos."

"It should be yours," she said bitterly.

They had never discussed the paternal side of Fiona's family. Keith had felt that it was too awkward, but now he decided she had opened the subject. "But you're a Lancaster – Margot's your aunt."

She hesitated, as if considering how to reply. "Doesn't matter. She stole *Acacia*," she said finally.

"Does that cause problems with your dad?" he asked, feeling that she had been about to tell him something.

"No. It wasn't his fault."

Keith looked thoughtful. "If it hadn't been for Margot your father and mother would never have met and you wouldn't have been born."

She didn't reply, but again she looked as if she wanted tell him something, but her expression changed and it was obvious she had decided against it.

"Oh, Fiona, I don't want to be like Dad. I want to have plenty of money. It's my ambition to buy *Acacia*. I've heard rumours that they might have to sell up. I don't know if it's true. They're so unpopular in the Darling Downs it might be wishful thinking. If it is true I'd give anything to be able to buy it. What's the bloody use. I'll never have enough money."

"You might one day."

"How? Apart from winning the lottery? Being a postman won't make me a millionaire."

"You enjoy gardening, don't you?"

"That didn't make Dad rich. He couldn't even afford to buy a house."

Fiona shook her head. "You'll never get rich working for someone else. I went to school with a girl whose father started off as a cleaner in a hospital. Then he began working for himself, cleaning houses of the rich. Now he's got his own cleaning company and he employs lots of people. You could start your own gardening business. Mum and Dad have got a man to mow their lawn and pull out the weeds once a week."

He looked at her with interest. "Quite an entrepreneur, aren't you? You've got the Lancaster head for business. You might be right."

"I am right," she said.

"I'll think about it."

"I thought there were lots of trees on *Acacia*," she said.

"There were. Dad told me that the whole boundary was planted with trees. The new owners chopped them down."

She turned and looked at the property on the other side of the road. "Now that's how I imagined *Acacia*."

He turned and looked across the road at the rusty gate leading to a winding track lined with trees. A rough wooden sign painted in uneven black lettering hung lopsidedly from the top rung. "*Eumeralla*. There was an article about it in this month's farming magazine. I'll show you when we get back."

Keith's pleas to Gabriella to have a shower had gone unheeded. When they arrived she was sitting on the verandah with an ashtray full of cigarette butts beside her. Greasy hair hung in a tangled mess down her back, and her unshaven legs looked more like a man's.

Fiona burst into tears.

Before going to bed that night Fiona wrote in her journal.

Dalby
February 1972

Gabby's in a terrible state. She responded to me a bit, but I'm sorry I cried when I saw her. I couldn't help it. She used to be so fastidious. She's five years younger than I am, but looks ten years older. We had salad and mangoes for dinner – it's too hot for anything else. Gabby didn't do anything to help, just sat around smoking.

Her house is beautiful. Dad did a brilliant job. Outside it's rustic and you can't see it through the trees. Inside it's sophisticated. The doors, window frames and skirting boards are unpainted, waxed timber. The door handles are white china with a gold rim. Mum's taste is evident, but she's incorporated Gabby's personality into the scheme.

Keith said that building the house with Brett's insurance money was the only sensible thing she's done since he died, but I think the money is the reason she's depressed. Because she doesn't have to work, she's got nothing to do all day. She's not even interested in the garden and she used to be crazy about gardening. If she hadn't got any money she'd have to work and if she'd had children they would keep her busy. Also, children would have been a part of Brett and she would feel that she had something of him left.

On the way back from the airport this afternoon I nearly told Keith I was adopted. But I remembered that years after I'd told Catriona and Kim, they used it against me. The memory of Catriona's face twisted with enmity as she said that the Lancasters were too good for me, still hurts. Why didn't I tell him? Probably because I would have had to tell him about my real mother being an alcoholic. If he despised me too, I couldn't bear it.

I'm looking forward to seeing Dad tomorrow. I bet Mum will

tell me I look thin or too pale, comments designed to make me think I'd be better off at home with her. But if I tell her I don't need to be looked after, she'll sulk, so I'll try and be nice and accept her smothering hugs with fortitude, even though they repel me.

The stars are so bright here – not washed out like in the city. I'd like to move here. I could ask *Ansett* for a transfer to Brisbane and spend the weekends with Keith or Gabby. Since we grew up we seldom see each other. We're in danger of becoming a family who only meet at weddings and funerals.

Ω Ω Ω

Virginia hugged Gabriella.

Keith marvelled that his aunt, who wore a smart white linen trouser-suit, neither flinched or recoiled from her rank body odour and breath. 'Maybe it's because she used to be a nurse,' he thought. His Uncle Alex looked at Gabriella with compassion and shook her hand. Gabriella flopped on the sofa, which was upholstered in cream cotton, and lit a cigarette.

Virginia went over to her. "You can't go to your mother's funeral looking like this. When you've finished that cigarette go and have a shower and dress in clean clothes."

"I haven't got any." Gabriella's tone was conversational and Keith was surprised. Usually she sounded sulky or defensive.

"Fiona will lend you something, won't you, darling?"

"Yes, of course."

Gabriella flicked the ash into the ashtray on the coffee table in front of her. "And a shower and clean clothes will make me feel better?"

Virginia sat beside her. "Yes."

"How?"

"When you look in the mirror, Gabby, what do you see?"

Gabriella smiled derisively. "I don't look in the mirror much these days."

"But when you do, what do you see?"

"A hag."

"What else?"

Gabriella looked at her defiantly. "A dirty hag, with greasy hair and a muddy skin. Satisfied?"

"Are you satisfied with looking forty when you're twenty-one?"

She sucked on her cigarette and inhaled deeply. "So ... I go and have a shower and wash my hair and shave my legs and dress in clean clothes and when I come back here Brett will be sitting on the sofa?"

Virginia shook her head.

"Didn't think so," said Gabriella.

Virginia reached over and took her hand. "If you go to bed tonight without having a shower or cleaning your teeth, and throw your dirty clothes on the floor instead of putting them in the washing machine – will Brett be here in the morning?"

They stared at each other. Keith, aware of the stillness in the room, held his breath.

"Will he, Gabby?"

"No," she whispered.

"Do you like looking like a hag?"

"No."

"If you have a shower and wash your hair and dress in clean clothes, you won't look like a hag, will you?"

Gabriella shook her head.

Keith expected her to break out of her compliant mood and say, "You're just like everyone else – if I get a job I'll get over it."

"You'll never stop loving Brett," Virginia continued. "But being on your own and brooding all day is making you more wretched. When you look in the mirror now you're Gabby, the grieving widow who does nothing all day but sit around lamenting. If you get a job you'll still be a grieving widow, but you'll be doing something important. Now, we'll sort out something for you to wear tomorrow. Do you have a black dress?"

"No."

"I packed two," said Fiona.

Virginia stood up. "Good. Come on, Gabriella. Fiona, you come too."

When his sister obediently went into the bathroom, Keith looked at Alex in astonishment. "Mum and I have been telling her that sort of thing for ages. How come she listened to Aunty Virginia?"

Alex smiled. "Her nurse-to-patient tone of voice. You don't ask a patient to do something, you tell them firmly but kindly. If Virginia had got upset and begged her, she would have ignored her too." He smiled drily. "And Virginia's got an air of authority. If she tells someone to do something they do it. Even me," he said, half jokingly.

"Do you want a beer, Uncle Alex?"

"Not just yet. I'd better get these cases unpacked."

An hour and a half later, when Keith had made a salad for lunch and Alex had set the table, they heard the click of shoes on the slate floor. Fiona and Virginia walked into the room smiling. A transformed Gabriella stood between them. Her hair had been cut and washed. Shining waves the colour of bronze fell to just below her ears. Her brown legs were smooth and she was wearing red shorts and a white camisole top. The olive-brown skin on her face glowed and her cheeks were pink.

Keith stared at her. "You've cut your hair."

"Is that all you can say?" asked Virginia.

"Typical man," said Fiona.

"You look great, Gabby," said Keith, giving her a hug. She smelt of soap and toothpaste and Fiona's perfume.

"Yes," said Alex. "You do."

Gabriella smiled self-consciously.

"I'm starving, " said Virginia, walking over to the table. "Let's have lunch."

"What's happening to your mother's house?" Alex asked,

picking up the jug of iced water.

Keith thought about the small weatherboard house, in the country town with its population of three hundred. The beautiful garden his father had planted, with its mixture of wildness and cultivation, disguised its plainness. In the seven years since his death it had become wild, owing to his mother's inability to keep the weeds at bay. The once neat vegetable garden with grass paths between the rows of beds was now an overgrown mess. The trellis their father had erected round the water tanks, to hide their ugliness, had collapsed beneath the weight of the vine she had not pruned. This time next month there would be nothing left of childhood memories or of his parents, just a vacant house for strangers to buy.

"I wanted to buy it. I asked the owner if I could rent it for two years till I'd saved the deposit, but he wants to sell it straightaway."

"Oh, Keith, for goodness sake, we'll give you the deposit," said Virginia.

Alex nodded. "Of course we will."

He shook his head. "It's very good of you, but when someone gives you something you're forever in their debt ... and I'd hate that."

"It's not as if you asked us – we offered. We're family," said Alex.

Keith grunted. "Family. Like Dad and Uncle Johnny and their father – and Margot. Sorry, Uncle Alex. Sometimes I forget you're Margot's brother. That was rude of me."

"You were right," said Virginia vehemently. "*Acacia* should be yours."

"Don't start that again," Alex said wearily.

Keith saw that Fiona and Gabriella were uncomfortable. Ashamed that he had churlishly turned the offer of a loan into a dispute, he sought to change the subject. "Aunty Virginia, did the Mitchells' own *Eumeralla* when you were on *Acacia*?

His mother's reaction had prepared him for evasion, but not the look of shock on both their faces. "They were written up in a farming magazine," he continued, looking questioningly at his aunt.

"We didn't know them." Virginia's normally well-modulated voice sounded high pitched and fraught. She picked up her glass and drank some water.

Keith was puzzled.

"We passed *Acacia* on our way back from the airport," said Fiona. "We couldn't see the house."

Keith noticed that Virginia's face was white.

"What's the matter, Mum?" asked Fiona.

"It's the heat." She stood up. "I'll go outside."

Alex followed Virginia. Fiona, Keith and Gabriella looked at each other.

"What was that all about?" asked Keith.

Fiona shook her head. "I haven't got a clue." When Alex and Virginia were out of sight, she lowered her voice. "Keith, let Dad give you money so you can buy your mother's house."

"I don't want to be in someone's debt."

"Listen, *Acacia* was nothing to do with Dad, but Margot's his sister and they get on well. When Dad started his property development business she gave him money to help him get started. Think of it as Margot's money."

"And therefore yours," said Gabriella.

Later that afternoon Alex sat on the verandah and tried to read the biography of Florence Nightingale that he had found in Gabriella's bookcase, but he was too perturbed to concentrate. The knowledge that Fiona had been so close to *Eumeralla* appalled him. He felt guilty whenever he saw Keith. If Jonathan and Laurence had inherited *Acacia*, Keith would have been a wealthy young man and *Acacia* would have been a better place under his guardianship.

Laurence and Jonathan's wildness, stubbornness and volatile tempers had been offset by an acute instinct of what was right for the land. They hadn't needed to go to Agricultural College. From early childhood they had learned everything about the running of *Acacia* from their father, his managers, the drovers, jackaroos and station hands.

From the moment he had met Jonathan and Laurence, six months after Margot's wedding to their father, he had envied their closeness. He wished that he and his brother David had shared the bond that made the Clarkson boys inseparable. Where David was concerned, Alex was just the younger brother. Alex had spent his youth regretting that he would have to leave *Kingower*, the family property, when he grew up. For Jonathan and Laurence there was no question of one of them leaving *Acacia*. Their father had made them his joint heirs. It was their tragedy that the one person for whom they had harboured an irrational hatred was Margot, their stepmother, who was admired by most people, but had been loathed by them. Being Margot's brother and Virginia's husband had put Alex in a difficult position when Jonathan and Laurence were disinherited and Margot was the sole beneficiary.

CHAPTER 4

Keith couldn't sleep. He was too worried about the effect his mother's funeral would have on Gabriella. It was almost midnight when he pulled back the mosquito net and sprayed himself with insect repellent. Opening the fly-screen door he flashed his torch along the verandah, checking for spider's webs or snakes. He crept round to the other side of the house so he could see the Southern Cross.

Expecting everyone else to be asleep, he stopped when he heard Alex's voice through the open bedroom window. Although he was speaking softly his voice was clear.

"If you hadn't started raving about *Acacia* – "

"My family have suffered because of Margot and another generation is still suffering," interrupted Virginia.

Keith had heard it all before from his father. Feeling like an eavesdropper, he turned to go.

"Virginia, stop it. We've got other problems. Keith might decide to go to *Eumeralla*."

He stopped and listened.

"Why?"

"To ask for a job. He's restless."

'What a great idea, Uncle Alex,' he thought.

To his exasperation a cicada began its ear-splitting chirping and the next few minutes of their dialogue were drowned out. The racket stopped abruptly. He only caught the last two words of Virginia's sentence, but then he heard Alex's reply.

"Sometimes I want to end the agony and tell her."

"No," said Virginia. "She'd go berserk. She'll blame me as usual." Her voice was bitter. "Funny, isn't it? She has so much more rapport with you."

Alex's voice was patient. "Stop it, Virginia."

"Sorry. It's not your fault. It's mine."

"It's all right, darling."

Keith lingered, hoping their conversation would return to *Eumeralla*.

Instead he heard Virginia say, "Things would have been so different if Cheska hadn't died."

There was silence so he crept away, puzzling about what he had overheard.

Fiona's bedroom was on the same side of the house as his and, as he passed it, he saw her writing in her journal, bathed in light from the lamp. All the rooms had doors opening onto the verandah. "Fiona," he whispered. "Come out and look at the stars."

"Okay." She put down her pen and closed her journal.

She wore a white sleeveless nightdress and her straight hair hung down her back. He felt a surge of desire, but suppressed it. They were cousins and Fiona was too townie and sophisticated. Even now she smelt of expensive perfume. He preferred women who smelt natural. To him the scent of soap and skin was erotic. In his opinion men who wore cologne or aftershave were effeminate. Soap, deodorant and toothpaste were the only toiletries he used. Fighting the temptation to reach out and stroke her hair, he lit a mosquito coil and pointed out the stars to her.

"If you were lost, could you find your way home by the stars?" she asked.

"Yes. Dad taught me. He and Uncle Johnny walked out of their boarding school in Sydney one morning and stowed away in the train to Brisbane. They found their way back to *Acacia* by the stars. It was the only time their father ever thrashed them. He took them back to Sydney and the headmaster beat them again."

"Ouch. I bet they never did that again."

He laughed. "They did – a month later. Their father gave up and let them stay on *Acacia*. He made them finish school though. They both matriculated. Not that it did them any good."

"No."

"Fiona, do you know who Cheska was?"

"Francesca – they called her Cheska."

"Who was she?"

Fiona gaped at him. "You don't know?"

Keith shook his head.

"But you must."

He looked at her in exasperation. "But I don't – so tell me."

"Um." She ran her hand over the smooth verandah rail. "Your parents must have told you. No, I don't – "

"I'll shake you in a minute. Come on, who was she? I know she's dead."

"She was your father's first wife."

Keith was too astounded to speak.

Fiona cleared her throat. "Didn't you know he'd been married before?"

"No. What happened?"

"She died just after the war ended. She had an asthma attack."

"God. Poor dad."

She grimaced. "Then you don't know the rest of it. She was Dad's sister – and Margot's."

"No. He wouldn't have married Margot's sister."

"Why not? Mum married her brother. And this was years before he was disinherited."

"I didn't know Margot had a sister called Francesca. Dad talked about Ruth – he liked her. He said that David was a schemer like Margot, but I'd never heard of Francesca. He never mentioned her. Neither did Mum. Are you sure about this?"

"Of course I am."

"Why didn't you tell me before?"

She shrugged. "I thought you knew and the subject never came up."

After he went back to bed Keith still couldn't sleep. He was wondering if Fiona had been mistaken about Francesca, when he heard the sound of crying. Assuming it was Gabriella he threw back the mosquito net and jumped out of bed. But as he tiptoed along the hall he realized the sound was coming from Fiona's room. He peered round her door. "Fiona," he whispered.

He heard her sharp intake of breath.

"Turn on the lamp," he said.

"No."

He closed her door, groped his way to her bedside table and switched on the lamp. She was curled up with her face buried in the pillow. He pulled the mosquito net aside and brushed back the hair covering her face. She turned towards him and screwed up her eyes against the glare of the lamp. Her face was wet and her dark eyelashes were clumped together.

She reached under the pillow and got out a handkerchief. "Sorry. Did I wake you?"

"No, I couldn't sleep." He sat on her bed. "What's wrong?"

She sat up and wiped her eyes. "It's silly."

"Tell me."

"I had this dream. I keep having this dream. It's not a nightmare. I feel happy ... more happy than I've ever been in real life." She hugged her arms to her body. "I'm looking in a mirror and my reflection does different things to me. If I put my hand up, it doesn't and it laughs or smiles when I don't or doesn't when I do. When I wake up I have this feeling that I've lost something. It's as if someone's died and I'll never see them again." She looked embarrassed. "I told you it was stupid."

"How often do you have it?"

"I used to have it all the time when I was a child. I don't have it much now ... about twice a year. Am I mad?"

"No. Lots of people have strange dreams."

"Do you?"

"Probably do, but I never remember them. My ex-girlfriend once had a dream that she was in a London workhouse."

"Keith, your mother's funeral is tomorrow. I'm being neurotic. Go back to bed."

But he spent the final hours till dawn thinking about an incident years ago. He had been on holiday in Sydney with Gabriella and his parents. Fiona was ten, he was seven and Gabriella five. Memories returned. Fiona screaming hysterically in the middle of the night. Footsteps running. Him getting out of bed and going into the hall. Gabriella coming up to him, her eyes wide with fright. Fiona's screams fading to mewls. Soothing words from Virginia and Alex. Fiona repeating a word he didn't understand and now could not recall. His parents coming out of her room, seeing him and Gabriella and sending them back to bed telling them she had only had a nightmare.

What was the word Fiona had kept saying? He couldn't remember. 'But I'd know if I heard it again,' he thought.

No breeze relieved the stifling heat in the cemetery. The sun reflecting off Laurence's and Jonathan's white headstones dazzled Fiona, who wished she had stood in the shade of the gum tree. The dozens of wreaths were already wilting. Their fragrance was almost swamped by the insect repellent the mourners wore.

'This is the worst part,' she thought, as the coffin was lowered into the hole. She glanced across at Gabriella who was standing between Virginia and Keith, but she looked composed. Fiona's relief turned to worry as she remembered Keith's letters to her after Brett's death. He had told her that Gabriella was being brave. Fiona chewed her lip. 'Maybe it would be better if she howled. Her grief gets stuck inside and chokes her soul.'

When the burial service ended people drifted away and stood in groups, leaving Keith and Gabriella alone. Virginia laid a red carnation on Laurence's grave.

Fiona stood next to her. "You're great with Gabby, Mum," she said awkwardly. She seldom complimented her mother.

"Thanks." Virginia's expression revealed gratitude tinged with surprise.

Fiona saw a withered posy of wattle and gum leaves lying on Jonathan's grave. She picked it up. The brittle gum leaves rustled and fragments of wattle fell back onto the marble slab. There was a card attached. *"To Johnny, from Eleanor,"* read Fiona. "Who's she?"

Virginia stared at the card as if in a trance. Then she shook her head and walked away.

'Is she my real mother?' Fiona thought. She tried to assess Eleanor's character from the neat, precise writing on the card. 'If she is, then at least she's not illiterate.' She looked at the inscription on Jonathan's headstone. 'Just his name and years of his birth and death,' she thought. 'My father. I wish I'd known you.' She saw Alex walking towards her.

"Are you all right, Fiona?"

"Yes, Dad." Although tempted to ask him who Eleanor was, she didn't want to hurt him. He had once told her that it was his greatest regret that she was not his real daughter.

After writing a page in her journal about the funeral, Fiona continued,

> My living in Melbourne has done Mum a lot of good. She didn't fuss over me at all. Mum and Dad are flying back to Sydney tomorrow. I haven't told them I'm moving up here yet – I want to make sure that Ansett can transfer me to Brisbane. I hope Gabby doesn't go into a decline after Mum leaves.

"Two more days and Fiona will be back in Melbourne," thought Virginia, hoping her optimism, that the danger was almost over, was not premature. She felt at home in Gabriella's house. She remembered them discussing colour schemes.

"Shall I paint all the walls white, Aunty Virginia?"

"No, the floors are grey and white would be too cold. You want to create a cool atmosphere, not a cold one. And all the rooms in one colour would be monotonous. I'd suggest the palest blues, yellows, pinks and greens. Just a hint of colour."

Virginia packed the last of her clothes in the case and put it by the door. She began to strip the bed just as Gabriella came in.

"Aunty Virginia, don't worry about that. I'll do it later. I wanted to ask you something."

Virginia tried to disguise her tension by tossing the sheet into the corner. "I can't let you do all the work, Gabby," she said, trying to smile normally. "And the sooner these get hung on the line the sooner they'll dry."

"Fiona told Keith something strange."

"Oh?" said Virginia, bracing herself for a question about Eleanor.

"She said that Dad was married to Margot's sister."

Virginia relaxed. "He was."

"Oh. We didn't even know he'd been married before. What was she like?"

"Enchanting. Nothing like Margot."

"Was Francesca a lot younger?"

"Yes – seventeen years." She shook the mosquito net. "Your father, Johnny and I were distraught when Dad married Margot. We thought we'd hate her brothers and sisters too. When they came to *Acacia*, six months after the wedding, we were determined to be ungracious." Virginia's laugh was droll. "And we were ... for a while."

"And what about Johnny?"

"What do you mean?"

"I was thinking about the other sister – Ruth, wasn't it?"

"Yes."

"Or did she look like Margot?"

"No. She and Francesca were alike, but Johnny – " she stopped, appalled by how she had let her guard slip. She had been going to say that he was involved with someone else.

"What, Aunty Virginia?"

Trying to compose herself, she looked at the shadows from the trees, dancing on the yellow walls. "Not interested ... in Ruth, I mean."

"Was she interested in him?"

Virginia tried to look vague. "I don't think so."

"Were Dad and Francesca happy?"

"Yes, very. Cheska was delicate in health and appearance, but she was fiercely independent." She rubbed lotion into her hands.

"They were well suited."

"How come Dad or Mum never told us?"

Virginia slid her ruby and diamond engagement ring onto her finger. "Your father couldn't talk about it. And your mother ... well she once told me that she'd always felt she was in Francesca's shadow."

"And was she?"

Virginia knew she had to be honest. "Yes." She picked up a bottle of Blue Grass perfume from the dressing table and sprayed it on her neck and wrists. "That's often the fate of second wives. Your father was never the same after Cheska died. He had that longing and lost look – she was the only thing he wanted but the only thing he couldn't have."

Gabriella bit her lip. "I know how he felt. Brett is the only thing I want I can't have." She shook her head. "Sorry, I'm being morbid again. Was Margot in your mother's shadow?"

Virginia hesitated.

"Did your father love her or was she just a convenience?" prompted Gabriella.

"We told ourselves that he married her because he needed a wife," she said as she collected her make-up. "But it wasn't true. He loved her. It was our mother who had been the convenience. That hurt us. He used to talk to Margot; he and Mum never talked – except about necessary things. They weren't cold with each other, they just didn't talk much. But he and Margot talked all the time ... about horses, agriculture, politics, literature, poetry – it was as if Margot was another man, and intellectually she was."

"I can see why that hurt you. But Dad said Margot was ugly."

"She wasn't exactly ugly ... although we thought she was when we first saw her. To be fair, she was just terribly plain. Laurence, Johnny and I assumed that her brothers and sisters would look like her, but they didn't even look related. Francesca was pretty, she was blonde and had a beautiful complexion." She shut the lid of her case and locked it. "It's Margot's niece Catriona who looks most like her – she's got the same square jaw, frizzy hair and small sharp eyes, like a bird of prey. And she's skinny like Margot, and tall too – almost six feet. Margot's five feet ten."

"I'll miss you, Aunty Virginia."

Virginia almost burst into tears. Fiona never said that she missed her; she was always pleased to escape. "I'll miss you too, Gabby. If you ever need me just phone and I'll come."

Gabriella's hug was uninhibited and warm. Fiona's rare hugs were grudging and brief. "I promise I'll sort myself out. I haven't been fair to Keith, have I?"

"No. But you weren't yourself. He understood that. Repay him by rebuilding your life."

"I'm scared that if I'm happy it'll all be taken away again."

"You won't find anything by staying home all day, Gabby, but you might find it if you go back to teaching or do anything else that appeals to you. You could go overseas."

"I'm not adventurous like Fiona. I've never had any desire to go anywhere else. I love the Darling Downs. Brett and I wanted to buy a house and have children. That's all we wanted. Was that too much?"

Keith appeared in the doorway. "The car's got to be back at the airport by eleven or they'll charge you a full day's hire." He picked up her case. "Um," he looked at her awkwardly. "You and Uncle Alex offered to lend me the money for the deposit on Mum's house."

"No, we didn't."

He looked mortified. "Sorry. I thought you – "

"We offered to *give* you the money." Virginia smiled. "That offer still stands."

"Thanks. I accept."

"Good." Feeling a wave of emotion, she kissed his cheek. "You look so like your father that sometimes seeing you makes me sad, but happy too, because part of him is still alive." She gave him a little shake. "And you're stubborn – just like him. But I'm glad you've been reasonable about this."

Fiona was waiting in the driveway with Alex. Virginia glowed with happiness as she received the only spontaneous embrace Fiona had ever given her.

Keith and Fiona had got into the habit of staying up and talking or playing chess after everyone had gone to bed. He reluctantly felt attracted to her in spite of her being sophisticated, spending too long under the shower and refusing to go anywhere without putting on make-up. At night when they talked, his daytime irritation with her vanished.

Keith took the chess set out to the verandah and put it on the table. After he had turned on the outside light and lit a mosquito coil he went back to the kitchen where Fiona was making them iced chocolate. He watched her filling the glass with milk. "I could get addicted to this," he said as she put scoops of ice cream on top and dusted them with cocoa powder.

"Did you check for snakes?"

He nodded. "There's only a death adder. Don't fret, it's at the end of the verandah."

She shuddered. "You are joking?"

"Yes, of course, Townie," he said with a grin.

"Townie nothing! They don't give you a playful nip, they sink their fangs into you and inject as much venom as they can," she retorted, handing him a glass. "And if you don't get to hospital in time you die an excruciating death."

He sipped the chocolate. "Yum. You can stay forever."

"Funny you should say that," she said as they walked onto the verandah.

"Why?" he asked, as he sat down.

"I'm going to ask *Ansett* for a transfer to Brisbane."

Her news didn't surprise him. Fiona had moved more often than anyone he knew. "I'd love to see more of you. Gabby would too," he said, moving his white pawn.

She advanced one of her central pawns two squares. "I can rent a flat in Brisbane and stay there during the week. I could buy a house near here for weekends and holidays. Or just stay with you or Gabby."

He moved his bishop. "The way you cook I'd pay you to stay weekends."

"Mum taught me."

It was rare to hear Fiona praise Virginia. "She must have been a good teacher."

"She was. It's the only thing we enjoyed doing together."

"Won't you miss the high life of the city?"

"No. I'll miss Aunty Ruth. I won't miss going to *Kingower*."

"Is Margot that bad?"

"It's not just her," she said, moving her knight. "I'm left out because I can't ride. My uncle and cousins go off riding all day and I'm left alone with Mum and Aunty Ruth. Even Aunty Margot rides and she's seventy-two."

"You can learn."

Fiona shook her head. "They tried to teach me when I was five. I was so terrified I screamed and the horse almost bolted. Uncle David was furious with me, and he and Mum had a terrible argument. She accused him of being a useless teacher."

"If you were that frightened it sounds as if he was." He studied the board.

"Catriona and Kim are clever. They look down on me because I haven't got a degree and don't have ambitions. I just want to find somewhere I feel I belong. Every time I come up here I feel at home. Maybe it's because I was born here."

"Were you? I thought you were born in Sydney."

"No, Queensland."

"Whereabouts?"

Her cheeks reddened. "I'm not sure ... somewhere round here." Her next move left her open to checkmate.

"Fiona! Do you really want to do that?"

"No. Thanks." Her hand hovered over her queen. "Ah, no not fair. I never warn you when you do something silly. You win. We'll start another game." Fiona put her pieces on their squares. "Listen.

You know you were telling me that *Acacia*'s in a bad way? Do you think that you, me and Gabby might be able to afford to buy it together one day?" she asked.

He felt a stirring of excitement. "Even if I did make a success of a gardening business it would be years before I'd be able to afford *Acacia* or a property like it. Fiona, are you serious?"

"Yes. I love the country, but I'm left out at *Kingower*. They despise me because I'm a coward."

"What? Just because you can't ride?"

"I'm scared of horses."

"So? That doesn't make you a coward."

"They think I'm like Uncle Johnny."

Keith stared at her. "He wasn't a coward."

"But he didn't fight in the war."

"He wasn't allowed to. He was needed on the land – some men had to stay behind. Who told you he was a coward?"

"Catriona and Kim – my cousins. Aunty Margot told them."

"But – a coward? You must know how he died?"

She nodded. "His house caught fire."

"Not his house. It was the house belonging to one of his neighbours in Brisbane. Uncle Johnny rushed in and got a little boy out and went back for the mother and a baby, but the roof collapsed and they all died."

Fiona looked baffled. "He didn't live in Brisbane."

"He did. He went there when our grandfather cut him out of the will. He rented a house and worked for the Department of Agriculture."

"Oh, God. Are you sure?"

"Yes. Dad told me. How come your mum didn't tell you?"

She shook her head. "Talking about him upsets her. Now I know why."

CHAPTER 5

At the beginning of March, Fiona flew up to Sydney for Virginia's birthday. Normally she dreaded these dutiful visits, but this time she was looking forward to it. She decided to stay for three days instead of flying back to Melbourne the next morning. Since returning from Queensland she rang her parents more often and found that, instead of Virginia reproaching her, they were able to have sensible conversations. The night she arrived in Sydney she wrote in her journal.

> I've been selfish. I used to resent Mum's questions, but maybe she wasn't being nosy; just interested. After all she is my mother – not my real mother, but my mother in every other sense. She loved me and sent me to the best school in Sydney. To make up for my ingratitude I've bought her a pearl brooch for her birthday.
>
> I'll ask her about Johnny. Keith might be wrong. Laurence and Johnny were inseparable and Laurence might have woven a fantasy about him. I'm constantly fantasizing that my real mother was a secret agent in the war, so I'll understand.

Fiona had been keeping a journal since she was eight, and had made her first entry the day her parents told her she was adopted. That evening, instead of doing her homework, she wrote about her distress in a new exercise book that had originally been destined for arithmetic. She ended with the sentence:

> My real daddy was Mummy's brother. His name was Johnny. He died. But who is my real Mummy?

Throughout her childhood Fiona had poured out her yearning for brothers and sisters and her abhorrence of Virginia's possessiveness into her diary.

Today Mummy told me what to put in my essay about the school holidays. She said I can write – *I had a lovely holiday. But the day I enjoyed most was when I went to the Botanical Gardens with my mother.* I want to write about the week we spent at *Kingower*.

She kept it hidden, knowing that if Virginia found it she would read it and accuse her of ingratitude. In her teens, just as she was struggling to become independent, the luxurious house in Vaucluse became a prison. Virginia grew more possessive. Fiona was forbidden to wear the mini-skirt and Virginia ranted against the Beatles, calling them uncouth savages. Boyfriends were inevitably too common, too dull or supported the Labor Party. When she was eighteen Fiona had rented a flat with a friend. On her first night in her new home she wrote,

Bondi
July 1964

I am free. There is no mother hovering around, prying and fussing. She cried when I left and she's certain that I'll let some man have his wicked way with me and get pregnant. Her opinion of me is insulting. Although I have swapped a large bedroom with antiques and views over Sydney Harbour for a small room with grotty furniture, I am happy. I can play my Beatles records without her complaining. I'll miss walking down to Rose Bay in the morning and catching the ferry to work. Instead I'll have to travel in a crowded bus.

She was irritated when Virginia phoned every day, begged her to come home and expected her to spend every weekend in Vaucluse. When her friend got married, Fiona decided to travel. Before she went to England for two years, she took all her diaries to

Ruth, Alex's sister who lived in Melbourne.

When she had returned to Australia four months ago with a pile of journals and photographs cataloguing her travel experiences, the thought of living in Sydney within easy reach of Virginia had been unbearable. She moved to Melbourne. Alex, happy that Fiona was back in Australia and hoping she would finally settle somewhere, bought her a two-bedroom unit in Hawthorn, near Ruth's Victorian terraced house.

Virginia rang twice a week, but the five hundred miles that separated Sydney and Melbourne made the contact tolerable. Fiona no longer had to invent excuses for not visiting, and her involvement with the tennis club prevented her from making regular weekend trips to Sydney.

Ω   Ω   Ω

Virginia enjoyed her fifty-fifth birthday. Fiona and Alex took her to Doyle's seafood restaurant, for dinner. Located on the beach at Watsons Bay, it had views over the harbour. They arrived in the early evening so they could watch the sunset and the moon rising over the water. Fiona looked happier than they had ever seen her. Virginia wondered if she had a new boyfriend, but experience had taught her not to ask.

"We've got some news," said Alex. "Catriona's getting married in September."

Fiona picked up the menu. "I hope he's horse mad."

Virginia saw her fleetingly envious expression.

Alex nodded. "They met at one of the trekking holidays at *Kingower*. He's a teacher at Wesley College."

"What's his name?"

"Stefan Jovanovics."

"Is he Polish?"

Alex shook his head. "He was born here. His father's Hungarian, but his mother's family are English."

"I don't suppose I'll be invited to the wedding," said Fiona.

"You will be," said Alex. "But if you're not, Virginia and I won't be going either."

"Dad, I don't want you to keep quarrelling with your only brother because of me."

"I won't if you get invited to the wedding."

Virginia made herself stay silent.

The next day Alex went to Randwick to look at a house that was coming up for auction. Virginia was delighted when Fiona suggested they go into Sydney to do some shopping. It had been over ten years since they had gone shopping together. Virginia remembered the laborious expeditions with Fiona moaning that she would rather play tennis or go to the beach with her friends.

After Alex left, Fiona knocked on her parents' bedroom door. "Mum, can I ask you something?"

Hearing the caution in Fiona's voice, Virginia tensed. "What about?"

"Jonathan. I didn't ask while Dad was around, because I didn't want to upset him."

"But you don't mind upsetting me?" She saw the familiar guarded expression on Fiona's face. "Darling, that was silly of me. What do you want to know?"

Fiona smiled tightly. "It doesn't matter."

'We're being formal with each other again,' Virginia thought. "Yes, it does. It matters to you and you were right to wait till your father had gone. What do you want to know?"

"How did he die?"

Virginia had never been able to talk about it. Knowing that Fiona was embarrassed by displays of emotion, she fought for control, but her throat tightened so much she could hardly speak.

"Sorry, Mum. It's just that I thought he was a coward, but – "

"A coward?" Virginia shook her head violently.

"Keith said he died trying to save someone from a burning

house. Is that true?"

Virginia tried to breathe evenly. "Yes." She went over to a camphor wood chest under the window, that had belonged to Alex's grandmother. It was so old its scent had faded. In the middle of the chest, under the photograph albums, she found an envelope. With trembling hands she took out a newspaper cutting and handed it to Fiona, who started to read it.

She looked at Virginia in consternation. "You were there?"

"Yes. Our father had cut him out of his will – "

"I thought he cut them both out."

"He did eventually, but he cut Johnny out first."

"Why?"

Virginia, unable to tell her the real reason, thought quickly. "He had a fight with Margot."

"I should have guessed."

"Laurence told me it didn't matter, because he intended to ignore the will and make Johnny a joint owner. He had it all worked out. I went to Brisbane to see Johnny and tell him. As soon as I turned into the street I saw ... " Virginia's voice faltered as she remembered the clouds of black smoke. "I couldn't smell anything, but the wind was blowing the other way. It was the house two doors away from where Johnny was living. I was relieved that it wasn't his house.

"People were yelling that the fire brigade was coming, but a woman and her children were trapped inside and a man had gone in to rescue them. I knew it was Johnny – it was the sort of thing he'd do. Then I saw him – he came out of the house carrying a little boy. He thrust the child into my arms. Johnny was dressed in white – he'd been going off to play cricket when the fire started. His jumper and face were all sooty and his hand had an awful burn on it. Burnt flesh, I could smell his burnt flesh. The child was screaming 'Mummy, Mummy.' I realized Johnny was going back to get the others. I dropped the boy and ran after him. I grabbed him, but he shook me off. He went in and it took two women and one man to hold me back to stop me from following him. The firemen arrived – but it was too late."

Virginia relived the terrifying moment when part of the roof collapsed. She could almost smell the smoke and hear the crackle of flames and feel the blistering heat. She saw the thousands of sparks explode into the air and blow away in the wind. Until the moment they had found Jonathan's body she had hoped that he had got away. She had considered all the possibilities. He had escaped out of the back door just before the roof fell in. He had been hit on the head and got amnesia and wandered off somewhere – perhaps he had even gone to his cricket match.

"Mum." Fiona sounded alarmed.

Virginia pulled herself back to the present. Fiona's arm was outstretched to touch. Never demonstrative, she looked as if she was about to stroke a strange animal.

"Why did you think Johnny was a coward?"

"It doesn't matter. I'm just so glad Keith was right. That sounds awful, but ... well ... for years I've thought that he was a coward, and I was too because I'm afraid of horses. I feel differently about myself now. It was bad enough knowing about my real mother."

Remorse flooded Virginia's conscience. "I've done lots of things that have been dishonourable, Fiona. I wish I could undo them."

"So have I, so has everyone. But you tried to stop him."

In this mood of Fiona's kindness, Virginia wanted to tell her the truth, but hesitated, terrified of the denunciation that would surely follow. Now was the time to confess. To say, 'I've got something to tell you. Years ago I did a terrible thing – I lied to you. It's been on my conscience ever since.' She bit her lip. 'Say it,' she told herself. 'Say it now – get it over with.' She exhaled.

Fiona went to the door. "Come on, Mum, let's go shopping."

And the right moment was gone.

That night, during dinner, Fiona told Virginia and Alex she was moving to Brisbane.

Virginia felt as if she'd been punched. "You can't!" She managed to put her wine glass down without dropping it. She saw that Fiona was scowling.

"Why can't I?"

"Don't be cranky, Pet," said Alex. "Your mother means ... what about a job?"

"*Ansett* are transferring me. I'm going in August."

"Have you told them you don't want to go?" asked Virginia indignantly.

"I do want to go, I asked for the transfer."

Virginia felt Alex kick her leg under the table.

"I thought you were happy in Melbourne," he said.

"You've only been there for five months," said Virginia. "All this moving around seems a bit unstable."

"I am unstable, Mum."

"I didn't mean it like that." Virginia, trying to hide her apprehension, cut a piece of steak and put it in her mouth.

"No, Mum. I'm not normal. I've never been in love."

"You've never met the right man," said Alex.

Fiona shook her head. "Catriona and Kim were falling in and out of love all the time when they were younger. I've never felt like that with any of my boyfriends."

Alex sipped his wine. "Everyone is different."

"But, I've never felt I've belonged anywhere. I feel as if I'm searching for something and can't find it ... I don't even know what it is. Somewhere in my mind I've got this inkling that I've lost something or someone."

Virginia heard the desperation in her voice. Worried that her guilt was obvious, she looked at her plate.

Fiona sighed. "Sane people don't feel like this. Should I see a psychiatrist?"

"No, of course not," said Alex. "You're entirely normal."

"Then why do I feel like this?"

He smiled. "Maybe lots of people feel strange things and they don't talk about it."

Virginia wished she could behave as calmly as Alex. She was still chewing her steak and hoped she could swallow it without gagging. 'Since she was eight, I've lived with the worry that she'd find out the truth,' she thought. 'Every time she went to Queensland it's been like playing Russian Roulette. When she left Queensland the game was over and I'd won – till next time. Then there had only been one bullet in the chamber. With Fiona living in Brisbane life will be a permanent game of Russian Roulette, but with five bullets in the chamber.'

"We have to tell her," said Alex as soon as they arrived home from driving Fiona to the airport.

Virginia paced round the bedroom. "She'll hate us – well she'll hate me."

"She won't hate either of us if we manage it properly."

She sat at the dressing table and put her head in her hands. "You're such an optimist."

"We've got till August – it's almost April so that gives us four months to plan."

"Oh, I can't have this hanging over my head that long."

"We're going on holiday soon – do you want to tell her before we leave or wait till we get back?"

"When we get back. We'll invite her here for the weekend."

"No. We'll go to Melbourne," said Alex. "If she flies into a fury she'll walk out of here. If we're in her unit she can tell us to leave, but she can't throw us out. We won't go till we've explained how things happened."

Melbourne
March 1972

Keith was right! Now I can face Catriona and Kim as equals. Catriona announced her engagement to Stefan Jovanovics yesterday. Next weekend I'm going to *Kingower* and I'll make an announcement in the middle of their Sunday lunch. I hope

Stefan's there so he'll see what a despicable family he's marrying into.

Ω   Ω   Ω

"Apart from natural disasters, people shape historical events," Stefan told his fourth form history students. "To comprehend history you have to understand the people who made it. Not just what they did, but why they did it. Imagine the world today if Oliver Cromwell, Charles Dickens, Lenin or Hitler had never been born." He wrote, IMAGINE IF, on the blackboard. "I want you to rewrite history. Any century, any country, any event, any person. For example, imagine if Alexander Fleming had employed a conscientious cleaning lady."

The boys laughed.

"Depending on who or what you choose, you might have to do research so I'm giving you eight weeks. I want you to be creative and show an appreciation of the delicate balance between how it is, and how it might have been."

The bell clanged, ending his last lesson for the week.

In his flat in Albert Park, Stefan showered and packed casual clothes, jodhpurs and riding boots, pleased to be free of the formality of a suit for two days. Before heading for *Kingower* he drove to Prahran, where he bought bottles of wine and chocolates for dinner and bunches of flowers for Catriona and her mother.

As well as breeding horses, *Kingower* was a riding school that ran horse-trekking weekends and holidays. Located in lush countryside at the foot of the Great Dividing Ranges in Victoria, it had belonged to the Lancaster family since 1853. Their ancestor had been a groom on an estate in England. He had emigrated when he heard about the gold discoveries in Australia. Within a month of his arrival in

Ballarat he had found a nugget the size of an orange at Kingower Gold Field. He bought twenty horses and one thousand acres of land.

Catriona and her sister Kim were veterinary surgeons who worked at a practice in Whittlesea, the nearest town. They lived in cottages on *Kingower*, two hundred yards from the homestead. Before the war, when the staff had lived on the property, their cottages had been occupied by the gardener and the housekeeper. Originally they had been painted white with red corrugated iron roofs. Catriona's was still white but she had chosen navy for the door, roof and woodwork. Kim's colour scheme was cream and chestnut brown. Forest lay behind the cottages and the gardener had planted their front gardens with lilac trees. Lavender hedges lined the paths leading to the front doors. Two cottages, which had once housed the chauffeur and cook, had been converted into one large house for Margot, who was Kim's and Catriona's widowed aunt.

On Friday night when Stefan arrived at *Kingower* he found the cottages and homestead deserted. Puzzled, he went to Margot's house and knocked on the door. There was no reply. On his way back to the homestead he saw her walking up the step to the verandah.

"Mrs Clarkson," he called, running up to her. "Where is everyone?"

"Oh, Stefan, one of the mares has given birth, but we can't find the foal. Someone left the paddock gate open. The gardener saw her with the foal and told me, but when we got back the foal had disappeared."

"Give me a torch and I'll help."

She shook her head. "We've all been searching for two hours. Catriona and Kim are in the stables – the mare's got a retained placenta."

It amused him that, although Catriona was called Tree by the rest of the family, Margot disliked the nickname and refused to use it.

Stefan ran over to the stables and arrived just as Catriona pulled out the placenta. He screwed up his face. "Ugh."

She held out her arm. "Kiss my hand."

"Yuck." He stepped back. "Get away."

"That's a romantic way to greet your fiancée," Catriona quipped.

He grinned. "I'll be romantic when you've washed. He looked at Kim, but her face was blank. He realized she hadn't moved since he'd come in. Her straight black hair shone in the light from the bare bulb. The pupils of her toffee-brown eyes were large and her face was paler than usual.

"Are you okay?" he asked.

"The creek – the foal's in the creek," said Kim.

Catriona rubbed soap on her arms. "It's too far away."

"Tree, she's in the creek."

"Did you look there?" asked Stefan.

"No," said Catriona as she pulled a nail brush through a cake of soap.

"Oliver said the foal is in the creek," said Kim slowly.

Catriona spun round. "Oliver?"

"Who's he?" asked Stefan.

Catriona picked up a horse blanket and thrust it into his arms. "Quick! We've got to get to the creek." She grabbed two torches and gave one to Kim.

Bewildered, Stefan followed them. As quickly as the darkness would allow, they ran to the creek and scrambled down the muddy bank to the stones below. The heavy rain that had fallen the day before had been the first for months and the water level was low. The night was cold and their breath emerged as white wisps.

Catriona flashed her torch downstream. "There it is!"

The foal was close to the opposite bank.

Stefan groaned. "It would be at the widest part."

They ran down the creek till they were opposite the foal. Stefan followed them into the water, wincing as it swirled round his calves. Kim slipped on the stones and fell before he could grab her.

"I'm all right," she panted, ignoring his outstretched hand. "No.

It's easier to crawl." She reached the foal first. "She's alive!"

Using the horse blanket as a stretcher they lifted the foal out of the water.

Kim checked its legs. "Nothing broken."

Stefan took off his jumper and put it over the foal.

Catriona contemplated the formidable slope of the bank. "We can't get it up that by ourselves. I'll run back and get help."

"No, Tree. We've got Stefan. Time's crucial. She'll die if we don't get her warm and fed."

Stefan thought she was going to die anyway, but kept his opinion to himself.

"She'll die if we drop her down the slope," argued Catriona.

"Shut up, Tree. She's not going to die!"

"Wait," Stefan said. "Let's work this out. We won't go straight up the bank – we'll traverse it." He heard Catriona's teeth chattering. "Tree, you and Kim take the front of the blanket and one of you shine the torch."

When they reached the top the journey to the stables was easy. They reunited the foal with its mother, but it was too exhausted to feed. It lay on the pile of straw and closed its eyes. Stefan thought it had died until he saw it was still breathing.

"Kim, I'm sorry, but she's dying," said Catriona.

"Stop being drippy and help me," snapped Kim, rubbing towels over its sodden fur. "Get me the milk pump and prepare a vitamin injection. Stefan, go and get Dad and Aunty Margot. And we all need dry clothes and jumpers."

In the homestead their mother was cooking the dinner. David and Margot were in his study doing the accounts. Watching Margot taking charge, Stefan realized Kim and Catriona had inherited her decisive nature. Compared to Margot, their mother was insipid and vague. It was Margot who told her to go to the cottages and get dry clothes. When she had gone, Margot planned the new dining arrangements.

"It will have to be in shifts. Two people need to stay with the foal all night. And one of them has to be Kim or Catriona in case there's a crisis. Thank goodness there's no ride this weekend." She looked at him. "You're soaked. Go and have a shower."

To Stefan's amazement the foal was alive in the morning. Although weak it was taking milk from its mother and looked brighter.

"Damn," said David. "Fiona's coming for lunch today."

"I'll ring her and put her off," said Catriona. "She's the last person I want to see after a sleepless night."

"It might seem rude," said her mother.

Kim stroked the foal. "She invited herself. We didn't ask her to come. Anyway, we'll be too busy nursing this little one to entertain Fiona."

It wasn't until Stefan was getting ready to go home on Sunday evening that he and Catriona were alone. They went to her cottage and Catriona spooned coffee grounds into the basket of the percolator.

"Tree, who's Oliver?" He saw her hesitate. "Have I got a rival?"

She shook her head and smiled. "Did you see another man in the stable?"

"He must have leapt behind a bail of straw when he saw me coming." He grinned. "Did I interrupt a romantic moment with a man who would have kissed your gory hand?" He stood behind her and put his arms round her waist. "A less squeamish man than I am?"

Catriona chuckled. "No."

He lifted a curl and kissed her neck. "Then who is he?"

"You won't believe me."

"I might."

She turned round and faced him. "All right. He was our brother." She slipped out of his arms. "Do you want biscuits or sultana toast?"

"Hang on. You haven't got a brother."

"He died of scarlet fever when I was a baby and before Kim was born." Casually, as if her statement had been normal, she filled the percolator with water and put it on the gas.

Stefan frowned. "This is ludicrous."

She took a deep breath. "Oliver's been talking to Kim all her life." She poured milk into the mugs. "Her first word was "Oliver" – not "mummy" or "daddy." I can see you think I'm bonkers. I knew you'd be sceptical so I never told you."

"You really believe in all that mumbo-jumbo?"

She folded her arms. "What about the foal? Give me a rational explanation."

"The only place you hadn't looked was the creek. Sounds logical to me."

"She knew the foal was alive and she knew its sex."

"It could have been dead or alive and it could have been male or female. She made a lucky guess."

"Look, Stefan, the chances of the poor little creature being alive were negligible."

He laughed uproariously. "Tree, you're a vet. How can you believe in all this garbage?"

"You've seen what she's like with animals."

"Animals like her – so what? Animals like lots of people."

"They more than like her. Animals like and trust me, but when Kim's around they ignore me. Every pet I've ever had ends up being hers not mine. Animals that are fraught, calm down when she's around. You've seen it yourself, and you've commented on it."

"But there's nothing spooky or psychic about it."

"What would you call it then?"

He shrugged. "Special or unusual, but not mystical. She's got a gift, just like someone has a gift for singing or athletics."

"No. It's more than that. When Kim was three and I was four we were playing outside one day. She ran over to Dad and told him that Oliver said there was a snake in the rhododendron bushes. There was. It was a tiger snake and I was about to go and hide there."

"She saw the snake herself. Lots of children have imaginary friends – Kim had one and she called him Oliver. She saw the snake and thought he had told her about it." He kissed her lips. "I'm glad you didn't get bitten, though." Slipping his hand under her jumper he unbuttoned her shirt. "Very glad."

Melbourne
March 1972

    Catriona rang this morning to tell me not to come for lunch, and told me some silly lie about a foal falling in the creek. Apparently Kim's had another premonition. They only have visitors' rides once a fortnight so I told her I'd come in two weeks' time. She sounded annoyed, but they can't put me off. The time has come for Aunty Margot to be shown for what she is.

Ω   Ω   Ω

Kim went to the mahogany sideboard in the dining room at *Kingower* and took out a lace tablecloth. "Where do you want Fiona to sit, Tree?"

    "As far away from me as possible."

    "What's wrong with this cousin of yours?" asked Stefan.

    "She's petrified of horses," said Catriona. "And she's boring. All she does is prattle on about her job at Ansett. She's only a clerk, but she carries on as if she owns the airline."

    "And she goes on and on about the tennis club," said Kim. "Being a member makes her feel so important anyone would think she was the Prime Minister."

    Catriona counted out seven pieces of silver cutlery. "Actually, she's not really our cousin. She's adopted."

    "A dumb blonde," said Kim, putting a crystal wine glass beside every place. "She wouldn't know what an oesophagus was if she fell over one."

He grinned. "Have you ever fallen over an oesophagus?"

"You know what Kim means ... she's a dope," said Catriona.

"And she's a slut," added Kim.

'And she's exquisite,' thought Catriona. 'And I'm terrified you're going to fall in love with her.'

CHAPTER 6

Catriona and Kim hadn't always hated Fiona. When they were children they had looked forward to her visits. She invented exciting games and, in spite of her volcanic temper, they got on well. When Fiona had told them she was adopted they had been fascinated. Because she was upset that they were not her real cousins, they became blood sisters in a ceremony held under the oldest tree on *Kingower*. Catriona and Kim had picked scabs from their knees while Fiona, having no scabs to pick, cut her finger with a knife. Fiona had been in raptures when, after mingling their blood, they had declared she was closer than a cousin. Her inability to ride was the only thing that marred their relationship, but whenever they tried to persuade her to try again, she refused.

Fiona was a year older than Catriona and two years older than Kim. But, as they grew up, Kim and Catriona had matured faster than Fiona, who was held back by Virginia's over-protectiveness. When Catriona and Kim discovered that animals were slaughtered for meat, they refused to eat it. Mealtimes became a battlefield, but after a week of wasted meat their parents gave in. Catriona and Kim had been vegetarians ever since. To their disgust, Fiona's resolve to follow them had lasted until she went home to Sydney. Under Virginia's threats she had caved in.

It was when Catriona was seventeen and going out with her first boyfriend, that the first incident that fractured their relationship with Fiona took place. At a party on New Year's Eve he pursued Fiona and overlooked Catriona. She knew she was plain, but her parents and Margot had told her that her personality, skill with horses, and intelligence were more valuable attributes than beauty. Seeing her boyfriend's reaction to Fiona had shattered this belief and made her conscious of her angular face, large jaw, small grey eyes and frizzy hair.

"I haven't even got a good figure like you," she had wailed to Kim. "I'm too tall, too thin and flat chested."

"Since Twiggy became famous, your figure's just right," Kim had consoled her. "You could be a model." She giggled. "Twiggy and Tree."

Catriona shook her head. "No photographer would want to take pictures of my face."

The next morning they ignored Fiona.

She railed against their unfairness. "He was a dag!" she shouted, following them to the paddock. "He chased me. I wouldn't be seen dead with him. He had pimples. If he's the only boy you can get I pity you!"

"Your real father was a coward, Fiona," taunted Catriona.

"He wasn't!" yelled Fiona, raising her hand.

Catriona dodged her slap. "He was. And you're a coward too – you're scared of horses."

"He wasn't a coward!"

"He wouldn't fight in the war," said Kim.

"Liar!"

"Aunty Margot told us," said Catriona triumphantly.

"She's a liar."

Kim climbed over the fence into the paddock then turned to face Fiona. "Have you ever seen a photo of Jonathan Clarkson in uniform?"

Catriona laughed when she saw Fiona's expression. "Of course you haven't – there isn't one. Your real parents were trash. The Lancasters are too good for you. You were born in the gutter and that's where you should have stayed."

Fiona's devastated expression sobered Catriona. Before she could apologize to her, Fiona turned and ran down the track. "Fiona! I'm sorry."

Kim and Catriona chased her, but Fiona was spurred on by rage. They got to the beginning of homestead gardens just as Fiona tore up the steps past the two sets of parents, Ruth and Margot, who had all been relaxing on the verandah. From the shelter of the trees they saw Virginia jump up and follow Fiona inside.

"Hell," said Catriona. "What will we do?"

Kim chewed her lip. "Aunty Virginia will be furious. And Aunty Ruth and Uncle Alex."

"If she tells," said Catriona. "She's not a sneak."

"No. She'll get over it, if we apologize."

Catriona shook her head. "If someone said that to me I'd never get over it."

"But it's true," said Kim.

"That's why I shouldn't have said it."

"Well she shouldn't have flirted with – " Kim stopped when she saw Fiona run onto the verandah carrying her suitcase. Alex and Virginia followed her to her car. She ignored them and flung her case on the back seat.

Kim and Catriona ran to the gate, but failed to close it before Fiona drove up. She blasted the horn and they jumped out of the way. Catriona was horrified by the speed Fiona was going. She saw everyone hurrying down the drive.

"What the devil's going on?" asked David.

Catriona turned red.

"We had a fight," said Kim.

"What about?" asked Virginia.

"Last night," mumbled Catriona.

"Fiona spent most of the night trying to keep out of his way," said Alex.

"Pretending to try," said Kim.

Virginia glared at her. "She wouldn't want a gawky boy with acne – she's got better taste. If she has an accident I'll never forgive you."

"Just a minute," objected David. "If she has an accident it's because she's driving too fast. And she almost ran over my daughters!"

"She's an excellent driver – under normal circumstances," said

Alex.

"Fiona's volatile whatever the circumstances," David retorted.

"No," said Ruth. "She sticks to the speed limit and never gets impatient. So – what have you two done to her?"

"Tree's upset after the way Fiona behaved last night!" said Kim. "We had an argument about it and she overreacted."

"We're leaving, David," said Virginia. "Alex will ring you when we get back to Sydney. And you had both better pray that Fiona arrives safely."

For a year Fiona sent back Kim's and Catriona's letters, and hung up when they rang her. Only when they begged Ruth to intervene did Fiona accept the invitation to the *Kingower* New Year's Eve Party. Gradually their friendship was restored, although it never had the same intensity. Two years later, Kim, her father and Margot had caught Kim's fiancé kissing Fiona. This time it was Catriona and Kim who returned Fiona's letters and hung up when she rang. Alex, Virginia and Ruth, who believed Fiona's version of events, had stayed away from *Kingower*. Then Fiona had gone to England. When she returned two years later she was permitted to visit *Kingower*, but it was made obvious that it was only because of Ruth and Alex.

Ω Ω Ω

Fiona chose a selection of her Beatles and Rolling Stones cassettes to entertain her during the two-hour drive to *Kingower*. She backed the M.G., that her parents had given her on her twenty-first birthday, out of her garage. She considered buying wine and flowers but, as it was her aim to discredit them in front of Stefan, decided that it would be hypocritical.

"Here comes the Sun," sang The Beatles.

'Here comes the Truth,' thought Fiona.

As she approached Whittlesea, the nearest town to *Kingower*, she recalled every detail of the incident that had led to her banishment. A family dinner had been held at *Kingower* on Saturday night to celebrate Kim's engagement. The next morning, a ride over the Great Dividing Ranges and a picnic lunch had been planned. As usual, Fiona, Virginia and Ruth stayed behind making sandwiches, pies and cakes. In the afternoon they would drive in the station-wagon to the place chosen for the picnic. Kim's fiancé was unable to ride because he had sprained his ankle earlier in the week.

After Kim had set off on horseback with the others, Fiona, Virginia and Ruth prepared the picnic. When they finished, Ruth and Virginia went for a walk. Fiona and Kim's fiancé sat in the lounge listening to Beatles records. For half an hour they talked about the engagement party which was two weeks away.

"You're the most gorgeous girl I've ever seen," he said, touching her hand.

She looked at him coldly and pulled her hand away. Before she could stand up he pushed her back on the sofa and kissed her. Trapped beneath him she struggled to escape.

"Fiona!" shouted David.

He sat up. Fiona leapt off the sofa, trying to tuck in her blouse. Kim, who had her arm around Margot, looked stricken.

Ruth and Virginia ran in from the garden.

"Are you ill, Margot?" asked Ruth.

"My horse saw a snake and bolted. I fell off."

"Are you hurt?"

Margot shook her head.

"But she was shaken so we came back here and caught these two writhing on the sofa," said David.

"No, I was trying to push him away!" protested Fiona.

"It was nothing to do with me. She just started kissing me," he said.

Fiona shoved him so hard he nearly fell over. "You started kissing me."

"Your daughters seem to have a preference for tom cats," said Virginia.

He limped over and put his arms round Kim. "If I'd known what she was trying to do I would have left the room, but she just jumped on me."

Fiona kicked him on his sprained ankle. "Liar! You're after her money, aren't you?"

David grabbed her wrist and pulled her away. "Fiona, leave *Kingower* and don't ever come back."

"No, David," said Ruth. "Why don't you believe her?"

"She's done this before! I'm not having my daughters made miserable because she seduces their boyfriends."

Margot sat down. "You've got no morals, Fiona. You're a cheat, a calculating cheat."

"You're a fine one to talk about cheating, Margot," said Virginia. "You cheated my brothers out of their inheritance. *Kingower* was saved by the money that should have been theirs. Clarkson money saved this property – Fiona's got more right here than any Lancaster!"

'Yes, I have got more right here than the Lancasters,' thought Fiona as she opened the black iron gates to *Kingower*. As she drove up the winding drive that was lined with rhododendrons and azaleas, her anger increased. Through the gap in the bushes on her left she saw Margot's house. The conversion of the two cottages into one had been designed by Alex. 'Done with the money she got from stealing *Acacia*,' she thought.

The homestead came into view. In Victorian times when the first Lancaster had built the house, the plain one-storey design, surrounded by a wide verandah, had been scorned as being boring. His descendants had not made the mistake of changing anything. The rooms were large and all had doors opening onto the verandah. Now its plainness was called elegance.

Fiona pulled up in front of the homestead. 'They've got all this, plus gardeners, grooms and cleaners, and Keith's got nothing.'

Catriona came onto the verandah and rested her hands on the cast-iron lace-work. Her diamond engagement ring flashed in the sunlight.

"Fiona, you're here. Lunch is nearly ready."

"Hello, Tree. Congratulations."

Catriona didn't smile. "Thank you."

Fiona doused the faint hope of reconciliation. 'Well, you asked for it,' she thought. 'If you just smiled at me I wouldn't have done it. We could have had a normal lunch, but now – '

"Good morning, Fiona."

She jumped and turned round. "Aunty Margot. Hello."

"You're very jumpy," said Margot.

Fiona smiled and walked towards the verandah. 'Not as jumpy as you're going to be soon,' she thought.

"Stefan, this is Fiona – our cousin," said Catriona when they went into the lounge. With a stab of envy she saw his expression of disbelief. She regretted that she and Kim had reviled Fiona, who was dressed in black velvet trousers and a polo-necked jumper in black angora with a red silk scarf. Her only jewellery was a pair of pearl earrings.

"Sherry, Fiona?" asked David.

"No thanks, Uncle David, I'm driving. I'll have lemonade at lunch."

He looked relieved. "You're not staying the night?"

Fiona smiled. "No."

Her enigmatic expression infuriated Catriona.

"Tree and I are having cheese, broccoli and tomato pie. Do you want that or roast lamb?" asked Kim.

"I'll have the pie, please."

Catriona looked at her uneasily as they all went into the dining room. 'Red and black – the colours for danger,' she thought.

Kim nudged her. "She's up to something."

"Fiona, you're sitting next to Mum. Let me take your handbag," said Catriona.

"Oh, no. I'll need it during lunch."

"What for?" asked Kim.

Fiona gave a secret smile and took her place at the table. She was silent while they ate their pumpkin soup, but her presence was uncomfortable. Knowing Fiona was an excellent cook, they had gone to a great deal of trouble choosing the menu for lunch. The chocolate and hazelnut filling for the pancakes was ready and the batter was in the refrigerator.

Catriona was annoyed by Fiona's failure to praise the pie. 'Why should I care?' she thought. 'The only thing she can do is cook.'

At the end of the main course Fiona looked at Stefan who was seated diagonally opposite her. "Do you have any idea what sort of a family you're marrying into?"

He grinned. "A very clever one."

"Do you believe in family traits?"

"I suppose so – as a general rule."

"So, if a man was a coward his daughter would be too?"

Stefan looked taken aback. "I don't know about that."

"But do you think that cowardice is as much a family trait as intelligence or the ability to ride?"

"He's a teacher not a psychologist," said Kim.

Fiona kept her eyes on Stefan. "Did Tree tell you I'm adopted?" She went on without waiting for him to reply. "My mother is really my aunt. The family relationships are convoluted. Aunty Margot was my grandfather's second wife so she's her stepmother as well as her sister-in-law. If Margot hears Mum referring to her as her stepmother she'll announce that she's Alex's sister. Mum's just as bad – they do it to rile each other."

He laughed. "Crikey – that's complicated."

"It gets worse. Three Lancasters married three Clarksons. My uncle Laurence married Margot's sister."

Catriona tried to think how to make Fiona stop talking, but Stefan looked fascinated.

"My real father's name was Jonathan – Margot was his stepmother too. I'm not illegitimate – my real parents were married." She picked up her handbag from the floor and opened it.

Catriona and Kim exchanged alarmed glances.

"What happened to your parents?" Stefan asked innocently.

Fiona took something out of her bag. When she unfolded it, Catriona saw it was a newspaper cutting. "My father died in a fire."

"How ghastly. I'm sorry," he said.

Catriona opened her mouth intending to ask her mother if they should start cooking the pancakes but, before she could speak, Fiona waved the newspaper cutting. "This is the account of the fire. Would you read it aloud, please, Stefan?"

He took the cutting as though hypnotized. Knowing it would look rude to try and stop him from reading it, Catriona listened in confusion. When he finished no one spoke. She heard the crackle of paper as he folded it up.

Fiona glared at Margot and then looked at Stefan. "Is rushing into a burning house to save someone's life a cowardly thing to do?"

He looked bewildered. "No, of course not. It was terribly brave."

"Aunty Margot told Kim and Catriona he was a coward."

Margot stared at her plate.

Kim broke the silence. "Are you all right, Aunty Margot?"

Fiona's laughter sounded harsh. "Of course she's not. She's been caught out. For years she blackened her stepson's name. If he was alive he could sue her for slander."

"That's enough," said David.

Fiona threw down her serviette. "Is that all you can say, Uncle David? No apology? Not even from you, Aunty Margot? And what about you, Aunty David?"

"Go back to Melbourne, Fiona," said David.

Fiona shoved back her chair. "Before I leave, I want to catch Margot out in another lie. Jonathan didn't fight in the war because he wasn't allowed to – he was needed on the land. You're not only a cheat, Aunty Margot, you're a liar too." She turned and walked out of the dining room and down the hall.

They heard the front door bang.

Catriona couldn't bear the mixture of embarrassment and admiration on Stefan's face. "Fiona's real mother was an alcoholic," she blurted out. "She was incapable of caring for a baby, so when

Jonathan died Aunty Virginia and Uncle Alex adopted her."

"Who told you that?" asked Margot.

"Fiona did."

Margot looked at her thoughtfully "When?"

"Ages ago ... when we were children," said Kim.

Margot laughed.

Except for Catriona, who looked dispirited, everyone else attempted to behave as if they had just had a normal family lunch. They made no reference to Fiona as they cleared the table and did the washing up. Stefan suspected that, when he left, she would be their only topic of conversation. Her antagonistic relationship with the *Kingower* Lancasters puzzled him. He wondered why Catriona and Kim, who were gentle with new or fraught riders and had many good friends, were vitriolic about Fiona.

Stefan liked and respected Margot, but Fiona's allegations mystified him as did the fact that no one had challenged them. He knew it had not only been his presence that had prevented them. 'They behaved as if they were used to the accusation. Yes. That's it, it's been said before. Why? Because it's true? Why did she lie about Fiona's real father?'

If Margot had cheated her stepsons out of their inheritance, then he had misjudged her and so had many others. He had once told her that she was the youngest old person he had ever met. Although she had taught juniors and he taught senior classes, their mutual occupation gave them a common interest. Her house was full of books, she was a good pianist, and their discussions were stimulating. Although she had given up teaching forty years ago, her old pupils often visited, bringing spouses and children and occasionally even grandchildren.

Margot was the matriarch of the Lancasters. In spite of her age she played an active role in the day-to-day workings of *Kingower*. She supervised the grooms, making sure they kept the stables and horse troughs clean, maintained the saddlery, and ensured the droppings in the paddock were removed every day. She handled all

Kingower's finances and did the tax returns. He knew she was a widow. He had seen her wedding photos and had been struck by how like the young Margot, Catriona was. What he had not known was that Virginia, whom he had heard about, but never met, was Margot's stepdaughter as well as her sister-in-law.

The family stuck together for the rest of the afternoon. Catriona seemed reluctant to be alone with Stefan, but he managed to guide her away from Kim on the walk back to her cottage in the evening. As they strolled along the muddy track he breathed deeply, sucking the pure air into his lungs.

As if deciding she could face any questions he might ask, she said, "I'm sorry about the scene at lunch. I'll try and explain."

He put his arm around her waist. "You don't have to tell me now, if you don't want to."

She looked at the ground. "It started before we were born. When Dad got back to *Kingower* in 1945 it was in a mess. Before the war he had a manager and lots of staff to care for the horses, gardens and homestead. But most of them joined the forces. It wasn't a farm so no men were kept back to look after it. Mum did her best, but it was impossible. *Kingower* was severely short of money when the war ended so Dad was contemplating selling the cottages and some of the land. But then Aunty Margot's husband died and left her everything. He cut his three children out of the will."

"That would cause a lot of bitterness," he said as they reached her cottage.

She wiped the mud off her shoes on the mat. "They thought she'd cheated them out of their inheritance." She opened the door. "They didn't want him to marry her – "

"Why not?"

"I guess they were worried that if she had a baby they'd lose the property."

"Didn't they contest the will?"

"Their solicitor advised them against it. Anyway she sold the property in Queensland and moved back to *Kingower*. Starting a riding school was her idea. It was successful so she suggested they branched out into pony trekking weekends and holidays. Dad realized he didn't have to employ a manager – he had Aunty Margot. And *Kingower*'s wealthy and her stepsons lost the property."

"Why did Fiona call your mother Aunty David?"

Catriona grimaced. "One Christmas, years ago, Aunty Virginia was ranting about how she hated her letters being addressed to Mrs A Lancaster because her name wasn't Alex. Mum said that she liked being called Mrs David and Virginia began to call her that just to be sarcastic, but the name stuck."

"It sounds as if you and Virginia have a lot in common. Do you like her?"

"I could, but she's very dominating. Whenever she comes here she makes her animosity towards Aunty Margot conspicuous."

Stefan wanted to ask why Margot had lied about Jonathan being a coward, but it was getting late and he wanted to make love before he left for Melbourne. "I never seriously thought she was a cheat," he said, leading her towards the bedroom.

She stopped in the doorway and looked at him intently. "Do you still want to marry me, Stefan?"

He knew the reason for her trepidation. Fiona could not be categorized as a dumb blonde. Anticipating a heavily made-up doll dressed in a mini-skirt, he had been astonished by her appearance. Her nails had been short, unpainted but well manicured. Long straight hair, tied loosely with a black ribbon, shone like platinum. Her eyes were an amazingly luminous shade of turquoise. If she had worn make-up it had been too subtle to be evident.

He feigned surprise at her question. "Of course I do."

She looked apprehensive. "I thought Fiona might have captivated you."

He laughed. "I've seldom met anyone less charming."

"Really?" For the first time since lunch, she smiled.

"Really," he said. 'Tortured, beautiful and fascinating, but not charming,' he thought.

Melbourne
March 1972

I've routed the *Kingower* lot. They can no longer brush me aside as being of no consequence. Today I made a fool of all of them in front of Stefan. If he hadn't been present they would have thrown me out. Tree looked radiant – till I created a scene. Her engagement ring is a solitaire emerald-cut diamond. It must be at least two carats. How I envy her. I long to find a fabulous man and get married and have children. Stefan's taller than she is, so I bet she's pleased about that. He's solid, with wavy hair. With his olive skin and brown eyes he looks a bit Italian or Greek, or would if his hair was a darker brown, but it's got a bit of red in it.

The doorbell rang. Fiona shut her diary and went to answer it. "Hello, Aunty Ruth. I'll put the kettle on. Tea or coffee?"

"Tea please." Ruth smiled wryly. "I've had Margot on the phone for the last hour. You caused a commotion at *Kingower*."

"Good. Why did she lie about Uncle Johnny?"

Ruth followed her into the kitchen. "I didn't know she had. If I'd known you thought he was a coward I would have told you otherwise." She sighed. "Laurence, Johnny and Virginia hated Margot for marrying their father. He'd been a widower for three years, but they behaved as if she had broken up the family."

"She must have done something to make them hostile," said Fiona, putting three teaspoons of Darjeeling tea into the pot. "They wouldn't have been so unreasonable – "

Ruth laughed. "Laurence, Johnny and Virginia were the most headstrong, intense, passionate and unpredictable people I've ever met." She opened her handbag and took out her cigarettes. "Where do you think you get your temper from? When have you ever been reasonable?"

"When I'm driving."

"Yes," Ruth admitted.

"Uncle Laurence was rational. I never saw him in a temper," said Fiona as she put an ashtray on the table.

Ruth flicked on her lighter and lit her cigarette. "Cheska mellowed him and her death doused a lot of his fire. I never met his second wife. He was gentle with women and animals. Every woman except Margot."

"Then it must have been her," said Fiona, taking mugs out of the cupboard. "She was probably jealous because he wouldn't let her replace his mother."

Ruth shook her head and sat down. "Margot isn't jealous – and I'm not saying that because she's my sister. They were the only people I've ever known her to be at war with. But she tried. When Laurence got married again she sent him a cheque for fifty pounds. He sent it back with a note saying, 'Keep it. You've got everything else.'"

"Good for him."

"No. He was being petty. He didn't have much – fifty pounds was a lot of money in 1949."

"And it was his money anyway."

When the kettle boiled Fiona made the tea.

Ruth frowned. "Who told you that your real mother was an alcoholic?"

"Mum did."

"She shouldn't have."

"Why not? It's best that I know the truth. How did Aunty Margot justify her lie?"

"She didn't ... but she's sorry you suffered."

"It's not the sort of thing you can boast about."

"But you told Tree and Kim about your real mother being an alcoholic."

Fiona chewed her lip. "That was when we were young, before they started hating me. Oh, Aunty Ruth, I've got something to tell you. I'm moving to Queensland in August. Ansett are transferring me to – "

"You can't," Ruth said, almost choking on the smoke from her cigarette. When she recovered she saw Fiona's perplexed expression.

"Mum said exactly what you said. She said 'You can't,' just like you did."

Ruth forced herself to smile. "I'm being selfish. I'll miss you."

"When I get settled you'll have to come up for a holiday."

"What about all the friends you've made here? You've got a good social life."

Fiona poured milk into the mugs. "My friends are just friends. I like being with them, but there's no one I'm close to. No one I can share secrets with." Her expression became pensive. "I miss Tree and Kim ... I never needed anyone but them. Did they ever like me at all?"

"Of course they did."

"But they wouldn't let me defend myself. If they'd felt about me the way I felt about them they'd have listened, wouldn't they?"

"It was hard for them – seeing their boyfriends falling for you."

"Yes, but they're happy without me. I'm not happy without them ... that's the difference."

As Ruth walked back to her house, she tried to think of a way to stop Fiona moving to Queensland. 'What would make her stay here?' she thought, opening the gate. 'A man?' She tried to think of any young doctor at the hospital who might interest Fiona. When she arrived home she went to the phone and dialled Alex's number. Not wanting to be made even more agitated by Virginia's dire predictions, she hoped he would answer. When there was no reply, she paced around the room. She caught sight of herself in the mirror over the mantelpiece and glowered at her reflection.

Apart from making sure she was clean and tidy, she did not bother with her appearance and rarely wore make-up. Expensive perfume and soap were her only indulgences. Her golden hair was streaked with grey. Because it was easy to pull back and twist into a bun, she wore the same classic but severe style she had adopted when she had been a trainee nurse. Her clothes were sensible and good quality. Today she wore a sage-green skirt with a matching cardigan over a cream silk blouse. Her loafers were brown leather and her winter tights were the same colour as her skirt. She wore the only pieces of jewellery she owned. Both had been bridesmaid's presents. The gold watch had been from Alex when he married Virginia. When she had been Francesca's bridesmaid, Laurence had given her the strand of cultured pearls.

"Poor Sister Lancaster," she said mockingly to her reflection. "All she's got is a career. Is that what they say at the hospital? I bet it is. They're right."

Life to Ruth was, and always had been, a disappointment. She had resented the privileges her brothers had been granted because of their sex. Margot, Francesca and Ruth had been educated at local state schools, but David and Alex had been boarders at Caulfield Grammar School in Melbourne. From her earliest school-days Ruth had consistently come top of her class. Teachers had spoken about her cleverness, followed by the statement, "What a shame she's a girl." Her desire to be a doctor had been squashed by both her teachers and parents. At first her father had told her that only men could be doctors. When she discovered this was not true she begged him to let her study medicine.

"You'll probably get married before you graduate and the whole thing will be a waste of time and money," he had said. "You'll have to be a nurse."

All five children matriculated and could have gone to university, but that prerogative went to Alex. David, as the oldest son, would inherit *Kingower*. Margot, who would have been an economist or a lawyer if she had been a boy, went to teachers college. Francesca and Ruth became nurses.

As soon as war was declared in 1939, Laurence, David and Alex had joined the army. The Nursing Corps accepted Ruth and Virginia, but turned down Francesca because of her asthma. Laurence wanted Francesca to stay on *Acacia* but, disappointed by her inability to do something for the war effort, she went to Melbourne and moved into Ruth's rented flat in Carlton. With nurses joining the forces it had been easy for her to find a job as a ward sister at the Queen Victoria. But Laurence was worried about her living alone. He had been joined by Alex, David and Margot in persuading Ruth to stay behind with Francesca.

Ruth resented having to stay in Melbourne. Jealousy complicated her feelings. Francesca was adored by her husband. Although she had been overwrought about him during the war, she had something to look forward to when he came home. She was constantly talking about the future. "We'll go back to *Acacia* and have lots of children." Ruth, trapped in Melbourne and denied the excitement of serving overseas, had mixed in a narrow circle that consisted exclusively of women. The only men she met were too old, married or wounded.

The day Francesca had died, the war was over and Laurence was on his way home. Ruth was in the middle of studying for her midwifery exam. To her irritation, Francesca had spent the whole day talking about their plans and how many babies they were going to have. "And of course, you must be a godmother, Ruth."

To her lasting misery she had turned on Francesca. "Must be! Why must I be? I'm sick of hearing those words – Ruth must. Ruth must do this. Ruth must do that. Why has no one ever cared about what I wanted? I wanted to be a doctor, but I wasn't allowed to be because I was a girl. I wanted to join the army, but I was told I must stay home and look after you. Now I'll probably never get married because lots of eligible men have been killed. I've wasted five years of my life."

Francesca had been upset, but her reply was spirited. "If you'd gone overseas you might have been killed. I suspected you resented me, but I didn't know how much. I didn't ask you to stay with me. If you'd told me how you felt I would have stayed on *Acacia* till you and Virginia had left, then I would have gone back to nursing. You should have told me, Ruth."

But Ruth felt too frustrated to apologize. She left for night duty and when she returned to the flat in the morning Francesca was dead. The doctor who came said she had been dead for at least seven hours. It still haunted her that the last words Francesca had heard her speak were angry ones. She had been persuaded to look after her sister, but she often asked herself if her anger had caused Francesca's death.

Now, twenty-six years later, guilt still lacerated Ruth's conscience. She turned away from the mirror. Her brief period of contentment was over. Fiona was leaving. Most of her colleagues at The Alfred Hospital were either much younger or had husbands and children. When Fiona had moved to Melbourne Ruth's life had been transformed. While other women talked about their children she could talk about Fiona. They met for lunch when Ruth had days off and they had dinner together at least once a week.

She grimaced. "I can't mean much to her. She's moving to Queensland without a thought for me. She didn't even talk to me about Johnny. She could have confided in me when she thought he was a coward, but she didn't. The whole structure of deceit is about to collapse on Alex and Virginia and Eleanor and Greg. Will any of us survive the falling wreckage?"

CHAPTER 7

"I can't believe it's mine," Keith said, standing on the verandah holding a copy of the deeds to the house.

Gabriella opened the front door. "There's a lot of work to do. Where will we start?"

He noted her use of the word 'we' and was grateful, not just for her help, but because she was showing an interest. Although she showered every day, made their meals and spent a great deal of time gardening, he still worried she would lapse back into apathy.

"The surveyor said it's structurally good," he said as he followed her down the hall. "The outside has to be repainted, but it's not urgent."

He was looking forward to decorating, but his anticipation was muted by sadness that he owned what his parents had struggled to rent. The house was full of cheap furniture and worn linoleum, but in a haphazard way his mother had imprinted it with her warmth. He was determined not to eradicate the atmosphere. The only furniture he intended replacing were the kitchen chairs that she had bought in a jumble sale before he and Gabriella had been born. The cushions she had made for them eased their hardness, but not the awkward angle of the backs. The lounge suite, although hideous, could be covered with cotton throws.

"I'll pull up the lino and have bare floorboards," he said. "And wax or seal them. I'm not going to have curtains, except in the bedroom."

The flypapers that hung from the ceiling in every room were thick with flies. Keith took them down and replaced them with new ones. "Too many for you to catch?" he said to the huntsman spider on the wall in the kitchen.

Gabriella poked her finger through the hole in the fly-screen over the window. "They all need replacing and everywhere needs painting."

He nodded. "But we must get the garden done first. If we leave it much longer I'll need a machete to get to the front door."

"When are you moving in?"

"The gas and electricity are being connected next week ... so sometime after that." Wanting her to feel that he trusted her strength of character, he didn't ask if she would be all right living by herself.

She went into the bedroom that had been hers. "Erk! Candy pink walls. How did I ever have such bad taste?" She laughed.

His anxiety diminished. "You were only eight when you chose the paint."

For a moving-in present Gabriella bought him a washing machine. Although she lived twenty miles away in Dalby, she drove to Cecil Plains every morning and had breakfast with him. When he left for work she tackled the garden. First she mowed the grass and pulled up the weeds. Then she relaid the winding paths. In the evenings and weekends he helped.

One Saturday while they were pruning, Keith climbed up into the fig tree to saw off a limb that was growing inward. "Pass me the saw."

She was staring into space. "Gabby, wake up and pass me the saw."

"Sorry."

Her manner was distant all morning.

Although concerned, Keith didn't mention it until they were having lunch. "Gabby, what's wrong?"

"Nothing." She pushed the plate of sandwiches over to his side of the table. "I just realized something."

"What?" he asked, trying to sound casual.

"She smiled. "I've just decided what I can do. I owe it to Francesca and Dad to make something of my life. I'm going back to teaching."

It was only when they had restored the garden to how it had been when their father was alive that they felt capable of sorting out their mother's possessions. Her wardrobes were not only crammed with her own clothes, but those that had belonged to their father. Cardboard boxes were piled in corners and there were more under the bed.

"Let's get the clothes sorted out first," said Gabriella. "You do the wardrobes and I'll do the chests of drawers."

The painful task of deciding what to throw away took all morning. The only things worth keeping were the blouses and silk scarves that Virginia had given her. Their mother had worn these to church, and the social events organized by the Country Woman's Association. Keith decided to keep most of his father's clothes and wear them when he was gardening.

"I'll make lunch. You start on the stuff under the bed," said Gabriella. "Are cheese and tomato sandwiches okay?"

He nodded and took the lid off a box that was full of old photographs and snapshots. Most he was able to identify by the writing on the back, but confusingly they were in no order. Snapshots of him and Gabriella as children were muddled up with photos of Virginia, Jonathan and Laurence at *Acacia*. At the bottom he found a photograph album. He opened it and saw a photo of three young men standing in front of a church. They were dressed in tails and had carnations in their buttonholes. The one in the middle was his father and the one on his right was Jonathan. The other man was much shorter and Keith recalled having seen him in other snapshots. He looked familiar and he was sure he had seen him recently.

On the next page was a bride with two bridesmaids. One was Virginia. In the background was a Rolls Royce festooned with white ribbons. On the opposite page he saw his father and the bride outside the church. "Francesca," he murmured. He was staring at the photo, gripped by his father's loss, when Gabriella came in with the sandwiches and tea.

"What have you got there?" she asked, putting the tray on the floor.

"Dad and Francesca's wedding photos."

She knelt beside him. "Gosh, she was lovely, wasn't she?"

Keith looked at the delicate face. "Yes."

"Dad looks so happy – they both do," she said huskily. She turned the page. "I wonder who the other bridesmaid is?"

"Probably Ruth."

Gabriella looked thoughtful. "One day all we'll be are images in old photos," she said. "What will people say about us when they're going through our things? Dad always seemed sad, even when he smiled."

"A bit like Fiona really," said Keith.

Gabriella tutted. "No comparison. Dad lost so much. Fiona hasn't lost anything."

He tried to remember what she had said when he had found her crying after a dream. 'Something about having lost someone,' he thought.

Before he could tell Gabriella, she had turned her attention back to the album. "That's Uncle Alex, isn't it?"

"Yes."

"Peculiar how three Clarksons married three Lancasters, isn't it?" she said turning to the last page.

"Geography had a lot to do with it, I reckon. *Acacia* was remote. I don't suppose there was much chance to get to meet lots of people," he said, putting the album back in the box. "It makes sense if you think about it. Margot was the oldest in her family. Our grandfather was fifteen years older than she was, so her young brothers and sisters were the right ages to pair up with her stepchildren. They married in the thirties; people didn't zoom round in cars and planes like they do now."

Gabriella picked up a sandwich. "But Dad loved Francesca. He didn't marry her because there was no one else."

"We'd better get a move on or we'll be here till next year."

They worked in silence until Keith found a wedding photo in a silver frame so tarnished it was almost black. "This must be our grandfather's and Margot's wedding."

Gabriella shook her head. "It can't be. Dad would have chucked it on a bonfire."

Keith removed the photo from its frame and looked at the back. "Cheska, All my love, Margot," he read. "That's why he kept it. It was Francesca's and he couldn't bring himself to destroy it. The evil stepmother." He studied Margot's plain face with its heavy jaw. Her teeth looked perfect. "How can someone as attractive as Francesca have such a plain sister? What shall we do with it?"

She snatched the photo. "Tear it up, polish the frame and put another photo in it. One of Dad and Mum."

"But it's our grandfather."

"He destroyed his sons. They grew up believing they'd inherit *Acacia*." She held the photo up. "So ... ?"

He nodded and she gave it back to him. "You do it. He deprived you of *Acacia* so you deprive him of his image."

"I can't."

She took it back. "I can."

Keith, feeling that it was an empty gesture, watched her tear it to bits. "It doesn't change anything."

"No, but we've got a valuable frame to put Mum and Dad's wedding photo in. I'll buy some silver polish next week."

"Right, let's get on," he said, opening another box. It contained bundles of letters tied with blue satin ribbon. He flicked through the envelopes. "They're Dad's and Francesca's letters they wrote to each other during the war. We should burn them."

Gabriella looked horrified. "Keith!"

"They might be private."

"He was our father. We've got to read them."

"Gabby, I don't feel like it just yet."

"Promise you won't burn them?"

"We'll read them together when we've sorted this out." Feeling a sense of curiosity that made him ashamed, he put the letters on the bed. For the next hour they tried to make a semblance of order out of the muddle. Loose snapshots were mixed with bills, letters and dress patterns. Disciplining themselves not to ponder over photographs, they skimmed through official letters and put most of them on the pile of rubbish.

"Why did Mum keep all these bills?" asked Gabriella as she screwed up another one. "That one was from nineteen sixty-five."

When all the boxes under the bed had been examined they began on the ones under the wardrobe.

"I wish I knew how our grandfather met Margot," said Gabriella. "It's bugging me."

"Fiona might know," said Keith. When she comes up we'll ask her."

"I want to know now."

"You'll have to wait till she moves here."

"That might be ages yet," she protested, picking up an envelope.

"Write and ask her."

"Blimey!" said Gabriella. "Look what I've found." She held up a snapshot of two baby girls. "Aunty Virginia denied knowing Eumeralla." She tossed it in his lap. "Read the back of that."

May and June, celebrating their 1st birthday.
Eumeralla. *1st June 1947*

"And this," she said, giving him a single sheet of paper.

Dear Laurence,

Hope the chocolate stains came out of your shirt! Thanks so much for their presents. The silver identity bracelets Virginia sent them are too big at the moment. I've just cut one of their fringes so I can tell them apart. The one with the fringe is May. I'm sure that in a few years time they will swap bracelets and both appear with fringes giggling at my confusion.

Love,
Eleanor

"What do you make of that?" she asked impatiently.

"This proves that Dad and Aunty Virginia knew the family on *Eumeralla*."

"More than just knew them, Keith. They must have been friends. Casual acquaintances don't give each other things like silver bracelets."

"Something about *Eumeralla* scares the hell out of Uncle Alex and Aunty Virginia. Let's go through the rest of this stuff – we might find something."

He soon found a letter addressed to Lieutenant Laurence Clarkson in Palestine. Part of the postmark was smudged, but the year 1942 was clear. When he turned the envelope over he received a shock. The letter was from Jonathan Clarkson and the address was *Eumeralla*.

"He must have worked there after he was disinherited," said Gabriella.

"Not during the war. Our grandfather didn't die till 1947." He opened the letter and read the events of one week of farming life. The letter was signed, *Love, Johnny and Eleanor*. "What's going on, Gabby?"

"Nothing's going on now. It's what went on all those years ago that interests me."

"No. Something's still going on – something to do with *Eumeralla*. We'll have to read every single letter in this room till we find out what it is."

Gabriella whacked his arm. "It's just as well we didn't burn them."

"Ouch! That hurt." But he laughed, pleased they were sharing their family history and that she was so engrossed.

It didn't take them long to find a letter of startling significance. It was addressed to Mr. and Mrs Jonathan Clarkson at *Acacia*.

2 / 9 / 1938

Dearest Johnny and Eleanor,

I'm so upset to hear about your father, Eleanor. We arrived home *from our honeymoon today and have just read Dad's letter. He told me that you'll be moving to **Eumeralla** now, but just in case you're not there yet I'll address this to **Acacia**.*

We look forward to seeing you both soon.
Lots and lots of love and sympathy,

Virginia and Alex.

"They were married," Gabriella said excitedly.

"Why didn't Dad tell us? He talked about Johnny a lot, but he never once said he was married or mentioned *Eumeralla*." He picked up the snapshot of the toddlers. "Were these his children?"

"They must have been. Twins. Did they die in the same fire?"

Keith shook his head. "Dad said Johnny died trying to rescue a boy and his mother." He jumped up. "A bloke named Greg Mitchell owns *Eumeralla* now. Hang on, I'll get the magazine." He went into his bedroom and came back flicking through the pages. "Here it is."

*Farmers should return to more traditional and less wasteful and greedy methods, Greg Mitchell of **Eumeralla** advises.*

Keith read the whole article, but there was no reference to Eleanor. "*Eumeralla* must have been sold. Eleanor might be dead."

"Let's keep looking."

Two hours later when they had almost given up, Gabriella found a letter.

12/12/1946

Laurence,

*Why do you resent me marrying Greg? Jonathan left me and only came back when he found out about the twins. If you want to see May and June, treat me and Greg with courtesy or you are not welcome at **Eumeralla**.*

Eleanor.

Gabriella gave a whoop of triumph. "This is it – the connection! She married Greg Mitchell. That means she's still on *Eumeralla*."

"If that other letter of hers is anything to go by, they were friends again six months later so Dad must have apologized," said Keith.

"Let's go to *Eumeralla* next weekend," she said.

Her animation reminded him of Gabriella as she had been before Brett's death.

"Shall we go in the car?" asked Gabriella when she arrived at Keith's on Saturday.

He picked up his leather jacket. "The bike."

She took her jumper from the front seat and pulled it over her head. "Do I look all right? Respectable, I mean."

"You look fine," he said, looking approvingly at her shining bronze hair that she had tied back with a brown ribbon that matched her trousers. Her cotton shirt was white and her yellow jumper was new. A few days ago, when she had gone into Brisbane and bought new clothes, he felt that her recovery was complete. Among her purchases were suits and dresses suitable for wearing to interviews.

They got on the bike. Although Keith never wore a crash helmet when he was in the bush because it spoilt the feel of the wind on his face and in his hair, he always made his passenger wear one. It was not until he was steering his bike through the gates of *Eumeralla* that apprehension gripped him. "Should we be doing this?" he asked when Gabriella had closed the gates.

"Yes," she said, prodding him. "Come on, we're nearly there."

Following the track for a mile, he stopped when he saw a white weatherboard house set on stilts. He propped his bike against a tree, took off his jacket and draped it over the seat. Gabriella balanced her helmet on it and they went up the flight of wooden steps onto the shaded verandah.

Before they could knock a woman came down the hall. "You've beaten Hazel – she's late as usual," she said, opening the door. She had dark hair that was turning grey, brown eyes and a tanned skin. Tall and thin, she wore jeans and a blue shirt. "I'm her mum. Come in."

"Mrs Mitchell, there's a bit of a misunderstanding," said Gabriella. "We're Laurence's children. Jonathan was our uncle."

Keith saw her welcoming expression change to shock. "Are you Eleanor?" he asked.

"You've got to go!"

He was startled by her fear. "I'm not going to hurt you. I read about *Eumeralla* in a farming magazine – then when our mum died we found some letters – "

"You've got to go!" She looked at her watch.

Keith could hear her panicky breathing.

She banged the fly-screen door shut. "Please, leave," she begged. "Please."

Gabriella touched his arm. "Come on, Keith." She ran down the steps.

He followed slowly.

"Hurry. She's probably watching us."

"Tough," he said. He mounted the bike, then turned and waved.

Gabriella slapped his back. "Stop it! Obviously her children don't know about Jonathan."

"But they were married. Why all the flaming secrecy? It's not as if he was a criminal or some uneducated lout."

"Get going."

He turned on the engine and drove down the track. Half a mile away he slowed down. The house was out of sight. He stopped the bike. "This is ridiculous. Why was she frightened of us?"

"I don't think it was us," Gabriella said thoughtfully.

"Who was it? There was no one else there."

She got off the bike and leant against a tree. "It was more that she was scared about someone coming and seeing us. She looked at her watch."

"She was expecting Hazel's friends and Hazel. Gabby, something's weird. Aunty Virginia and Uncle Alex were frightened of me coming here, and look at the reception we got. Three frightened people. For God's sake, what's frightening them?"

"Let's go, Keith, I can hear a horse."

"So what? I'm fed up with this."

She jumped back on the bike. "Quick. We don't want to be done for trespassing – they might shoot us."

He turned round and to his astonishment saw Fiona riding towards them.

"Hi!" she called as she reigned in the horse. She waved her hand. "The house is that way."

Keith got off his bike. "What are you doing here?"

She looked at them blankly. "Are you ... Hazel's friends?"

"Stop mucking about, Fiona," said Gabriella. "What the hell are you doing here?"

She appeared baffled, and her horse tossed his head.

Realization flashed through Keith's mind. Apart from her beauty, Fiona had two distinctive features. Her vivid turquoise eyes were one. The other was her dark eyebrows and lashes that were in dramatic contrast to her fair skin and platinum-blonde hair. Although the rider was identical to Fiona, there were two discrepancies. The girl on the horse was an expert rider. Unless she had lied to him, Fiona was scared of horses. Fiona spoke quickly almost in staccato. This girl spoke in a typical country drawl.

"June," he said. "You're June, aren't you?"

She nodded. "Who are you?"

"Keith, and this is my sister Gabby. We're your cousins."

She shook her head. "We haven't got any cousins."

"Look," he said, "I don't know how to tell you this – "

Gabriella grasped his arm. "Don't!"

"What's going on?" asked June.

They all stared at each other until the sound of a car diverted them. It came into view and stopped. A girl with dark curly hair got out. She was a young version of the woman up at the house. "Juju!" she called.

"Hi, Hazel," said June.

Hazel walked over to Keith and Gabriella. "Are you lost?"

"No, we thought you were someone else," said Keith.

"He thought they were our cousins," said June.

"I made a mistake."

Hazel gazed at him admiringly.

Keith did not notice. His memory jolted, he remembered the word Fiona had cried repeatedly, sixteen years ago.

'Juju.'

CHAPTER 8

Keith drove straight back to his house. He and Gabriella got off the bike and looked at each other, still awed by their discovery.

"We're stupid," he said. "It was so obvious. I can't believe we didn't guess when we saw the photo of the twins."

"We would have if Fiona's name had still been May," said Gabriella. "Fiona's birthday's the thirty-first of May. The date on the photo was the first of June. What are we going to do?"

He wheeled the bike to the side of the house. "Haven't got a clue."

"Who's Fiona's real mother?" she asked as they went inside.

"Eleanor must be."

"But she looks like Virginia."

He grinned. "Drongo. She's Uncle Johnny's daughter."

Gabriella frowned. "What are we going to do?"

"I still haven't got a clue." He took a bottle of beer out of the fridge. "Do you want anything?"

"Tea." She put the kettle on. "Have you got any biscuits or cake?"

"Both." he said, putting a packet of chocolate biscuits and a slab of banana cake on the table. "We've got to tell Fiona."

"How?" She leant against the worktop. "This will cause turmoil."

"We can't keep this from her."

Gabriella chewed her lip. "I could go down to Melbourne and tell her. But I'll have to see Uncle Alex and Aunty Virginia first." She lit a cigarette and paced round the room. "Let's piece as much of this together as we can. You think Eleanor is Fiona's mother, but

Virginia could be. What would drive a mother to give away a baby?"

"The twins were identical – maybe she thought one was expendable. Johnny left Eleanor – she had the twins and gave one to Aunty Virginia."

"Not straight away," said Gabriella. "According to that photo she had both twins on *Eumeralla* in 1947, when they were a year old."

Ω Ω Ω

"Mum, he was such a gorgeous hunk, wasn't he, Juju?" said Hazel as she added vinegar to the chopped mint.

June cut a potato into quarters. "I suppose so."

Eleanor tried to sound amused. "Is there a boy on this earth that you don't think is gorgeous, Hazel?"

"He wasn't a boy, he was a man," said Hazel. "He looked like a Viking."

Eleanor put dripping into the roasting pan. "Was he wearing a horned helmet?"

"No, he had long blonde hair."

"Long blonde hair?" Eleanor tried to keep her hands steady as she put the leg of lamb in the oven. "Are you sure it was a man? Sounds more like a girl."

"Mum, it wasn't that long. Just a bit longer than fashionable. And his eyes ... they were smoky green ... like gum leaves, weren't they, Juju?"

June weighed the flour. "I don't know, I didn't look into them," she said drily. "Haven't you finished that mint sauce yet?"

Eleanor opened the door to the stove. "We need more wood. This isn't burning very well."

"How can I find out where he lives?"

June added more flour to the weighing bowl. "You just stand

and dream – Mum and I'll do all the work."

Hazel scooped up the vegetable peelings. "Sorry. Did he tell you his name?"

June smiled. "He did."

"Tell me."

"Aloysius."

"Well that's the end of that," said Eleanor, able to joke in spite of her guilt. "I'm not having a son-in-law called Aloysius."

"Al," said Hazel. "I could call him Al."

"No you couldn't," said June.

"Why not?"

June spluttered with laughter. "Because his name's Keith."

"Juju!" said Hazel, flicking a piece of potato peel at her. "Who was that girl? Wasn't his wife was it?"

"His sister."

Eleanor turned to the cupboard so they wouldn't see her face. "It sounds as if you asked him for his family tree."

"Did you find out his surname?" asked Hazel.

June giggled. "No."

"How remiss of you, Juju," said Eleanor. "You should have asked him for his address so Hazel could hunt him down."

"He thought they were our cousins," said Hazel. "Maybe we're distantly related and they're searching for their family tree. That'll give me an excuse to get in touch with him."

"We might be." June looked thoughtful. "He knew my name. I thought it was strange, but if we're related – "

"We must be! He looked a lot like you, Juju."

Eleanor was thankful she had put the mixing bowl down without dropping it.

"His hair was a darker blonde than yours ... it was more gold, but your features are the same," Hazel continued. "You look more like him than his sister does. You must be a throwback."

"For goodness sake, Hazel, let's get on with the dinner. Your friends will be here soon," said Eleanor, trying to sound exasperated, not unnerved.

June went to the door. "I'll go and get the wood."

"No I will," Eleanor said, wanting to get away. 'She's no throwback,' she thought as she went down the steps to the shed. 'She's like Johnny.' As she collected the wood, she remembered Keith and Gabriella's bewilderment when she told them to go. If Keith's features had not been dappled by shadows, she would have known who he was immediately. She hadn't wanted to send them away. Foreboding had fought with regret as she watched them go down the steps. She had wanted to hug them and tell them she was sorry about their mother. She had wished she could invite them in and talk about their father and Jonathan and Virginia. "I upset them for nothing," she murmured, "They saw Juju anyway."

"Are you all right, Mum?" asked Hazel when she came back to the kitchen.

She sighed. "I will be if you stop waffling and get the pastry for the apricot pie made."

Eleanor kept up the pretence all afternoon and through dinner. She listened to Hazel's chatter about life in Brisbane, asked her friends sensible questions and laughed at the right time. Even Greg didn't notice her strain. Hazel's friends were not the townies she normally brought to *Eumeralla*. One of the men was saving up to buy a farm and one of the girls, who said she was fed up with the city, flirted with Tom. Normally Eleanor would have hoped a romance was beginning, instead of longing for the evening to end. It was after midnight before she and Greg were alone.

As soon as she had shut their bedroom door, Eleanor clutched his arm. "Keith and Gabriella were here today," she whispered.

"What?"

"Sh, keep your voice down."

"Did they see Juju?"

"Yes. They told her she was their cousin. When she was telling me I tried not to seem interested. Luckily Hazel kept raving about Keith." She smiled ruefully. "Not only does she think he's a gorgeous hunk – he's the most gorgeous hunk she's ever met. He looks so much like Laurence."

"Bloody hell." Greg sat on the bed. "Keith and Gabriella are sure to tell Fiona. We'll have to tell Juju."

"I can't."

He put his arm around her. "I will."

"We promised Virginia and Alex – "

"We'll have to warn them."

Eleanor rubbed her throbbing head. "No. There must be another way. Go and see Keith and ask him keep quiet."

He nodded. "I'll go tomorrow."

It gave Greg a strange feeling to see the house again. Twenty-five years ago he, Laurence and Virginia had stood in the overgrown garden.

"We must be able to find something better than this," Virginia had protested, looking at the peeling weatherboard and the corrugated iron roof that had once been red, but which the sun had bleached to pink. All the fire had gone out of her. Until the solicitor had advised them not to contest the will she had been ready to fight.

Greg shook his head. "If Laurence does all the painting, the owner will pay for the paint. The place belonged to his parents and he wants to keep it. It's clean inside." Desperate to cheer them up he latched onto the few good things. "And the garden's big. Wait till you go round the back."

"It'll do," said Laurence. "Anything will do." Devastated by the deaths of Francesca and Jonathan, his love for *Acacia* had been the only thing that kept him going. Being disinherited had reduced him to a stupor. The potential heir to ten thousand acres of rich farming land and a beautiful homestead was so impoverished he had to rent a small house in the nearest town. The only things he had taken from *Acacia* had been his clothes, books, photos, letters and the onyx chess set his parents had given him one Christmas. He had refused to let Virginia buy him anything.

Until January 1949, when he had married again, the house was sparsely furnished. It had been Keith's and Gabriella's mother who had scoured second-hand shops and filled each room with cheap but solid pieces. When Keith was a year old the Clarksons and Mitchells realized they must never see each other again. It had been hard for all of them. Greg missed Laurence's companionship. He knew that Keith and Gabriella would have been marvellous friends for his children. Instead of being able to visit *Eumeralla* and learning to ride, Keith and Gabriella had lived a parochial existence. What they knew about agriculture and horses had come second-hand from their father.

It was twenty two years since Greg had visited the house. The gate was pitted with rust, the white picket fence was sagging, but the garden Laurence had created, with trees, shrubs and winding paths, was as he remembered. The gate squeaked when he opened it. Tins of paint, labelled antique ivory, were on the verandah. Keith, dressed in overalls, came outside with a pile of brown linoleum and dropped it in the skip. His hair was longer and darker, but he looked so much like Laurence that Greg felt he had gone back in time.

Keith turned round and saw him. "Hello?" he said, sounding puzzled.

"I'm Greg Mitchell. Can I speak to you?"

"Oh. Sure."

Keith towered over him. He was even taller than Laurence had been.

"Come in. Do you want a cup of tea?"

"Thanks."

"Careful, some of the paint's still wet," Keith warned as he opened the fly-screen door.

Greg followed him inside. 'He moves like Laurence and he talks like Laurence,' he thought. "You're doing a good job," he said, stopping to look at the freshly painted walls and ceiling in the hall. The skirting boards, architraves and doors were shiny with white gloss and the exposed floorboards looked far better than the linoleum had. A huntsman spider ran up the wall.

Keith looked at it. "It's been disrupted by all the painting. I'm pleased it didn't leave. I need one in every room. They look better than flypapers."

"I'm interrupting your decorating."

"You came at the right time. I'd just put the kettle on."

The kitchen smelt of turpentine and paint, in spite of the open windows. Units lined the walls. Some of the cupboards were painted white, others were the original brown.

Keith was looking at him as if trying to memorize his features. "Were you my father's groomsman when he married Francesca?"

Greg nodded. "That was when I worked on *Acacia*. Laurence was a good cove. Not like the scum that own it now."

Keith put three spoons of tea into the pot. "Bloody Margot had no thought for anyone except herself."

"Well," said Greg. "I was fond of Margot."

"Get out of my house then."

"Calm down, Keith. I was upset when your dad lost *Acacia*, but it wasn't only because of Margot. Jonathan was cut out of the will because he deserted his wife."

Keith looked uncertain. "Was he?"

"Yes."

"What about my father? He didn't desert his wife. For God's sake he was married to Margot's sister!"

"It's not that simple."

"It is that simple. Dad had to rent this dump because of his stepmother. He died of a stomach ulcer because of her. If he'd inherited *Acacia* he wouldn't have had to worry about money. But his life was one big worry and that's why he got an ulcer and that's why he died." The kettle boiled, but Keith ignored it. "Margot didn't just wreck my father's life, she wrecked mine too. Do you think I enjoy being a postman? And it's not just me, it's *Acacia*. The new owners have ruined it. Margot sold it to them so it's her fault." Water bubbled out of the spout and made a hissing sound as it flowed down the sides. He turned off the gas. "Anyway, you didn't come here to talk about Margot, did you?"

Greg shook his head. "Have you told anyone about who you saw at *Eumeralla* yesterday?"

"Not yet," he said, pouring boiling water into the teapot. "But I will."

"Please don't."

Keith took a bottle of milk out of the fridge. "Who's Fiona's mother?"

"It's nothing to do with you."

Keith looked incredulous. "She's my cousin. Don't you think that the fact she's got a twin sister is anything to do with her either?"

"She's happy – "

"How would you know?"

"Isn't she?"

"Not particularly. She hated being an only child. She has dreams about when she and June were babies – "

"Rubbish," Greg said. "She was too young."

"Now look here, Mr. Mitchell, don't speak to me as if I'm one of your employees. If I tell Fiona she's got a twin sister she'll be thrilled. Is Eleanor her mother?"

"Mrs Mitchell to you, lad."

"Don't call me "lad". And I won't call her Mrs Mitchell. She was married to my uncle so I'll call her Aunty."

In spite of his disquiet, Greg was amused. "You sound like your dad. That's just what he would have said."

Keith smiled. "Yes. Well ... so, I'm trying to make sense of all this and I'd like to know who Fiona's mother was. Was it Eleanor?"

"Yes."

Keith put a mug on the table in front of him. "Was Jonathan her father?"

"Yes." Greg sipped the strong tea. "Please don't tell Fiona."

"I've got to."

"You'll cause a lot of unhappiness."

"Fiona will be overjoyed. But even if I kept quiet you've got a big problem."

"What?"

"Cecil Plains is the nearest town to *Eumeralla*, right?"

"Yes."

"Fiona's moving to Queensland in August."

Greg managed to put down his mug without spilling any tea. "To live?"

Keith nodded. "She's getting a transfer to Brisbane, but at weekends she'll stay with me or Gabby – she lives in Dalby. One day someone who knows June will see Fiona. Or worse, June and Fiona will see each other. You've got about four months to work something out. I'll tell her as soon as she gets here. You'd better warn June, because Fiona will want to meet her."

Ω Ω Ω

When June and Greg finished checking the fences in the western section of *Eumeralla* they let the horses wander towards the creek.

June saw some sheep and dismounted. She stroked the lambs that had been born in the spring. "Better fleeces – finer. That new breeding ... "

Greg nodded absently.

"Dad, what's – ?"

"Juju, I've got to tell you something."

"Are we bankrupt?"

He shook his head.

She held her breath. "Has Mum sold *Eumeralla*?"

"No, no."

"Thank God for that – you had me worried." His distracted expression stayed the same and her relief dwindled.

"Race you to the creek, Juju. Bet you Digger can beat Monty." His attempt to smile made him look worse.

"No, Dad, tell me now." He looked trapped and she panicked. "Has Mum got cancer or something?"

"No. It's old news." He dismounted. "It's about you."

"Me?" she laughed. "That's all right then."

Greg gazed into the distance.

"Dad?" she prompted.

He patted his horse. "We never told you before, Juju, because we didn't want you to feel different. I was the only dad you ever knew and we wanted you to feel you were as much mine as the others. I've never treated you any different, have I?"

Her heart raced. "Am I adopted?"

"No, but I'm not your real dad."

June looked at him in shock. "Who is?" Her horse jerked his head and she dropped the reins. "Why are you telling me now?"

"Because the other day you saw your cousins."

"They were my cousins – how come?"

"Your mum's been married before."

"What? Who to?"

"She married Jonathan Clarkson when she was eighteen – "

"What happened to him?"

"Juju, wait. It's a complicated story. Your mum and Johnny both wanted children – she just wanted them, but he was desperate for them. After nine years he left her. Well, the war had just ended – I was in the Middle East at the time. Johnny left and there was no one to run *Eumeralla* but your mum. There was no phone, she didn't have a car, and she struggled alone for months. Because Johnny's leaving had been such a shock she thought that was why ... " He looked embarrassed. "Well, something that usually happens every month hadn't. It was quite late when she realized she was pregnant. It must have been because she was freed from his desperation. Anyway, she gave birth to you and ... and another baby – alone in the house."

"Another baby? Did it die?"

"No."

June felt breathless. "I've got a twin?"

"Yes."

"An identical twin?"

Greg nodded.

"Fiona?"

"Yes."

"So that's who they thought I was!"

He put his arm around her. "I know it's a bombshell, Juju."

She pulled away. "Was this Johnny bloke our father?"

"Yes." He went to touch her hand.

She pushed his arm aside. "Tell me the rest."

"She was born ten minutes before midnight on the thirty-first of May and you were born twenty minutes later on the first of June. Her name was May at first. I came home from the war shortly afterwards. My feelings towards your mum had always been strong and when she married Johnny I felt glum. When I left for the war I was that miserable I didn't care if I got killed. But when I came home I heard he'd left her. I told your mum how I felt and we planned to marry as soon as she was divorced. Then Johnny heard about you and Fiona and he came back. I thought I'd had it – he was a handsome cove, and a good one too, but she wouldn't forgive him."

"Where is he now?"

"I'm sorry, Juju. He died in a fire."

"When?"

"A few months after you were born. Then your mum and I got married."

"Did Jonathan work on *Eumeralla*?"

"No." Greg smiled. It was a proper smile not a forced one. "It was Jonathan's dad who used to own *Acacia*."

June's fury turned to astonishment. "What?"

"Jonathan and his brother were disinherited in favour of their stepmother. When their dad died she sold *Acacia*."

"Hang on. What happened to Fiona?"

"Johnny's sister adopted her."

"Why?"

"She couldn't get pregnant. She and your mum were like sisters – they grew up together. Virginia was as obsessive about having children as Johnny was. She came to stay with us to help your mum when she was eight months pregnant with Hazel. The pregnancy was difficult and she was exhausted. You and May were eighteen months old. Eleanor had a rough time with Hazel's birth. She was a big baby and she was overdue.

"Things got worse after she was born. Your mum had a breast abscess and Hazel was a tiresome baby. They both spent most of the time bawling. We wouldn't have been able to cope without Virginia. Not only did she cook and clean, she looked after you and May and Tom. When Hazel's grizzling got too much she'd take her for walks so your mum could get some sleep. She'd done midwifery and she advised Eleanor to stop breast-feeding. It was Virginia who got Hazel onto the bottle. After that things improved, although she was still weak. You and May and Tom had been such good babies, we weren't prepared for one who cried all the time. Then Alex came – "

"Who's Alex?"

"Virginia's husband. As the time drew closer for them to go back to Sydney, Virginia got really unhappy. I felt that sorry for her – for both of them. It was your mum who suggested that we let them have May. She had a great rapport with them – you were shyer. Your mum had been through it and she understood how Virginia felt. So when they went home to Sydney they took May."

"Just like that?" June said. "How could she?"

"It wasn't easy for your mum. It wasn't easy for me either."

"Dad, she gave her baby away. A baby – not a sack of wheat or a horse. Why didn't you stop her?"

"I don't know."

"You didn't care because we weren't yours. I bet you wouldn't have let her give Tom away."

"I'm making a hell of a mess of this, Juju. I'm no good at explaining." He ran his hands through his hair. "Look, your mum was finding it rough. From being married for ages and not getting pregnant, she had three pregnancies in three years. It was overwhelming. We never thought she'd get pregnant so fast so we never did anything to stop it."

"Why didn't you give them Hazel?"

"Because she wasn't related to them. Virginia was Johnny's sister and she was beside herself when he was killed. Eleanor thought she and Virginia could share the only thing that was left of him. You and May ... Fiona."

"Why didn't Mum tell me herself?" June, her mind exploding with questions, didn't wait for a reply. "What did I do after she'd gone – did I miss her?"

Greg nodded. "You cried a lot. But you had Tom. You taught him things. It was as if you were impatient for him to catch up with you."

"Did Virginia give you money? Did you sell my sister?" She saw his defensive expression change to anger. "Sorry, Dad."

"How could you think such a thing? Juju, it's not as if we gave her to strangers. Eleanor and Virginia had been friends since they were born. Virginia's your aunty – your real dad's sister. And they were wealthy. They could give a child so much more than we could. Fiona went to one of the most exclusive schools in Sydney."

"I want to find her."

"You won't have to. She's coming up here to live in August."

"No. I want to see her now. I'm going to go to Sydney."

"She lives in Melbourne. But, listen, Juju, wait until – "

"No."

"You just can't turn up on Fiona's doorstep. People have to be warned."

"You warn them!" She ran over to Monty, who had wandered off.

Greg caught up with her as she flung herself into the saddle. "Don't be angry with your mum."

She turned Monty's head and galloped away.

Letting Monty go where he wanted, June rode for two hours. When he went to the creek to drink, curiosity nudged aside her anger. "I've got a sister, Monty. She's like me ... not just like me, but identical. Is she like me in other ways too? Would she come to *Eumeralla* to live?" The unknown had never excited June. Now it did. When Monty finished drinking she rode back to the paddock. She had just taken off the reins when she saw Tom vaulting the fence. As he ran towards her she could tell that he knew. Turning away she went into the tack room and put the saddle on the rack. When she came outside with the brush, he was giving Monty a carrot. For the first time in her life she felt uncomfortable with him. She could tell that he was uncertain about what to say. Normally they would have talked about the quality of the wool, but now he was silent. Monty finished the carrot and Tom stroked him.

"Well," he said finally. "We know why they were acting strangely. It's better than Mum selling some of the land, isn't it?" His smile was tentative. "Or having an affair."

June stood with the brush in her hand. "I feel dislocated," she burst out. "My real father's dead. Dad said he was a good bloke ... that's why I'm upset. Tom, I feel as if I've lost two fathers. And I've got a twin I've never known and cousins. I feel that they've been lost too."

Tom looked relieved that she had spoken. "It's a shock, Juju. More for you, of course. Gee, it's like one of the Agatha Christie mysteries. Except no one's been murdered."

"Yet," said June.

"You're still my sister."

"Only half of me is." She began to groom Monty. "I'll never forgive Mum, never."

Tom looked at her thoughtfully. "Why not?"

"I'm not who I thought I was."

"No one's going to turf you off *Eumeralla*. It's not as if Mum once robbed a bank or killed someone."

"She lied to me and robbed me of a sister."

"She never lied to you, Juju."

"Okay – she deceived me."

"Why?"

"Why what?"

"Did she deceive you?"

June grunted. "Ask her."

"Do you think she wanted to make you unhappy? Do you reckon she hates you?" He opened Monty's mouth and inspected his teeth. "Well?"

She couldn't think of a reasonable answer. "She robbed me of a sister."

"So you keep saying."

"Well she did. I could have had a sister that I could have been close to instead of a frivolous thing like Hazel who's only interested in boys and clothes. I bet Fiona would have loved this place as much as I do."

"Juju, if Mum had sold your twin or given her to someone horrible, it would have been terrible. But she gave her to her friend because she couldn't have a baby of her own. Was that so bad?"

"She shouldn't have done it."

"Ever done anything you shouldn't have done, Juju?"

She caressed Monty's ears. "It's different."

"Of course it is. All situations are different. Are you staying on *Eumeralla*?"

"Yes."

"Well, we'll still play cards and chess after dinner, won't we? We'll still ride together. Nothing's changed. It's just that you know something now that you didn't know before. You've got to admit it's exciting. Dad said that you want to find Fiona."

She nodded. "I'll go to Melbourne as soon as I get her address."

"Don't be too disappointed if she's a townie."

"Some townies are okay."

"You will come back, won't you?"

She was grateful for his look of anxiety. "I hate Brisbane so I'll probably hate Melbourne even more. I won't stay any longer than I have to." She smiled. "And maybe I'll bring Fiona with me."

"Come up to the house and have a look at the photos of Jonathan."

"Photos?"

"Yes, lots of them – some in posh frames. They've been hidden away since your twin was adopted. Mum couldn't wait to get them out and show us. Wedding photos too – Mum was a real looker in those days."

Eleanor, unaware that Virginia and Alex were on their way to New Zealand for a two-week holiday, tried to phone them. She tried all day and then gave up and wrote to them.

10th April 1972

Dear Virginia and Alex,

June knows about Fiona. She's flying to Melbourne on Monday. Sorry this gives you so little time to prepare her.

Ω   Ω   Ω

"Alex, I won't be able to enjoy this holiday. I'm too worried about what Fiona will do when we tell her," said Virginia as they arrived at the hotel in Wellington.

He put the cases on the bed. "Let's forget everything at home," he said firmly. "Fiona will be upset at first, but she'll understand."

But that night Alex lay in bed unable to sleep. Despite his comforting words to Virginia he was perturbed about Fiona's reaction. He would never forget the terrible weeks after they had taken her from *Eumeralla*. They had travelled on the overnight train from Brisbane and at first Fiona had been excited by the new experience. She slept well, but woke in the morning, disorientated and crying. Nothing they did would pacify her.

From Sydney Station they had taken a taxi back to Vaucluse with the hysterical toddler. Alex carried her into the house. As soon as they went inside her screaming stopped. She had seen her reflection in the hall mirror.

She held out her arms. "Juju, Juju!"

Her joy had changed to anger when she could not touch her sister. For weeks the torment continued. Fiona sought out mirrors, beat her fists on the glass and sobbed. Her vocabulary was reduced to a single word – Juju. She disregarded the toys and dolls Virginia bought her and cried until exhaustion overtook her and she slept. When she woke, she began crying again.

Alex decided to take her back to *Eumeralla*. Virginia begged him to give her more time, but he was intransigent. "It's cruel, Virginia. I'll take her back at the weekend."

When he returned from work the next day Virginia had taken down all the mirrors. Fiona was awake and calm.

"I took her to the beach and she paddled in the water," Virginia told him. "I'll take her out every day. Don't worry, Alex, she'll soon forget."

Two weeks later Fiona called him Dada. Then she called Virginia Muma. Soon she had regained all her previous vocabulary with the additions Virginia had taught her.

They took her to a mirror. "Fiona," said Virginia.

"Juju," said Fiona.

For months she said, "Juju," when she saw her reflection, but she was bewildered not excited.

Eight weeks after her second birthday she looked in the mirror and said, "Fiona."

CHAPTER 9

As Stefan drove out of Melbourne on his way to *Kingower* on Friday afternoon he got stuck in a traffic jam. Usually this irritated him, but as he waited in the barely moving line of cars his thoughts strayed to Fiona. The way she dominated his psyche unsettled him. His mind, usually so focused on what he was doing, was now prone to wander, even in the classroom. The five o'clock news came on and began to report the progress of the bombing raids in Vietnam. Snorting in disgust, he switched stations, and Marianne Faithfull's sensual voice filled the car.

He attempted to analyse his feelings. 'I'm too sensible to fall for someone because she's stunning,' he thought. 'And I'm not in love with her, of course I'm not. I love Tree. Fiona just interests me. But why? She's got more than just superb bone structure. She's shrouded in mystery. And I don't like the way the *Kingower* family treat her,' he admitted as the traffic crawled towards the lights.

"If you'll come and stay with me," sang Marianne Faithfull.

He drummed his hands on the steering wheel. 'I'm happy with Tree. We've got a good relationship based on the things that matter.'

The driver behind him blasted his horn and Stefan saw that the lights were green. Finally the traffic thinned and he was able to change out of first gear. Half an hour later he was in the country.

The only thing he disliked about Catriona was her style of decorating. Her cottage, with its primrose walls and white woodwork, was surprisingly feminine. Romantic Victorian prints of children and animals hung on the walls. As a historian, he knew that the children were more likely to have been down the mines or sweeping chimneys than playing outside idyllic thatched cottages.

The elaborately carved rosewood furniture in her bedroom had been hers since childhood. Yellow and blue floral curtains hung at all the windows and the sofa and armchairs were upholstered in the same fabric. He hated floral patterns. In Stefan's opinion, her cottage looked as if it belonged to a fluffy girl who would have hysterics in an emergency, knew nothing about politics, never read a book and had no interests apart from fashion. When they had been going out together for six months, he had told her so. It was the first time he had seen her angry. His comment that pastel colours, floral patterns and lace did not suit her practical nature or intelligence, incensed her even more.

Striding to the bookcase she had pulled out a thick volume. "Would a fluffy girl read this?" she had demanded, shoving *Equine Anatomy and Physiology* at him.

"No, I'm not – "

"How would you decorate this place?"

"Like Kim's." As soon as he had said it he wished he hadn't. The last thing he wanted was for Catriona to think he was unfavourably comparing her with her sister. To his surprise her anger abated.

She looked amused. "Earthy colours? Beige, ochre, wheat, terracotta? Scandinavian furniture?"

"Yes."

"Why?"

"Because they're natural."

She pointed to the walls. "What colour is this?"

"Yellow."

"Be precise, Stefan. What sort of yellow?"

"Primrose? Lemon?"

She smiled. "What is a primrose?"

"A flower."

"Exactly. And what is a lemon?"

He guessed she and Kim had debated this subject already. "A fruit."

"Is a flower a product of nature and therefore natural?"

"Yes," he conceded. "It's just that I like browns and stuff that looks as if it's come out of the ground. My primitive genes must be dominant. Mud huts and all that. It must be why I like simple lines, not furniture that's elaborately carved and curvy."

To his relief she had laughed. He recollected that even in the midst of their disagreement he had been pleased that she had not started weeping like most of his previous girlfriends.

As he took the turning to *Kingower*, he tried to sort out his tangled thoughts. 'Tree and I talk to each other, laugh together and spend our leisure riding horses. There aren't any snags. I get on well with her family, my family adore her. Our politics are the same. I bet Fiona agrees with conscription and the Vietnam war. The thought of aborigines having the vote probably horrifies her.' He got out of the car to open the gates. 'I don't know her. And I don't want to.'

He drove up to the cluster of cottages and parked next to the Mercedes that Kim and Catriona shared. Kim's dog rushed out of her cottage, barking. When Stefan got out of the car the warning bark changed to welcome. 'Hi, Toby old feller,' he said, giving him a pat.

Catriona came out of her cottage and threw her arms round him. "Ready for dinner?"

He kissed her. "I'm ready for something."

"Good."

He carried his case into the spare cottage and put it in the bedroom. Out of respect for her parents, when Stefan came to *Kingower*, Catriona went through the charade of preparing the spare cottage for him. She made up the bed and opened the windows to air it. When he arrived he went through the charade of unpacking. Kim knew he spent the night with Catriona and returned to his cottage before dawn. She had done the same when she had had a serious boyfriend.

Stefan looked at the bed and grinned. "Looks comfortable. I'm sure I'll sleep well tonight."

"Mine's warmer."

"I don't get sufficient sleep in your bed." He smiled at her through half-closed eyes. "You distract me."

"Are you complaining?"

"Bitterly."

She led him into her cottage and shut the door. "Dinner's at the homestead at seven thirty." She reached the bedroom and pulled back the white lace bedspread. Her cheeks were flushed and her eyes sparkling with anticipation. "We've got time for something."

He kissed her and they fell onto the single bed.

That night Stefan was roused from sleep by a howl. "What was that?"

Catriona sprang out of bed. "Toby," she said, pulling on her nightdress.

He grabbed his dressing gown and picked up the rock that she used as a doorstop. "Get behind me."

Kim didn't have any curtains at the front of her cottage, and the light from the lamp shone through her windows. He looked inside, expecting to find her struggling with an intruder, but she was sitting on the sofa with Toby. He tapped on the window and Toby barked.

Kim hushed him and opened the door. "Sorry, did he wake you? He knew I was upset." Her distressed expression became sheepish. "Did you tell Stefan who Oliver is?"

Catriona nodded. "But he thinks it's nonsense."

"Well it is," he said. "What's happened this time? Not another foal in the creek, I hope. Or did he tell you there's a tiger snake under your bed?"

"What did he say, Kim?" asked Catriona.

"Two things."

"Terrific," he said. "There's a foal in the creek *and* a tiger snake under the bed?"

"Sh, Stefan," said Catriona.

He sat in the armchair by the fireplace. "It's half past one – we've got to be up at six."

"Aunty Ruth's going to die. I think he said within the year, but it might have been in a year," she said at last. "So she'll either die before the end of December or before April next year."

"Oh, God," murmured Catriona.

Seeing how troubled she was, Stefan stopped himself from being sarcastic. "Has she got any problems – is she asthmatic?"

Kim shook her head. "But she smokes."

"How old is she?"

"Fifty-three or four."

"What else did Oliver say?" asked Catriona.

"May is going to tear this family apart."

Catriona frowned. "Who's May?"

"It's a month," said Stefan. "It could mean that there'll be a terrible storm in May and the homestead will be struck by lightning and burn down – that would tear the family apart, especially if there was someone in it."

Catriona looked horrified. "I thought you were sceptical about all this."

"I am, but I'll join your morbid flights of fancy." He stood up. "Kim, you had a vivid dream. Let's try and get some sleep or we'll be falling off our horses tomorrow." He gave her a hug. "Aunty Ruth will be alive and as fit as ever this time next year."

Stefan went to sleep immediately, but Catriona was too fraught. Not wanting to disturb him, she went into the kitchen and made some hot chocolate. It was Ruth who had championed her and Kim when they wanted to go to university. Like his own father, David had the view that women were happiest when they were married with children.

At thirteen Catriona didn't know if she wanted to get married. She didn't know if she wanted children. She did know that she wanted to be a vet.

It was during dinner, on one of her weekend visits, that Ruth had asked her what she wanted to be.

"A vet," she replied promptly.

"So do I," Kim said. "But Daddy said only men can be vets."

"He's mistaken," said Ruth. Her acerbic tone had puzzled

Catriona, who had expected her to agree with their father. "There is nothing to stop either of you becoming vets if you want. Tell me if there's anything I can do to help."

"Don't encourage them," their father had said sternly.

"I will, David. Our father said I couldn't be a doctor. He lied to me and you are lying to your daughters." She lectured him for the next fifteen minutes, demolishing his arguments and making them seem ridiculous.

"You're crazy, Ruth," he said finally.

"No, she's not," protested Margot.

Ruth had looked amused. "He can't wriggle out so he's being pathetic."

"Only a crazy person would disappear for four months."

Catriona saw that Kim was as startled as she was.

"It was three months, David," said Ruth. Catriona remembered that she had blushed. "I bet that your daughters know more about the anatomy of a horse than you do."

"Yes! We know the names of all their bones," said Kim. "And their digestive – "

"That's enough," said their father. "If you're so keen for them to go to university, Ruth, you pay their fees. I'm not wasting my money."

"I'm sure they'll get scholarships, David."

It was then that Catriona had become interested in Ruth as a person and not just a spinster aunt. When Ruth returned to Melbourne, Catriona, who was helping Margot in the tack room, had bombarded her with questions.

"When did Aunty Ruth disappear?"

"In 1946."

"Why?"

"When Francesca died, her husband was on his way home from the war," said Margot, putting the horse brushes in soapy water. "We tried to send him a telegram, but communications were down so we wrote to him. Unfortunately he didn't get the letter. He turned up at Ruth's flat expecting to see Francesca. Ruth was so shocked that he didn't know, she just blurted out that Francesca was dead. He was mad with grief and disappeared – "

"He disappeared too?" Catriona said as she filled the second sink with water.

Margot nodded and gave her one of the brushes to rinse. "Ruth blamed herself for telling him so badly. She went away. The only person she told was the Matron, who was concerned enough to tell us. She said that Ruth had been unwell, had lost a lot of weight and had been behaving strangely for months. We were terribly worried. We'd almost made up our minds that she had killed herself. Three months later she wrote to me at *Acacia* saying she was coming up on the train and could I meet her at the station. After that she was better."

"Where had she been?"

"She never told us. We didn't press her – because we were in the middle of a – "

"What?"

"Um ... " Margot looked evasive. "Crisis. Someone got bitten by a snake."

"Who? Did they die?"

"I don't know." As if realizing that was unlikely, Margot said, "They died later. It was one of the jackaroos."

"What happened to Francesca's husband?"

"He turned up at *Acacia* eventually."

"They must have gone somewhere together." Her eyes widened. "Maybe they were going to jump off a cliff – "

Margot laughed. "Impossible. Laurence turned up before Ruth disappeared."

"Where had he been?"

"He refused to tell us." Margot frowned. "He was a contentious man." She took the brushes Catriona had rinsed and put them out in the sun to dry. Now, you deserve some cake and lemonade."

"Tree?"

She jumped. She had been so wrapped up in her memories that she hadn't heard Stefan coming.

"Are you okay?"

She nodded. "I couldn't sleep."

He sat next to her. "Be realistic," he said, taking her hand. "Oliver's not being helpful, is he? He tells Kim that someone's going to die and something vague about the family being in jeopardy, but not what anyone can do to avert it. That alone shows that it's rubbish."

"He might be preparing us for grief."

"Tree," he said putting his hand on her shoulder and giving her a little shake. "She has dreams, not premonitions. Come back to bed."

She began to tell him about Ruth's disappearance, but he yawned.

"I'll tell you another time," she said. As she washed her mug, she concluded that Margot had not been telling the truth. 'There was a crisis, but I bet it was nothing to do with someone being bitten by a snake,' she thought.

In the morning the alarm went off at six. In spite of his interrupted sleep Stefan felt energetic and optimistic that a weekend of hard riding would erase thoughts of Fiona. On trekking weekends they had to be ready for the riders who would arrive between eight and nine. After dressing in jodhpurs and riding boots they left their cottages and went to the homestead for breakfast. Kim and Catriona were so preoccupied that Margot asked them what was wrong. Kim told them about her premonition. To Stefan's surprise, they all took her seriously. The mention of May agitated them even more than the premonition about Ruth's death. David was the last person he would have thought capable of believing that the dead gave messages to the living. His reaction made Stefan's scepticism falter.

"Do you know who May is?" Catriona asked.

Stefan saw their glances flicker to each other and then away.

"It's a month," Margot said.

Stefan thought that her attempt to sound nonchalant failed.

David stuck a fork into the poached egg and looked mesmerized by the yoke seeping into the toast. "No," he said.

Their mother's laugh sounded unnatural.

'They know who May is,' he thought. 'Or what it is. If they'd discovered that *Kingower* was bankrupt they couldn't look more upset than they do now.'

Stefan was the only one who finished his breakfast. Most of the eggs and tomatoes on the other plates were scarcely touched. The toast racks and dishes of marmalade and butter were full. When the cook that they hired for trekking weekends worried that the food was inedible, Kim reassured her and admitted that they'd had a bit of bad news.

"Is May a person or the month?" Catriona asked, as they walked to the stables.

Stefan thought about it. "A person," he said eventually. "You can be frightened of a person, but I don't see how you can be frightened of a month. Unless someone else in your family has the same power as Kim and has had the same premonition."

"No one else is psychic," said Kim.

"What about the sister who died? What was her name?"

Catriona looked thoughtful. "Francesca. We don't know much about her ... just that she was married to Aunty Margot's stepson and died of an asthma attack at the end of the war."

"Your Aunty Ruth seems to be a bit distant from the family. She doesn't come to *Kingower* that much."

Catriona sighed. "Fiona's her favourite, I don't know why."

"She used to come all the time before Fiona wrecked everything," Kim added. "It upsets Aunty Margot because Aunty Ruth was more like her daughter than her sister. When our grandmother died Ruth and Francesca were only little girls. Margot was old enough to be their mother and she practically brought them up."

"What did Fiona do?"

Catriona scowled. "She caused a family row. Two family rows."

"What about?"

"It was so long ago," she said with a shrug.

When they arrived at the stables, Margot was organizing the grooms.

"How many people are coming?" Stefan asked.

"Ten," said Kim. "So we need sixteen horses. Let's go and round them up."

They went to the paddock. It had rained overnight and the April sun sparked on the grass. Stefan marvelled how the landscape changed from brown in the summer to green in autumn and winter. As usual, the horses came to Kim with no coaxing. Catriona had to entice them with carrots while Stefan only succeeded in catching one. When the horses had been led to the fence the grooms put on their bridles and saddles.

The trek set off at ten and was scheduled to return at four, with a break of two hours for lunch. The place chosen for the barbecue was a clearing in a forest. The deciduous trees were at their autumnal best. As Stefan trotted his horse into the clearing he looked at the golden and russet ceiling of leaves contrasting with the blue sky. Dismounting, he led his horse to the stream and let her drink, then tied her reins to a tree.

Margot, who had driven to the area in the station-wagon, had the fires burning in the brick barbecues. Paper plates and napkins, bowls of salads and fruit, and sandwiches for Catriona and Kim were arranged on the picnic tables.

"Left the others behind, Stefan?" Her smile was strained.

"I accidentally took the short cut. What can I do to help, Mrs Clarkson?"

She handed him a plate of sausages and chops. "Could you start cooking these?"

"Mrs Clarkson, can I ask you a question?"

"You'd better be quick. Here come some more riders."

He smiled disarmingly. "It isn't important." The chops and sausages hissed as he put them on the metal racks over the flames.

Catriona trotted over to him. "Where did you get to?"

"Lost!"

She hooted with laughter. A few minutes later she walked over and looked disapprovingly at the sausages and chops. "Dead animals," she declared.

"Catriona, don't stand there like a stick of liquorice," snapped Margot.

Her outburst was so out of character that even Catriona was taken aback.

'She's rattled,' thought Stefan. 'She knows who May is and it's frightening her. It's frightening the hell out of all of them.'

It was not until after the barbecue that he caught David alone.

"Who's May?" he asked bluntly.

He looked thoughtfully at Stefan. "I don't want you telling Tree and Kim until we decide what to do. But I don't know that there is anything we can do."

"If you try and prevent it you can. Only the past is fixed. So, who is May?"

"Fiona," he said finally. "Her name used to be May. Virginia and Alex didn't like it so they named her after Virginia's mother. Kim's premonition makes sense. Fiona's a wrecker and that's why she's not welcome at *Kingower*."

On Sunday afternoon, Stefan and Catriona cantered across the hill in the glow of the late afternoon sun. It was the final stretch back to *Kingower*. He slowed his horse to a trot and followed her along the track leading to the paddock. They were the last to arrive. Most of the horses were at the water troughs. Normally he was sorry when the weekends ended, but this weekend had been so oppressive he was looking forward to going home. He had not succeeded in obliterating Fiona from his thoughts and Kim's eerie contact with her dead brother was rocking his belief that the paranormal did not exist. The other explanation, that the family he was marrying into was weird, made him feel worse. For once he did not dread the journey back to Melbourne and the thought of the busy week ahead with his students, who were preparing for the second-term exams.

The first thing he did when he arrived at his flat that night was look in the phone book for Fiona's address.

Ω Ω Ω

15th April 1972

Dear Mum and Dad,

I've been in Melbourne for six hours. It's noisy, dirty, cold and crowded. People swarm along the pavements, pushing and shoving. Mothers plead with demanding brats. I want – I want – is echoed all over the streets of this horrible city. I had a cup of coffee in a cafe and the waitress was too busy to chat. People are unfriendly. How can Hazel stand living in Brisbane? I bought a cheese sandwich – the bread was tasteless and the cheese was rubbery. I should have done what you said, and waited till Fiona came to Queensland. This morning I went to the Ansett offices and stood outside, but I didn't want to meet her with lots of people around. I'm so fraught. What if she doesn't want to know me?

June went over to the window of the Youth Hostel in South Yarra. By her calculation, Fiona would arrive home at about six in the evening. It was lunchtime and she did not want to be cooped up inside for the rest of the day. She studied her map and walked to the Botanical Gardens. For three hours she strolled round the green lawns. She fed the black swans on the lake and gloried in the rich autumn colours of the trees that were so different to the grey-green leaves of the native gums on *Eumeralla*. Even their deciduous trees did not turn to such vibrant colours.

At five o'clock she walked to St. Kilda Road and caught a crowded tram. 'Wouldn't it be funny if Fiona was on the same tram,' she thought. It was fifteen minutes before the conductor had struggled through the mass of people. She handed him her fare. "Hawthorn, please."

"You're on the wrong tram. Get off and go back three stops."

By the time June had caught the right tram it was almost six o'clock.

Fiona lived in a quiet street, which was lined with mature sycamore trees. Stefan had expected the units to look modern, but they had been built of red brick with Victorian-style windows. Moss growing between the cobblestones of the pathway enhanced the illusion that they were a row of old cottages. Even the garages had rustic wooden doors, which made them look like stables. Terracotta pots planted with white geraniums and ivy stood on Fiona's window sills. Her garage door was open. As well as her royal-blue MG he saw two tennis rackets, an ironing board, skis and ski boots.

Fiona opened her door as soon as he rang the bell. She wore a holly-green velvet suit and a white blouse with a high neck. The cut of the jacket was almost masculine, and her blouse was uncompromisingly plain.

"What the hell are you doing here, Stefan?"

He was taken aback. "Can I talk to you?"

She stayed in the doorway. "What about?"

"Have I come at a bad time?"

"Any time you came would be a bad time."

"Are you going out?"

"Yes."

"Can I give you a lift anywhere?"

"No."

He grinned. "You're totally without charm, aren't you?"

Her scowling expression remained. "Yes. Now scram." She went to shut the door.

"Fiona, I must talk to you. It's important."

"What about?"

"Your family."

She gave an exaggerated sigh. "What about them?"

"I'd like to bring you together."

She yanked the door wide open. "Come in."

As she turned around he saw black leather boots with flat heels showing beneath the skirt that fell to just below her calves. There was no hallway and the front door opened onto the lounge. His feet sank into the thick blue carpet.

"Leave the door open, Stefan. I warn you that if you touch me I'll scream the place down."

If he hadn't been so confused he would have been angry. "I have no intention of touching you, Fiona."

The phone rang. Before she left the room to answer it she said, "Don't sit down and don't make yourself comfortable." She banged the lounge door shut.

It was evident that a great deal of money had gone into furnishing the room, which smelt of new fabric. The sofa and armchairs were upholstered in burgundy-and-navy-striped chintz, and matching curtains hung at the windows. A large bookcase stood against one wall. Remembering Kim and Catriona's scathing remarks about Fiona's lack of intelligence he looked at some of the titles. There were biographies of Winston Churchill, President Kennedy and T E Lawrence. Her collection of novels included titles by Henry James, Thomas Hardy and Daphne du Maurier. A paperback copy of the novel *Exodus*, by Leon Uris, lay on the sofa. The bookmark showed that she had almost finished it. 'Hardly light reading,' Stefan thought. Red and white roses, which perfumed the air, were arranged in a crystal vase. He wondered if she had bought them herself or a boyfriend had given them to her. Oriental pictures in black lacquer frames hung on the powder-blue walls. The room was tidy, but the atmosphere was welcoming. Although he would never have painted walls blue, her style of decorating was more sophisticated than Catriona's.

"Nice paintings," he said when she came back. "Where did you get them?"

"At an art gallery," she said caustically.

"It's an attractive unit."

"I'm so grateful that you approve." Fiona stalked over to the window and turned to him with her arms crossed. She stood as rigidly as a soldier. "Let me tell you about my relationship with Tree and Kim," she said acidly. "When we were young we were friends. I loved going to *Kingower*. I wanted to live there all the time and wished they were my sisters. I hated being an only child –

hated the loneliness and longed for the comradeship of a sister. At school I used to lie about having lots of brothers and sisters, I even invented names for them. When my mother found out, she was angry with me and I was ostracized at school because I was a liar.

"I knew Tree and Kim weren't really my cousins, but I wished they were. I told them things I've never told anyone. Uncle David despised me because I was afraid of horses. Aunty Margot didn't like me because I was the daughter of her stepson, but I didn't care. All I cared about were Tree and Kim. Then we grew up. And what happened? Men. Bloody, rotten men." She walked towards him so belligerently that for a second he thought she was going to hit him. "Their boyfriends, who wanted a bit on the side with me. All the *Kingower* lot blamed me. Did they tell you that?"

He shook his head. "I knew there was some row, but I thought it was something to do with your grandfather's property."

"If they ever find out you were here, they would presume I had lured you. Tree would never believe that you came of your own accord and neither would anyone else."

"I'm sorry, Fiona, I shouldn't have come." His sense of shame forced him to lie. "You've misjudged my motives, though. I thought that as I was almost part of the family I could help." His attempt at justifying his actions did not dent his conscience. He had insulted Fiona and betrayed Catriona. "It was arrogant of me."

"Yes, Stefan, it was. The best thing you can do is stay away from me. I'll next see you at your wedding to Tree."

"You're very unhappy, aren't you?" he asked gently.

Tears gushed into her eyes. He was not surprised that his method of disarming her had worked. Teaching had taught him that angry or aggressive pupils were usually unhappy.

She turned her back on him.

"Fiona."

"Go away."

Stefan turned round. He gaped in amazement at the young woman standing in the doorway. She was wearing jeans and a red jumper over a check shirt. The jeans had frayed hems and her jumper was faded, but apart from the way she was dressed she was identical to Fiona. "Strewth!" he said.

"Go away."

"Fiona, you've – "

"Get out, Stefan! Get out!"

"You've got a visitor."

Fiona spun round. Stefan, who was blocking her view of the doorway, stepped aside. He watched, fascinated, as they stared at each other.

A faraway look came over Fiona's face. She shut her eyes. "Juju," she whispered. "Juju."

Part Two

THE PROPHECY

1972

April to October

CHAPTER 10

Eumeralla
April 1972

I must be a dill. It took me ages to catch on. I assumed that Juju was adopted too. But I was staggered – wonderfully staggered when she turned up – and there was so much to do I didn't have time to ask many questions. I had to pack and go to work and tell them what had happened. They let me take leave and will hurry my transfer to Brisbane. I rang Aunty Ruth, but she wasn't home, so I wrote her a note and put it in her letterbox.

I could have flown to Brisbane with Juju, but as soon as she saw my MG she wanted to drive it. So we drove here and stayed in motels overnight. It only took us three days.

When I arrived at *Eumeralla* this morning I was touched by the welcome they gave me. Neil and Tom called me Sis and I was pleased that they accepted me. But I thought they were Juju's adopted family. I thought my real mother was an alcoholic and I imagined she'd be living in a filthy slum. When I realized what Eleanor's name was, I remembered the card attached to the posy on Jonathan's grave. "Did you know Jonathan?" I asked. She looked confused. Then Juju told me everything. Even then it took me a while to grasp the fact that Eleanor was my real mother. I just managed to stop myself from blurting out that I thought she was an alcoholic. She said that she's so excited that she can see Virginia again and I didn't want to tell her how her 'friend' betrayed her.

I'm so happy, but angry with Mum. I'll never forgive her for lying to me. I'm going to stop calling her Mum and call her Virginia from now on. I was born here. Not in a slum. And my real mother is not an alcoholic. But when I walked into the house this morning the smell was familiar. Every house has a smell, especially older ones. The ingrained scent of the building materials and the walls and the air. And of the people who live in it. This house smells of baking bread, soap and oil from the lamps. It was here – along the hall and the verandahs – that I crawled as a baby – with Juju. We slept contentedly in our bassinets and had loving parents. All these years I've thought that I lay disregarded and hungry while my real mother sat oblivious and drunk surrounded by empty bottles while flies buzzed in the mess.

Eleanor and my mother (I mean Virginia) are the same age, but Eleanor looks older. Her dark hair has got lots of grey streaks. Her eyes are brown. She's not elegant like Virginia – she wears jeans and men's shirts, but smart dresses and suits and silk blouses would be impractical here.

The house at *Eumeralla* is not beautiful like *Kingower* – it's small and there are only three bedrooms, but it's freshly painted and clean. It's built on stilts in case the river floods. It looks a bit clumsy and there's a verandah at the back and front. There is no electricity or gas and we have oil lamps and torches. It's like living in the olden days. It's fun.

Virginia would scorn this place because the floor's covered in lino, the sofa and chairs don't match, the cutlery is stainless steel not silver, and the glasses are just glasses not crystal, and the crockery is cheap instead of the bone china she cherishes, but I wish I'd lived here all my life instead of in the luxurious house in Vaucluse.

There are two dogs. Toddles is a border collie and Red's a kelpie. Toddles took to me straightaway, but Red is wary. Juju said I should be flattered – he growls at strangers.

Now I've found my family I'm not sure what to do. I can't ride a horse and I'm ignorant about agriculture. Tonight I helped Juju cook the dinner. I could help around the house. Until I get used to country life it might be better if I stay in Brisbane during the week and come to *Eumeralla* at weekends.

There's only one thing wrong. The toilet is outside – a long way from the house and it stinks so much I nearly vomited. It's primitive, but there are only a few flushing toilets out here. All the water for the house comes from the tanks which collect rain. There's a lot I'll have to get used to. Because of the importance of water conservation I won't be able to spend ages under the shower. Juju almost had a fit when she was in Melbourne. She couldn't believe I'd spent so long under the shower. And I couldn't believe she spent so little. No sooner had she gone into the bathroom than she came out again. Hair washed and everything! If I come to live on *Eumeralla* for good I'll have to get my hair cut. The boys – my brothers, look like Greg, but are much taller and apparently Hazel is the image of Eleanor.

Today has been the happiest day of my life. *Eumeralla* – my home. My sisters and brothers. It feels so good to write that. I'm so lucky. The house is silent. Everyone's in bed. They go to bed early and get up at six. I'll have to finish now even though I could write for hours.

As Fiona dressed in jeans and a shirt the following morning, the curtainless windows disconcerted her.

"You'll have to get used to the isolation," said June. "The nearest house is over the creek."

"When I get my hair cut, do you think anyone will be able to tell us apart?"

June rummaged through her drawer for a jumper. "We'll have to try it. Aren't you putting on a jumper?" she asked.

"No."

"It's cold."

Fiona laughed. "You don't know cold."

"Yes, I do, I've been in Melbourne."

They went into the kitchen. The table on the verandah was set for breakfast.

Tom was spooning porridge into bowls. "Hi, Sis."

"Hi, Townie," said Neil.

Fiona laughed delightedly at this symbol of her acceptance. "Hi, brothers."

"Fancy a ride round *Eumeralla* today?" asked Tom.

Fiona bit her lip. "I can't ride."

"Nothing to it – we'll teach you," said Neil sprinkling brown sugar over his porridge.

"I'm scared of horses." The confession shamed her.

"No you're not," said Tom, passing her the milk jug.

She felt her face turning red. "My uncle tried to teach me to ride and failed. I was frightened."

Greg smiled encouragingly. "We'll sort you out."

Fiona felt daunted. 'It's going to be like last time I tried to learn – they'll despise me too.' Her jubilation shriveled. 'I should have known better than to think I'd found happiness,' she thought.

Tom drained his mug of tea. "Finished, Sis?"

"Yes."

"Come and meet the horses."

"I won't have to ride one, will I?" she asked, loathing herself for her feeling of panic.

"Nope. Not till you're ready."

'I'll never be ready,' she thought.

Tom took two apples out of the fruit basket. "Catch," he said, tossing her one.

She caught it, relieved that she hadn't dropped it.

Tom ran down the back steps and Fiona followed. They were joined by Toddles and Red who bounded along beside Tom. He strode to the paddock which was three hundred yards from the house. Fiona almost had to run to keep up with him. He vaulted the fence then lifted her over as easily as if she'd been a child. He whistled and some of the horses trotted over.

"Monty, say hi to our long lost sister. Here comes Digger." He broke the apples into quarters and gave some pieces to Fiona. "Offer treats on the palm of your hand or the horse might accidentally bite your fingers. I'll do Monty, you do Digger."

Fiona copied Tom. Digger demolished the apple and looked for more. She gave him the other pieces, enjoying the feel of his tongue on her hand. She was aware that Tom was watching her.

"Scared of horses, eh?" He shook his head. "No you're not. I knew yesterday you weren't scared. You let me come right up to you when I was on Zorro and you stroked him. If you'd been scared of horses you wouldn't have let him near you."

"Then what am I scared of?"

"Maybe it was the person who tried to teach you," he said.

"It was my uncle. He's a good teacher. No one else had any problems – just me."

"Sis, you were born on *Eumeralla*, Mum's a smashing rider and so was your real dad. Riding's in your blood. You had a bad experience. Was he impatient with you?"

Fiona grimaced. "He was furious when I screamed and the horse almost bolted."

"Did you ever try again?"

"No. He said I was bad for his horses."

"He should have tried something different with you. I've got to saddle up Zorro and ride round the place checking the water tanks. How about getting on his back and just sitting. I'll hold him and he won't go anywhere. What do you say?"

Feeling slightly more confident, she nodded.

Tom grinned. "Good on you, Sis. You're not bad for a townie."

"How many townies have you known?"

"Too many. Hazel's always bringing them here for weekends. One even turned up in a dress, high-heeled shoes and stockings. She minced round like a princess all weekend and squealed whenever the dogs went near her. Then she saw a snake and ... "

"And what?"

He looked as if he was trying not to laugh. "Wet herself."

"I don't blame her." Fiona shuddered. "Was it poisonous?"

"It was only a carpet python."

"Why does Hazel live in Brisbane?"

He pulled a face. "She's weird. Even when she was a kid she wanted to go and live somewhere else. She couldn't wait to get away. Bit strange really – Juju, Neil and I would rather drop dead than live in a town."

"I can see why."

He checked the water troughs. "Are you going to stay, or what?"

"I haven't decided yet. I don't want to be a burden."

He grinned. "You won't be. We won't let you."

"I could do what Hazel does and come here for weekends."

"She doesn't come every weekend. What would you really like to do, Sis?"

"Stay here."

"Then do."

"Have you got a girlfriend, Tom?"

"Not at the moment. I just ditched one. She wanted us to get married and move to Toowoomba. No one could persuade me to live in a town. Besides we'd only been going out for six months. I don't believe in rushing things. How about you?"

"No. Chaps bore me."

He looked at her in mock alarm.

She blushed. "It's just that they talk about cars and football. I went out with an airline pilot for a while. He was only interested in himself, cars and his uniform. All the girls used to go for the pilots as if they were God. He probably noticed me because I wasn't impressed."

"What impresses you, Sis?"

"*Eumeralla.*"

He ruffled her hair. "Let's get the saddle."

Eumeralla
April 1972

Today I sat on a horse! Tom showed me how to handle the reins and how to mount and dismount. Tomorrow I'm going to ride round the paddock. He said I'd have a half-hour lesson every day. Because I'm a townie he was amazed that I knew so much about horses, so I'm pleased I took notice of Tree and Kim.

Juju drove me round *Eumeralla* in the truck. I saw the wheat silos and flocks of merinos. Sheep are taken to the property over the creek to be shorn. They used to go to *Acacia* when my grandfather was the owner.

I use the toilet as little as possible. Every time I go in there I feel queasy. Luckily we've each got a potty under the bed so we don't have to go out at night. Everything, including our urine, goes on the compost heap, except food scraps suitable for the chickens. It's strange knowing that my urine is useful. The garden is enclosed by a picket fence to keep out the sheep.

Although the soil in the Darling Downs is fertile, Greg says that it must be looked after and respected. Like the aborigines, his attitude to the land is that he is nurturing it for the next generation. Keith told me about the article in the farming magazine, but I wasn't really interested. That was only in January – it seems like years ago. What a naive townie I was.

Ω   Ω   Ω

"She's got some carrots for you, boy," Tom said as he led Flicker over to Fiona. "One of the best ways of making friends with a horse is to give him treats."

Fiona smiled as Flicker ate the carrots on the palm of her hand.

"Today you won't leave the paddock. I'll hold the reins for you," said Tom.

She felt a twinge of fear she was determined to hide.

"Up you get, Sis. Flicker's gentle. He's twenty so we don't ride him far now, but he likes a bit of exercise."

Fiona mounted and sat still while Tom adjusted the stirrups. 'I'm only going round the paddock and Tom will be with me,' she thought.

"Sit up straight when you're walking or trotting. You lean over the horse when you're cantering and galloping." He grinned. "And you won't be doing that for a while. All you'll be doing today is walking. Right, let's take you round a few times."

As soon as Fiona realized she wasn't going to fall off and break her neck, she felt more composed.

When they went round for the second time Tom let her take the reins. "These are to guide the horse. Never yank on them because it'll hurt their mouths. All our horses have good temperaments so, if you're riding one and it starts acting up, it's probably sensed or seen a snake, so slacken the reins and hang on tight. Always trust their instinct."

When they had been round the paddock twice Tom said, "You're a good pupil. How about going round by yourself?"

"Yes. It's not as scary as I thought it'd be."

"Off you go."

She went round twice and was disappointed when the lesson was over.

"We'll have another go tomorrow," said Tom. "I'll teach you how to trot. Say goodbye to Flicker. Part of the friendship thing."

"Thanks for being such a good horse." She stroked his muzzle and he nudged her.

She saw Tom's expression of anger and thought it was directed at her. "Tom?"

"It's okay, Sis. He's a good horse because we treat him well. I was thinking of those ignoramuses on *Acacia* ... not your family – the ones who own it now. Know anything about horse breaking?"

"My cousin Kim's only got to look at a horse and it's broken in. She's got this extraordinary way with animals. She and her sister Catriona are vets."

"Is that how you know so much?"

"Yes, and through Mum and Dad too," she said, reluctant to give all the credit to Kim and Catriona.

"Sis, what would you do if a bloke came up to you, hit you, grabbed you by the hair and dragged you off?"

"I'd kick his precious bits to pulp."

Tom laughed. "Would you submit to his will?"

"Not if I could help it."

"It's the same for a horse. Bridles and saddles aren't natural for them so you've got to coax them. The scum on *Acacia*, and lots of other people too, think horses must be bullied into submission – they take the word *breaking* seriously. Right, now I'll show you how to take off the bridle and saddle."

"Trotting is the most difficult part of riding," Tom told Fiona the next day.

She mounted Flicker. "It's getting easier. I could hardly haul myself up a few days ago."

"Before you set out on a ride, check you can lift yourself out of the saddle," he said as he adjusted her stirrups. "Try it."

Fiona rose effortlessly.

"Good. If you can't, you'll be shaken about and end up aching all over. With trotting, the trick is to rise when the horse does and lower yourself when he does. It's got a rise-on-one and down-on-two sort of feel about it. Ready?"

She nodded.

"Away we go." He ran beside Flicker.

Fiona immediately got into the right rhythm.

"That's beaut," he said encouragingly. "Whoa, boy. Now you can go round by yourself. Okay?"

"Okay." Heartened by her spurt of confidence, she pressed her heels lightly into Flicker's side. He set off and trotted round the paddock. Halfway round Fiona was gripped by instinct and a wild impulse to go faster. She urged him on. He broke into a canter and she laughed, overcome by an incredible sense of freedom. The trees round the perimeter of the paddock sped past and her hair streamed behind her. 'If Tree, Kim and Uncle David could see me now!' she thought. She gently pulled on the reins as they approached Tom.

"Born to it, Sis!"

She looked down at him. "That was out of this world!" Kicking her feet out of the stirrups she threw her leg back and slid down the horse.

He picked her up and swung her round. "Whacko, Sis. Whacko! You can ride. It'll be a while before you can go off on your own, but in a year you'll be able to round up sheep."

'Now I understand Tree and Kim's passion for horses,' she thought.

We moved the horses to a new paddock today. *Eumeralla* has three paddocks – home, which is closest to the house, middle and far. They are huge, much bigger than the one at *Kingower*. There are no stables, they have foul-weather shelters with old car tyres on the roof to insulate against lightning. To promote good grazing pasture, they rest each paddock by moving the horses into the adjoining one. When most of the grass and dandelions have been eaten the horses are put in the new one.

Greg said that sometimes you just open the gate to the new paddock and they wander in of their own accord. Once one horse goes in the rest often follow. Other times, and today was one of them, they need persuading with treats of carrots and apples. I led Flicker in by myself and was so proud.

I haven't worn tights or dresses or put on make-up since I got here. How different from my old life. Instead of a perfectly-ironed blouse, smart uniform and tights I put on un-ironed shirts and jeans. No solo breakfast of orange juice, cereal and coffee in my unit, but porridge, eggs, thick slices of homemade bread with jam or marmalade and big mugs of strong tea. The milk is creamy and the brown sugar is sticky and fragrant. We eat on the verandah in the fresh air. The view is trees and pasture not houses, and the sounds come from birds and horses not traffic. I walk over to the paddocks instead of waiting for a tram and am outside most of the day instead of being cooped up in an air-conditioned office.

After my riding lesson with Tom, I helped Juju in the house. I learnt to make bread. We made two loaves. It's delicious – much more flavour than the bread I used to buy in the shops. Then Juju said that we had to mow the lawn. She looked furtive and told me to wait while she got the lawn-mowers. When she left the garden, instead of going to the shed, I thought she was going to borrow them from the family over the creek. Ages later she and Toddles came back with four sheep! I had to supervise them so they wouldn't eat the vegetables.

I cut my hair this afternoon and it's a sort of pageboy style now. Juju did the back for me. When Tom came back I was on the verandah and he looked up and called me Juju.

We get all our dairy produce from the property over the creek. In exchange we supply them with eggs, fruit and vegetables. We don't go to the shops much, we just go into the garden or across the creek. All the jam, marmalade and lemon curd is homemade. Food here has a lot more flavour. The egg yokes are so dark they are almost orange.

Fiona groaned as she poured the bucket of water into the copper. "It's full at last!"

June, who was sitting on the stone floor splitting kindling with a tomahawk, remembered Fiona's washing machine and her own amazement at how easily the washing was done.

"I'm a bit of a weakling," Fiona said as she poked newspaper into the fireplace under the copper and arranged the kindling on top.

June handed her the matches. "As soon as that catches we can put a few logs in."

When the water in the copper was boiling Fiona poured in a cup of washing powder and stirred it with a wooden pole until it dissolved.

"How long do they have to boil?" she asked as June put in the sheets.

"About five minutes."

"How do we get them out?"

June turned on the taps over the double sink. "With the pole. We put them in this sink to rinse them and feed them through the wringer. Rinse them again in the second sink. Empty the first sink and wring them again. It's easy really." She laughed at Fiona's expression. "But not as easy as your washing machine."

When the washing was pegged on the line, June said, "Let's go and catch tonight's dinner." She went to the shed and took out two fishing rods. "Can you fish?"

Fiona shook her head. "Something else I've got to learn."

"It's easy. But we've got to keep quiet or we'll frighten them away."

I caught two fish this afternoon! Juju caught the other four. They don't suffer for long. As soon as we get them off the hook Juju bashes them on the head with a rock. I was horrified at first, then she made me do it. So I did. Tonight we had fish fried in butter, with peas and mashed potatoes. And for dessert I made a bread-and-butter pudding, which we had with cream.

It rained last night while we were having dinner. The smell of the wet grass and earth was better than the most expensive perfume. I stood on the verandah and watched the water dripping off the trees. In Sydney and Melbourne rain never interested me unless there was a drought. The weather used to affect me only in relation to my leisure activities. If it snowed in the mountains that meant the ski season would be good. If it rained I couldn't play tennis or go swimming. Here if anyone talks about the weather it's in relation to the crops and water planning.

I'm going to see Keith and Gabby at the weekend.

Fiona found Keith and Gabriella in the garden. They sat on the verandah and Fiona told them what had happened. "So I wrote to Virginia last night and told her I never want to see her again," she finished.

Gabriella looked horrified. "You're being callous, you can't just cut your mother off like that."

"I'm not, am I, Keith?"

"Yes."

Their attitude bewildered Fiona. "But she told me my real mother was an alcoholic. She deprived me of my twin sister and she dominated and bullied me."

"She doesn't strike me as a bully," said Gabriella. "Did she beat you?"

"No. You don't have to beat someone to bully them. You don't know how it feels to have your life ruled by someone who wants to imprison your thoughts. She said that my political views were deranged and asked who'd brainwashed me."

"You're being a bit melodramatic," said Keith.

"My teenage years were a nightmare. All my friends were allowed to wear mini-skirts, but I wasn't."

"What a tragedy," said Gabriella. "Listen, Fiona, you've regained all that you lost. I'd give anything to have Brett back."

"Gabby, it's not the same," argued Keith.

"Too right, it's not!"

"Fiona," said Keith. "Don't send the letter to Aunty Virginia ... she'd be heartbroken"

"I posted it on my way here."

Gabriella stood up so quickly her chair fell with a crash. "You're heartless, Fiona. I don't know that I ever want to speak to you again."

"Hang on, Gabby," said Keith. "Aunty Virginia did tell lies."

Gabriella turned so that her back was to Fiona. "But she did her best and so did Uncle Alex. They loved her, she went to a private school, they bought her a car for her twenty-first birthday. She decided to go overseas and they paid her fare. When she came home they bought her a unit. She had everything anyone could want. She's an ungrateful – "

Fiona stood up and faced Gabriella who immediately turned

away. "Except what I wanted most of all – brothers and sisters," she said.

"You can't tell me that she didn't love her father's wealth. She made the most of it. She wore exclusive clothes – "

"Today she's dressed in jeans and a shirt," he said, taking Gabriella by the shoulders and turning her towards Fiona. "Have you ever seen her looking happier?"

"No," she conceded.

CHAPTER 11

Stefan was unable to obliterate the scene in Fiona's unit from his memory. When her twin had arrived Fiona had been transfixed. He had no idea how long he had stood staring at them. His presence had been irrelevant. The stillness of the twins had not been broken by the few words that passed between them.

Eventually Fiona's twin had said, "Come back to Queensland."

"Yes," had been Fiona's reply. Then she had smiled.

Her radiance had sent quivers down his spine. Feeling like an interloper, Stefan had left. As he drove back to his flat he wondered if they had been aware of his departure, but suspected that they had immediately forgotten him.

Now he felt trapped. If he told Catriona he had been to see Fiona, she would think he had betrayed her. But if he didn't tell her, Fiona might. Even if she had gone straight to Queensland she could write a letter.

'If I tell her father, would he believe my motive?' He mulled over the best way to mention it. 'When you told me that May was Fiona, I was worried about it so I went to see her.' He shook his head. 'That's no bloody good. But it's why I went to see her. No, that was the excuse.'

He tried to concentrate on his students' essays written on the theme of *What If*. So far most of them had been imaginative. A couple were so preposterous they made him laugh. He picked up the next essay, entitled *World War Zero*. Notwithstanding the compelling writing about Gavrillo Princep being killed in a brawl before he could shoot Archduke Franz Ferdinand, Stefan's mind drifted to Fiona. Hoping a walk would help him find a solution, he left his flat and went across the road to the Albert Park Lake. The late afternoon was cool, but the slanting sun was bright. A few people were walking their dogs and a child floated a toy yacht on the water.

By the time he had strolled around the lake he realized he had more problems. Everything was nearly ready for his wedding to Catriona in September and to call it off would be devastating. He castigated himself for his preoccupation with someone he scarcely knew. Before he had met Catriona he had been infuriated by virgins who thought their modesty was incomparable, and her earthiness was refreshing. She was honest about her sexuality and had not pretended to be a virgin. Stefan disliked promiscuity, but felt that sex completed a serious relationship. He remembered the first time they had made love. It was six months after they had started going out together. Overcome with passion they had stopped their horses in the forest. The current joke had been that, when a man went to bed for the first time with an English girl, the first thing she would say afterwards was, 'Like a cup of tea?' A Russian girl would say, 'You have conquered my body, but not my soul,' while the Australian girl, years behind in the sexual revolution, would burst into tears and say, 'Now you'll think I'm awful!'

Catriona had laughed and said, "Don't fret. I still respect you."

He had looked forward to the exhilaration of being married to an intelligent woman with ambitions. Ultimately, Catriona and Kim wanted to start their own veterinary surgery. His new teaching position at the local high school would commence when he returned from their honeymoon. Holidays and weekends would be spent horse riding. Catriona was tidy and efficient and never kept him waiting. Combined with her common sense was a romantic streak. When she cooked for him she put flowers on the table and lit candles in the winter. Before he had met Fiona the prospect of marrying Catriona had been so appealing. Now he wanted to postpone it.

'Why?' he thought. 'Tree's the sort of woman I admire. She's got a tremendous personality and we have fun together. We want children, but that's not the reason for the marriage. We spend hours just talking. Fiona's got nothing compared to Tree. She's abrasive, insulting and misunderstood. Oh hell, hell. I bet she hasn't thought of me once.'

Ω Ω Ω

When Alex and Virginia arrived back from New Zealand they saw, on the hall table, the pile of mail that had been collected by their neighbour. Virginia took the smaller cases into their bedroom. Alex flicked through the mail to see if there was anything important. He saw the letter from Fiona and wondered why it was addressed only to Virginia. Then he saw the Queensland postmark. With a feeling of trepidation he ripped it open.

Eumeralla
24th April 1972

Virginia,

I'll never call you Mum again. You never loved me. You wanted a baby for yourself and you didn't care that you ravaged my soul with your lies. Why did you tell me that I would have grown up in a slum if it hadn't been for you? **Eumeralla***'s not a slum and you knew it. Eleanor's not an alcoholic, and you knew that too. How could you say something so appalling about a friend who gave you her baby because you couldn't have one of your own?*

I never want to see you or speak to you again, but I will on family occasions, for Dad's sake. In spite of what you've done, I don't want Margot to crow over you. For the first time in my life I'm happy. I've found what I've been looking for.

Fiona.

He saw Virginia coming out of their bedroom. "What's – ?"

"Fiona's on *Eumeralla*," he said, giving her the letter. He put his arm around her while she read it. He could feel her trembling.

"She blames me," Virginia whimpered. "I knew she would. You've escaped. You're still her saintly father."

"Darling, we'll sort this out."

"How?"

He saw there was another letter from Fiona. It was addressed to him.

Dear Dad,

Some of this must be your fault, but unlike Virginia you loved me and compensated for some of the unhappiness I suffered. Did you know she told me my real mother was an alcoholic? I have to go back to Melbourne at some stage to sort out my unit and job. I haven't decided what to do yet. Can I see you in Melbourne? I'll ring you when I arrive. Don't try and make the peace between Virginia and me. If she comes with you I'll refuse to see either of you.

Fiona.

He handed her the letter. "I'll go and see her. Today – if I can get a flight to Brisbane."

"I'll come too."

"No, Virginia. Stay here. Leave her alone for a while."

"I'm coming with you!"

"You'll make things worse. For God's sake, for once in your life, listen to me. If you'd listened to me years ago we wouldn't be going through all this now."

She dropped the letter. "And we would have lost her then."

"Not if you'd done it the way I wanted. What could an eight year old do – walk all the way to Queensland?"

"Knowing Fiona she probably would have tried."

"Virginia, I'm going to *Eumeralla* and you're staying here, and that's an end to it." He looked through the rest of the mail. At the bottom was the letter from Greg and Eleanor. "We just missed it," he said when he read it.

"If we'd known we could have ... " She went into the bedroom and sat on the bed. "I've lost her," she moaned. "She hates me."

Alex sat beside her and took her hand. "You know how melodramatic she is. She feels betrayed, but she'll get over it."

She shook her head. "I doubt it. And she's right. I did tell lies. Terrible and damaging lies."

"You were frightened. I'll tell her why. She won't relent immediately, but she will in the end." He squeezed her hand. "Trust me, Darling."

The phone rang. It was Ruth. "Alex, thank God you're back. Fiona's gone to Queensland, she's – "

"I know," he said. "She wrote to us from *Eumeralla*. I'm going to see if I can get a flight to Brisbane today."

"Wait till tomorrow and I'll come with you. I'm on night duty tonight, but I've got the next four days off. I'll try and get an early flight to Sydney tomorrow. I'll ring you back to let you know what time, and you can book a flight to Brisbane for both of us."

Gabriella met Alex and Ruth at Brisbane airport.

"This is very good of you, Gabby," said Alex. "This is my sister Ruth."

"Hello, Miss Lancaster."

"Hello, Gabriella, and please call me Ruth."

They walked out to the car park. "Do you want to go straight to *Eumeralla*, Uncle Alex?"

"I reckon that'd be best."

"Keith rang them this morning and spoke to Eleanor." She prayed he wouldn't ask how Fiona had found out about June. She dreaded telling him the part she and Keith had played. "How's Aunty Virginia?"

"Distraught," he said. "Gabby, how much do you know about all this? Have you seen Fiona since she went to *Eumeralla*?"

She wanted to avoid the first question. "Yes, we saw her last week. She told us that June had arrived at her unit."

"How did June find out?"

"Keith and I saw her and thought she was Fiona," she said, hoping Alex would assume they'd seen June in Cecil Plains.

"Where did you see her?"

Gabriella felt uncomfortable. "*Eumeralla*."

"Why did you go there?"

Hearing the accusation in his tone, she blushed. "When we were sorting out Mum's belongings we found out that Uncle Johnny had been married to Eleanor, so we went to see her. Sorry, Uncle Alex."

"Sometimes it's better to leave things alone, Gabby," he said.

To Gabriella's surprise Ruth said, "And sometimes it's not."

The exterior of the house on *Eumeralla* and the lush garden was much as Alex remembered, so he was unprepared for the shabbiness inside. He and Virginia had their own house painted and redecorated regularly and he was shocked by the way the Mitchells had neglected to re-upholster the lounge suite, paint the flaking walls and replace the worn linoleum. Eleanor's lined face and greying hair were an even greater shock. She looked twenty years older than Virginia.

After the reunions and introductions, Greg put some apples in a paper bag, gave them to Fiona and said, "Take your father for a walk to the paddocks. We'll have lunch when you come back."

As Alex and Fiona walked through the garden, he noted the stubborn set of her lips. When they had arrived at *Eumeralla* she had been waiting on the verandah with June. Until she had run down the steps to greet him, he hadn't been able to tell which twin was which. Her eyes had lost the haunted look that had been her hallmark. Now she looked tranquil.

'We destroyed her spirit,' he thought. 'And I'm more guilty than anyone. If I'd agreed to go to an adoption agency Virginia would have been happy and some unwanted baby could have had a good life with us. Instead we put a little girl through hell. And just two weeks here has wiped away her unhappiness.'

Fiona opened the gate and Alex deliberated how to begin. Although he and Ruth had discussed the best way to approach Fiona, he felt muddled. The change in her made him hopeful that she would be more understanding.

"It's good to see you, Dad."

"Your mother wanted to come too."

"I'm glad she didn't." She shut the gate and they walked towards the paddock.

"She's wretched about all this. She didn't mean – "

"It's no good, Dad. I can't forgive her and I can't call her Mum ever again," she said, throwing an apple up in the air and catching it.

"But you forgive me?"

"You didn't tell me my real mother was an alcoholic."

"I didn't tell you she wasn't either."

"Why did she lie?"

"She was frightened of losing you."

"Then why didn't she tell me my real mother was dead? That wouldn't have been as bad as me thinking she was an alcoholic."

"You would still have been angry when you found out the truth."

"Not as angry as I am now."

They reached the paddock and Fiona leant on the fence and called the horses. "Here they come." She gave Alex an apple.

He broke it in half. "Now who are you?" he asked the horse taking the apple.

"Monty. He's the greediest one. Come on, Flicker, there's plenty for you too."

"Fiona, your mother loves you."

"She can't have. She would have known that telling me my real mother was a drunk would have had a bad effect on me. She should have – "

"Should have – would have – could have. Fiona, the world's full of people who should have, would have, could have but didn't. I should have told you the truth – I could have, but I didn't. Virginia tried to make you happy. Remember Marmalade getting cat flu when you were seven?"

Fiona nodded.

"Who stayed up all night spooning medicine into him, forcing water down his throat so he wouldn't get dehydrated? Who cleaned up his vomit and diarrhoea? Who saved his life?"

"She did," Fiona admitted.

"Yes. Because she couldn't bear your unhappiness if he'd died." He looked into her eyes, hoping to see a sign that she was softening. Encouraged by the uncertainty he saw, he continued. "I hope you never have to suffer the agony of wanting a baby and not being able to have one. It was even worse in those days. Married women didn't usually work and your mother had time to brood. Her friends and neighbours were having babies and she was surrounded by serene mothers. Virginia wanted to adopt, but I didn't want a baby whose background I didn't know. She wanted to get a job and I wouldn't let her."

"Why not?"

He stroked Monty's muzzle. "After work I wanted to come home to a tidy, clean house and a nice dinner. I didn't want an exhausted wife too tired to talk to me – "

Fiona nudged him. "Too tired to do the housework, you mean."

"Yes. Call me a chauvinist, but that's how it was in those days. In my opinion it was better – look at all the divorces there are now."

"Women can look after themselves financially now. They don't have to put up with men bossing them around. But stop making excuses for her, Dad. I can't forgive her."

"Do you expect people to forgive you?"

"Tree and Kim never forgave me when they thought I'd stolen their boyfriends."

'There's no answer to that,' Alex thought.

"Dad, I'm so happy here. Virginia would scoff at the house – "

"No she wouldn't."

"She would, because it's not filled with antiques and silver and crystal."

He put his hand on her arm. "Virginia and Eleanor were friends," he said firmly. "Their parents were friends and they grew up together. She's never scoffed at *Eumeralla*."

"But all my life she's drummed into me the code for gracious living and I was so shallow I went along with it. But all the beautiful clothes and furniture and stuff I bought for my unit didn't bring me happiness. Oh, I enjoyed buying them and showing them off. When I had dinner parties for the people from work or the tennis club, they'd admire everything and envy me, but now I see that it meant nothing. A fork is just a fork and the food tastes the same whether it's eaten with silver or stainless steel.

"Juju's the only person who's ever been in my unit and not commented on how beautiful it was. To her it was a unit in a cold and crowded city. She was impatient to get back here. It doesn't matter what the inside of the house is like if when you wake in the morning you look out of the window and see trees and birds and horses. One morning I heard a kookaburra. I jumped out of bed and ran to the window, and it was sitting in the gum tree. It filled me with such joy. All these years I've valued material things. Is Tree's wedding still on?"

The abrupt change of subject disconcerted him. "Yes. Why?"

"Stefan came to see me. He's just like the others."

Alex frowned. "He seemed a decent sort. Poor Tree."

"He was in my unit when Juju turned up."

"So he knows," said Alex thoughtfully. "I don't think he's told Tree."

Fiona grunted. "I hope he never does. They'll accuse me of causing another broken engagement. It's not my fault Tree and Kim are attracted to philanderers. Dad, I didn't know that Eleanor and Aunty Ruth knew each other."

"No, I don't suppose you did. We've had to keep lots of things secret."

"They don't like each other, do they?"

"Yes they do. They were good friends. Ruth was looking forward to seeing Eleanor again."

"Eleanor seems hostile towards Ruth. They must have had a row or something. Eleanor's my real mother and Aunty Ruth's my favourite aunt, and I don't want them to be enemies."

"Darling, they're hardly enemies."

"They might not have been once, but they are now," she said.

When Keith arrived home from work that afternoon, Gabriella was sitting on the verandah waiting for him.

"Keith, I'm going to Sydney tomorrow to see Aunty Virginia."

"Good idea." He opened the front door and they went into the kitchen. "What's Ruth like?" he asked, filling the kettle.

"You'll find out soon, she's coming here for dinner tonight. She wants to give Alex and Fiona plenty of time together and she doesn't want to impose." She put a shopping bag on the table. "I've bought lamb chops and I thought I'd make a trifle for dessert."

"When's she coming?"

"I said I'd go and pick her up later. She can stay the night with me and we'll go to the airport together. She's nice."

"We'd better not say anything about Margot then. Don't want to hurt her feelings."

"Keith?"

"What?"

"You could ask for a job on *Eumeralla*."

"Yes." He smiled. "It'd be better than being a postman."

"Ask Fiona to talk to Greg."

"No, Gabby. I'll do my own asking."

Ω Ω Ω

Ruth hoped that she was imagining Eleanor's coldness towards her. She finally caught her alone when she was collecting eggs. "It's wonderful to see you again."

"Is it?" Eleanor snarled.

Ruth was taken aback. "It wasn't me who told Keith and Gabriella about Fiona."

"I know."

"Then what's wrong?"

Eleanor put another three eggs into the basket. "Do you think I'm blind as well as stupid? I'm astounded you had the nerve to turn up here today." She went to the door of the coop and waited impatiently for Ruth to come out.

Hurt and bewildered, Ruth watched her stalk back to the house. She was thankful when Gabriella arrived at *Eumeralla* that evening. She had hardly seen Fiona, who spent most of the day alone with Alex. Gabriella stayed for an hour and then drove her to Keith's house. When Ruth saw him she was so shocked she was unable to speak.

He smiled. "I'm like Dad."

"Yes," she said breathlessly. "Gabriella isn't, so I wasn't ... "

Gabriella smiled ruefully. "No, I take after Mum's side of the family. People who knew Dad when he was young, and haven't seen Keith before, think he's a ghost."

Ruth saw the photograph of Laurence on the sideboard. It was the same one that had stood on Francesca's bedside table.

"How did Margot meet our grandfather?" asked Gabriella.

"At a horse sale."

Keith looked surprised. "What was she doing at a horse sale?"

"Buying horses for *Kingower*."

Ω Ω Ω

Alex had been gone for three days and there had been no word from him. Virginia knew that if the news had been good he would have rung. She went out to the letter-box praying for a letter. It was empty and she almost cried. She was the treasurer of the local branch of the RSPCA and was supposed to attend a committee meeting that afternoon, but she rang and told them she had a cold.

If anyone had asked her how Fiona was she would cry and she dreaded making a fool of herself. She felt useless. There was nothing to do. Her cleaning lady had cleaned and tidied the house and done the ironing, and the gardener had mown the lawn. Trying to occupy herself, she went into Alex's office. On the walls were photographs of houses taken before and after the renovations he had organized. She sat at his desk and studied the details of a red brick house the estate agents had sent them.

'We could really do something with this,' she thought.

The estate agent had described it as suitable for demolition, suggesting that units could be built in its place, but she knew that she and Alex could turn it into a comfortable family home and sell it for twice what they paid for it. She studied the plans and looked at the photographs. 'Paint the window frames and doors, new carpets, it needs a new kitchen and bathroom. Garden's a bit bare, it needs trees and shrubs. We could build an extension.' She was working out an estimate of what it would cost to renovate when the doorbell rang. Thinking it was a neighbour wanting to hear about their holiday, she was not going to answer it. When it rang persistently she opened the door.

Gabriella was on the doorstep. "I thought you might need me."

Virginia burst into tears. Ashamed of her fragility she turned away, struggling to control herself. She felt Gabriella put her arms round her. "Silly me," she said, dashing away her tears.

"It's not silly at all," whispered Gabriella, guiding her into the kitchen and pulling out a chair. "Sit down. Let's have some tea."

Virginia found a handkerchief. "Have you seen her?"

"Yes."

"How is she?"

"Happy at the moment. I don't know how long it will last." When the kettle was on, Gabriella sat at the table. "Aunty Virginia, she said you told her that her real mother was an alcoholic."

"I did." She wiped her eyes, unable to look at Gabriella's expression. She knew that if she had denied it or fabricated some story, Gabriella would have wanted to believe her. She dreaded what she would think of her when she told the truth. Finding courage, she blew her nose. "Alex and I knew we had to tell her we weren't her real parents one day, but we kept putting it off. Finding the right time to tell a child something that will disrupt their perceptions is hard. When she was eight we decided to tell her. It was terrible. She was upset because Alex wasn't her father. We managed to comfort her ... well Alex did. Next morning I asked her how she felt about me not being her real mother. Children are so brutally honest. She said she was pleased, and asked if she and Alex could go and live with her real mother. So I told her that her real mother didn't want her. I told her she was a drunk. I said she lived in a slum. I wanted her to love me. I tried to be a good mother, but I failed."

"No you didn't."

"I did, Gabby. I was possessive. She once said that this house was her prison and I was her warder. If I'd had more wisdom I would have controlled my possessiveness. I tried to mould her. I smothered her. She would have been happy at *Eumeralla* and I denied it to her. Worse, I lied about Eleanor and made her unhappy."

"It's not that you wanted Fiona to be unhappy. You wanted her to be happy here – with you and Uncle Alex."

"Yes. But she never was, Gabby. She never was."

CHAPTER 12

Fiona shrieked. "My God, you were serious."

Tom put the dead hen on the table.

"That was Blanche. You've strangled Blanche. Tom, how could you?"

"Not easily, Sis, but it had to be done. She was too old to lay."

"Why couldn't you have let her die of old age?"

"We can't afford to keep anything that's not useful. It was quick. Dad taught us how to wring their necks when we were young. I killed my first chook when I was ten. I was so upset I made a botch of it and she suffered. Learned a big lesson that day – one I never forgot. Take them gently out of the coop, walk away with them and then do it – fast. Don't get sentimental or you'll hash it up. We say good-bye to them the night before."

"Do Eleanor and Juju wring their necks too?"

"No. Do you think we're savages? When there's killing to be done – the men do it. Now help me pluck her."

Fiona gulped. "We're not going to eat her, are we?"

"What do you want us to do? Bury her and sing hymns?" He patted her shoulder. "Come on, this is tonight's meal. She'll be tough, but better tough than wasted."

Fiona decided to be pragmatic. "If we marinate her overnight she'll be more tender."

"What's that?"

"You make a marinade with cider vinegar or lemon juice, olive oil, and herbs. We can have it tomorrow. If you pluck her and cut her up I can make a casserole." She opened a cupboard. "Where are the casserole dishes?"

"We haven't got any."

"Well whatever you make casseroles in."

He looked nonplussed. "We've never made casseroles."

"Oh. Let's go into town and buy some."

"Sis, we can't afford it."

"I can," she said gleefully. "It's time I started paying my way."

"Can we take your MG?"

"Yes. Would you like to drive it?"

He grinned. "What do you reckon?"

"I can't get over how friendly everyone is," said Fiona as she and Tom left the bank. "They all know you."

"I couldn't live anywhere where people were unfriendly, Sis."

She hesitated in the doorway of the general store. "Eleanor won't be offended, will she? I don't want her to think I'm interfering."

Tom laughed. "She's been nagging Dad to get new saucepans and things for ages."

"Hi, Tom," said the owner.

While he and Tom talked, Fiona explored the store and came back to the counter laden with saucepans, a frying pan, casserole dishes, a measuring jug and a set of sharp knives.

"Is this the lot?" Tom asked.

"No. I want tea towels and mixing bowls."

The owner helped them carry everything to the MG.

Tom enjoyed having Fiona around. Since her arrival the standard of cooking had dramatically improved. She had introduced them to garlic, yogurt, a variety of herbs, olive oil and real coffee. The Sunday roasts had been transformed. Leg of lamb was now baked on a bed of rosemary, and roast beef was served with horseradish sauce. To the basic salads of lettuce, tomatoes and cucumber, she added carrots, beetroot and potatoes mixed with yogurt, mint and garlic. She taught them how to toss lettuce leaves and make dressings using cider vinegar and olive oil. Coffee no longer came out of a jar, and at mealtimes the kitchen was full of the aroma of ground beans. Before Fiona's arrival the only herbs in the garden had been mint and parsley. Now two rosemary bushes were flourishing, and there were clumps of thyme, sage, basil and oregano. The garlic she had planted was showing green shoots.

Although she was a year older than Tom was, she was like a younger sister. He and June were equals. June could do most of the things that he could, but Fiona had to be taught. Her joy when she had learnt to ride had touched him and he was proud that he had succeeded where her uncle had failed. She still had a great deal to learn and when she rode he had to accompany her, but she cantered round *Eumeralla* fearlessly. She was quickly approaching the stage where she and the horse seemed as one, although it would be a year before she would be able to manage a more highly-spirited mount.

"You know, Sis, for someone who's spent most of her life in cities, you've taken to country life faster than I would have thought was possible," he told her as they drove back to *Eumeralla*. "Soon I'll be able to teach you to round up sheep."

She looked out of the window at the fields. "I belong here. The years I spent away were an accident."

As Tom had predicted, Eleanor was delighted by the things Fiona bought. Clearing the cupboards of the old saucepans she replaced them with the new ones.

"What can we use the old tea towels for, Mum?" asked Neil.

"Nothing," she replied. "They're not even fit to dry the dogs with."

Tom sat at the table on the verandah and read the paper. "Hey, Neil, look!" he said coming into the kitchen. "A house in Dalby. Just what we've been waiting for. It's got three bedrooms."

Fiona looked puzzled. "I thought you were never leaving *Eumeralla*."

"We're not," said Tom. "We want to live in a house that's in Dalby."

"What are you going to do? Pull it down and rebuild it here?"

"Sort of." Neil laughed. "When someone buys an old weatherboard house and they want to demolish it and build a new one, it's cheaper to get someone to take it away and move it to a new location. Lots of newly-married couples buy a block of land and wait for one of these houses to become available. All they've got to pay for is its relocation. They – "

"Now look here, boys," said Eleanor. "If a flushing toilet costs too much then we can't afford to move a house here just so you can have somewhere private to take your girlfriends."

"We haven't got any girlfriends at the moment," said Neil.

"It won't be long before you do. So we're not – "

"Dad said – "

"I don't care. If I can't have a flushing toilet you can't have a house, and that's final."

$$\Omega \quad \Omega \quad \Omega$$

As Greg was riding towards the paddock at the end of the day, he saw Keith approaching slowly on his motor bike.

"Mr. Mitchell, could I talk to you, please," he asked, turning off the engine.

"What about?"

Keith propped the bike against a tree. "Would you be willing to give me a job?"

The irony that Laurence's son was asking him for a job saddened Greg. "Doing what?"

"Anything."

Greg dismounted and led the horse into the paddock. "Can you ride?"

"I can learn."

"Know anything about wheat, sheep and wool?" he asked, removing the bridle.

"What I've read in books and what Dad taught me."

"We do need help," Greg said thoughtfully, not wanting to

dishearten Keith with an immediate refusal. "But, I can't afford someone full-time. I sure couldn't afford to pay you what you get at the Post Office. After we've paid the bills there's hardly anything left. Most of the money goes straight back into the land."

"What if I bought my way in – like buying a share in a co-operative? I could sell my Mum's house – "

"Steady on, Keith. It's risky." He undid the girth. "One bad season and you've had it."

"I want to take the risk."

"Why?"

"Two reasons. I love the land and I've got faith in you."

Greg smiled. "I can't stop droughts or floods. I can't make it rain at the right time just by looking at the sky and praying."

"No, but your methods are right. You planted lots of trees, practise crop rotation and feed the land."

"Yes, and everything I do I learned from your grandfather."

"Did you like him?"

"Yes. He could have been a snob, but he wasn't. All his workers had good living conditions and wages. Unusually for round here they had servants – a cook, gardener and a housekeeper, but they were more like part of the family. Your dad's grandparents had been servants in England and were badly treated, so when they came to Australia they were determined to treat their workers well. They drummed that code into their own children. Even though your dad and Johnny boarded at the most exclusive boys' school in Sydney, never once did they or Virginia make me feel inferior. I was their friend, and when I dined at *Acacia* it was at the same table. I'd like to help you, Keith, if I can."

"Can I ask you one question?"

"Go on."

"This might sound impertinent, but do you all own *Eumeralla* outright?"

"Yes."

Keith stroked the horse. "So, if there is a run of bad seasons and the crops get wiped out and the sheep die, provided we can feed ourselves, I'll have somewhere to live?"

"Yes."

"Then I want to take that risk."

"The house has only got three bedrooms," said Greg taking the reins and saddle into the tack room. "There's no space for another bed in Tom's and Neil's room. Where would you live?"

"I could buy a caravan."

Greg washed and dried the bit. "I've just thought of something. Come with me."

They walked along the creek. Greg stopped at a log cabin which was surrounded by trees, and grass that was knee high. "This is the first house Eleanor's ancestor built on *Eumeralla*. I used to live here with my dad. We could fix it up for you." He smiled. "I was used to living in a crude caravan pulled by two horses ... this was luxury. It didn't leak when it rained and I had a room all to myself. Needs new windows, but the roof's okay. There are two rooms. No kitchen – my dad and I used to cook meat and fish over the fireplace, but you'd eat with us and use our bathroom. There's a tap and a sink. Want to take a look inside?"

"Yes."

They went through the long grass. "Snakes are hibernating, but be careful when we go inside. Don't disturb anything as they might have found a way in."

He opened the door. A carriage and dray took up most of the room. "When we got our first car, we kept those in case we ran out of petrol. Now we keep it for fun. Hazel's friends sometimes want a ride in it when they come for the weekends."

Keith looked around and smiled. "Yes, I could live here. Doesn't need much ... just cleaning and fly-screens over the windows and a fly-screen door. How old is it?"

"About a hundred years."

"Were Eleanor's family the first owners of *Eumeralla*?"

Greg nodded. "There's a convict ancestor somewhere, but I don't know if the first Osborne was a squatter or a free settler."

"A pioneer's house," said Keith. "It'll give me a good feeling to be living in a piece of history. When did you start working at *Acacia*?"

"As soon as I left school. Your grandfather needed someone who knew about horses. He saw I was wanting to learn and get on so he promoted me." He shook his head. "I never would have thought that his grandson would be living here. I owe a lot to your dad and Virginia. When I came to *Eumeralla* I'd never been to school. Mum taught me to read and write and add up and subtract, but that was all. I couldn't multiply or divide, I knew nothing about history or geography or literature.

"Because Laurence, Johnny and Virginia went to school I wanted to go too. So I went with Virginia. The teachers were appalled at my ignorance and the children teased me." He looked rueful. "I couldn't bring myself to tell a girl, specially one younger than me, how hopeless I was at lessons, but she found out and she and her mum taught me. When Laurence and Johnny came home from Sydney for the holidays they lent me their books and gave me lessons too. By the end of the year I'd learnt so much I passed all the exams except art." He sighed. "Queer how things turn out. Come to the house and talk to Eleanor. If she agrees, we'll have to consult with Tom, Neil and Juju."

Keith held out his hand. "Thanks, Mr. Mitchell."

"Call me Greg. Tom and Neil will be crazy about your bike."

"I'll sell that too if – "

"No. It'd be useful in the wet season when the cars and trucks get bogged."

Ω Ω Ω

"I've decided to sell my unit," Fiona announced when they were having dinner. "I want you to put the money into *Eumeralla*."

Eleanor envisaged all the improvements that could be made. To her dismay, Greg, Tom and Neil had decided what to do with the money Keith was putting in without consulting her. Once she had decided that Keith could buy into the property, Greg had discussed the financial aspect of the partnership with his sons. They would buy a new tractor, stock saddles and a truck. A new toilet was not even on the list. She was adamant that this time her wishes would be fulfilled. 'We could have a new bathroom,' she thought when she heard how much Fiona's unit was worth. 'And we could buy a new bed and paint the inside of the house.'

"Fiona, you don't have to contribute financially, this is your home," said Greg. "Anyway look at all the things you've bought."

"But I've got a unit, and money in the bank lying idle. It's getting interest, but – "

"Look," said Greg. "You might start missing your friends and tennis, going to the movies and out to dinner. I hope you don't, but you might."

Fiona shook her head. "Never."

"I know what Dad means," said June. "At the moment all this is new, but you might get sick of it – Hazel did."

"I'm not Hazel."

"Thank God," said Tom. "Sis. You've taken to everything here well, but give it a year. Wait till you've experienced the heat and the spiders, snakes and mozzies, then sell your unit if you want."

Eleanor saw her wishes slipping away. "We must – " she began.

"Tom's right," said June. "I stayed with a friend in Brisbane when I was fifteen. The novelty soon wore off and after a week I was so homesick I was nearly demented."

Fiona grinned. "Okay. But I've got lots of money in the bank and I've decided what to do with some of it."

"What?" asked Eleanor hopefully.

"I'll pay to move that house in Dalby to here."

"Ah, Sis, would you really?" said Neil. He nudged Tom. "A house of our own. No more waiting in a queue to get into the bathroom!"

On the verge of screaming with frustration Eleanor went into the kitchen.

Eumeralla
May 1972

Hazel came for the weekend. She's elated that Keith's moving to *Eumeralla*. She said he's the best looking guy she's ever seen.

Tomorrow I'm going to the cemetery with Eleanor. It's the date of her parents' wedding anniversary – my grandparents. No one else ever goes with her. Tom and Neil reckon it's morbid, Juju says it's spooky and reminds her of where she's going to end up, and Greg thinks visiting a grave is a waste of time because the dead don't know you're there. But I'm looking forward to going. It will give me a chance to be alone with Eleanor. I don't know how she feels. I've not been paired with her on a rota yet, so we haven't had much time to talk.

Eleanor didn't want Fiona to come with her to the cemetery. In many ways she was pleased to have her on *Eumeralla*. Her good cooking made mealtimes more pleasant and varied, and now the person on home rota was never alone, which eased the loneliness and made the tasks easier. But Fiona's rapture about the lack of electricity frustrated her. The sophisticated city veneer had almost vanished. She had slipped into life on *Eumeralla* with the ease of a chameleon. She knew that if Fiona sold her unit the money would not go into anything Eleanor wanted, but would be absorbed into the land. They had already paid for the house in Dalby to be moved to *Eumeralla* and she was furious that Greg was enthusiastic about it.

"They need some independence," he had argued when she protested.

As they drove to the cemetery she suspected that Fiona would bombard her with distressing questions. 'But Johnny was her father ... it's natural that she wants to know all about him,' she thought.

When they reached Jonathan's grave Fiona looked at her intently. "What was he like?"

She tried to think of a reply that would satisfy Fiona and stop further questions.

"Eleanor, I'm sorry. Does it upset you to talk about him?"

"I've never talked about him."

Fiona looked bemused. "Not even to Greg?"

"Just that he'd left me because he thought I couldn't get pregnant."

"Why didn't you write to him when you realized you were?"

"I didn't know where he was. I was alone. The men hadn't come back from the war, and my father was dead. We didn't have a car."

Fiona put her posy on the grave. "Why didn't you go to *Acacia*?"

"That was the last place he would have gone. His father was furious that he'd left me. I knew he wasn't there."

"But my grandfather would have helped you. He would never have let you stay alone on *Eumeralla*."

"He didn't know I was pregnant. There was no phone. The distance from the front door of *Eumeralla* and the front door of the homestead at *Acacia* was over three miles. I was so ill that I didn't feel like getting out of bed in the morning let alone walking three miles," Eleanor said, attempting to hide her irritation. "Come on, let's go."

"Why didn't anyone from *Acacia* come and visit you?" asked Fiona, as they walked to the other side of the cemetery.

"They were busy. By the time Laurence got back from wherever he'd been, he was immersed in his own unhappiness ... and he was thin and exhausted. He came a few times, but at that stage I didn't know I was pregnant. I felt ill, but put it down to misery not pregnancy. I upset him by ranting about Johnny."

"It's odd, isn't it? Laurence, Ruth and Johnny all disappearing."

"Johnny didn't disappear, he left me and I didn't know where he'd gone. I found out later that he was in Brisbane."

"Did Uncle Laurence tell you where he went?"

"No, he was peculiar about it." Fiona's questions had triggered a memory. "He said that he'd told someone, but they didn't believe him, so he wasn't going to tell anyone else."

"Who did he tell?"

"I don't know. It must have been Margot or his father, but he was friendly with the manager and the jackaroos so it might have been one of them. I should have asked him again, but I was so pleased that he was home, that I didn't pursue it."

"He did get back to *Acacia* before Aunty Ruth disappeared, didn't he?"

"Yes, why?" asked Eleanor as they reached her parent's graves.

"One of my cousins thought they might have been going to jump off a cliff together. Maybe Aunty Ruth had amnesia."

Eleanor shook her head and pulled up some weeds.

"What did Johnny do in Brisbane?"

"Got a job as a clerk. He knew his father had disinherited him," she said, taking a pair of secateurs out of a bag and pruning the rose bushes. "I'll have to buy a new rose for Dad. This one only had a few flowers last year."

Fiona ignored the invitation to change the subject. "I bet Margot cajoled his father to cut him out of the will. Loathsome woman."

"I liked her."

"But she stole *Acacia*."

"No she didn't," said Eleanor. "It was Johnny and Laurence's own fault they lost it. She was kind to me. I wouldn't have minded if she'd been my stepmother. It used to embarrass me the way Virginia, Laurence and Johnny treated her. They weren't rude to her – their father wouldn't have stood for that, but somehow that almost made their behaviour worse – when they had to speak to her they were chillingly polite. It hurt her. She tried so hard to win their affection. She was an excellent rider and could break-in horses. But instead of respecting her for it they resented it. They said she should stay in the homestead and sew and manage the house instead of riding out with their father and checking the sheep and fences. But that was what Johnny, Laurence and Virginia were like – whatever Margot did would have been wrong. My dad said that if William had known how they were going to react he would have done things differently."

"How?"

"If she'd come to *Acacia* as an employee, they would have liked her."

Fiona looked skeptical. "Would they?"

"Yes. It was because she was replacing their mother that they were against her. William would have introduced her to them as the accountant or something, and they would have got to know her. Then they could have announced they were getting married."

"Huh," said Fiona. "What makes you think they would have liked her?"

"She was sincere and intelligent," said Eleanor patiently. "They would have realized that if they'd got to know her. They only saw her as their mother's usurper. Things could have been so different. We had plans to turn *Acacia* and *Eumeralla* into one property. It would have been a good union." Her old feelings of anger burst out. "They had so much in common with Margot ... the same way with horses – breaking them in by kindness not force. They could have been such a happy family ... instead we've all suffered because they were unkind to her." She unscrewed the top of a bottle and poured water round the bottom of the bushes. "Let's go – there's heaps to do back home."

Fiona touched her arm. "Please talk to me. I don't know you and I want to."

The intense turquoise eyes looked into hers. She sighed. "You're so like Johnny. Much more than Juju – you've got his mannerisms and passion."

"What was he like?" Fiona insisted. "He must have had some good points."

"Of course he did. He was sensitive, he couldn't kill anything. If *Eumeralla* had been a cattle station he would have changed it. He wrote poetry, he spent a lot of time dreaming, he was more out of this world than in it. He was terrific with animals. And women," she added bitterly.

Fiona looked startled. "Women? What do you mean?"

"Isn't it obvious?"

"Was he unfaithful?"

"Yes. Let's go, or else Greg will be thinking a bunyip's got us."

Today Eleanor was strange when I asked her about Johnny. I was probably too inquisitive, but I want to know about my real father. I was shocked when she told me he'd been unfaithful. I wonder if he had lots of women or just one.

I can't understand why she liked Margot. But if Margot was as kind as Eleanor thought she was, she would have gone to *Eumeralla*. Then she would have found out that Eleanor was pregnant and someone could have looked after her.

Ω Ω Ω

Keith took time off work to paint the outside of his house. As soon as he finished he put it up for sale. The estate agent enthused about the polished floorboards, freshly painted rooms and the garden. As he predicted it sold quickly and for a higher price than forecast.

"I feel a bit sad," said Gabriella as she helped him pack. "This is where Mum and Dad lived."

"It wasn't where Dad wanted to live," he said.

"Are you taking their bed?"

"It won't fit. I'll just take the furniture from my bedroom, the bookcases, the table and chairs and an armchair."

"Is that all?"

"That's all I need. The sofa and the rest of the stuff can be chucked. Gabby, don't look like that. Mum and Dad only had this furniture because it was all they could afford. I'm not getting rid of family treasures."

"I know it's junk, but it was their junk."

He picked up a framed photograph of his parents. "These are what count ... and I'm taking them all. And Dad's chess set. Think how pleased he'd be about me living on *Eumeralla*."

"Do you reckon the rumours about the owners of *Acacia* being nearly bankrupt are true?"

"I hope so," he said with a grim smile. "It'd be great if we could all buy *Acacia*. It doesn't feel like a crazy dream any more."

Eumeralla
May 1972

Keith's signed the papers that make him a one-seventh owner of *Eumeralla*. Greg, Tom and Keith are working on the log cabin. They've put in a new sink, tap, windows and fly-screens. They've cut the grass and made a pathway to the door. We call it *Keith's Cabin*. A film company bought the dray and carriage. Before they took them they had to check there were no snakes hibernating in them – ugh.

The water tank's in good condition so he'll have running water, but there's no toilet so he'll have to go native. I'm giving him a shovel and potty as a moving-in present! Because the cabin is so close to the creek we built a mound around it as a precaution against flooding. We've sown it with grass seed to keep it together. The last time the creek flooded was years ago and the floor was damaged but it didn't matter too much as no one was living in it.

The other day Gabby told me about her talk with Virginia. I remember my parents telling me that I was adopted and getting upset that Dad was not my real father, but being pleased that Virginia was not my real mother. Gabby told me how hurt she was. But she shouldn't have told such terrible lies. She could have just told me that Eleanor had died.

Ω Ω Ω

Tom arrived back from the gate with his hands full of birthday cards for June and Fiona. "If I'd known there'd be this much mail, I'd have taken a sack with me."

"Oh!" exclaimed June as she opened her card from Virginia and Alex. "Fifty dollars! I've hardly ever seen so much money."

Fiona opened her card and took out five twenty-dollar notes. The card from Ruth contained another fifty dollars. She smiled and handed it to Greg. "You take it."

Eleanor snatched it back. "No! Buy something for yourself."

"What?"

"You know what I dream of having?" June said excitedly. "Jodhpurs and riding boots."

Eleanor nodded approvingly. "Yes. Let's go into Brisbane and get some tomorrow. We can have a day out and have lunch with Hazel."

Eumeralla
1st June 1972

Today is Juju's birthday. Yesterday it was mine. But I wanted us to celebrate on the same day. So we tossed a coin and we celebrated today. It was fun opening our presents together. We went into Brisbane yesterday with Eleanor, and Juju and I bought ourselves jodhpurs and riding-boots. All the others are envious – I know what I'll be buying them for their birthdays. Buying a present for Juju was almost as hard as buying for a man. She doesn't use perfume or wear jewellery and she only buys men's shirts. Her pyjamas are wearing out so I bought her new ones and three shirts. I also got her some moisturizer and hand cream.

Keith and Gabby came to dinner and everyone got on well. Neil made us a birthday cake, he iced it in white and wrote our names in blue. Having my name and Juju's on a cake gave me a real feeling of belonging. Hazel brought twenty-six candles and two bottles of champagne. She flirted with Keith, but he didn't react.

Last birthday Virginia and Dad bought me a stereo and Aunty Ruth gave me a cameo brooch. We all went out to dinner at The Windsor Hotel. The surroundings were sumptuous, but I enjoyed this birthday far more. It was warm enough to have dinner on the verandah, but we had to wear jumpers.

Hazel commented that it's strange having twins born in different months. Tom pointed out that twins could be born in different centuries.

Keith is moving into the cabin at the weekend.

CHAPTER 13

Margot was given the task of telling her nieces about Fiona.

Kim looked at her in astonishment. "A twin sister? She's gone to live in Queensland?"

"Was this *Eumeralla* place near *Acacia*? asked Catriona.

"Yes."

"Ah, I understand now," Catriona said. "Aunty Margot, who died of snakebite on *Acacia*?"

"What are you talking about? No one was bitten by a snake."

Catriona smiled knowingly. "Years ago you told me about Aunty Ruth disappearing."

Margot was bewildered. "So?"

"You said that when Ruth turned up, no one asked her where she'd been because you were in the middle of a crisis," said Catriona. "You looked flustered. Then you told me that someone had been bitten by a snake on *Acacia*, but that wasn't the crisis, was it? It was because Fiona and her twin had been born."

Margot nodded. "You've got an excellent memory."

"Not really – it's been bugging me for years."

"What's that got to do with Aunty Ruth?" asked Kim.

"She wrote and told us she was arriving in Brisbane," explained Margot. "She was waiting at the station and we forgot to meet her because of the twins. No one knew Eleanor was pregnant."

"Golly," said Kim. "Eleanor's the alcoholic?"

"Well, that's the other thing. She's not and never has been. I liked her very much."

Ω Ω Ω

Stefan drove through the gates of *Kingower*, dreading the weekend. The incessant talk about the wedding irritated him. Last weekend he had been unable to face two days of discussion about invitations and reception arrangements. On Friday morning, safe in the knowledge that it was a horse trekking weekend and Catriona would be too busy to come to Melbourne, he had rung her and told her he had the flu. Her sympathy increased his guilt. As he drove towards the cottages, he wondered if he would be more tolerant if he had never met Fiona.

There was no one in whom he could confide, because all his friends and family thought Catriona was amazing and that Stefan was fortunate to have met her. 'They'd only tell me I was suffering from wedding nerves and if I told them about Fiona they'd think I was infatuated.' He knew if he called off the wedding and never saw Catriona again, he would regret it, but to marry her while he felt like this about her cousin would be reprehensible. "If I never had to see Fiona again I could suppress my feelings, but she'll be at our wedding," he told himself, pulling up in front of Catriona's cottage.

When he turned off the engine, he sat for a minute trying to work himself into a buoyant mood. Catriona and Kim came rushing out to meet him. Usually Kim, knowing they wanted to be alone before dinner, stayed away. 'They've been told about Fiona,' he thought.

"You'll never guess what's happened!" exclaimed Catriona as soon as he got out of the car. "Fiona's got an identical twin!"

For weeks he had been wondering when they would find out. He judged by their attitude that Fiona had kept his visit to her a secret.

"And Fiona's real mother's not an alcoholic either," said Kim. "Aunty Virginia must have lied to her. I don't know why."

Catriona pulled a face. "One of her is bad enough. Of all the people to have a twin sister."

"It's tragic if you ask me," he snapped.

Catriona looked startled. "What the matter?"

"You two. You're full of spite about your cousin."

"She's not our real cousin," said Kim.

"You grew up with her! It's monstrous that Margot lied about her real father being a coward and someone lied about her mother being an alcoholic. What sort of a family is this?"

Kim and Catriona looked stupefied.

He pulled the car door open. "I'm going back to Melbourne."

"Stefan, please ... don't. I'm sorry," said Catriona.

He knew that to use this as an excuse to get away was underhand, but he could see no other way. If he told Catriona the truth she would blame Fiona.

Kim's face was red. "I'm sorry too. I suppose we did sound spiteful, but we were flabbergasted by all this."

'So was I,' he thought bleakly, remembering Fiona's expression when she had seen her twin. He closed his eyes. "I've got to get away and think, Tree."

Kim went into her cottage and Catriona stared at him. "What about?" she asked breathlessly.

"I'm sorry, Tree."

She bit her lip. "Are you calling off our wedding?"

"I don't know. I need to be by myself for a while."

'If I don't marry Tree, I'll never see Fiona again,' thought Stefan on the way back to Melbourne. The realization gave him peace. He hated the way people tended to gang up on someone because they were weak or different. As a teacher he ruthlessly stamped out such behaviour in his classes. As a man he abhorred the way the *Kingower* Lancasters treated Fiona. 'Tree and Kim can't face the fact that their boyfriends are overwhelmed by her, so they accuse her of seduction. Fiona's not a vamp. I know her power to unwittingly enchant.' He remembered that Kim had called her a slut. 'She's more likely to be a virgin.' As he mulled it over the more convinced he became that Kim's premonition had been a dream, caused by her jealousy. 'David and Margot know that Fiona's original name was May. It's inconceivable that they never mentioned it. Even if Kim's forgotten, the name could have been buried in her subconscious and surfaced in a dream.'

As he drove through the city the thought of going home to an empty flat depressed him. He parked near the Houses of Parliament and walked down Bourke Street past the cinemas, boutiques and shops. As he was passing a cafe the smell of coffee and food made him feel hungry. He went in and ordered spaghetti. The cafe was full of couples. He wondered if they were waiting for the traffic to clear before they went to their beach houses for the weekend, or if they had met in the city straight from work and were having dinner before they went to the pictures. A young man said something to his girlfriend and she laughed. Others were earnestly talking while another pair held hands across the table. 'Tree and I used to be like that,' he thought.

He had been back in his flat for two hours when the doorbell rang.

It was Catriona's father. "Stefan, we need to talk."

"I'm sorry about this, David," he said, taking him into the lounge. "Sit down. Can I get you tea or coffee?"

"No thanks," he said brusquely. "What's the problem?"

Stefan knew that if he told the truth, Fiona would get the blame. "The wedding," he said. "It's getting too elaborate. Every time I arrive at *Kingower* I'm told about the plans – told, not asked. It's my wedding too." He saw that David had not been anticipating his reply.

"Why didn't you say something?"

'Yes, why didn't I?' he thought.

"Do you think that we're so dictatorial we would have ignored you? Do you?" he insisted when Stefan didn't answer.

"No. You're right."

"What would you like?"

"A smaller wedding, one bridesmaid instead of four, and a reception for close friends and family. At the moment it seems like everyone you know is invited."

"Country communities are friendly, Stefan. We've known most

families in the district for years. I've been friends with some since I was a boy. I'm paying for the reception."

"And I have to pay for the bridesmaids' presents and wedding cars," said Stefan, feeling more sure of himself. "Four bracelets or necklaces won't be cheap. All the expense for just for one day is futile. I want to spend the money on our future. I'm not mean, David, but I'm careful with money. I want to buy a house so we can move into it when we get married."

"There's no rush. You can stay in Tree's cottage."

Stefan shook his head. "I'm not living off her and I've got no intention of depending on you. When Tree gets pregnant I want to be able to support her. The important things about getting married are the ceremony and the honeymoon. All this other stuff is a waste of money. I'd rather get married in a registry office. The whole business is aggravating me."

"Are you sure that's all? Catriona thinks it's something to do with Fiona."

Stefan knew that he would be unable to make a convincing denial. "Well, I seem to be seeing things I never saw before. Tree's got a side to her that I find repugnant."

"We've all got a bad side, Stefan, even you. Did you behave well tonight? You were expected for dinner. Your behaviour was discourteous."

"Yes. I apologize. But this spite against their cousin worries me."

David looked dubious. "I can't believe that one episode of insensitivity on Catriona's part has made you react like this."

"It was the culmination. I used to think that you were a happy, successful family, who had an interesting way of life. Now, I realize that there are deep fissures and undercurrents."

"Caused by Fiona. She is the only problem this family has. Has she been to see you?"

"No." He imagined how David would react if he told him that he had been to see Fiona. 'He'd probably punch me,' Stefan thought.

"She makes a habit of seducing my daughter's boyfriends," he said, staring accusingly at Stefan.

"I can assure you that she has not tried to seduce me." He wanted to look away, but succeeded in maintaining eye contact.

David stood up and paced the room. "But she is one of the reasons you've got misgivings. I'd bet she's the main reason."

"One thing without the other wouldn't matter too much ... but, yes, the family's attitude towards her disturbs me. Your sister lied about something serious. Not only was Fiona's real father not a coward he died a hero. It's as if she doesn't matter because she's adopted and can't ride."

"Stefan, you've only met her once, you don't know what went on before. She was nasty to Margot too. The family are not against her. She was welcome at *Kingower* till she was caught kissing Kim's fiancé. Ruth adores her and Alex treats her like his real daughter. The antipathy some of us have towards Fiona was caused by her behaviour."

For the first time it occurred to Stefan that Fiona might have distorted the truth.

"I don't want you marrying Catriona if you're going to make her unhappy. Do you want to call off the wedding?"

"I need time to think."

David went to the door. "Don't leave it too long. Catriona's got lots of male friends who would be happy to take your place."

Catriona was sorry when the juniors' riding lesson came to an end. For one and a half hours she had been able to push thoughts of Stefan into the background. While the grooms supervised the children as they took off the bridles and saddles, she chatted to some of the waiting mothers.

One little girl rushed over. "Miss Catriona, Miss Catriona, Mummy said I can have my own pony when you tell her that I'm responsible enough. Am I? Am I yet?"

"Have you put everything away?"

"No, but nearly."

Catriona jiggled the child's plaits. "Go and finish and I'll discuss it with your mummy."

"She's not ready yet, is she?" the mother asked, laughing as her daughter rushed away.

"Not quite, but she's very conscientious, and she's got a natural ability. I'd say that the ideal time for her would be Christmas."

As she watched the last mother drive away she felt an ache of regret as she pondered over the likelihood of her and Stefan having children. It made her realize how often she envisaged the future with him and at least two children. Ideally she wanted four. There were many pupils in the riding school about whom she would think, 'I'd love a child like that.' Occasionally she would look at one and vow, 'I'll never let my child be a brat.'

When Kim came home from the surgery she insisted that they play canasta, but Catriona was unable to concentrate on the game. She put down her cards and wandered restlessly round the lounge. "If I wasn't on emergency call I'd go out. Shall I ring him?"

"No," said Kim. "It's only been three days. Try not to give in. Let him start missing you."

"What if he doesn't?"

"Then there's nothing you can do," said Kim gently. "Come and finish. You're winning."

"It's Fiona. He hasn't been the same since he met her."

"But you told me he didn't seem impressed."

"He'd hardly say he thought she was gorgeous, would he? I saw how he looked when he met her. It's Fiona. It's always Fiona and it always will be. He won't marry me because he's obsessed by her. She's got 'it' and I haven't. Sometimes I'm so jealous I want her to die. Then I hate myself for being evil. Stefan's right – she doesn't flirt. But that makes it worse. I hate her more because she doesn't try. She doesn't have to." She walked over to the mirror. "Look at me. I'm plain. The only thing I've got is brains."

"Poppycock. You've got perfect teeth and beautiful lips."

"And that's all."

"No. Your hands are beautiful too."

"So are Fiona's. And her teeth and her lips. And everything else."

"You've got good skin."

"So has she. I'm nearly six feet. Stefan's one of the few boyfriends I've had who's taller than I am. I'm so flat chested I can't wear a bra. Aunty Margot says that looks don't count, but she's wrong."

"No, Tree, she's right. She looked just like you when she was young and she got married. If photos are anything to go by, Fiona's grandfather was incredibly handsome."

Catriona sighed. "He probably needed someone to look after his children and manage the house."

"Don't ever let Aunty Margot hear you say that," said Kim with a sharp intake of breath. "Anyway, if that's true why didn't he marry someone else? There must have been lots of spinsters who'd have been happy to marry him ... he was a wealthy grazier."

The phone rang and she let Kim answer it.

'Let it be Stefan,' Catriona prayed. Sense told her that as she was on call it was more likely to be an emergency.

Kim put the phone down. "Someone's found an injured dog – it's probably been hit by a car. Do you want me to go?"

Catriona went into her study and picked up her medical bag. "Stefan won't ring. And if he does I don't want him to think I've been sitting here fretting. Let's go together."

By Saturday Catriona could stand it no longer. Stefan had not rung or written so she decided to go and see him. She got up early, had a shower and tried to decide what to wear. She deplored the superficiality of her thoughts, but she wanted to look good. At the surgery she wore a uniform and the only suits and dresses in her wardrobe were those she had bought for weddings and parties. Not wanting Stefan to think she was desperate, she rejected them in favour of navy corduroy trousers, a white shirt and a jumper the colour of raspberries. She went through her jewellery box and chose the gold sea-horse pendant he had given her for Christmas.

Normally she never bothered with cosmetics, but knew they

noticeably improved her looks. Her fair lashes and eyebrows benefited from a coat of dark mascara and eyebrow pencil. After applying make-up and twisting her frizzy hair into a sophisticated knot she looked critically in the mirror. Her reflection pleased her, until Fiona's image danced into her mind.

Knowing Kim would try and talk her out of going to see Stefan she put a note under her door.

In the car she listened to a Seekers cassette. 'All over the world, people must meet and part,' sang Judy Durham.

'Is that what Stefan and I are going to do?'

She arrived in Melbourne at eleven. The city was crowded with Saturday morning shoppers and it took her half an hour to get through the traffic. By the time she reached Albert Park her neck was stiff with tension. She sat in the car for ten minutes, trying to calm herself. The sunlight caught the diamond in her engagement ring and she remembered her happiness when she and Stefan had chosen it. Afterwards they had lunch in The Windsor Hotel to celebrate and he teased her because she had looked at the ring more than at him.

Steeling herself, she went up the three flights of stairs and rang the bell to his flat. The first time Catriona had seen his flat she had thought that he had just moved in. Now she knew that was how he liked it. There were no photos on display or pictures hanging on the beige walls. The windows were bare because he lived on the top floor and was not overlooked. Books and records that would have revealed his tastes were in cabinets with doors. He had paid a lot of money for the brown upholstered sofa and armchairs. Stefan called it minimalist. Catriona called it dreary.

When he answered the door his expression was serious, but he smiled when he said, "Tree, come in."

"Stefan, I thought we should talk before we reached any decisions." To her relief she sounded composed.

He nodded. "Would you like tea or coffee?"

"Coffee, please." She sat at the kitchen table.

He filled the percolator with water. "How've you been?"

"Okay. Busy," she said, trying to keep her voice light.

He sat opposite her. "Tree, marriage is such a gigantic step that any reservations must be sorted out."

"That's why I'm here. Dad told me what you'd said and I've been thinking. Firstly, I was a bore going on and on about the wedding. You should have said something."

"Yes, I'm sorry."

"Secondly, and this is difficult for me ... it's about Fiona." She looked down at the table. "I'm jealous of her beauty and the effect she has on men."

He took her hand and squeezed it. "That's quite an admission to make."

"If you still want us to get married, we can cut down on things," she said, happy that he had touched her. "I've spoken to the bridesmaids and they understood. It's just Kim now."

He ran his thumb over her finger. "You're a hopeless fibber. What did they really say?"

"One called me a cow, one thought she'd done something to upset me. The other one understood – she called you a bastard."

"She's right, I am a bastard, putting you through all this."

"No, you're being sensible. Have you told anyone else about your doubts?"

He shook his head. "Not even my parents. They would have come storming over and tried to talk sense into me."

"Stefan, what do you like about me?"

"Lots of things."

"Be specific. When you first saw me what did you think?"

He smiled. "Who's that divine girl on that enormous horse?"

"Be serious."

"I am."

"I'm not divine, I'm plain."

"Don't talk twaddle. Your skin's flawless and your lips are the type sculptors carve on their statues. The first conversation we had I wanted to kiss you. I was impressed by you ... the whole of you – the way you handled the horse, the way you moved and your voice. You sound definite. Breathy, little girl voices revolt me. When I went home after the weekend I knew I wanted to see you again. Two weeks later, you were so immersed in the new riders you scarcely noticed me. I was disappointed, but I came back every fortnight until you did. When I asked you out I was worried you'd tell me you had a boyfriend."

She heard the coffee percolating. "And after we went out?"

"I was even more impressed. Especially when I saw your legs."

"Why?"

"You're different. Lots of girls – even intelligent ones – are subservient, insipid and constantly on some infernal diet. You were living an exciting life and you had ambitions. You weren't waiting for some man to come along and rescue you from tedium. And you don't mope about like a limp lettuce leaf once a month like many girls do. If I had to describe you in one sentence I'd say you had the body of a woman and the intellect of a man."

She raised her eyebrows. "Is that supposed to be a compliment?"

"Yes. You're my mate – my friend."

"The coffee's ready," she said.

He stood up, but instead of going to the stove he came to her side of the table and put his hands on her shoulders. "Do you really want coffee?"

She fought the temptation to kiss him. "Yes."

He bent over and lifted her pendant, kissing the place on her throat where it had been. "Tree." He undid the top button of her shirt and stroked the lace on her camisole.

She stood up. "I'm leaving while I've got some willpower left."

"I've been an idiot. Give me time to chuck a few things in my case and I'll come back to *Kingower* with you."

"No," she said, striding to the door. "You're in a state of arousal and men will do anything like that."

He tried to persuade her to at least stay and have coffee, but she was adamant. It was the first time she had ever been calculating, but she had wanted to leave him hungry. As she drove back to *Kingower*, she didn't know whether to congratulate or despise herself.

During the week, Stefan rang her every day. The phones in the two cottages were connected and she asked Kim to answer all calls and say she was out if it was Stefan.

"He sounds perturbed," Kim reported. "Serve him right if he thinks you've found another man. But, Tree ... "

"What?"

"You don't have to resort to tricks. You're not being you."

"Being myself didn't work once he'd met Fiona."

"Don't be cunning like her."

Catriona smiled sourly. "She's not cunning. She doesn't have to be. Life's easy for beautiful women."

On Friday night Stefan arrived at her cottage with a bunch of flowers and a bottle of champagne. "Will you still marry me?"

She had planned to tease him, but was too overcome with happiness. She kissed him and said, "Yes."

Kim had felt stifled all weekend because she couldn't talk about the wedding. "Are you sure he's what you want, Tree?" she asked when Stefan had gone back to Melbourne on Sunday night.

"Yes."

"He put you through a hell of a lot," she grumbled as she poured milk for their Ovaltine into a saucepan. "And why shouldn't we talk about the wedding? Weddings are fun."

"Maybe more so for women than men," said Catriona. "He was terrific this weekend, wasn't he? It's natural to have doubts."

"Have you had any?"

"No."

"If having doubts is so natural you'd have them too."

"Look, Stefan's life is going to change drastically. Not only will he have to adjust to a new job and a new area, he's got to establish his reputation again. He's giving up teaching at a school he loved."

"You didn't force him – "

"No, he offered because he knows how much my family and

riding mean to me. The only thing that'll be different for me is a new house. Maybe I'd be wavering if I was moving to Melbourne."

"Am I allowed to buy you a wedding present, or would Stefan deem it too extravagant?"

"Kim, stop it."

"Sorry. What about a dinner service? A posh one for parties, like Royal Doulton."

"That'd be great." She hesitated. "Something white with a gold or silver rim, I think."

Catriona's favourite china had a floral pattern, so Kim knew she was giving in to Stefan's preference for simplicity. Concerned that she was being swamped by what he wanted, she made herself say, "Go to Melbourne, order it, and I'll pay for it."

"That's awfully generous. Thanks."

"I don't care what Stefan thinks," said Kim. "I love weddings and when I get married it's going to be a grand occasion."

The next weekend Stefan and Catriona went to look at a weatherboard house in Whittlesea that had been built in the 1890's. Empty, and cheaper than most houses they had seen, it was owned by a widow who had moved into her son's granny flat. Stefan was impressed by the size of the rooms and the large front and back gardens. His parents struggled financially and he was determined that by the time he was forty he would have no mortgage. "With our combined salary and savings we'll only need a small loan from the bank," he said.

"It's ideal," agreed Catriona. "Four bedrooms means we can have a study each as well as a guest room. And we can both walk to work."

He grimaced. "It needs redecorating – I can't stand all this floral wallpaper."

"We'll get the painter and decorator who does *Kingower*. He's a friend of Dad's and he'll give us a good rate. Deciding on the colour scheme will be a bit of a problem. I don't want to live in a place that looks like a cave and you hate yellow and blue ... my favourite colours."

He put his arm around her. "As long as you don't want floral patterns we can compromise."

She looked doubtful. "Kim and I couldn't. We shared a bedroom till we were ten ... it was pink and had been the same since we were babies. Our parents were going to have it done up for Christmas. I wanted blue and Kim wanted beige walls with brown bedspreads. We had such a fight about it that Mum said we'd have to have separate rooms."

He kissed her lips. "Name a colour."

She snorted with laughter. "Red."

"Red it is. Walls, doors and ceilings."

Stefan had tried to push thoughts of Fiona out of his mind. Mostly he was successful, but they rose at unexpected moments. On the way back from the estate agent that morning they went into the hardware store and got some colour charts.

"Could you cope with blue for the lounge? And striped curtains and upholstery?" Catriona mused. "Regency stripe? Or navy and emerald to contrast with the walls?"

The image of the blue in Fiona's lounge and the navy and burgundy striped curtains and upholstery shot into his mind. He remembered the room and her fury in photographic detail. "No, not blue."

"What then? Please don't say ochre or brown." She looked at him. "What's wrong?"

"Nothing. Green. What about green?"

Catriona wrinkled her nose. "It's a difficult colour. Sage is dreary and apple's ..."

"We'll find one we both like. Green would suit the house. What about pale green walls, white woodwork and dark green velvet curtains and upholstery?"

"Velvet's too opulent for a weatherboard house. Stripes would be more cosy." She squeezed his hand. "We can have velvet when we buy a mansion."

His guilt was crushing. "I want you to be happy, Tree."

"We will be. You can indulge yourself in mud-hut colours in your study," she said enthusiastically.

'Thank God I didn't see Fiona's bedroom,' he thought as they reached the car.

"When do you want to go and look at furniture?"

He knew he had to make an effort. Her parents were buying their bedroom furniture and Margot wanted to give them a dining table and eight chairs. "Tree, how about you and me taking your parents, Kim and Aunty Margot to the city one Saturday to look at furniture, then we can treat them to lunch afterwards."

"That's a lovely idea."

"You've got a tremendous family. Not many married couples start off with a house that belongs to them and good furniture bought for them by relations. My parents have worked hard for years and will never have the things we'll start off with."

Catriona's expression was radiant. "We're going to be so happy, aren't we?"

"Yes, Tree, we are."

CHAPTER 14

Alex debated how to begin his letter to Fiona. 'We' might make Fiona think he was ignoring her wish to dissociate herself from Virginia. 'I' would respect her wish, but went against his instinct. 'Virginia's my wife and my loyalty is to her,' he thought.

We are pleased you're continuing to enjoy your new life.
I've bought four terraced houses in Fitzroy. From being a slum, it's an up and coming area so I got in quickly and bought them cheaply. With the exception of one, all the old cast-iron balconies have been boarded up and glassed in, but they are still there and in good condition so they can be painted which will save a lot of money. So many old terraces have had their intricate cast-iron lace-work ripped out, and replacements are expensive. I'm going down to Melbourne next week to see the builders and hire the decorators and landscape gardeners. I'll stay at your unit.
We'll see you at Tree's wedding. David wants to know if you are bringing anyone.
Virginia sends her love.

'How normal it sounds,' he thought. 'If I was truthful I'd write – We're in purgatory. Virginia has been silent since I got back from *Eumeralla*. She blames me for failing to get you to forgive her. You Clarksons are too intense. She's not as bad as Gabby ... she's meticulous about the way she dresses and she pretends when we're with other people, but when we're alone it's a different matter. I don't know how much of this I can stand. I've lost my daughter and my wife.'

Alex arrived in Melbourne early in the morning. He caught a taxi from Tullamarine Airport to Fiona's unit. He phoned Virginia to let her know he'd arrived safely. Dejected by her monosyllabic replies he rang Ruth and arranged to have dinner with her. After unpacking, he went to look at the houses in Fitzroy where work had begun the day before. The builders had pulled up the linoleum and ripped out the stained baths, sinks and toilets. The tiny backyards were full of rubble.

Restoring dilapidated houses usually excited him, but now he felt weary. Being away from Virginia was a relief, but he worried about her and their relationship. His decision to marry her had been based more on passion than on reasoned thought. Sometimes he had longed for the peace another woman might have given him. When Virginia was at her most tumultuous he envied his brother whose wife was gentle and unselfish, but he found her dull. Annoyed by her inevitable response of, "I agree with David," he had given up asking her opinion when controversial subjects were discussed.

Compared to Virginia, many women Alex knew were dull. His life with her was unpredictable, stimulating and often dramatic. Her rages were verbally violent, but she never hit him or threw things. When she was upset she punished him with long spells of silence, occasionally they lasted as long as a week. But this time her misery was so acute he could not break through it.

'I'm too old for this,' he thought. 'If Fiona had cut me off too we could have shared the pain. But Virginia feels that she's on her own.'

He remembered Margot's warning before he and Virginia married in 1938. "You'll never have any peace, Alex. She's too tempestuous and never considers the consequences of her actions. She'll leave chaos in her path, but deny she's caused it and she'll believe she was innocent – that's what is so frightening. She'll get what she wants at no thought about the cost to others. The Clarksons are like that."

"Is William?"

"No. They must take after their mother. Why are you grinning? This is serious, Alex, it's not a joke. You must take Virginia seriously."

"I am taking her seriously, I'm marrying her. You can't get more serious than that."

"Look beyond her beauty and ask yourself what else she has that attracts you."

"Courage, intelligence and compassion."

Margot had looked sad. "I hope you'll still have that lovely smile in a few years."

As soon as war was declared Virginia had volunteered for overseas nursing service when she could have stayed at home. After the war, it was an experience they shared and they talked about it knowing how fortunate they were to have survived.

He remembered their first meeting in 1933 after Margot had married William Clarkson, Virginia's father. Margot had met them in Brisbane. The train journey from Melbourne had taken two days and when they arrived Alex was cheerful, Francesca wheezy and Ruth excited.

When the car had left the city Francesca's breathing eased. "Margot, you've hardly told us anything about your step-children in your letters," she had remonstrated.

Alex grinned. "She's been sighing over the photos of Laurence and Jonathan."

Ruth giggled. "Cheska's in love, but she's not sure who with."

"Oh, no. Don't go getting romantic about them, Cheska."

"What's wrong, Margot?" Alex asked.

"Being a stepmother is awful. They resent me."

Alex was surprised. Margot's students had wept when she left the school in Whittlesea and most of them had come to see her off on the train. As far as he knew no one had ever disliked her. "Perhaps they're still missing their mother."

"I'm so glad you're here. I've missed you."

Once they had reached the unmade country roads conversation was impossible. The car lurched and by the time they reached the road to *Acacia*, it had a flat tyre. After Alex had changed it, Margot couldn't start the engine. Alex, Margot and Ruth pushed the car the last half mile to *Acacia* while Francesca steered. Sweaty and dirty, they left the car at the gate and trudged up the long track to the homestead.

As they walked under a group of trees near the paddocks they heard a giggle. They looked up. In the middle of a giant eucalyptus tree, sitting on a limb, was a girl dressed in jodhpurs and a white shirt. Her silver-blonde hair hung in two untidy plaits.

"Hello, you must be Virginia," said Alex. "I'm your step-uncle and Francesca and Ruth are your step-aunts."

"I know," she said disdainfully. She grabbed a higher branch and swung from it then hooked her legs over another branch and hung upside down.

"I've been looking forward to meeting you."

Virginia manoeuvred herself into a standing position. "I haven't been looking forward to meeting you."

Margot sighed, but Alex laughed. Used to submissive, neatly dressed girls, her wildness intrigued him. Virginia looked at him in astonishment. Suddenly there was a cracking sound. The branch on which she was standing broke and crashed through the tree. As he caught Virginia, he felt the jagged end of the branch hit his forehead. With her in his arms he fell backwards and rolled over. They landed side by side on the grass.

Margot knelt beside them. "Alex, are you hurt?"

He scarcely heard her. He found himself looking into a pair of emerald-green eyes, framed by dark lashes and brows.

"Your sister's worried about you," said Virginia. "She doesn't care if I'm injured."

"Are you?" he asked softly.

She looked scornful. "Laurence and Johnny taught me how to jump a long way and not hurt myself. But you've got blood pouring out of your head."

He chuckled.

"What's so funny? You might be dying."

"I don't reckon either of us is dying, do you?"

When they got to the homestead Margot took him into the kitchen and, pushing back his black hair, cleaned his lacerated forehead and applied ointment.

Virginia watched from the doorway. "Only sissies put that stuff on."

"If your scratches get infected that's up to you. Where are Jonathan and Laurence?"

"Hiding from you."

Margot's voice was icy. "Take Ruth and Francesca to their rooms, please."

Alex shook with laughter.

"Stop it," she said when Virginia had gone. "You'll encourage her to be even more insolent than she is already."

"She's honest."

Margot flicked his hair back into place. "Oh, Alex!" she said in exasperation.

The next day Virginia had been more enthusiastic about their presence and took them riding over to *Eumeralla* to visit Eleanor. To Margot's amazement she smiled during dinner instead of sitting silently with an expression of endurance on her face.

Alex noticed that when Francesca played the piano Laurence looked mesmerized.

Two years later Laurence and Francesca had married, and in 1938 Alex married Virginia. During the war they hardly saw each other. Alex served in the Middle East. Virginia was one of the last nurses to be evacuated from Singapore before the Japanese arrived.

After the war Alex had joined a firm of architects in Sydney, but designing skyscrapers that would replace fine Victorian buildings repulsed him.

"Sydney's being ruined, and I'm part of it," he had told Virginia. "Everywhere's the same. Look at the friends I made at university – they work for different firms, but they're as disaffected as I am."

"Start your own firm," she suggested.

"There's no demand for graceful buildings nowadays. Even the new houses are hideous boxes."

Virginia had looked thoughtful. "What about buying old houses, doing them up and selling them? That way you'd be using your architectural knowledge and you'd be happier."

Much of the success of his property development business was due to Virginia's ideas. When he had finished restoring their first house he had been unable to sell it, although a lot of people had looked at it. After a month he was about to lower the price when she proposed furnishing it. "That will give it an atmosphere. The white walls make it look large and clean, but sterile."

Alex had disagreed. "People can use their imagination."

"A lot of people don't have any imagination."

"It will cost too much."

"Let me try."

She had bought second-hand furniture, hung curtains, made up the beds, put pictures on the walls and bought vases and books. Two hours before people came to view it she put flowers in the vases, opened the windows and polished the furniture. To his astonishment the first person who came to see it bought it straight away.

"We can't go to that expense every time we do up a house," Alex said later.

"Don't sell the furniture – keep it and put it in the next one."

"Where can we store it?"

"Anywhere. We've got a spare room. It won't be for long. When you do up your next house put this furniture in it. Judging by the profit you've made on this one, soon you can buy two houses at a time and when one is sold just move the furniture into the other one."

It was a simple concept that worked every time.

Virginia's taste was elegant and innovative, and was reflected in their house and the way she dressed. In public she was gracious and dignified, in private she was often the opposite. But she was enthralling and beautiful and he loved her.

Ω Ω Ω

"How are you, Alex?" Ruth asked as she carried the plates of chicken casserole into the dining room.

He poured wine into their glasses. "Fine."

"Truly?"

"No," he confessed with a wry smile.

"You look terrible."

He picked up his knife and fork. "I'm in hell."

"So am I. But, I've been in hell for so long now I'm used to it."

He looked at her in concern. "Why?"

"I'm missing Fiona. She gave me something to talk about at the hospital. Now I'm back to being a lonely middle-aged spinster." She sipped her wine. "Old sins cast long shadows."

"What were your sins?"

"My first one was resentment."

"Who did you resent?"

"You and David because you were boys and didn't have to do any housework."

He laughed.

"It wasn't amusing, Alex. I got the highest marks at school, but our mother and the housekeeper did your ironing and cleaned and tidied your rooms, but Cheska, Margot and I had to do our own chores because we'd have to do them when we got married. Cheska was ill with asthma a lot so I ended up having to do her share most of the time. And yet I still came top of the class every year. But because I was a girl Dad wouldn't spend money to send me to university. And then when the war came I had to stay here and look after Cheska. The one thing I did for the war effort – looking after Laurence's wife. I failed. She was put in my care and it was my fault that she died."

"No one blamed you," protested Alex.

"I blamed me."

"I had no idea you felt like this. What did Laurence think?"

She shook her head and picked up her packet of cigarettes.

"Can I have one?" he asked.

She gave him the packet. "When did you start smoking again?"

"Just now." He lit a cigarette. "You could go to *Eumeralla* for a holiday."

"I can't. Eleanor was antagonistic."

"Oh. Fiona told me that, but I thought she was imagining things."

"No, she was right."

"What about writing to Eleanor – "

"I have. When I got back I wrote to her and she replied that she didn't want to see me on *Eumeralla* and if I want to see Fiona I'll have to meet her elsewhere."

Alex frowned. "Strange. Write to Fiona and ask her if she can find out anything."

"Yes. I will. How's Virginia?"

"She's in hell too."

"With hindsight, would you have married her?"

"Yes."

"Would you change anything?"

"Only things to do with Fiona. Nothing else. What about you?"

"Everything. Every single thing."

"Ah, Ruth. It's not that bad."

"Yes it is. It's been that bad for years."

Realizing she was slightly drunk, he dared to question her. "After Cheska died and you got ill ... where did you go?"

"Does it matter?"

"Not now. But I'm curious. We were worried about you."

"I had to get away. I couldn't bear the guilt and pain. Everyone was happy because the war was over and I wanted to escape so I didn't have to see anyone."

"You disappeared for four months."

"Three months," she said sharply. "I was away for three months."

Eumeralla
1st July 1972

Dear Dad,

Juju's teaching Keith to ride. Hazel's hilarious. She's blatantly attracted to him. When she came for the weekend Juju told her she was behaving like a tart. My relationship with Juju is strange in many ways. I don't feel the need to ask her about her feelings because I sense what they are. I often know what she's going to say before she says it. We are comfortable together and don't talk much.

Keith and Tom are good mates already, and Tom's mad about Keith's motorbike. Keith's happy and I'm happy – now all we need is for Gabby to find happiness again. I asked her the other day how she was feeling and she said 'neutral'. She's got a temporary teaching job for one term and she's finding it stimulating. Tom's going to give her riding lessons and she's looking forward to it.

Tom's coming to Tree's wedding with me. Can he borrow one of your suits? And a shirt and tie. He's the same height as you and about the same build. It's fabulous having a brother – they come in useful when you need a partner.

Love,

Fiona.

Alex picked up the phone and dialled his number in Sydney. When Virginia answered she sounded normal, but as soon as she knew it was him her voice became apathetic. He read Fiona's letter to her.

"She didn't mention me," she said. "Or ask how I was."

"No, but she didn't tell me not to refer to you, and that's a good sign."

"It's not," she said and put the phone down.

'I give up,' he thought. 'If she wants to speak to me she knows the number. I'm not pandering to her any more.'

He realized with an extreme sense of loss that he didn't want to go home. 'I'll stay in Fiona's unit until the houses in Fitzroy are finished. At the weekends Ruth and I can go to *Kingower*.'

CHAPTER 15

June was riding around *Eumeralla* with Keith, showing him how to check the sheep. "Look out for ones that are too far away from a flock – they might have strayed and got lost. They'll run off when we approach so watch to see none are limping. If one trails behind or is uninterested in us they might be sick or injured."

He listened intently and nodded.

Suddenly she realized why Hazel's amorous advances to Keith aggravated her. 'Is this how it feels?' she wondered. 'I've never experienced this ... not with any of my boyfriends.' She blushed and let her horse fall behind his.

As they neared a group of sheep they slowed their horses to a walk.

"We're also making sure there's plenty of green grass for them."

"It's as good as I imagined," Keith said, slowing his horse so she could catch up.

Satisfied that the colour in her cheeks had subsided, she looked at him. "What is?" she asked, although she thought she knew.

"The life. Getting up in the morning and knowing that soon you'll be on horseback. The sense of purpose and doing something real."

"Wasn't being a postman real? People getting their mail's important."

"We were looked down on by the office workers. It was seen as menial work, something a bloke did because he was too stupid to do anything else. Here I look on myself as being a guardian of the land and a provider of food and wool."

"Did you enjoy your go on home rota last week?"

He nodded. "Especially the gardening."

She looked sceptical. "Even the laundry and cooking?"

"Doing the laundry was tedious, but I had this to look forward to. Cooking's okay and Fiona's given me a few tips. You'd all been outside working hard and you needed a clean house and good food to come home to. Here I feel that my life's got a reason."

"You sound like Fiona."

He nodded. "I'm amazed at how well she's taken to all this – she used to be such a townie."

"Yes, the first time I saw her, she was so glamorous. She looked like someone in those magazines Hazel reads. We had to buy her a whole lot of new clothes."

She dismounted to check a sheep that was lagging behind the flock. Keith. held her horse's reins while she felt its legs and parted the fleece, looking for ticks.

"Is it okay?" he asked.

She nodded. "Probably just lazy. "Do you like Hazel?" she asked as he handed her the reins.

"Not as much as I like you."

She smiled up at him. He slid off the horse, put his arms round her and kissed her lips.

"We're cousins," she murmured when they stopped for breath.

"Cousins can kiss."

"What else can they do?"

He ran his hands through her hair. "Lots of things, Juju, lots of things," he whispered.

Eumeralla
July 1972

How thrilling! This afternoon Juju and Keith came back holding hands. Juju tells me she adores him.

The financial situation at *Eumeralla* looks promising. With some of Keith's money they've bought a new harvester, more sheep for breeding and new saddles.

"I'm pleased about you and Juju," Tom told Keith one night when they were setting up the chess board. "I detested her last boyfriend."

"How did she meet him?"

Tom grimaced. "Hazel introduced them. *Eumeralla*'s remote so we're a bit limited when it comes to meeting people our own age. My first girlfriend lived over the creek. After she moved to Brisbane we stayed friends and she comes to see me when she visits her parents. Our hatred of the people on *Acacia* has wiped out one social alliance."

"Do you reckon the rumours about them being almost bankrupt are true?" Keith asked.

"Could be, but it might be wishful thinking. Their wheat crop failed last year. It depends how much money they've got as back up. They must have investments. In your grandfather's day the soil was fertile, but it's been plundered for over twenty years. Instead of putting money back into the land they spent it on cars, overseas holidays, and they employ lots of staff to do the things they should do themselves."

"If they sell it could we all buy it together?" Keith asked.

"It depends on the price. We don't want to get too much in debt. The house from Dalby is arriving tomorrow and Neil and I will have to buy a few things for it. Mum's only letting us take what's in our bedroom. We'll have to dismantle part of the fence so the trailer can get through."

Fiona was laughing so much she couldn't hold the camera steady. "Usually people move to houses," she said, as the driver inched the trailer through the gates. "Is there a flushing toilet?"

"There was one outside, it and the laundry and a shed were attached to the main house, but it would have cost more to bring so we said to leave it behind," said Tom.

"Drat!" said Fiona.

"Typical selfishness," Eleanor said to Greg. "Thanks very much. The one thing I wanted you make sure is left behind!"

Fiona, seeing Greg's embarrassment at being censured in front of strangers, said, "How much will a new one cost?"

"Too much," Greg replied.

Eleanor sighed. "Naturally."

"It's just that I thought that I could buy one." To her relief Eleanor smiled.

The house's new location was close to middle paddock well away from the creek. As soon as it was put into place they all went inside. To their astonishment it was full of furniture.

"We didn't pay for this," Tom said.

"Do you want it?" asked the driver of the trailer.

"How much will it cost?"

"Nothing. The old lady who owned the house died and the family don't want the furniture, so they left it. It's quite good stuff."

"It is," said Eleanor. "We'll keep it. And it's not staying here," she said when the men had left. It's coming to our house. You can have all the old junk."

Tom held up his hands. "Okay, Mum. Whatever you want. We'll move it tomorrow, it's too late to do it now."

"Actually, I think your father and I should move here and the rest of you can stay in the old house," she said when she saw the modern bathroom.

Neil looked furious. "No!"

"I don't see why you should live in the best house."

"This was meant to be a happy day for them ... don't spoil it," said Greg.

"She already has," said Neil.

Fiona could think of nothing conciliatory to say. 'Now I know how Dad felt when Mum and I quarrelled,' she thought.

Ω Ω Ω

Gabriella and Tom rode side by side.

"You're really enjoying this, aren't you, Gabby?"

She nodded. "It's fantastic. Thanks for teaching me."

"It's nice to see you smile. Keith told me you've had a rough time."

Her smile ebbed away.

"Sorry. That was clumsy of me."

"It's hard to talk about. It's when people give me sympathy."

"Hard not to be sympathetic, I reckon. It's not something you can be offhand about."

"No. Leukaemia. Suddenly he was tired all the time. His mates used to tease him about being a newly-wed and tell me I was exhausting him. Then he got all these bruises. That's when he went to the doctor." She turned her head away from him and looked at the sky. "The clouds are moving fast."

"Are they?" He stopped his horse. When she stopped hers Tom reached over and touched her shoulder. "Gabby, don't be ashamed of crying in front of me."

She bit her lip and he saw her swallow hard. "I'm okay. I've done too much crying and self-pitying. Can we canter?"

Eumeralla
July 1972

Today I got a letter from Aunty Ruth. I knew I was right. There *is* something wrong between her and Eleanor. Positive that it was a misunderstanding, I thought I'd be able to sort it out, because Eleanor and I are on rota together. We were gardening when I told her about Aunty Ruth's letter.

"I never liked Ruth," she said, looking as if she wanted to whack me with the spade for even mentioning her name.

"But, Dad told me that you used to be friends," I said.

"We were polite to each other ... neither of us has uncontrolled passions like you Clarksons. Besides, Alex wouldn't know – he was so fascinated by Virginia he wouldn't have noticed if the sheep had metamorphosed into elephants and the wheat had turned purple."

"Why didn't you like her?"

"For heaven's sake, Fiona, why can't you just accept that we didn't like each other?"

"Aunty Ruth likes you – she wouldn't have written this letter if she hadn't. She wants to know what she's done to upset you."

With that, Eleanor yanked up a clump of weeds and shook them so viciously the soil went everywhere. She said, "It's nothing to do with you. Nothing." Then she laughed wildly. Weird.

Ω Ω Ω

On Saturday morning in the second week of July, Gabriella drove up to Keith's cabin. She jumped out of the car, ran up to his door and banged on it. There was no reply. As she raced to the house she saw they were all on the verandah. "Coo-wee!" she called.

Greg waved. "Want some breakfast, Gabby?"

"*Acacia*'s for sale!" she shouted, jumping up and down.

Keith stood up. "How much?"

"I don't know." She bounded up the steps and stood beaming at them.

Greg pulled out a chair for her. "Damn. We've just bought a load of new machinery and sheep."

"And paid a fortune for that house to be moved from Dalby," said Eleanor.

Neil groaned. "Stop going on about it. It wasn't your money, it was Fiona's."

"*Eumeralla*'s owned outright," said Keith. He looked at Greg. "Would you mortgage it?"

"Yes," said Eleanor. "If we had to."

"I'll sell my unit," said Fiona. "And my car and my furniture."

"I can sell my house," said Gabriella. "If you all buy *Acacia* I want to be in too. I want to be the eighth partner."

Tom shook his head. "They'll balk at selling to us. They think we're interfering busybodies and the fact that we've been proved right will stick in their guts."

"They won't have any choice," Gabriella said. "They're bankrupt."

"How do you know?" asked Tom.

My next door neighbour's an estate agent. He told me all about it last night."

"Is it going to be auctioned?" asked Keith.

"I don't know."

"Why didn't you ask?"

"Tactics," she replied smugly. "I didn't want to look too interested."

Eumeralla
July 1972

After Gabby's monumental announcement we spent most of the morning doing our sums. We all got different answers so we gave up. Greg said that before we decide Gabby and I have to get our places valued. Keith and I went back to Dalby and helped her clean and tidy up. The place was a mess. It looks great now. There are no worries about the outside – the garden's beautiful even though it's winter. Gabby spends most of her time in the garden and that's why the housework never gets done.

I'm going to Melbourne on Tuesday to see an estate agent.

Ω Ω Ω

Fiona caught a taxi from Tullamarine Airport to her unit. She put her key in the lock, but it wouldn't turn. When the door opened she jumped. "Oh, Dad, I thought you were a burglar. I didn't know you were still here or I would have rung. The most wonderful thing's happened. *Acacia*'s for sale. I want to sell this place. Is that all right with you?"

"Of course. It's yours."

"But you bought it for me." She pulled her key out of the lock. "Mum will be thrilled."

He smiled and went over to the phone. "Ring her now."

She looked sheepish. "I forgot for a minute."

"Forget forever, Fiona." He picked up the receiver. "Please – for my sake and your mother's. She's in a terrible state. I'm still here because I don't want to go home. You've forgiven me, forgive her."

"I can't, Dad."

"You can, but you won't," he shouted. "What would it cost you? Nothing."

Fiona stared at him in shock, unable to believe that her tolerant, humorous father had lost his temper. "It'd cost me the truth."

"You bloody Clarksons are all the same," he shouted, dropping the receiver. "Go back to *Eumeralla*. I'll sell your unit and send you the money and anything else you want."

"Dad, please." She had been so excited she hadn't noticed how drained he looked when she arrived.

"Get out of my sight."

After she left, Alex deplored his explosion. 'If I'd been calm she might have been persuaded to at least ring Virginia. Then I could go home and get back to normal,' he thought, tossing a newspaper across the room. 'Normal? When has anything to do with Virginia ever been normal?'

The phone rang half an hour later and he picked it up. It was Ruth. Fiona had arrived in a state and they were both worried about him. He reassured her and hung up.

An hour later Virginia rang. "Alex, why haven't you rung me? Why haven't you come home?"

"I'm sick of ringing you and tired of hearing your peevish voice. I'm staying in Melbourne till I feel like coming home – if I ever do. I might not because I'm sick of the sight of your miserable face." He threw the receiver back in its cradle.

Eumeralla
July 1972

    I got an impersonal letter from Dad yesterday telling me that he's had my unit put on the market. That's all. He signed himself Alex and didn't even put love. Last night I couldn't sleep. Usually I just crash out, but I lay awake for ages. I'm so far away from him and not just in miles. I wish I knew what I could do to make things right. But I do know, don't I? Forgive my mother. There ... I've written it. I said it to Dad and now I've written it. My mother instead of Virginia.

    All this has spoilt my excitement about *Acacia*. The bank manager said that with the sale of my unit and Gabby's house and putting up *Eumeralla* as collateral we will be able to manage the repayments provided the fates are kind. Can we take the risk? Are we greedy to want more? But what a slap in the eye this would be for Margot. What a triumph for the Clarksons. We mustn't get our hopes up too much. Someone else might offer more. The waiting is nerve-racking. Mum would be so happy if we got it. I don't miss her, but I think about her a lot and not all my thoughts are angry ones.

Ω   Ω   Ω

"Fertilizer-collecting time?" Fiona said when she and Tom had finished weeding the garden.

    He got the wheelbarrow from the shed. "You're toughening up."

    Fiona carried their shovels to the paddock. The first time she had helped collect the horse dung she had felt queasy. Now she found the smell more pungent than vile.

    Tom leant on his shovel. "How come your family were so much

richer than ours? Were they squatters?"

"No." She grinned. "The first Australian Clarksons were crooks."

"Convicts? Really?"

She scooped up a pile of dung and put it in the barrow. "Crooks not convicts."

"What's the difference?"

"They were crooks, but didn't get caught. He was a coach driver for a family who had country estates in Sussex and Scotland and a house in London. He was in cahoots with a maid. They planned it for ages, and practised their employer's la-di-da accent till they got it right. When the family went out one night she stole lots of jewellery, money and clothes. She wore the clothes, pawned the jewellery and they came to Australia. When they got here they bought the land and built the house with the money."

Tom looked shocked.

"What's the matter with you?" she asked. "They didn't kill anyone. The Victorian aristocracy paid their servants paltry wages and made them work long hours, while they lazed around all day. If the master of the house got a maid pregnant she was thrown out without a reference and became a prostitute or went to the workhouse. And they had the gall to preach morality. Pah! If my ancestors were thieves they earned every penny they stole."

"Don't get mad at me, Sis," he said with a laugh. "None of my ancestors were toffs."

She smiled. "Sorry."

"Is that how they could afford servants?"

"I suppose so. I went to see the places they lived when I was in England. It gave me a weird feeling to stand in front of the London house. It was not far from Buckingham Palace."

"How come you knew the address?"

"Family history. They wrote it all down."

"Wasn't it dangerous to brag about what they did?"

"They didn't tell anyone. Our grandfather found their ... confession I guess you'd call it ... when he was sorting through some trunks when he was young. It was addressed to the descendants of Ellen and James Clarkson. They hid their tracks well – Clarkson wasn't their real name."

"What was it?"

"They didn't say. But they wrote in graphic detail about their working conditions and their callous employers and why they did what they did."

"If they'd got caught would they have been hung?"

Fiona nodded. "They wrote about what they'd stolen – rubies, sapphires, pearls and diamonds ... necklaces, bracelets, rings, brooches and tiaras. The whole lot would probably be worth millions today, so I think their crime would have been judged heinous enough."

"And you wouldn't be here and neither would Juju." He sighed. "What a pity they didn't hang." He jumped sideways as Fiona tossed a pile of dung from her shovel at him.

Eumeralla
July 1972

Today we went to see *Acacia*. The owners and their workers have left and the sheep have been sold. The new homestead that was built in 1950 is vulgar and modern. Eleanor went mad at Tom when he said it could be pulled down. She wants to live in luxury so we're going to keep it and grow creepers up it to hide its ugliness. There are two tennis courts, a pavilion, garages and a massive swimming pool. No wonder they went broke.

The old homestead has survived. Guests stayed in it when the main house was full. They must have had heaps of visitors. It's similar to *Kingower*, but it's built of timber and it's smaller. There are seven bedrooms, a vast kitchen and a bathroom with a flushing toilet. Heaven! Now I've been to the old homestead I hate Aunty Margot even more. Seeing where our family lived has given Keith, Gabby and me a peculiar sensation. For years we've heard about *Acacia*, now we've been there and hopefully we'll live there. It hasn't affected Juju like it's affected us – she hadn't been brought up on the injustice done to her real father.

Neil's going to move into this house and Tom will stay in the house they moved from Dalby. The rest of us will live in the old homestead. Greg wants to keep Keith's cabin because it was the first house to be built on *Eumeralla*. We're going to plant hundreds of trees. Greg said the wheat fields will have to be manured and left alone for a year. He is the only person who's being sensible about this. If we don't get it Keith will be the hardest hit. We must get it – we must!

CHAPTER 16

Greg opened his eyes and stared into the darkness. He had almost been asleep when Eleanor had called out, "Johnny." During the first years of their marriage she had often said 'Johnny' in her sleep. He knew by her tone when she spoke Jonathan's name that she still loved him. Sometimes she sounded happy, sometimes anguished, but never neutral. The first time she had woken sobbing, he comforted her, but realized his intrusion was unwelcome. While appreciating that her intense feelings for Jonathan would never fade and that he would always be second best, Greg hoped that she did have some kind of love for him. In pessimistic moments he decided that his wish that her feelings for him would develop into love had never materialized. Even now, when she addressed him, it was in a careful way as if in an unguarded moment she might call him Johnny instead of Greg. When Eleanor was at her most withdrawn, he tried to cheer himself by remembering that when Jonathan had come back she had sent him away. 'Why?' he had asked himself hundreds of times.

Now, she spoke his name less often, and the times that she did settled into a pattern. It was usually after a visit to the cemetery. But tonight was the third time in succession it had happened. He knew that visiting *Acacia* had brought back the dreams.

Ω Ω Ω

"Hi, Aunty Virginia, it's Gabby. Listen, I want to buy a new house, and I'd like your opinion. Have you got time to come up?"

Virginia's voice became brighter. "Yes. When?"

"Any time. Book a flight and let me know."
"Where's the new house? Why are you – "
Gabriella laughed. "Wait and see."

The last weeks had been the worst Virginia had ever experienced. Whatever her troubles, there had been Alex to share them. Now there was no one. He put the phone down whenever she rang Fiona's unit. 'I've driven him away,' she thought. 'I've pushed my kind, gentle and humorous husband too far.' She wondered if Margot knew about their problems. 'How she'd gloat if he wanted a divorce.'

If it hadn't been for the fear that he would slam the door in her face she would have gone to Melbourne. Gabriella's invitation gave her something to look forward to. She would only stay a few days. If she stayed longer the temptation to get in touch with Fiona would be overwhelming. She could not endure another rejection.

When Gabriella met her at the airport she was bubbling with excitement. She jangled a bunch of keys in front of her. "I got these first."

"Is the house vacant?"

Gabriella smiled mysteriously. "Yes."

She was obviously revelling in her secret so Virginia decided not to question her. "You're looking well, Gabby," she said, as they walked to the car.

"Tom's teaching me to ride."

"Splendid. It's exhilarating, isn't it?"

"Sure is," Gabriella replied, putting Virginia's bag in the boot. "He's a fantastic teacher."

"Perhaps Fiona would like to have another try. She had a bad experience with David. She was so excited about learning to ride, but he intimidated her. Just because Catriona and Kim were tomboys didn't mean Fiona was. She might have more success with Tom."

As they drove down the road towards *Eumeralla*, Virginia said,

"Are we going to *Eumeralla*?"

Gabriella grinned. "No."

"Oh, I thought Fiona – " The gates of *Acacia* were open, and to Virginia's astonishment she drove through them. "Gabby, this is – "

"I know."

"Gabby, don't. I couldn't bear it. I don't want to see the new owners."

"Depends what new owners you're talking about. The last new owners or the future new owners."

"You don't mean ... you're buying this?"

"If we can. Keith and me and the Mitchells and Fiona. We don't know if it's a private sale yet. We hope so, but they might decide on an auction."

"It looks so bare without the trees."

"We'll plant lots more. In ten years' time it'll be just like it was when you and Dad and Uncle Johnny lived here."

Keith was waiting outside the old homestead. When Virginia got out of the car he hugged her. "Welcome home, Aunty Virginia."

She felt too emotional to speak. As they walked onto the verandah she felt a surge of optimism. 'They'll buy *Acacia*, Alex will come home and Fiona will forgive me,' she thought.

Virginia indulged in nostalgia as they wandered through the echoing rooms. She showed them which bedroom had been their father's and told them stories about when she, Laurence and Jonathan were young.

"Dad told me how you fell out of a tree when you first met Uncle Alex," said Gabriella.

Virginia was indignant. "I didn't fall – the branch broke." She walked over to the kitchen window. "Without all the trees it's hard to get my bearings. They were our landmarks. There were ghost gums and blue gums. And peppercorn trees – we used to play under them when we were little. There were lots of bushes round the house too and we had fig trees. It looks so bleak now." She sighed. "Margot's actions destroyed more than her stepsons' lives."

There were chairs on the verandah so they went outside and sat down.

"Did any of you ever like her?" asked Gabriella. "At first, I mean."

"No, she was bossy. We hated her for making Dad forget our mother. Margot was very brainy – all the Lancasters are. She knew as much about farming as Dad did."

"What was your mother like?"

"Beautiful. She had very blue eyes and silver-blonde hair. Dad had green eyes. Your father got that amazing mix of blue and green – so did Fiona. I've got Dad's eyes and Johnny had Mum's. Dad's hair was blonde too, but darker. Mum was gentle and she deferred to Dad. Margot changed all that – he deferred to her."

"Did she marry him because he was rich?" asked Keith.

Being on *Acacia* for the first time since 1947 brought all Virginia's outrage flooding back, but knowing how her consuming behaviour had alienated Alex and Fiona she struggled to be dispassionate. "No, she loved him, there's absolutely no doubt about that. She would have married him even if he'd been destitute. And Francesca and Ruth were her treasures and she adores Alex too. To be fair, Margot wouldn't have done what she did, if Francesca had been alive. But what she did to your father was morally criminal. Apart from the six years of the war, he'd worked here all his adult life." She sighed. "When the war ended we should have been happy, but Johnny left Eleanor and Laurence came home to the news that Francesca had been dead for two weeks. Ruth had to tell him. He stumbled out of her flat and didn't come back. She sent a telegram to *Acacia*, but he didn't turn up for months. We were frantic ... we thought he might have killed himself. As soon as I knew he was back I came up. He was depressed and thin. God knows where he'd been. He wouldn't say. *Acacia* and the horses were the only things that kept him from permanently plunging into despair. He threw himself into the land ... he said if he didn't go to bed exhausted he'd be awake all night."

"Greg told me Johnny was disinherited because he left Eleanor. Is that true?" asked Keith.

Virginia nodded.

Gabriella looked perplexed. "So Johnny being cut out was nothing to do with Margot?"

"Yes it was. Because Laurence told me that he'd ignore Dad's wishes and he and Johnny would share *Acacia*. Johnny had earned his inheritance – he and your father had never had a wage. I'm certain Margot heard our conversation and told Dad and that's why he left everything to her. They didn't have the decency to tell Laurence. They let him work for what would never be his. It could have gone on for years, but then Dad died suddenly ... he was only sixty-two and seemed healthy. Margot was distraught and it brought us all together for a few days. It was ironic. Laurence told Margot that if she wanted to stay on *Acacia* she could. We should have guessed by her expression then. She looked sly. I'll never forget the reading of the will. But shocking as it was, we consoled ourselves with the thought that Laurence had a home here. We assumed Margot would keep *Acacia* and let him run it."

"Surely he wouldn't have wanted to work for her," Keith said.

"He didn't have any choice. The only money he had was from the army, but it wasn't enough to buy even a small house. He was going to make her pay him. He had the idea that eventually he'd be able to buy her out. But *Kingower* was in debt so she sold it. She said that if Laurence hadn't called her a scheming gold digger she would have used *Acacia* as collateral to save *Kingower*. But she was justifying her actions. Your father had nothing and she knew it."

"Why didn't he contest the will?" asked Keith.

"A solicitor advised us against it. He said that although Laurence hadn't had a wage at *Acacia* he had never had any expenses. It was true. He'd lived rent free and his food and clothes came from the household budget. If he lost he'd have had a huge legal bill. I offered to pay, but Laurence wouldn't let me. Margot was cunning ... she'd gambled on his pride."

Ω   Ω   Ω

"Right, Sis, soon it'll be spring," said Tom as they walked to the chicken coop to collect the eggs. "It's time to teach you about our native fauna. In September all the hibernating snakes come out – they're dozy for a bit, but still dangerous. What will you do if you see one?"

"Run like hell," said Fiona.

"Right. But if you take precautions you won't have any problems. In the summer if we're working anywhere with long grass we wear long trousers and socks. It's hot and uncomfortable, but if we tread on a snake we'll have some protection. The one you're most likely to tread on is the Death Adder. They're difficult to see and can whip round like lightning and strike. They hide under leaves and the end of their tail looks like a worm. It's a lure for birds and frogs. When you're walking in long grass stamp your feet and most snakes will go away. They don't want to see you any more than you want to see them. They'll only bite when cornered, but some are more aggressive than others. Some are venomous and some aren't, but treat every one you see as if it is. Spiders are something else. Check your shoes and shake your clothes before you put them on. If one falls down your neck – "

Fiona shrieked. "Are you trying to make me die of fright?"

Tom grinned and opened the door to the coop. "No, I'm teaching you bush law."

"Okay." She shuddered. "What do I do if one falls down my neck?"

"Try and stay calm."

"How can I stay calm when there's a poisonous spider down my bloody neck?"

"Judging by the state you're in just thinking about it – you'll faint." He laughed. "By the time you recover, the spider will have run out."

"Have any spiders ever fallen down your back?"

"Last year when I was shifting sacks of wheat, a red back ran up my arm."

"Oh, my God. What did you do?"

"Flicked it off. Come on, Sis, how many people do you know who've been bitten by a spider or a snake?"

"None, but I've lived in a city all my life."

"Don't fret too much. Children and animals are the most vulnerable. A few years ago one of our dogs got bitten by a brown snake. But she tried to kill it. We were on the verandah having tea and we heard her barking. We called her off, but it was too late."

"Did she die?"

"Yes."

"Did you kill the snake?"

"No. Never kill a snake. If there were no snakes we'd be overrun by mice and rats."

She grunted. "I'd rather see a rat than a snake."

Eumeralla
August 1972

Damn, damn, damn! *Acacia's* being auctioned. The agent told us today. There are lots of people interested. Keith reckons we've got as much chance as anyone else, but we haven't. I said that whoever's got the most money will get it, but he said the person with the most money may not want it enough to go over what we can afford. Compared to other properties round here, *Acacia's* not got much going for it. Whoever buys it will have to wait at least a year before they plant crops. That's before they even think about droughts, bush fires or floods.

Fiona's pen ran out of ink. "Poxy thing," she muttered, realizing that she had run out of cartridges.

Ω Ω Ω

Keith woke and felt June's hair spread across his chest. With two of them in his single bed it was cramped.

"Juju," he whispered.

She opened her eyes and stretched. "I wish I could stay all night."

He kissed her. "I wish you could too."

"We didn't finish our game," she said, looking at the chess set on the table.

He nibbled her ear. "How can I concentrate with you sitting in the moonlight looking more beautiful then ever?"

She propped herself up on one elbow. "I'm so happy."

"So am I. I feel I've known you all my life."

"In a way you have – Fiona I mean."

"Physically yes. But you're different." He got out of bed and pulled on his shirt. "She a lot more like you now than she used to be. She's happier and more casual. She used to be sophisticated. But I can tell you apart ... not from a distance though."

They walked in silence back to the house. Keith watched June creeping up the steps. When she reached the verandah she turned and blew him a kiss, before opening the door and going inside. He strolled back to his cabin in the moonlight lost in the fantasy of him and June living on *Acacia*.

When Fiona rode to the post-box the following morning there was a letter from Virginia addressed to Greg and Eleanor.

"I haven't a clue what it's about," she said, giving it to Greg at the breakfast table.

"I think I do." He tore the flap open. "I was right. She wants to give us money so we can increase our bid on *Acacia* if necessary."

"Did I hear that right?" said Eleanor, coming onto the verandah with bowls of porridge.

Fiona, feeling torn, nodded.

"We are going to accept, aren't we?" Eleanor said.

"I don't know," said Greg.

"No," said Keith. "We've got to do this on our own."

Greg nodded. "I agree."

"But we mightn't even need the extra money!" protested

Eleanor. "We can give it straight back – it's just insurance to give us a better chance."

"Much as we want *Acacia*," said Tom. "Keith's right. We've got to do this ourselves."

"You wretched men," exploded Eleanor. "She's giving us a chance and you're chucking it away. Fiona, talk some sense into them."

Keith, looking embarrassed, said, "Aunty Virginia gave me the money to buy my parents house. Just because she's my aunt doesn't mean I have to sponge off her."

"Then borrow it and pay it back," said Eleanor.

"No," said Greg. "We're not borrowing anything from anyone."

Fiona, seeing Eleanor's fury and Greg's determination to be independent, felt that they were both right. "Let's vote on it."

"All right," said Greg. "Who says we should let Virginia give – "

"No." Eleanor put her hands on her hips. "Not like this. Think about it during the day and we'll vote tonight in a secret ballot. There are things you men have to consider. *Eumeralla* is five thousand acres. *Acacia* is ten thousand. Think ahead to when the boys get married and have children. They both want to stay on here. How long will it be before it gets too small for all of us?" She looked at Keith. "You and Juju are keen on each other at the moment, but it could fizzle out. You both marry someone else and you all stay here. That's before we include Fiona and what she wants to do. If she marries a man who wants to live here we'll end up with so many houses there won't be any room for crops and livestock. Think hard before you turn down Virginia's offer. And Gabby should vote too."

Eumeralla
August 1972

We voted no. I was in a dilemma all day. One minute I was going to say yes, the next no. In the end I voted no. Keith's right. We've got to do this by ourselves. And Mum used to bombard me with cries of, 'After all I've done for you.' I don't want her to ever throw that at Keith or anyone else. Eleanor's refusing to talk to anyone.

Keith found Eleanor in the kitchen washing the dishes. She hadn't spoken for two days and he hated the atmosphere.

"Do you know if this is real?" he asked, hoping curiosity would make her turn around and look at him. "I looked up gemstones in the encyclopedia," he continued, when she failed to respond. "It said the darker the sapphire the better the quality. This one's navy. If it is real I'll sell it so we can increase our bidding limit."

When she faced him and looked at the ring he held in the palm of his hand, he tried not to look satisfied. "It was Mum's, but I doubt if Dad could afford – "

She picked up the sapphire and diamond ring and held it to the light. "It's real all right. Your father didn't buy it ... it belonged to his mother and his grandmother before that. It was passed down to the wife of the eldest son."

"So it was Francesca's first?"

"Yes. When Ruth heard that your Dad was getting married again she gave it to Aunty Virginia to give to your mother. Would you really sell it?"

He nodded. "How much do you think it's worth?"

"I haven't got a clue. You'll have to get it valued."

Eumeralla
August 1972

Keith came back from Brisbane with a huge cheque for the ring. Now we can up our bid. Eleanor's happier. It was ghastly when she wasn't speaking to us. The estate agent wrote to tell me they've got a buyer for my unit. Dad hasn't answered my letters so I'm going to see him. When he was here I didn't tell him I could ride, I wanted to surprise him when I was at *Kingower* for Tree's wedding, but with me not speaking to Virginia and Dad not speaking to me, maybe it would be wiser if I didn't go. It's Tree's big day and I'd hate there to be a sour atmosphere. What with our quarrel and the auction, I'm a nervous wreck.

CHAPTER 17

When Fiona arrived at her unit on Friday afternoon Alex was not there. The lounge was untidy with newspapers scattered all over the floor and the ashtrays were full. She opened the windows to get rid of the stale smell of cigarettes. In the spare bedroom she found the bed unmade and piles of dirty clothes all over the floor. Pleased to be able to do something positive she tidied the room and put his shirts into the washing machine. By the time she had vacuumed all the rooms she felt better.

Two hours later when all the washing was hanging on the line and she had tidied and cleaned the whole unit, Alex had still not arrived. Disappointed, she walked to Ruth's house.

"He's gone to *Kingower* for the weekend," she told Fiona.

"Has Dad said anything about our quarrel?"

"No. He's said nothing about your mother either," Ruth said, handing her a glass of sherry.

"You don't think he'll leave her for good, do you?"

Ruth looked at her thoughtfully. "Do you want him to?"

"No, he's all she's got."

"She's got lots of friends."

"Friends can be replaced – husbands can't. If he divorced her she'd never marry anyone else." She looked perturbed. "Do you think he will divorce her?"

Ruth lit a cigarette. "In his current mood he could do anything."

"Would he cut me off permanently?"

"The same answer as before, Fiona. I've never seen him like this. Never. I'm going to *Kingower* tomorrow morning; why don't you come with me?"

"Thanks, Aunty Ruth."

"I won't tell them you're coming ... it might be better to catch your father unawares."

They arrived at *Kingower* at lunchtime.

David looked at Fiona in annoyance when she got out of Ruth's car. "I didn't know you were coming."

"Hello, Uncle David, how nice to see you. I haven't come to seduce Stefan. Where's my father?"

"I see you're still as inconsiderate as ever."

"Your greeting was hardly courteous."

"Stop it, both of you," said Ruth. "Fiona wants to talk to her father – where is he?"

"In the paddock with Margot and Kim."

Fiona looked despondent.

"I'll come with you," said Ruth.

"Ruth," said David. "Are you well?"

"Of course I'm well. What are you looking at?"

"Nothing ... you look a bit pale."

She turned to Fiona. "Do I look pale?"

"You look fine to me. Uncle David probably presumes I've upset you like I seem to upset most of the Lancasters."

"How long are you staying?" he asked Fiona.

"The whole weekend."

"If you'd told us we would have got a room ready for you," he said coldly.

Ruth and Fiona set off towards the paddock. Half way there Fiona slowed down. "What if he won't speak to me? I don't want Aunty Margot and Kim to know."

"The Clarkson pride. I don't think he's told her – he's got his pride too. He won't want to admit that his marriage is rocky."

Fiona chewed her lip. "You said last night that he's likely to do anything. What if he leaves Mum and moves to *Kingower*?"

"Be realistic, Fiona. Where would he live?"

"Tree's cottage when she and Stefan get married."

"He wouldn't be happy in a small cottage when he's been used to living a life of luxury with Virginia."

"As you said about his current mood – "

"Yes, all right. I'm sorry I said it now."

Fiona wandered over to a log and sat on it. "We've never had a serious fight before. I don't know what to do. Dad can't look after himself – the unit was in a mess. But that hasn't made him go back to Mum."

"No," said Ruth, sitting beside her. "He married her because he idolized her not because he wanted to be looked after. He found her brutal honesty and wildness refreshing. She was a fantastic rider, but she was undisciplined, and rode for the sheer hell of it – the thrill of speed and the danger. He'd never met anyone like her ... neither had I. I found her overpowering at first. But Alex, Francesca and I were better riders. Our technique was good and we won her respect."

Fiona picked up a gum leaf and crushed it. "Should I forgive her?"

"Yes. She loves you very much ... probably too much. Nothing can excuse the terrible lie she told you, but she's been a good mother. Do you know why she doesn't ride here any more?"

Fiona had never thought about it. "No."

"Because you couldn't."

"Oh. Why don't you ride here?"

"For the same reason as Virginia."

"Oh, I didn't know. I've been ungrateful."

"Come on, let's go to the paddock."

"I can't face him in front of Aunty Margot and Kim."

"You must, you've come all this way to see him."

Fiona threw the remains of the gum leaf on the ground. "What if he shouts at me again?"

"Shout back."

"Aunty Ruth, am I selfish to want everything?"

"Lots of people less deserving than you have it all so I don't see why you shouldn't. Now come on."

Normally Fiona enjoyed walking at *Kingower*, but she was too apprehensive to appreciate the green of the winter grass and the slanting sunlight through the bare branches. When they reached the paddock she saw Margot, Kim and Alex standing with a horse.

From a distance Margot, tall, straight backed and thin with her grey hair done in a bun, looked younger than her seventy-two years.

Kim saw them first. "Hi, Aunty Ruth, you look well."

Alex turned and looked quizzically at Fiona.

"Is there any reason I shouldn't look well, Kim?"

"No, I'm just pleased you do, that's all." She turned back to the horse, lifted up its leg and examined the hoof.

"We weren't expecting Fiona," said Margot.

"It was a last-minute decision," Ruth told her. "How many foals in the spring?"

Kim patted the mare's rump. "Six."

Fiona saw that Alex was dispirited. When Kim finished her inspection they walked towards the gate.

"Alex, I want to talk to you," said Ruth.

Kim looked alarmed. "What about?" she blurted out.

"Something private," Ruth replied irritably.

When Margot and Kim were out of earshot Fiona turned to Alex. "Dad, I'm sorry."

"What for?"

She was confused. "I don't understand."

"Neither do I, Fiona. I haven't got the foggiest idea why I'm behaving like this. I'm ashamed."

Ruth walked towards the gate. "Now I know you don't need a referee, I'll leave you."

"Why didn't you answer my letters?"

"You've exonerated me, but not Virginia. It's divided us. We're both to blame not just her. She's suffering and she won't let me help."

"I'm sorry you're so unhappy, Dad, and I'm sorry I've caused it."

"Fiona, you didn't cause it, the whole thing is mostly my fault."

"If it will make you happy I'll forgive Mum."

He shook his head. "It's got to come naturally. Begin by at least talking to her," he said, putting his arm around her shoulder. "But do it in your own time or it will sound artificial."

"All right. Dad, have you told anyone about our fight? Anyone here, I mean."

"No."

"Thanks."

Stefan first knew that Fiona was at *Kingower* while he, Kim and Catriona were walking to the homestead on Saturday evening. He and Catriona had spent the afternoon at their house checking to see how the work was progressing. "Now all that awful wallpaper's off the rooms look much bigger," he told Kim.

"Fiona's here," she said cautiously.

He was pleased it was dark.

"I thought she was in Queensland." Catriona sounded equally cautious.

"She's staying the weekend."

Certain that his voice would betray his guilt, Stefan said nothing. He took Catriona's hand and squeezed it. They reached the homestead and walked up the steps to the verandah in silence. He braced himself to meet Fiona, aware that neither Catriona nor Kim knew she was May. The eight weeks since he had almost broken their engagement had been happy ones. He spent the weekends at *Kingower* and had begun packing his possessions in Melbourne. They had bought material for the curtains, chosen carpets, and wedding presents had begun to arrive.

Keeping thoughts of Fiona at bay had been easier as the time passed. Their imminent meeting filled him with trepidation. 'She can never be mine. And I don't want her,' he told himself as he entered the lounge.

The convivial atmosphere of the night before had vanished. A huge fire blazed in the fireplace, but the cosy ambience was replaced by coldness. Even where they stood proclaimed which side they were on. Fiona, Alex and Ruth were by the fire while Margot, David and his wife stood apart near the French windows. Stefan tried to avoid looking at Fiona, but could not. His spirits plummeted. She wore a Black Watch tartan skirt, black tights and patent leather shoes, and a yellow jumper over a white blouse with a round collar. The pleated skirt was six inches above her knees and revealed her long shapely legs. She could have been a model at a photo shoot. As he took in her appearance it occurred to him that, if asked, he would not be able to say what Catriona was wearing. He had seen Fiona twice before and could remember exactly what she had worn on each occasion.

After stilted greetings they went into the dining room where the table was set with a lace cloth, silver and crystal. Fiona's offer to help carry in the serving dishes was rejected. Stefan usually savoured family dinners at *Kingower*, especially in the winter when the room was illuminated by the log fire and candles.

"How are the wedding plans, Tree?" asked Fiona.

Catriona smiled at her and Stefan appreciated her effort. "Fine, thanks. How do you like Queensland?"

As Fiona enthused about *Eumeralla*, Stefan noted her voice had changed. It was softer and less staccato. 'She's got a slight drawl,' he thought.

"Queensland's so warm compared to Victoria. Even at this time of the year we have our meals on the verandah, we only eat inside if it's pouring with rain."

"How are the horses, Kim?" asked David.

The rebuff angered Stefan. Fiona said nothing more until they were having coffee and liqueurs in the lounge. When Ruth went to bed, and Alex left a few minutes later, Stefan was surprised that Fiona stayed. She stood with her back to the fire and from the sofa where he was sitting with Catriona he had a good view of her face.

"Is there a ride on tomorrow?" she asked.

"Not a public one, but if the weather's good we'll be going," said Kim. "So you might as well leave after breakfast – we won't be home till after five."

"I'll come too," said Fiona, sipping her curaçao.

"You can't," said Kim scathingly.

"Why not?"

"You can't ride," said David.

"Oh, I can sit in a saddle now."

Kim smirked. "Was it on a horse?"

"We do hard riding – not just walking round the paddock," said Catriona placatingly. "We go over the Great Dividing Ranges – it's steep and can be hazardous."

Fiona wandered over to the coffee table and took a chocolate mint from the silver dish. "I'd like to try."

'She's acting,' thought Stefan. 'Like when she let them know her father was a hero not a coward. She's got the same expression as she had then. She can ride now and probably quite well. Good for her.' Then he felt appalled by his disloyalty to the family. David's next words soothed his conscience.

Looking at Fiona with derision, he said, "You can sit in a saddle. Yippee. It's not sitting in it that counts – it's staying in it."

'You idiot,' thought Stefan. 'Why are all these usually kind, discerning people, imbeciles when it comes to Fiona?'

"Try me out on a gentle horse tomorrow morning," she said sweetly.

"I will," said David. "You're not riding anywhere without my permission. I'm not having my insurance premiums skyrocketing because you fall off and break something. And I don't want you screeching and frightening the horses."

'I'm looking forward to tomorrow,' thought Stefan, pleased that Catriona had not joined in the sarcasm. 'But here I am again taking Fiona's side against theirs.'

On their way back to the cottages Kim said, 'Didn't Fiona look like a tart? If that skirt had been any shorter you would have been able to see her knickers."

"I suppose everyone wears that length in Melbourne," said Catriona. "If I wore dresses I'd probably wear them short."

Stefan hugged her. "So would I."

Catriona laughed and after a few seconds so did Kim. But their laughter sounded forced.

"Anyway, Kim, I've seen you in a mini-skirt," he could not resist saying.

The next morning Fiona arrived at the stables dressed in jodhpurs, a white shirt and riding boots. Stefan, thinking how much the outfit flattered her, saw her wink at Alex.

Catriona handed her a hat. "This should be your size."

"I don't want a hat."

"No one gets on a horse without a hard hat," snapped David.

Fiona shrugged and put it on. Ruth, looking anxious, helped her adjust the chin strap.

David led a horse over to her. "We'll put you on Sugar."

Fiona stroked the horse's nose. "Hello."

"Mount and ride to the paddock," ordered David.

Fiona, apparently unaware of the audience, went on stroking the horse.

"Hurry up, we haven't got all day," said Kim.

"Just getting to know Sugar," Fiona said.

As soon as she turned her back towards the horse's head, Stefan knew she could do it. New riders invariably faced the wrong way and put the wrong foot in the stirrup. In a flowing movement she swung herself into the saddle. Inexperienced riders hopped around on one leg unable to find the strength to haul themselves up.

David looked dour. "Come to the paddock."

Obeying his instructions Fiona walked, trotted and cantered. Stefan had never seen anyone look so chic on horseback.

She rode back to David with a triumphant expression. "Well?"

He turned away. "Right, everyone, we're leaving in ten minutes."

Fiona's expression changed to anger. "Uncle David!"

He turned round.

"Interesting, isn't it?" she said. "How I learnt to ride when I had a good teacher?"

"Shame she didn't fall off and break her leg," Kim muttered.

Ruth, who was about to mount her horse, glared at her. "You spiteful girl!"

Kim went red.

"I'll enjoy riding with my daughter," said Alex as Fiona came through the gate.

Catriona trotted over. Stefan could see she was torn between the insult to her father and the need to be sporting. "Well done," she said neutrally.

'Fiona is May and she's going to tear this family apart,' Stefan thought. 'And they'll give her the means. Should I tell Tree who May is or will that make things worse? Can premonitions change anything? Did Oliver tell Kim about the snake or did she see it and imagine that he told her?'

"You look pensive," said Catriona.

"How old was Kim when she said Oliver told her about the snake?" he asked.

"Three. Why?"

"I was thinking about her May premonition."

"We still don't know who she is," said Catriona. "Let's go."

Stefan guided his horse towards the track wondering how she would react if she found out. 'Should I tell Fiona and ask her to stay away from *Kingower*? It's seeing her that makes me have these treacherous feelings,' he thought.

"You did well going up the mountain," Alex told Fiona as they rode side by side through the gum forest. "I'm proud of you."

"Thanks, Dad. I'd only ever ridden on the flat before." She sniffed the eucalyptus-scented air. "Tree was helpful. Do you think we can ever be friends again?"

Alex looked doubtful. "Kim's still hostile."

"She really believes I tried to nick her fiancé. Funny, now I can ride she loathes me even more. It hasn't endeared me to Uncle David either. I thought he'd admire me."

"David hates being wrong."

"Did you get on well when you were young?"

Alex shook his head. "He was very much the older brother, even though there are only three years between us. I loved *Kingower* as much as he did and regretted that I wasn't the heir. When I met Laurence and Johnny, I envied the way they shared everything. They were going to inherit *Acacia* jointly and it occurred to me that David and I could do that. When I suggested it to him, he reacted as if I'd said something obscene. Things got worse when I married your mother. He doesn't like her, he prefers passive women."

Fiona knew that the words 'your mother' were a test, so she chose not to react.

"They tolerated each other till after your first riding lesson," he continued. "She accused him of being a useless teacher. She's been proved right, hasn't she?"

"Well, I am the only failure he's ever had."

"That's charitable of you."

"It's the truth. He was okay for everyone else. Dad, why do you come to *Kingower* so much?"

"To ride, but mainly to see Margot," he said as they guided their horses through the shallow stream. "She was like a mother to us younger ones when Mum died."

Catriona trotted up to them. "This is where we have a race," she said, as they approached a clearing. "Do you want to join in, Fiona?"

She nodded. "I'm sure I'll come last, but I don't care."

"Sugar's speedy," said Alex. I've been on her a few times."

When they rode into the clearing the horizon was stained red from the setting sun. Fiona saw six kangaroos at the water hole. She felt ecstatic as she watched them bound away. "What a breathtaking sight."

"Line up for the race!" called David.

Alex pointed. "See that tree ... that's the finish. It's half a mile."

"Ready – go!" said David.

When Fiona found herself in the lead she put her head down over Sugar's neck. "Come on, girl!" She finished second, beaten by Catriona.

"Congratulations, Fiona," said Stefan.

"I don't think I really came second ... they must have let me."

Then she saw the expression of rage on Kim's face. She knew she shouldn't gloat, but the opportunity to get back at Kim for her gibes the night before, proved too great. "My brother's a fantastic teacher. Do you want me to ask him to give you some lessons?"

Stefan laughed.

Kim was furious with herself. She knew that it was her own fault she had lost Stefan's respect and affection. On Sunday night after he had left for Melbourne, she walked with Margot back to her house. "When Fiona beat me in the race I wanted to kick her. Now she can ride I hate her even more. If I was a good person I'd be pleased."

"If she'd been a good person she would have kept her hands off your fiancé," said Margot, opening her fly-screen door. "Come in, I'll make us some Ovaltine."

Kim sat at the kitchen table. "Last night I said Fiona looked like a tart in front of Stefan. How could I be so crazy? She looked classy. Her jumper looked like cashmere."

Margot nodded and poured milk into a saucepan. "Her skirt was too short, but I'm old and shocked by modern fashions. We should have guessed she could ride when she said she could sit on a saddle, but I thought her fear of riding was ingrained."

"So did I. Tree and I tried for years to get her to have another try, but she was too frightened. How on earth did she overcome it?"

"I've been thinking about that all day," Margot said. "Everyone overreacted after Fiona's riding lesson. Your father was furious with her for screaming and Virginia should have either stayed out of it or told Fiona that David would not have let anything happen to her. I felt sorry for Fiona that day. She was so excited about learning to ride. Virginia insisted on watching, which didn't help ... and her blaming your father turned a failed riding lesson into a family row which festered for years because she dragged Alex and Fiona back to Sydney. No one had time to calm down and talk things through."

Kim frowned. "I don't remember any of this."

"You had mumps."

"I remember having mumps."

"So do I," said Margot with a grimace. "You were a terrible patient – bored, miserable and demanding. If Fiona's riding lesson hadn't coincided with your mumps, things might have been different. You and Catriona would have been with her and she might not have felt frightened."

"Why wasn't Tree with her?"

"She was with you, because you refused to be left alone. I taught her to play Canasta so she could teach you and keep you both occupied. She was as bored and miserable about your mumps as you were."

"Wasn't Virginia worried about her precious Fiona catching them?"

"She'd had them. I also think that Fiona associated riding lessons with quarrels. Virginia in a fury is upsetting for adults, for a child it would have been worse. When Virginia told her to pack her case she cried and said she wanted to stay on *Kingower*. Even Ruth couldn't reason with Virginia."

"Aunty Ruth heard me being nasty this morning. I don't want her to think badly of me. If Oliver's right she won't be alive for much longer. Why does she favour Fiona – she's not a Lancaster, but she defends her every time, even when her guilt is conspicuous."

"Ruth thinks that being uprooted when she was a baby has blighted Fiona's life," Margot said.

Kim sighed. Until her broken engagement she had never experienced misery. Her childhood had been happy and her school-days, like Catriona's, had been a triumph of sporting and academic achievements. Because she had what even her tutors called a brilliant brain, she had found her veterinary studies easy and university had been fun. She was popular and had many good friends. Although Catriona had been upset when her first boyfriend preferred Fiona, she quickly recovered. The experience had made her wary, not bitter. But Kim had known her fiancé since their first day at university. He had never flirted with other girls and she trusted him. Finding him and Fiona kissing had devastated her.

Since then, she had had boyfriends, but none she wanted to marry.

"Things are going wrong," Margot said, putting their mugs and a plate of biscuits on the table.

Kim put her head in her hands. "I'm sure Stefan's besotted with Fiona. He tries to fight it, but he can't."

Margot nodded. "I felt that last night. I'm sure he'll call off the wedding."

"But what about the house they've bought in Whittlesea?"

"It can be sold. He can change his mind right up to the day of the wedding," Margot reminded her.

"I feel this family's walking along a cliff that's about to crumble. My premonition about Aunty Ruth was precise, but the May one was hazy. 'May is going to tear this family apart.' How? What does it mean?" She stirred her Ovaltine. "Do you and Dad know who May is?" she asked watching Margot's face. "You do, don't you?"

"Yes," Margot said after a long pause. "We didn't know if we should tell you. Can you stop a disaster from happening?"

"I have before, haven't I? The snake – it was a tiger snake. Tree was about to crawl into the bushes. It would have bitten her. I stopped that. And the foal – I saved her. Tell me."

"It's Fiona. When she was born her name was May."

Kim stared at her in horror.

"Some people cause destruction," Margot said slowly. "And fate helps them."

"Then we've got to stop her coming to *Kingower*."

"Difficult considering the way Alex and Ruth feel about her. And she's coming to the wedding."

"Then after the wedding she must be told that she can't come here any more."

"Oh, Kim, I don't know. Sometimes it's lethal to push against such people. It's wiser to get far away from them so they can't touch us."

"But we can't escape," Kim whispered. "She comes to us. What happens, will happen here – because of her."

CHAPTER 18

Fiona stared at the plate of porridge in front of her. "I'm too nervous to eat. My stomach's knotted."

"Don't waste good food," said Greg.

"What'll will we do if we don't get *Acacia*?"

Tom pushed the milk jug toward her. "Same as we're doing now. Tomorrow morning we might own it or we might not, but we'll still be sitting here having our breakfast."

"I hope no one else comes," said Gabriella who had stayed the night on *Eumeralla*. "Just us and the auctioneer."

Fiona looked at Keith. "How can you be so calm?"

June laughed. "You're too nervous to eat ... he's too nervous to talk."

"I'm not happy about the Clarkson contingent coming to the auction at all," said Greg. "I'm sure you'll get too excited and bid. Why don't you all stay here?"

"No!" they protested together.

"Come on, Sis, eat," Tom urged her.

She sighed. "I'll be sick if I do."

"Don't vomit anywhere near me," said Gabriella. "Stop the melodrama. We're going to an auction not a hanging."

"If we don't get it someone else will, so just pray that they will be better than the last lot," said Greg.

"And also pray," said Tom, "That they've got two gorgeous daughters – one for Neil and one for me."

"And two eligible sons," said Fiona. "One for ... " she trailed off, regretting her thoughtlessness.

"One for you," Gabriella said with a smile. "And one for me."

For the first time Fiona reflected on a positive outcome of losing the auction.

They arrived at *Acacia* so early Fiona had thought they would be the first. To her dismay the area around the new homestead, where the auction was being conducted, was crowded.

"Hell," said Keith. "Let's wander round ... it might be our last chance."

When the auctioneer walked up the steps to the verandah, Greg pointed to Keith, Gabriella and Fiona. "Why don't the three of you go back to *Eumeralla* and wait?"

"No," they said.

"I'll do the bidding. Is that understood?" he demanded.

They nodded.

"Don't look at the auctioneer, and if you do don't move your heads," said Tom.

Greg led the way to the back row.

"Aren't you sitting in the front?" asked Fiona.

"No," he said softly. "The less people who know I'm bidding the better."

As they sat down, Keith took out a good luck card.

"Who's that from?" Fiona asked.

He gave it to her and she opened it.

To you all, I'll be praying on the day. Love, Virginia.

Feeling a rush of emotion she handed it back to him.

At first the bidding was slow. Fiona's hopes soared. She wished she could see if Greg was bidding, but he was sitting slightly back at the end of the row. Aware of Tom's warning, she was too frightened to move. She knew he would only bid if the auctioneer's hammer was about to come down. They still had not reached their limit, and the hammer had almost come down four times. Clenching her fists so tightly they hurt, she gazed at the pattern of horseshoes on the card Keith was holding.

The price crept up to their limit.

And reached it.

And passed it.

Fiona buried her head in Keith's shoulder. She felt his arm go round her. Virginia's card fell to the ground. When the auction ended June flung her arms around Keith.

Tom put his fingers under Fiona's chin and gently lifted her head. "We've still got *Eumeralla*. We've lost nothing. We just haven't got what we wanted."

Tears ran down her face. "I know. A few months ago I was an only child. Now I've got a twin sister and brothers and I can ride."

He hugged her. "That's the spirit. Keith's better off too."

Greg stood in front of Eleanor. "We didn't want to live in that hideous new house, did we?"

She looked crestfallen. "Yes. I reckon we've earned a bit of luxury. We were so close ... only five thousand dollars over our limit! Surely we could have gone over that much?"

"No, Eleanor, we would have been too much in debt."

"Not if we'd accepted Virginia's offer. She was giving us money, not lending it."

"It would have been a debt of a different kind," he said. "Keith was right. We had to do this by ourselves."

"We didn't do it at all," she snapped.

"Who bought it, Greg?" asked Gabriella.

"No one we know," he replied. "What are you going to do now, Gabby?"

"Cancel the sale on my house or else I'll end up with nowhere to live."

They walked out to their cars. Keith pulled Fiona aside. "I'm going back with Gabby – I'll stay the night with her."

"Can I come too?"

"Sure. Greg, the Clarkson contingent are going to Gabby's. We'll be back tomorrow."

Gabriella took a bottle of champagne out of the fridge. "Shall we drink it anyway?"

"I'll ring Aunty Virginia first," said Keith.

"I'll do it," said Fiona.

He looked at her in surprise. "Good on you."

"It's silly," she said, picking up the receiver, "but my first thought when they went over our limit was how disappointed she'd be."

As she dialled the number she heard Keith and Gabriella going outside.

"Hello," said Virginia.

"Mum?"

There was a moment's silence. "Yes."

"It's me." Fiona always said that when she rang either of her parents.

Usually her mother said, "Hello, me." Now she said, "What's the matter?"

"We've just got back from the auction – we've lost *Acacia*."

"But are you all right?"

"Yes."

"That's the main thing. I thought something was wrong."

"There is. We've lost *Acacia*." She found it hard to speak.

"There are worse things to lose." Virginia's voice sounded as strained as her own.

"Thanks for offering to give us money."

"Fiona, it's lovely to hear your voice. Where are you ringing from?"

"Gabby's."

"Well, I mustn't run up her bill. Thanks for letting me know about *Acacia*."

"Before you go – Keith and Juju are mad about each other."

"Really? That's good. Give Keith my love. Tell him I'm sorry. And Gabby too."

"I will. Bye, Mum."

"Good-bye, Darling, thanks for ringing."

Fiona put down the phone and went out to the swimming pool.

Keith handed her a glass. "To us, the Mitchells and *Eumeralla*," he said. "And the new owners of *Acacia*."

"Very sporting," said Gabriella.

"Some of the reasons I had for wanting *Acacia* were unworthy," he confessed. "I wanted to get back at a few people."

"Who?" asked Fiona.

"My first girlfriend's parents. They were rich. We wanted to get married, but her father didn't want his daughter to marry a postman. His house was vulgar and so was he. He didn't even hold his knife properly. I've put up with slights from rich snobs who think their money makes them better than me. But that was a poor reason for wanting *Acacia*."

"But you had other reasons too – good ones," said Gabriella.

Eumeralla
August 1972

How I wish I could write – The Old Homestead, *Acacia*. Greg found out who'd bought it and he's written to them welcoming them to the Darling Downs and inviting them to visit when they've settled in.

Mum asked Gabby if she'd like to go to Sydney for a holiday, but her temporary teaching job's been extended till Christmas, so Mum's coming up to Queensland for two weeks. She's lonely in Sydney without Dad.

Gabby's cancelled the sale of her house, but I'm selling my unit. I've got a buyer and it wouldn't be fair to pull out. I asked Greg this morning about me putting money into *Eumeralla*, but he still thinks I should give it a year. He must doubt me. I'll show him. The big news is that we're getting electricity in two weeks, but only in this house. We had a vote on whether to get a flushing toilet or electricity. Eleanor and I wanted a new toilet, but we were outvoted. Tom, Neil and Keith will still be on lamps and torches, but as they eat here it doesn't matter. Keith's washing machine is standing ready in the laundry. Electricity will save lots of time, but I'll miss the lamps – they were romantic. But none of us will miss taking all day to do the washing.

Ω   Ω   Ω

As soon as darkness fell, Eleanor flicked the switch and the room flooded with light from the naked bulb in the middle of the ceiling. "It's as bright as day."

Fiona screwed up her eyes. "It's awfully harsh. We need light shades."

"Let's try out this washing machine thing. You and Keith can show us how it works," Eleanor said as they all went into the laundry.

Fiona put a pile of sheets in the machine. She put in the washing powder and turned on the switch. "That's it," she said.

Eleanor looked incredulous. "We don't have to do anything else?"

"No," Keith assured her. "All we have to do is hang them out."

Greg looked dubious. "I'm sure it'll use too much water."

"Don't be such a drag," said Eleanor.

"It'll be worse than a drag if we run out of water."

Keith, seeing Eleanor's mutinous expression, spoke before she could say anything more. "The drum of the machine is a lot smaller than the copper and those two sinks. Shall we measure the water levels and see how things are after a few weeks?"

Greg grunted. "All right, but if that thing uses too much – it's going."

"If the cavemen had had your mentality, we'd still be living in caves," said Eleanor.

Eumeralla
September 1972

Today we met the new owners of *Acacia*. They are in their thirties and have three young sons. They came in a Bentley. They seem nice, the children are well behaved and the dogs liked them. They're living in the old homestead, which they adore, and they're going to demolish the new one. Mum will be pleased that the home she loved so much is appreciated by someone else. One of their first priorities is to begin a tree-planting project. Because they don't want to compete with us they'll grow cotton instead of wheat, but they will have sheep for wool. And they are enthusiastic about our barter system. They have a big shearing shed and said we could use that. It's good that they've got lots of money – they'll spend it on things that are important.

We went on a shopping spree and bought a fridge to replace the ice chest and an electric cooker to replace the wood stove. We bought bedside lamps, a supply of light bulbs and shades too. Greg tried to curb our spending, but Eleanor wouldn't let him.

$$\Omega \quad \Omega \quad \Omega$$

"Keith, you look so well," said Virginia when he met her at Brisbane airport. "How's Fiona?"

"You'll see for yourself soon."

"Really?"

He put her cases in the boot of Fiona's MG. "It was going to be a surprise, but, yes she wants to see you."

Virginia felt a flood of happiness. On the drive out of Brisbane, she tried to work out what she was going to say. 'Hello, Fiona, how are you? No, I can't say that ... not after all the bitterness between us. Oh, Fiona, I'm sorry.' She took a breath intending to ask Keith what he thought, but asking a twenty-three year old for advice seemed ridiculous.

By the time they reached *Eumeralla* Virginia's excitement had evaporated. 'I'm sure to say something rash and upset her again,' she thought.

"Are you okay, Aunty Virginia?"

"I've longed for this meeting, but now the moment's almost here, I'm ..."

"Just be yourself."

"Being myself has never worked with Fiona."

Keith stopped outside his cabin. "This is where I live."

"Greg lived here with his father," said Virginia. "He was ancient – well he probably wasn't really, he just seemed it to Eleanor and me. He used to tell us stories about when he was a drover." She looked at the beginnings of a garden and the path edged with seedlings leading to the front door. "This will be lovely when it's finished."

They went inside. "It looks better than it did in his day." She looked at the oil lamps hanging from hooks in the ceiling. Even with limited furniture Keith had made it homely. A bookcase was full of paperbacks, Laurence's chess set was on a low table and the only armchair was covered with a cream cotton throw. Other spaces were filled with family photographs. To her surprise Francesca's photo stood on the window sill. She picked it up.

"Part of Dad's history ... it seemed wrong to keep it hidden," he said.

She nodded.

"Now we won't be moving to *Acacia*, I'll make improvements. I'm going to build a verandah. Let's go for a bit of a walk." He looked at her smart white linen suit and high heeled shoes. "Will you be okay?"

"Yes, fine. I didn't know we were coming to *Eumeralla* or I would have worn more sensible clothes." They went outside and she looked round appreciatively. "This reminds me of *Acacia* – all the glorious trees." She heard a horse and shaded her eyes. "It's June. I nearly said Fiona."

Blonde hair flying behind her, the rider cantered up to them.

"Hello, June. I'm Virginia – your aunt."

"Hi, Mum."

Virginia looked at her in astonishment. "You can ride!" She turned to Keith, but he had gone.

Fiona grinned. "Tom taught me. I take it Dad didn't tell you?"

"No. Whenever I ring him he hangs up." Virginia looked at the ground. There was an awkward silence. "What's the plan now?" she asked. "Is Keith taking me back to Gabby's?"

"No way! Eleanor's itching to see you again. You're staying for dinner. Neil and Juju are cooking something special." She dismounted. "Let's go up to the house."

Virginia stroked the horse's head. "What's his name?"

"Monty," Fiona said, taking the reins.

"How's your father?"

"Not his usual self. I'm sure he's missing you."

They walked in silence for a while. Virginia was terrified of saying the wrong thing and she knew Fiona found it hard to make up after a quarrel. 'I've got to tell her I'm sorry,' she thought. "I haven't apologized yet," she began hesitantly. "But I can't make excuses for the lies I told. To say 'sorry' sounds trite – but I am sorry I was a bad mother."

"I was a bad daughter."

"No you weren't ... it was me."

Fiona stopped to let Monty graze. "You and I should never have been mother and daughter. I was a disappointment – "

"No you weren't."

"I was. You needed a well-behaved child. It must have been awful being besieged by complaints from the teachers whenever you visited the school. And I needed a relaxed mother. You were too fussy and forever worrying. I felt you were always watching me."

Virginia chose her words carefully. "I had this fear that something would happen to you. When you were ill I fretted in case it was fatal, when you were late home from school I thought you'd had an accident. I hoped you'd just missed the bus, but I dreaded that you'd fallen under it. Whenever you were late back from the beach I thought you'd been attacked by a shark. When you started going out with boys, if you weren't home by midnight I worried that he'd crashed the car and you were dead or in hospital. It sounds absurd, but you were precious to me. I had no idea I was damaging you."

"Monty, hurry up. There's better grass in the paddock."

"Er, does Eleanor know that I told you she was ..."

"An alcoholic? No."

"Thanks for not telling her."

"Did you know that Jonathan was unfaithful?"

Virginia was startled. "What? Fiona, you change the subject so dramatically. You never warn anyone – you just plunge in. What makes you think he was unfaithful?"

"Eleanor said he was. How did you feel when he left her?"

"Upset and furious with him. I went to Brisbane to persuade him to come back. He said he loved Eleanor, but was desperate for children."

"So he must have been intending to find another woman?" Fiona said as they reached the paddock.

"Well ... yes. But there wasn't anyone on the scene when I was in Brisbane with him. He was dejected and missing her and *Eumeralla*. Even if you and June hadn't been born, I'm convinced he would have come back eventually. He wasn't suited to suburban life, even though he'd made friends and joined cricket and tennis clubs." She opened the gate and followed Fiona through. "If he had found another woman I doubt the marriage would have lasted long."

"Maybe he was planning on getting some girl pregnant and then bringing the baby back to Eleanor," mused Fiona, as she took off the bridle and reins.

Virginia shook her head. "That would have been despicable."

"But he wanted Eleanor and he wanted children. He might have seen it as a way of getting both," argued Fiona, hanging the reins over the fence.

"Johnny didn't use people. He wouldn't have put a woman through hell just to get what he wanted. And he was so straightforward I can't imagine him being devious enough."

Fiona bent down to undo the girth. "But some woman might have loved him to distraction. It would be her suggestion, you know – a noble sacrifice. She would see her reward as being his gratitude. Perhaps they had a pact. She could see the baby and be its godmother or something. And at the end of the war there was a shortage of men. Especially handsome ones."

"Oh, Fiona, you're letting your romantic imagination run riot. If that was so, he would have told Eleanor and he didn't."

They left the paddock and walked to the house.

Eleanor waved from the verandah. She ran down the steps and threw her arms around Virginia. "It's wonderful to see you." She laughed. "Stop crying, you'll set me off."

Virginia's tears were partly emotion and partly shock as she looked in vain for the young woman she had known. It was not just the grey streaks in Eleanor's hair: she looked weary and the skin under her eyes was wrinkled and smudged with dark rings. Her hands were mottled with liver spots and her face and neck were leathery. Only her brown eyes with their clear whites were the same. 'She's let herself go,' thought Virginia. 'But at least she's still got a husband. Have I? Probably not.'

Eleanor linked her arm through Virginia's and walked to the steps. "Tomorrow we'll go for a ride ... just the two of us and we can catch up on the last twenty four years."

"Fiona told me you thought Johnny was unfaithful," said Virginia as they rode the horses at walking pace beside the creek the next day.

"He left me because he thought I couldn't have children, so he wasn't going to live like a monk, was he?"

Virginia wondered if Fiona's theory was correct. Jonathan had loved Eleanor since they were children and his devotion had never wavered.

"When he came back, why did you send him away?"

"I couldn't hurt Greg. We were engaged. He was a good man."

"Did you love him ... Greg, I mean?"

Eleanor stopped and dismounted. Crossing her arms she leant on the horse and buried her face in his mane. "Oh, God," Virginia heard her murmur.

She slid out of the saddle. "Eleanor. I'm sorry."

"I was going to tell him I couldn't marry him. I sent Johnny away to punish him and show him that he couldn't just pick me up when he felt like it. Greg doesn't know, but I was going to break our engagement and have Johnny back."

"Did he admit he was unfaithful?"

"No. I only found out a year after he'd died."

"Who told you?"

"No one."

"Then what makes you think he was?"

Eleanor's expression was bleak. "I just know."

CHAPTER 19

Eumeralla
September 1972

The garden is ablaze with colour. The yellow of the wattle and the purple and blue of the jacaranda and virgilla trees contrast with the green leaves and grass. Spring has always been my favourite season – here it's even more so. But, as Tom reminded me when I was raving about the beauty, the snakes are coming out of hibernation. We've got to be extra careful because they are a bit dopey so we're more likely to tread on them.

I've been helping to get the sheep over to *Acacia* for shearing. Red's fantastic at rounding them up. The men hardly had to whistle at all. Toddles was good too, but not as nimble as Red, who was more alert. He's got remarkable reflexes. The sheep went into the shearing sheds dirty and scruffy and came out white.

My unit has been sold, and Dad is renting a flat near Aunty Ruth. I was hoping he'd go back to Sydney. I got a letter from Mum and she's upset about it. She's written to him and he replied, but she said it was a brief letter. Fortunately he didn't mention divorce, just told her they would see each other at Tree's wedding and he'll meet her at the airport.

Now I look back on the weekend I spent at *Kingower* I can see that my behaviour was petty. Instead of leading them on, I should have told them I could ride. I want to put the past behind us and start again. I'll try hard at the wedding. I've written to Tree and Kim to let them know how I feel.

Ω Ω Ω

Kim finished reading Fiona's letter. "Huh, I doubt she's sincere."

"We should try trusting her," said Catriona who was opening wedding presents.

"Don't be naive. We trusted her once and she betrayed us. Not just me, but you too."

"People change. She's happy now." Catriona added a name to the list of thank-you letters she had to write. "She's found her real family and she can ride. Maybe she was jealous of us and that's why she nicked our boyfriends. And she's apologized for the way she behaved in August, and I think you and Dad should say sorry too."

"Why should we?"

Catriona folded up the wrapping paper. "Think back to that night, Kim. You and Dad were obnoxious to her."

"She set out to make fools of us."

"It wasn't hard to do, was it?" said Catriona, putting the wedding cards on the mantelpiece. "We should have asked her if she'd learned to ride. After all she'd been living on a big sheep station since April."

Kim chewed her lip. "Tree?"

"What?"

"She's May."

"She can't be."

"She is. When she was born her name was May. Aunty Margot told me."

Catriona snatched Fiona's letter and tore it up.

"Is it too late to tell her not to come to the wedding?" Kim asked, grateful that the revelation had altered her attitude.

Catriona went over to the window and stared into the garden. "Yes."

"Why?"

"She bought us a damask tablecloth and serviettes."

Kim threw up her hands. "Give them back."

"It's not that. It would be an aggressive act to tell her not to come." Catriona ran her hands through her hair. "She's been generous, and so have Uncle Alex and Aunty Virginia – they gave us a canteen of silver cutlery. We can't upset them."

"Tree, this family is in danger from her."

"No, Kim. It would make us look vindictive. Aunty Ruth would go mad. She'd never speak to us again."

"We'll have to tell her about my premonition ... just the May bit."

"Fiona's mostly up in Queensland now so hopefully we won't see much of her."

Kim, thinking that a great deal of damage could be done in one visit, said, "After the wedding Dad can tell Uncle Alex and Aunty Ruth what Oliver said. We can't risk having her here."

Eumeralla
September 1972

Kim and Tree have not replied to my letter. I hope it's because they're too busy. The wedding is this weekend. Tom and I are flying to Melbourne tomorrow and staying the night with Aunty Ruth and then we'll drive to *Kingower* together. He's getting excited – he's never been on a plane.

If everyone ignores me I'll be mortified. I hope they like Tom. It would be even worse if they ignored him.

The weather has warmed up. The mozzies and flies are out in force and we've stocked up on insect repellent. Fingers crossed, I haven't seen any snakes yet.

Ω   Ω   Ω

'I've never felt so fraught,' Virginia thought as she got off the plane at Tullamarine Airport. The sight of her thin face in the mirror that morning had not been reassuring and make-up did little to conceal the dark shadows under her eyes. The skirt of her mauve linen suit was so big she had to adjust the button and zip. There was nothing she could do about the jacket, which was now almost two sizes too large.

When she walked into the arrival lounge she saw Alex.

"Hello, Virginia. How are you?"

"Very well. How are you?"

"Fine." He took her case and they walked out to the car park.

The silence filled Virginia with misgivings. 'This is mad,' she thought. 'We've been married for thirty-four years – back there we sounded like strangers.' They got into the car and Alex drove towards Melbourne.

"I thought we were going straight to *Kingower*," she said, praying that he was not taking her to a solicitor to discuss divorce.

"We're going to have lunch first. You look as if you could do with a good meal."

"So do you." She relaxed a little. "How are you really, Alex?"

"Rotten. And you?"

"Rotten," she said, not caring that her voice was husky.

They went into an Italian restaurant in Carlton that Alex had discovered a week before. The red tablecloths gave it a cheerful atmosphere and the smell of garlic and tomatoes was appetizing. It was eleven o'clock and only one table was occupied.

As Alex chose a seat in a corner by the window Virginia felt her spirits lift, but she decided to keep the conversation light. If she apologized and talked about their marriage she would become overwrought. 'I'll never take him for granted again,' she thought, picking up the menu. 'He might have brought me here so he can talk about divorce without me making a scene. No, he wouldn't do that. Oh, God, what if he does? I will cry, I won't be able to help it.'

"Virginia, you look scared stiff."

She tried to smile. "Do I? No, I'm just a bit ... I'm sorry I drove you away. Yes, you're right ... I am. I've never been so scared. Even when I was in Singapore and the Japanese were coming I wasn't this frightened. I'm terrified you want a divorce."

"Why?"

"Because I've been so horrible." She looked him straight in the eye. "I don't want to lose you, but I know I deserve to."

The waiter came over.

"What are you having, Darling?" asked Alex.

Elated because he had called her darling, she said, "Minestrone soup and cannelloni, please."

When the waiter left, Alex said, "For years we've had this secret hanging over us. Now Fiona knows the truth, and we're both suffering from the repercussions. We've got to adjust."

"Yes." She buttered a roll. "Alex, have you missed me?"

"I didn't at first – it was a relief to be away. Sometimes I miss you. I'm pleased we're together now."

"I've missed you terribly."

He smiled. "Have you? Have you really?"

"Yes," she whispered. "Oh, Alex."

$$\Omega \quad \Omega \quad \Omega$$

'It's too late to back out,' Stefan thought as he stood under the shower on the morning of his wedding day. 'Leaving a bride at the altar is worse than divorce. I just hope I can get through the day without seeing too much of Fiona.'

After his shower he roamed around the house, which he had moved into a week ago. The decorators had finished, the carpets had been laid and the curtains hung. Catriona said that she could live with Scandinavian-style furniture if he could tolerate her colour scheme. Their bedroom was furnished with oak wardrobes, bedside tables, a chest of drawers and a king-sized bed all bought for them by her parents. Margot had given them a dining table and eight chairs. He and Catriona had hardly had to buy anything. Friends and his relations had bought them breakfast crockery, glasses and shining saucepans, which were neatly arranged in the large yellow and white kitchen. It would be years before they ran out of towels and bed linen.

"Everything's perfect," he said loudly. He sighed, went back to the bedroom and dressed in the expensive white shirt, silk tie and new suit that he had bought specially for the wedding. "I'm lucky," he told his reflection. "If I'd never met Fiona I'd be happy. Why am I thinking like a lunatic?"

While he waited for his best man to arrive he put a record of The Beatles' Ballads on the stereo. He was tempted to have a drink, but resisted. Turning up at the church drunk would be almost as bad as not turning up at all. While the *Song For No One* was playing he was aware of every word.

'A Love that should have lasted years,' sang Paul McCartney.

Stefan shut his eyes. "Oh, God, what am I doing?"

The first person he saw when he arrived at the church was Fiona.

His best man parked the car in the shade and followed the direction of his gaze. "Is that her?"

Stefan nodded.

"Wow. But she's too good for you or me, Mate." He went to open the door, but Stefan stopped him.

"Why?" he asked belligerently. "What's wrong with me?"

"She'll probably marry some millionaire or film star. And what's wrong with you, Mate, is that in an hour's time you'll be married. Smile. It's your wedding day."

"How the hell can I smile?"

"You know, Stefan, when we were at school and uni together, I admired you. You were clever, good at sport, and popular. When you and Tree got engaged I envied you. I don't envy you now, and I sure don't admire you. You've succumbed to the cheap allure of a flibbertigibbet."

Stefan felt like hitting him. "There's nothing cheap about her."

"How quickly you defend her honour."

"Well she's not flaunting anything, is she? If she was cheap she'd have a low neckline and a high hemline."

"True." He looked out of the car window and observed Fiona. "But I bet she's frivolous and self-centred."

"No, she's not. You said she was too good for you and me, so make up your mind."

"Okay. Shall we drive to *Kingower* and tell Catriona you want to call the wedding off?"

"I couldn't do that to Tree – it would humiliate her. She doesn't deserve that."

"She doesn't deserve to marry a man who doesn't love her."

"I do."

"No. You used to, but what you felt didn't prevent you from becoming smitten with someone else." He put the key back in the ignition. "You've stopped loving Tree – so let's drive to *Kingower* and tell her. She'll be humiliated and distressed, but she'll get over it and find someone better than you."

"That wouldn't be difficult."

"No. Lots of men are better than you at the moment, including me."

"You wouldn't."

"I might. Who's that man with Fiona?"

"I don't know," said Stefan. "It might be her boyfriend. I hope it is."

"Is the wedding on?"

He sighed and nodded.

"Don't be too enthusiastic, Stefan. Overexcitement's bad for you."

"Oh, very funny."

Fiona was standing so close to his car it was impossible for Stefan to pretend he had not seen her. She wore a yellow silk dress. A small cameo set in silver, and suspended on a navy velvet ribbon, hung round her long neck.

"Hi, Stefan. This is my brother Tom." She said 'my brother' with pride, the way a newly-married woman might say, 'my husband.'

Throughout the marriage ceremony Stefan was in a daze. When they came out of the church, people who had not been invited were waiting outside for Catriona. Children whose pets she had saved or had comforted when there was no hope, thrust gifts into her hands. Stefan felt mean that he had made her scale down the wedding. Although they had been excluded, their lack of resentment made him realize the extent of the goodwill the Lancaster family generated throughout the district.

"Do you like my dress?" Catriona asked as they posed for photographs.

"Yes," he lied, realizing he didn't have a clue what Catriona or Kim were wearing, while imprinted on his memory was every detail of Fiona's outfit. Round one wrist was a silver bracelet and on the other was a marcasite watch. He even noticed that she wore sheer pale-grey hosiery and that her handbag and high heeled shoes were navy. Her shining hair swung and the skirt of her dress moved enticingly when she walked.

Catriona's dress was a disaster of lace and frills. He had never seen her look worse. Her hair was piled high with corkscrew curls and topped with a lace veil and a headdress that added two inches to her height. 'The bloody hairstyle looks like Medusa's,' he thought. Her few attempts at dressing up were rarely successful. She looked best in jodhpurs, slacks or tailored suits worn with a plain shirt.

"Who's that chap with Fiona?" asked Kim as the photographer organized them into groups.

"Her brother," Stefan said. He saw the gleam of interest in her eyes.

After the photos they got into the wedding cars under a shower of confetti and drove to *Kingower*. As the vintage Rolls Royce drove slowly up the drive Catriona squeezed his hand. "The rhododendrons and azaleas are at their best ... divine, aren't they?"

He nodded, and saw the bees flying into the flowers that ranged in colour from white and cream and the palest pink to the deepest red. This time last year he had gloried in the spectacle. Now he felt that the myriad colours were imprisoning him. He stared at a bush heavy with flowers that were the same yellow as Fiona's dress.

To his dismay the seating arrangements at the wedding breakfast meant that Fiona was in his direct line of vision. Trying not to look at her absorbed him so much, he was scarcely aware of what anyone was saying. He roused himself sufficiently to make his speech, but knew that his words lacked credibility. When the room was cleared for dancing, his best man had to prompt him to lead Catriona onto the floor. When they cut their wedding cake Fiona was the first person he saw when he looked up.

Kim was debating whether to go over and introduce herself to Fiona's brother when Fiona saw her looking at them, and came over.

"This is my brother Tom," she said. "He taught me to ride."

Kim braced herself for a sarcastic remark.

He held out his hand. "Hi. You and your sister are vets, right?"

She looked at his genuine smile and decided that they were not going to gloat at her. "Yes."

"Bet that's handy, I wish we had one in our family. Fiona told me all about the riding school and treks. It sounds great."

As they chatted Kim became increasingly interested. His relaxed personality combined with his looks made him attractive. Wavy dark hair just touched his collar. Its haphazard cut added to his air of carelessness, which was at odds with the sophistication of the grey suit, white shirt and red silk tie he had borrowed from Alex. His skin was tanned and his hands were calloused and strong. She noticed that many of the females in the room were looking at him.

Stefan was pleased when it was time to leave the reception. As he waited for Catriona to change into her going-away outfit, he hoped that their two-week honeymoon on The Great Barrier Reef would enable him to recapture his old feelings of contentment and love for her. 'And I will forget about Fiona,' he vowed.

David's voice broke into his thoughts. "Make her happy, Stefan."

"I will," he promised.

When she walked into the drawing room his smile was genuine. Divested of the unflattering wedding dress, she wore a suit in honey-coloured velvet and a black satin blouse. The gold horseshoe pendant, that was his wedding present to her, hung round her neck, emphasizing its length and slenderness. She slipped her arm through his.

He kissed her. "You look ravishing."

Kim ran forward with the bridal bouquet. "You've got to throw this!"

Catriona laughed. "I'd forgotten. Ready, girls?" she called.

The bouquet of irises and daffodils sailed over Kim and Fiona's heads and was caught by the receptionist who worked at the veterinary surgery. Amid cheers Stefan and Catriona ran out onto the verandah, down the steps, and to the car that was waiting to take them to Melbourne.

It was after midnight by the time all the wedding guests had left or gone to bed. Kim walked with Margot back to her house. She hitched up the skirt of her bridesmaid's dress.

"You danced with Tom a lot. He seems a pleasant young man."

Under the neutral tone, Kim detected despondency. "I like him, Aunty Margot."

"Fiona's brother."

Kim sighed. "It complicates things. He doesn't look anything like her, does he?"

"No. When are you seeing him again?"

"I'm going to show him our horses after breakfast and we might go for a ride. Depends how we all feel."

"What did you talk about?"

"He told me all about *Eumeralla* and I told him all about our riding school and the trekking holidays and weekends. We've got a lot in common."

"Yes. But, with you feeling like this, your father and I can't tell Fiona not to come to *Kingower*."

"Maybe it'll come to nothing. He might have a girlfriend in Queensland," she said, as they reached Margot's house.

"I don't think so ... not the way he was looking at you." She patted Toby. "No, you can't come in, go home with Kim."

"See you tomorrow, Aunty Margot."

When Kim got back to her cottage she took the pins out of her hair and tried to comb it, but it was so teased and lacquered she gave up. 'I'll do it in the morning when I have a shower.' She tried to sleep, but was too stimulated by thoughts of Tom. Shadowing her fantasy about him were darker thoughts of Fiona.

Tom had found Kim invigorating. She was as engrossed by the land and horses as he was. Looking forward to seeing her again he got out of bed and had a shower, hoping that they would go for a ride. When he went into the kitchen she was laying the table for breakfast. He stared at her. Dressed in jodhpurs and a white shirt she looked different. Her black hair, that yesterday had been dulled by spray, was now straight and glossy. "Gosh, Kim?"

She blushed. "I look different now I'm not dressed up," she said, sounding disillusioned.

"You look a hell of a lot better."

"Do I? How come?"

"Your hair's soft and I can see your figure now you haven't got that awful dress on."

"It wasn't awful!"

"Yes it was. You shouldn't have had all those frills and stuff. You should have kept things simple like Fiona."

Kim banged a packet of cereal down on the table. "You arrogant, rude, chauvinist!"

"No, I'm honest. And I said you look nice now, didn't I? You don't wear fancy dresses every day, do you? So I'm saying that you look good more often than you don't."

She went over to the dresser and took plates and mugs off the shelves.

"I can't wait to see your horses," he said, disconcerted by her silence.

"The invitation has been withdrawn. You can go straight back to Queensland."

"Okay." He looked sardonic. "Can I have some breakfast first?"

She glared at him.

"I'm not a chauvinist. I'm the first one to admit that you're brainier than me. I've got no gripe with women going to uni. They shouldn't be tied to the house, it makes them dull. I don't mind you being mad with me either, it shows you've got spirit."

She smiled.

"That's better. So, can we go riding today?"

"Yes. Help me set the table."

Kingower
September 1972

Tree's wedding dress was abysmal. It had a straight skirt which made her look taller and skinner than ever. A fuller skirt and slightly puffed sleeves would have suited her. Her headdress was the crescent moon shape that Anne Boleyn used to wear. It was satin and sewn with seed pearls, but although it was lovely it was too high for someone of her height, and the Tudor and modern styles clashed. Kim's bridesmaid's dress was supposed to be dusky pink, but it looked more dirty than dusky.

I must stop being negative. It sounds spiteful. The hymns and wedding marches were stirring and the quartet they'd hired for the reception played a good variety of music. The caterers were efficient and the food was delicious. A farmer, whose valuable breeding bull Catriona saved earlier in the year, paid for the three tier wedding cake, which was horseshoe-shaped. What an original and fitting touch.

The homestead was decked in superb floral arrangements, mainly daffodils and irises which were the flowers in Tree's bouquet. As that was the dominant colour scheme, Kim's dress should have been blue or yellow. The weather was fine with a cool breeze. All the windows in the dining room were open and there were tables and chairs in the garden.

I thought that it was going to be a huge wedding and they were going to hire a marquee, but there were not as many people as I expected. I asked Dad if he knew why, but he is as puzzled as I am. Aunty Ruth doesn't know either. I hope they're not having financial trouble. Stefan looked distracted, he was probably overwhelmed by all the fuss.

Tom is impressed by *Kingower*. I also think he's impressed by Kim! I hope he is. We're all going for a ride this afternoon.

Mum looked happier and so did Dad, but she's too thin. I was watching them at the reception. They were together most of the night. Sometimes when Mum looked at Dad, she was like a star-struck schoolgirl.

Fiona nudged Ruth when she saw Tom holding Kim's hand as they walked through the forest after lunch the next day. "Isn't it exciting?"

"You're pleased?"

"Yes. If they got together maybe we could be friends again."

"Kim's so cynical she might think that you'll try and turn him against her."

"I won't. I'll be happy if they start going out together. I want things to be like they were when we were young. At last everything's going in the right direction. Mum and Dad look like newlyweds and guess what? Juju and Keith are in love. Eleanor's a bit concerned about them being cousins, but I don't think it matters. Cousins are allowed to marry, so there can't be much risk of – Aunty Ruth," cried Fiona in alarm. "Aunty Ruth!"

Kingower
September 1972

Aunty Ruth fainted yesterday. Anyone would think she'd been bitten by a snake the way Kim and Uncle David panicked. We brought her back to the homestead, but she refused to let us call a doctor. She snapped at poor Kim. "I fainted, I didn't have a stroke or a heart attack." Today Aunty Ruth's looking preoccupied, but says she's just tired. I hope that's all it is. She's promised to have a check-up when she goes back to Melbourne.

Tom and Kim are getting on fantastically. Maybe she'll come to *Eumeralla* for a holiday. She and Tom are suited to each other. If they married she'd be my sister-in-law. That would heal our rift, especially if she knows I'm keen on the union. There's no way she'd think I'd want to seduce my own brother. I'm sure Eleanor would like her too.

It's strange here without Tree. It's the first time I've been on *Kingower* when she's not around. I hope she and Stefan are having a wonderful honeymoon.

Mum's just been in to tell me that she and Dad are back together again. Dad is going back to Sydney with her. She said that although she's been distraught it's been good for her. I'm glad they are not getting divorced and Mum does seem to have learnt a lesson. Tom and I are going to Sydney instead of Melbourne.

$$\Omega \quad \Omega \quad \Omega$$

When Tom saw Vaucluse, with its hilly streets, trees and lush front gardens, he revised his opinion about suburbs. Virginia and Alex lived in a house that had been built in 1900 and there was a spectacular view of the harbour from the back garden. Inside were thick carpets, velvet or brocade curtains and antique furniture. They went to Doyle's Restaurant in Watsons Bay and chose an outside table on the beach.

"I've never seen the sea before," he confessed as he gazed at the crescent moon's reflection on the water.

The next day, Fiona took him on a ferry from Rose Bay across the harbour to Sydney's Circular Quay. "If I had to live in a city I'd choose this one," he said as they sailed past all the green coves and bays. He pointed. "What's that thing?"

Fiona looked at him in astonishment. "The Opera House. It's famous, it's opening next year. You must have heard of it."

He shook his head. "It's amazing."

"So are the dramas. They began building it thirteen years ago. It should have taken three years to finish, but the architect had a fight with the government and resigned. It's financed by the Opera House Lottery." She became serious. "There was a terrible tragedy. The son of one of the first winners was kidnapped. When the ransom was paid the boy was murdered – he was only eight."

"I heard about that. It was on the news. They caught the man, didn't they?"

"Yes. He said he didn't mean to kill him, but he'd threatened to throw him to the sharks."

"They should have hung him."

Thirty minutes later they walked through the crowded city streets.

Tom looked up at the skyscrapers. "I feel hemmed in, Sis. Can we go somewhere quiet?"

She took him into the Botanical Gardens. They sat on the grass with sandwiches and iced coffee they had bought from the kiosk.

"I like your cousin," he said. "What's funny?" he asked when she smiled.

"You're so frank. City men would have brought up the subject of Kim more subtly."

"Do you reckon she'd come to *Eumeralla* for a holiday?"

"Ask her."

"I don't know." He felt troubled. "I've never lived anywhere else and when I stayed with school friends in town I pitied them because they lived in such a tiny place. Apart from *Acacia*, most of the properties round us are much the same as ours, but now I've stayed at *Kingower* and your parents' house I've seen real luxury. Not trash like that new homestead on *Acacia*, but the sort of things I'd buy if I was rich. I'd hate Kim to despise me."

"She's not a snob, Tom, and she won't despise you. No one would. They'd not be worth anything if they did."

"What do you reckon she'll think about our toilet?"

Fiona grinned. "She'll envy Keith his shovel."

Part Three

THE TRUTH

September 1972
to
February 1973

CHAPTER 20

"Fiona."

Catriona froze. She opened her eyes and saw Stefan's face. "What did you say?"

He turned his head into her shoulder.

"You called me Fiona."

"I'm sorry, Tree."

"Get off me," she hissed, shoving him away. Jumping out of bed she ran into the bathroom and turned on the shower. When she came out, wrapped in the white hotel towel, he was sitting slumped on the bed. He had put on his dressing gown.

"Tree," he said, standing up and holding out his arms.

She dodged out of his way, grabbed her nightdress and pulled it on. "Don't touch me. Don't come near me," she said through gritted teeth, as she strode to the door leading onto their private balcony.

"I can explain."

She spun round. "Go on then."

"It was a sort of joke. I started to say 'Tree,' but got muddled and meant to say, 'Catriona,' like that little girl at the wedding did, you remember, pronouncing the o. She sounded so cute."

She longed to believe him, but he was so transparent. If that had been the truth he would have been laughing about it and looking foolish instead of desolate. "Good try, Stefan." She went onto the balcony. He didn't follow her.

It was the fourth day of their honeymoon. Until that moment she had been blissfully happy. Everything had begun so well. As soon as they left *Kingower* Stefan had relaxed. The days had been an idyll. They had swum, snorkelled, sunbathed on the beach or made love. The sun was warm and not too hot and she had a pale golden tan.

Stefan's olive skin glowed with health. Their room was luxurious and overlooked the sea. The hotel served delicious food and they feasted on freshly caught fish, and pineapple, mangoes and pawpaws. Owing to the absence of vegetarian dishes in restaurants and hotels, Catriona always ate fish when she went out.

"I bet you're glad there's no vegetarian choice," Stefan had teased her on their first night when she ordered barramundi. "It gives you an excuse to forgo your principles for two weeks." He lifted his champagne glass to hers. "I admire you, Tree,' he had said as he poured out the champagne. "More than anyone I've ever known."

She had wondered then if she was imagining the regret in his tone. 'Now I know I wasn't,' she thought. She sat on the balcony waiting for the dawn. Through the open door she heard Stefan tossing and turning, getting out of bed and pacing the room. Once he came out and looked at her beseechingly. When she shook her head he went back inside and the cycle of pacing and getting in and out of bed began again. It gave her satisfaction that he was as sleepless as she was.

The following morning they tried to appear normal when they went down to breakfast. In the afternoon they sat in a glass-bottomed boat with the other tourists gazing at the vivid corals and brilliantly coloured tropical fish, which darted in and out of the reef. Catriona tried to listen to what the guide was saying. 'Fiona, Fiona, Fiona.' The words sang in her mind as she stared into the water attempting to banish the memory. Stefan reached out and put his arm comfortingly around her. 'The gesture from a friend, not a lover,' she thought.

The boat pulled into the jetty. He helped her out, guiding her away from the other passengers. They strolled along the beach.

He kissed her hand. "I'm sorry, Tree."

She looked up into the gently stirring palms. 'This is paradise,' she thought. 'We're two people suffering. We should be two lovers loving.'

He squeezed her fingers. "Let's go for a walk." When they reached a secluded cove he stopped. "I'm a bastard."

Catriona looked at her feet, which were powdered with fine white sand. "Do you want a divorce?" she asked.

"No."

"A separation?"

"No."

She fixed her eyes on a sailing boat near the horizon. "What do you want?"

"Us to be happy."

"You and me?" She swallowed. "Or you and Fiona?"

"You and me. I want to erase her from my mind, but it's hard. If only I didn't have to see her again – "

"If you'd been honest with me in June, I would have broken our engagement. I would have been unhappy, but not as much as I am now. I could have been going out with someone else instead of being married to a man who thinks about Fiona while he's making love to me."

"No, Tree, I don't."

"You did last night. So why didn't you tell me how you felt about her?"

"I didn't want to lose you. I still don't."

She folded her arms. "If we get divorced, I won't tell anyone about Fiona. I'll tell them you were impotent or I discovered you were a homosexual."

He laughed. "I love your sense of humour."

"I wish you loved me." She ran down to the water, trying to blink away the tears that flooded her eyes. "Damn you men," she cried when he caught up with her. "Why do you all have to fall for her?"

"I'm sorry, Tree."

"Stop saying sorry!" She pushed him away. "I don't want your pity. I want your love."

"You've got that – and a whole lot more too. Respect and admiration."

"But someone else has got your love as well as me."

"I don't know that she has. It's probably just lust."

She wiped away her tears. "Lust's easily cured ... supposedly. You just gratify it."

"That would mean being unfaithful to you and I couldn't live with that."

"I could if it cured you."

He took her face in his hands. "It's our honeymoon and we've discussed divorce, separation and unfaithfulness." He ran his fingers through her hair. "Can we combat this together, Tree?"

"Your fixation with her is nothing to do with me." She tossed her head and broke away from his hold. "We've been married less than a week and already we've got another woman haunting us." She pulled off her white T-shirt revealing her bikini top. "I'm going for a swim."

"Can I join you or do you want to get away from me? I'll understand if you do. I wish I could get away from myself."

She gazed at his remorseful face in despair. "Our friends think we're so lucky. My parents like you, you like them – I like your parents and they like me. We own an attractive house and in a few years we'll be able to afford an even better one. We've got no worries at all ... except your obsession with Fiona."

Eumeralla
October 1972

June and Keith are getting married next May. We're all so excited. Gabby's going to be the matron of honour and I'm going to be the bridesmaid. As soon as Keith and June told us, Gabby mysteriously said that she had something old for Juju. She came back the next day with the tiara that Eleanor, Francesca, Mum and then Gabby wore on their wedding day. Now all June has to do is find a dress that does it justice.

Kim's arriving in two weeks. Perhaps when she's away from

Kingower and the memories of our past we can forge a new friendship.

Eleanor and June were sitting on the verandah looking through the wedding magazines Hazel had bought.

"I don't like any of these," said June. "They're too fussy. And the prices ... I don't want to spend all that for something I'll only wear once." She looked at the tiara Eleanor had placed on the table to gauge what dress would look best with it. "Those pearls look real."

"They are," said Eleanor. "And so are the diamonds. It was part of the haul that made the Clarksons rich."

"Keith said they sold all the jewels in London and bought *Acacia* with the money."

"They sold most of them. The tiara was one of the pieces they kept as a memento. And I suppose they had to have some jewellery to support their claim to be aristocracy. There were cuff links too, but I don't know what happened to them. Margot's got the pearl necklace and ruby and diamond brooch."

"The horrible stepmother?"

"Contrary to what you've heard from Keith and Fiona, she was very kind."

June pushed the magazines away. "Have you still got your wedding dress?"

"Yes, presuming you mean my first one."

"Could I wear it?"

Eleanor often opened the suitcase when she was alone and took out the dress, but not wanting June to know the depth of her feelings for Jonathan, she said, trying to sound vague, "If I can remember where I put it. But it's probably moth-eaten."

June looked disappointed. "Maybe it wasn't a good idea. Dad might be hurt."

"I doubt it," Eleanor said, pushing back her chair. "He'll be grateful that he won't have to spend money on a new one. Let's have a look. It's more your style ... very plain. We got married in the winter too so it's got long sleeves."

The suitcase was on top of the wardrobe. Relishing the feeling that there was no need to be furtive, Eleanor took it down. "I think it's in here," she said, opening the clasps. It lay among tissue paper and cakes of lavender soap.

"It looks perfect," June said when Eleanor lifted it out and gently shook it. Made of polished Egyptian cotton it had a square neckline and a full skirt. "It's divine – more elegant than anything in the magazines. It must have cost a fortune."

"Margot made it for me."

"She sure could sew," said June, stepping out of her shorts.

Eleanor chuckled. "She knew that, left to myself, I'd turn up to the church in jodhpurs. 'Eleanor,' she said, 'You'll have to have a full skirt, because you're such a hoyden, you're bound to dash about in your wedding dress and I don't want you falling over.' She was convinced that I was going to run down the aisle so she gave me deportment lessons."

June pulled off her shirt. "What? Walking round with a book on your head?"

"No. Taking small steps instead of strides and walking slowly. Funny, she'd given up trying to gain Virginia's affection so she didn't include her in the lesson. But Virginia, perverse creature that she was, came to watch and joined in. We were all having fun, then it was if Virginia remembered that Margot had replaced her mother and she became sullen again. I'll always remember poor Margot's expression ... she'd started to hope."

While June got into the dress, Eleanor reached into the case and took out a small leather box. "Would you like this too?" she asked, putting the twenty-two carat gold wedding ring on the palm of June's hand.

"Yes, I would, if Keith doesn't mind."

"It was his grandmother's." Her throat tightened as she watched June slip it on her finger. Eleanor had wanted to keep it and felt treacherous removing it, but Greg had insisted on buying her a new one. It was only nine carats and, to Eleanor, it looked and felt cheap. She turned away and opened the drawer of her bedside table. The wedding photo in its enamel frame lay at the back. She gave it to

June.

"Mum, you were beautiful. You look so happy. You loved him a lot, didn't you?"

Eleanor nodded.

"Heaps more than you love Dad."

June's expression was sympathetic not accusing. Eleanor knew she did not expect an answer and would not have believed a denial.

"Old age is so sad."

"I'm not old, I'm middle aged."

"Yes, I know, but ... "

"I look older than I am."

"No, I didn't mean – "

"I'm not offended, Juju. I know Virginia looks twenty years younger than I do, but she's had an easier life."

When Eleanor had finished fastening the hooks on the back of the dress June slid the tiara onto her head and looked at herself in the mirror. "I feel like a princess."

"Greg will be pleased when we tell him how much money we're saving on your wedding."

Ω Ω Ω

"That's the washing done," Tom said, as he and Fiona pegged the sheets on the line. "It's unbelievable. The machine saves so much time."

"I think that your father's coming to like it," Fiona said as they went up the steps. "Even though he won't admit it."

Tom looked round the kitchen. "All the chores are done. Time for a cup of tea."

She picked up the wicker basket. "I'm going to pick the vegetables."

"Okay," said Tom. "I'll put the kettle on. Then we'll go fishing."

Fiona ran down the steps and walked to the vegetable garden.

"I've never seen weeds grow so fast," she said to herself.

A week ago it had rained heavily and the soil was peppered with green dots.

'Would Kim like it here?' she mused as she picked the tomatoes. She selected a lettuce and pulled two lemons off the tree to go with the fish. "What shall I make for dessert?" Imagining that the conflict with Catriona and Kim was healed she went over to the fig trees to see how the fruit was ripening. She was so absorbed in her daydream she was oblivious to the rustle in the long grass. When she saw the rearing snake it was about three feet away. As it lunged forward, she threw the basket at it and screamed. Toddles barked and burst into view.

Tom came tearing down the steps. "Sis!" He grabbed Toddles' collar.

"Snake," she gibbered.

"Stay, Toddles!" He shouted. "Did it bite you?"

"Don't know."

"What colour was it?"

"Brown."

"Stay still, Sis. If it got you, it's essential you don't move. Heel, Toddles!" He picked Fiona up and carried her up the steps.

Eumeralla
October 1972

The snake didn't bite me. Tom was marvellous. He took control of the situation and was very calming. Even if I had been bitten he would not have let me die.

Is that why I fell in love with him? Or would it have happened anyway? He was my mentor and gave me so much. It was when we were talking about the snake and he leant over and hugged me and said, 'I'm so glad it didn't get you, Sis,' that I wanted to respond to his brotherly hug in an un-sisterly way. I wanted us to kiss and more than kiss. The feel of his arms around me and his scratchy chin on my cheek aroused me more than I've ever been aroused. I remembered in time that he is my brother.

I'll have to leave *Eumeralla*.

When Gabriella arrived home from school she saw Fiona sitting on the verandah surrounded by suitcases. Her MG was parked in the driveway.

"Hi, Gabby. Can I stay with you for a while?"

"What's wrong?"

"A brown snake nearly bit me yesterday." She shuddered. "It reared up and its mouth was open."

"Sounds as if you were lucky to escape." She saw Fiona's bloodshot eyes. "There's something more, isn't there? Is Keith – "

"Everyone's fine. It's me, but I can't talk about it." She got up and walked over to the swimming pool.

Gabriella stood beside her and gazed at a gum leaf floating on the water. "When Brett died I didn't talk about it and look at the mess I got myself in," she said. "Have you and Juju had a row?"

"Don't, Gabby."

"Whatever it is you have to go back to *Eumeralla* and face it sometime."

"I'm not going back."

"Have you had a fight with anyone?"

"No."

They stood in silence for a few minutes.

'The happy Fiona's gone. The old Fiona's back,' thought Gabriella.

"Sorry, Gabby."

"It's all right. I'll get some wine." She returned with a bottle of wine in an ice bucket. "If you haven't had a row with anyone there's only one other thing that can be wrong." She filled a glass and handed it to Fiona who looked sceptical. "You've fallen in love with Tom."

"How did you know?"

"He's terribly masculine and genuine. You've been together for five months and he taught you to ride."

"Are we Clarksons doomed?" Fiona said. "Your father's first wife died, he lost *Acacia*, and never saw old age. Johnny died in a fire. You were a widow by the time you were twenty. I was separated from my twin when I was a baby and now I've fallen in love with my brother. Tragic footsteps, Gabby. We're cursed."

"Keith and Juju are happy."

"They're the only ones."

"Your mum and dad are too ... now. What are you going to do?"

Fiona shrugged. "Go back to Melbourne and stay with Aunty Ruth while I look for a job and a flat. I can't live in Queensland. Tom's too close and I'll be tempted to go back to *Eumeralla*."

That night when Fiona had gone to bed, Gabriella sat in the kitchen trying to concentrate on a crossword puzzle. Too many thoughts were swirling in her head so she abandoned it. Feelings of guilt and elation swirled through her mind. Her grief for Brett was fading. Now she could look at his photo without the gut-wrenching sorrow that made her contemplate suicide. She looked forward to visiting *Eumeralla* and it wasn't just to see Keith. It was because she would see Tom for her twice-weekly riding lesson.

It had been easy to guess the reason for Fiona's unhappiness. Apart from Brett, Tom was the nicest man she had ever met. It was not surprising Fiona had fallen in love with him. She was developing strong feelings for him herself. She didn't want to deceive Fiona, but she feared her reaction.

Fiona's departure mystified Tom. As well as savouring their chats and camaraderie he felt protective towards her. Being needed by a woman was an unusual event for him. His mother owned *Eumeralla* and he felt this put his father at a disadvantage and gave her a degree of dominance in the family. Their mother, not their father, was its head.

No one could understand why Fiona had left. June and Keith were upset and Greg was concerned. Neil was disappointed and said he missed her. To Tom's disbelief his mother was cavalier about her going.

"Mum, she's your daughter. Don't you care? I thought she loved *Eumeralla*."

Eleanor was in the middle of kneading the bread. "She didn't grow up here. She's a townie who convincingly played the part of a country girl and then got bored with it."

"You sound as if you don't like her much."

"Sometimes I don't."

"Mum! Why not?"

She threw the bread down on the board and a cloud of flour flew up in her face. "She doesn't belong here. She's like her father!" She began to cry. "He deserted too."

Tom was too angry to comfort her. He ran out to the car and drove to Gabriella's.

Fiona and Gabriella were in the swimming pool when he arrived. Fiona looked embarrassed and swam to the other end of the pool.

"Feel like a swim, Tom?" asked Gabriella.

He shook his head. "I haven't got any trunks."

"I'll lend you some."

He was just about to make a flippant remark about girls' stuff not suiting him when he remembered Brett. "Okay, thanks."

She hauled herself out of the pool and he followed her tanned, bikini-clad figure into the house. She found a pair of trunks and showed him where the bathroom was.

"Beautiful house," he said.

"Thanks. Come out to the pool when you're ready."

When he went outside Fiona was swimming and Gabriella was sitting on the side dangling her legs in the water. He dived into the deep end and surfaced gasping at the shock of the cold water. He swam over to Fiona. "Come back, Sis. We've got used to having you around."

"I can't. I'm too scared. I really am a coward."

"Not you're not. Is she, Gabby?"

"No."

"Juju's lost without you."

She looked despondent. "She'll get over it. She's got Keith. You and Greg were right to doubt me."

"You were nearly bitten by a dangerous snake. It'd put anyone off. I've never come that close."

"I forgot about the long grass. You warned me and I forgot. I can't come back this summer. Can I try again in the winter when they're all hibernating?"

"If that's what you want, Sis." But he gauged from her tone that she had no intention of returning.

After Tom left, Gabriella and Fiona went inside and changed out of their bikinis.

"What will we have for dinner?" asked Gabriella, pleased that Fiona was looking happier.

"Let's go out and celebrate."

"What for?"

Fiona smiled. "You like Tom – more than just like him."

Gabriella heard the choke in Fiona's voice. "I was going to tell you, but I didn't want to hurt you," she said, blushing. "I'm sorry."

"Don't be sorry. Be happy."

"You're a good sport, Fiona. How did you know about Tom?"

"I saw it in your eyes. You said the other night that he was – bloody hell!"

"What?"

"Tom's interested in Kim. She's coming to *Eumeralla* for a holiday."

Gabriella's spirits plunged. "She's a good rider, isn't she?"

"She lives in Victoria. You've got the advantage of being here."

"But she's clever."

"So are you."

Gabriella shrugged. "They met at the wedding, didn't they?"

"Yes."

"So he knew me, but he's interested in her, which means he's never been interested in me."

"He wouldn't have wanted to rush things with you. Kim's carefree and single – you're a widow."

"She's amazing with animals, isn't she?"

"It might put him off. He might think it's weird ... her mother does."

"Compared to her I'm just a boring teacher. What you said yesterday was right. We are cursed."

"Gabby, I was being melodramatic. There's no such thing as curses."

Gabriella looked grim. "What about curses one hundred years old? I bet those Victorian aristocrats cursed our ancestors when they discovered they'd stolen their jewels. They were powerful in the flesh ... what if they were powerful in the spirit too?"

As soon as Fiona arrived in Melbourne she began looking for a job. She avoided Ruth's subtle questions and tried to pretend she was cheerful. When Ruth commented that Fiona looked emotionally battered, she almost broke down, but felt too raw to confess what had happened. When she found a job with QANTAS Ruth bought a bottle of champagne which they drank with their dinner. When the bottle was empty, Fiona, slightly drunk, began to cry.

"Do you want to tell me about it?" asked Ruth.

Fiona blew her nose. "My brain knows Tom's my brother, but my hormones don't."

"Oh, Fiona."

"I long for *Eumeralla*. I miss them all. The only thing I didn't like was the toilet, but right now I'd give anything to be walking down the track and smelling its stench. I miss the horses and the freedom. Will I ever stop longing for it? Lucky that Juju and I are identical. Imagine if we didn't look much alike. Tom might have begun to have un-brotherly feelings. It would have been a disaster. I try to be grateful for that. After *Eumeralla* it's hard living in a city. I know what will happen when I start working at QANTAS. I'll make the same superficial friendships that I had at Ansett. We'll go to the pictures and the theatre and dinner and I'll be dissatisfied like I was before. I can feel myself becoming shallow again."

"You're not shallow and you never have been."

"I am, Aunty Ruth. When Juju came to Melbourne she helped me pack. My clothes were too delicate for *Eumeralla*, so we went into town. She told me to buy men's shirts and jumpers because they're hard wearing so we went into the men's department. As I was trying to work out what colours to get, she said, 'Does it matter?' I couldn't understand her because I saw clothes as a fashion item whereas to Juju they're just clothes. Now I'm back to caring about my appearance and what I wear. On *Eumeralla* I never did. I'm not doing anything important. If I had a better relationship with Tree and Kim I'd ask them if I could have a job in their veterinary clinic."

"What about nursing?"

"I'd have to train with young girls."

"Would that be so difficult given that you'd have a worthwhile career at the end of it?"

"I hate taking orders – I was always in strife at school. I'd find it humiliating being supervised by Sisters years younger than I am."

"Think about it. You've got a good brain."

"No I haven't. Tree and Kim are right. I'm dim. The teachers were forever complaining I didn't concentrate."

"You didn't do well at school because you were worrying about who you were. Thinking your real mother was an alcoholic must have disturbed you, whereas Tree and Kim knew who they were. They had the luxury of being able to concentrate on their school work."

Ω Ω Ω

When Ruth discovered a lump in her breast she went to the doctor who gave her an immediate referral to the outpatient clinic at the hospital where she worked. Tests and a biopsy were performed and the specialist sent for her as soon as he got the results. She could tell by his expression what he was going to say. She had known him for a long time and had once been the Sister in charge of one of his clinics. "It was malignant?" she asked, trying to make it easier for him.

"Yes. I'm sorry, Ruth. It's inoperable and I'm afraid it's spread. It's not a primary site."

"Good."

"Ruth I ..."

She knew that this was the first time any of his patients had claimed to be pleased when told they were dying. "I've never seen you so ruffled. How long have I got?"

"Six months at the most."

She was dismayed. "As long as that?"

"You've had a shock."

"No, this is the best news I've had for a long time." She stood up. "I'll resign immediately. A sick Sister could be a liability."

On the way home she bought a pad of the best quality writing paper. When she arrived home she went into the lounge and sat at her desk, pleased that Fiona was out. Filling her fountain pen with black ink she began to write. She wrote several drafts before she was satisfied. The final rewrite took two hours.

The next day she made a photocopy and put the pages unfolded in two large envelopes. With one she included an old letter. The postmark was smudged, obliterating the day and the month, but the words Brisbane and the year 1945 were clear. She sealed the envelopes. On the one containing the original and the letter, she wrote, *To be handed in person to Fiona Lancaster*. The other she addressed to Eleanor. She gave them to her solicitor with precise instructions.

CHAPTER 21

Melbourne
October 1972

Last night when Kim rang we were nice to each other. When Aunty Margot rang this morning I was nice to her. Aunty Ruth's illness is mending our conflicts. Uncle David asked her to move to *Kingower* and stay in Tree's old cottage. She's agreed. She'll be better off in the fresh air and she'll have more company. I'll miss her, but will visit every weekend. Although I'm terribly upset, Aunty Ruth's attitude is making things easier. She told me to think about her being in another country. She says she's happy to die. Perhaps she's being brave, but she does look serene. I was stunned when she told me that she's left me this house and all her money. I hope Tree and Kim don't resent me or think I've coerced her. Aunty Ruth says I'm the only person who knows, but they'll find out soon.

When I worked in Sydney I had a friend who believed in reincarnation. Some things she said made sense. People are born with debts and credits from previous lives. If we don't pay or get our rewards in this lifetime we pay or get them in another. It's called karma. It's scary because you don't know about it. But she said that your soul remembers. It's comforting to think that Aunty Ruth might come back, but when I told her this she said she wanted to die and stay dead and that only fools rave about life being sacred. She said that this life has been bad enough and she doesn't want another one, but refused to tell me why it's been so awful. It must be something to do with her not marrying.

The country is already gripped by election fever. The newspapers are predicting a Labor victory. I hope so. The Liberal Party has been in too long and since Menzies retired they haven't had a decent leader. Aunty Ruth is going to vote Labor, because she knows how much I want them to win. 'Don't tell David or your parents,' she said, 'They'll have coronaries.'

Mum hasn't mentioned the elections to me. Once she would have provoked me into defending Labor's policy and called me a communist.

Ω Ω Ω

Although Tom was looking forward to Kim's visit, he was apprehensive. It was her reaction to *Eumeralla*'s toilet that worried him most when he compared it to the modern bathroom in her cottage with its white tiles, shining chrome taps and hygienic-smelling lavatory. His father was annoyed with him for mentioning it in front of his mother, because she renewed her campaign for a new one. They compromised by deciding to paint it.

"A vet will be used to worse stinks," Keith assured him as they washed the car. "When did you last do this?"

"Two years ago. Might have been three. Kim's got a Mercedes. All we've got is a clapped out old rust bucket."

"Why are you so bothered?"

Tom rinsed the suds away. "What if she thinks I'm after her money?"

"You're not, so she won't."

"For the first time in my life I want to impress a girl." He frowned. "Hell, it looks worse clean ... the mud was covering the holes."

"We can polish it."

"Nah. It might fall apart with all the attention. Let's go and clean the dunny."

"What a fabulous place," said Kim as Tom drove down the track.

Relieved that the car had not broken down, he dared not stop in case it stalled, but he slowed so she could see her surroundings. Her enthusiasm sounded genuine and he was impressed that she noted the differences between *Eumeralla* and other properties they had passed. She remarked on the smaller wheat fields and the way they and the grazing pastures were interspersed with areas of woodland. The house came into view and he hoped she would not make unfavourable comparisons with *Kingower*'s homestead. He parked under a tree. "We made it." He grinned and switched off the engine. "We rarely go as far as Brisbane."

"Ah, look at the dog. It must be Toddles, because I'm assuming Red is red."

June came onto the verandah and waved.

Kim expelled her breath. "She's so like Fiona. I knew they were identical, but ... gosh."

As they went through the gate, Toddles bounded down the steps. Instead of running to Tom she went straight to Kim, who squatted to pat her.

"Watch out – here comes Red," June called in warning.

"Steady ..." Tom began to say, but to his astonishment Red was walking sedately towards them, his eyes riveted on Kim. He stood in front of her wagging his tail.

June came down the steps. "Crikey, he's usually hostile to strangers." She smiled at Kim. "You've got a fan."

Tom scratched his head. "Fiona told me you had a special way with animals, but ... I didn't think it was this special."

"Lunch is nearly ready," said June.

Tom was delighted by the way Kim fitted in at *Eumeralla*. Any natural awkwardness when a stranger is thrust into the midst of a close-knit family was erased by Toddles and Red's attachment to her. Knowing the history of the Lancasters and Clarksons, he had been worried that Keith might be cool, but he was diverted by Toddles and Red's refusal to leave Kim's side.

After lunch Tom took her to the paddock to see the horses. As soon as he opened the gate they trotted over. This was unusual unless they were hungry. Normally he had to whistle to get their attention. But they ignored him and greeted Kim with rapture.

He started at her in amazement. "You're magic."

She stroked the horses in turn. "Mum thinks it's spooky."

"Have you always been like this?"

Kim nodded. "When we were children Tree wanted a kitten so Mum and Dad got her two for her birthday. They carried them into our room and put them on her bed. But the kittens just gazed at me. They became mine."

"Did she mind?"

"She was upset at first, but she got over it. Now she accepts that every animal on *Kingower*, whoever it belongs to, is really mine. A few years ago Toby was dumped at the vets where we work. I was on holiday in Sydney and she brought him home hoping that she could make him her dog, but when I got back he moved into my cottage."

Tom smiled down at her. She smiled back and he kissed her. "Magic," he murmured.

That night Kim wrote to Catriona. After describing *Eumeralla* she continued:

> *Tom's teaching Gabby to ride. She and Keith are polite to me, but I can feel underlying antipathy, especially from her. To their credit they try to disguise it. Isn't it sad how the rancour from one generation spills into the next? Personality-wise June and Fiona are very different. June's friendly and, unlike Fiona, she has no idea how beautiful she is.*
>
> *Am I'm courting danger by having a relationship with Tom? Now that my premonition about Aunty Ruth has come true I'm uneasy about having anything to do with Fiona's family. But it's a divine place and I would be happy here. Tom's parents are great and we get on well*
>
> *There's no T.V. or stereo, just a radio. After dinner they play cards, chess, scrabble or read. They are all poetry fanatics. Greg's favourite is*

Banjo Patterson and Tom's is Henry Lawson. Juju and Neil like the war poets.

At the end of Kim's holiday Tom drove her to the airport.

"I'll miss you, Magic," he said as they sat holding hands in the departure lounge. "You'll come again, won't you?"

Kim put her head on his shoulder. "Yes. Will you come to *Kingower*?"

"As soon as I can."

She considered telling him about her premonition. That Fiona had obviously not told him about the conflict between them puzzled her. Remembering how she and Catriona had maligned her character before Stefan had met her, she felt a twinge of guilt. 'She told Tom that I was terrific with animals. We didn't say one nice thing about her to Stefan.'

When her flight was called they stood up and kissed.

"I'll miss you, Tom."

"Not for long, Magic." He wiped away her tears. "Now skedaddle, or the plane will leave without you."

Tom had never written to a girlfriend before. 'I've always said I would, but never got around to it,' he thought as he opened a writing pad. 'The excuse was that I was too busy, but now I reckon that I didn't want to.' He unscrewed the top of the ink bottle and filled the fountain pen he had borrowed from his mother. There was a name engraved on it and when he looked he saw that it had belonged to Jonathan.

Dearest Magic,

If I was a poet I'd write you a poem, but if I attempted it you'd laugh or cringe, depending on how bad it was. I miss you already and so do Toddles and Red. They ran up to the car when I got back and were miserable that you weren't with me. Not having you here is lonely. I've never been lonely before. I'm not a romantic bloke, but the night when you came back here and we read poetry to each other will always be one of my best memories. And you started reading **In Flanders Fields** *and got emotional and couldn't finish it. And then ... Wow! Those memories will have to keep me going till next time.*

"Gracious," June teased him the next morning when he arrived for breakfast and put the letter on the pile to be taken to the post office. "You've actually written to her."

Neil grinned. "You're smitten."

"Good," said Eleanor. "This place could do with a girl like Kim."

Tom frowned. "Her money, you mean?"

"No. For herself. I thought she was wonderful. Her way with animals was extraordinary. Id like to see you settled."

Ω Ω Ω

When Margot finished icing the chocolate cake she had baked for her friends, who were coming to play bridge that afternoon, she went into the garden to cut some flowers. 'Gold and white chrysanthemums for the lounge and red roses with fern for the dining room,' she thought. She was pulling on her gardening gloves when she saw Kim walking up the path. "Hello, sweetheart." She saw Kim's happiness with a feeling of dread, but managed to smile and say, "Your holiday was obviously a success."

Kim hugged her. "It was brilliant." She bit her lip. "Part of me was hoping that I'd lose interest in him once we spent a week together."

"All of me was," confessed Margot. "But I knew you wouldn't. He's an impressive man and you've got a great deal in common. I was immensely fond of his mother."

Kim picked up the wicker basket and held it while Margot cut the flowers. "But having such a close association with Fiona's family might bring the factors together that could destroy the Lancasters. I didn't tell Tom. If only Oliver would tell me what to do."

"Is Fiona going back to *Eumeralla*?"

"I don't know. Tom misses her and so does Juju, but Eleanor didn't want to talk about her. I thought it was strange."

Margot went to the rose bushes. "The whole thing's strange. If she's left *Eumeralla* for good maybe that's the safest place for you to be."

"But it's not just me, it's the whole family. I haven't counted Aunty Ruth. Mum's only a Lancaster by marriage. Does that count?"

"I don't know, Kim. She was Oliver's mother." She cut long-stemmed roses and laid them in the basket. "Don't fret about me, I'm too old. Catriona and Stefan aren't happy. They put on an act, but they're not convincing. I thought things would be all right once they got married."

"So did I." Kim buried her nose in one of the roses and inhaled its perfume. "But I suspect that Stefan's still infatuated with Fiona."

Margot pulled off her gloves. "Everything in this family begins and ends with her. Have you got time for coffee?"

"No, I said I'd got to the clinic and help Tree when I got back."

Margot watched her walk down the path. The sun caught her hair making it gleam like black enamel paint. 'God, please keep her safe ... and Catriona. I'll sacrifice myself to save them from danger.' She went into her bedroom and picked up the photo of Oliver that had been taken a few weeks before he died. As an infant he had looked as if he was deep in thought, as a child he was fey. "Protect them from peril, Oliver," she whispered.

$$\Omega \quad \Omega \quad \Omega$$

When the school day ended Stefan was reluctant to go home and when he did he shut himself in his study pretending to mark essays or set homework long after he had finished them. His reputation as a teacher was flourishing. He had set up coaching sessions after school for students who needed extra tuition for the end-of-year exams. In reality these were so he could avoid Catriona. 'Great teacher – useless husband,' he berated himself as he sat staring out of the window. 'Once I couldn't wait to see Tree at the weekends. Now we live together in a lovely house, with a lovely garden. We've got a cleaner and a gardener and plenty of money. There are no interfering in-laws. Just Fiona. And how the hell am I going to survive the summer holidays?'

Before their marriage Catriona had been radiant. Now, although she tried to pretend otherwise in front of others, with artificial laughter and smiles, she was miserable and jealous. Hearing her footsteps in the hall he pulled a sheaf of papers towards him and picked up his red pen. "Come in," he said when she knocked.

She opened the door. "Dinner's nearly ready."

"Oh, thanks, I didn't realize the time."

"I thought we could have it outside. How about some wine?"

He tried to look enthusiastic. "That'd be good."

She had put the garden table and chairs under a tree and the air was perfumed by the flowerbed, which was planted with stocks, dahlias and roses. The dinner should have been a joy, but their conversation, as they ate the cheese salads, was strained. Once, he knew, they would have discussed politics and the news and exchanged stories about their days at work. They would have looked forward to going to bed and making love. Almost without being aware of it, he finished his salad.

Catriona got up and took his plate. "Was that all right?"

"What? Oh ... the salad. It was delicious. Thanks."

She came back with bowls of strawberries and ice cream. "You're working very hard," she said. "Did you have to do all this coaching at Wesley?"

He put down his glass. "Is this an interrogation?"

"No! I just – " Her expression became combative. "Why the guilt, Stefan? Thinking about her?"

He pushed back his chair. Only the presence of the neighbours in the next garden stopped him from shouting at her.

Catriona followed him inside. "What is it about her?" Her voice trembled. "What is it?"

In the doorway of his study he turned round. "If you saw people throwing stones at a kitten, what would you do?"

"Try and rescue it, of course."

"That's how I feel about Fiona."

She looked incredulous. "It's my family that need rescuing from Fiona."

He shook his head. "You mentally torture her. All of you, except your mother who tolerates her, but only just. I've seen the supercilious way your father looks at her. I've witnessed some of the scenes. Margot, who you see as a saint, lied about her real father – "

"And Virginia, who's not a Lancaster, lied about her mother."

"Kittens have two weapons," he said. "Sharp teeth and claws. Fiona fights the *Kingower* clan with the only weapons she's got ... the truth and your inability to see her as she really is."

"We see her as she really is, Stefan. It's you who has illusions about her."

CHAPTER 22

On Saturday the second of December Catriona made the breakfast for herself and Stefan. She wore the cream silk nightdress and kimono that her mother had bought her for her trousseau. She squeezed the juice from four oranges, and began cooking scrambled eggs with the new utensils that had been wedding and engagement presents.

'I've got so much, but so little,' she thought. 'Now Aunty Ruth's coming to live at *Kingower* and Fiona will visit her every weekend and that will unsettle Stefan again. When he sees her today I'll want to look away, but I won't be able to. I'll look at him looking at her. He won't want to look at her, but he won't be able to help it. And she'll look at him and he'll feel unravelled.'

Stefan came into the kitchen wearing a burgundy dressing gown. 'Why do men look okay in the morning before they've showered and shaved and why do women look a mess? Or is it just me? I bet Fiona looks sexy.'

"Want me to do anything?" he asked.

'He's trying so hard and he shouldn't have to. It should come naturally,' she thought desperately. 'If I was Fiona he'd smother me with kisses and the eggs would burn.' "Could you stick the bread in the toaster and put the butter on the table, Darling?" she asked brightly. 'I sound false,' she thought. 'Why am I so controlled? If I did what I felt, I'd yank the cloth off the table and hurl plates at the wall.' She giggled.

He looked at her. "What's funny?"

"Nothing."

They sat at the table and drank the orange juice and ate the scrambled eggs.

"Are the eggs okay?"

"Yes," Stefan replied absently.

'Give up,' she thought. 'He's thinking about Fiona. He'll see her again in a few hours. If I'd asked him if his elephants on toast were all right he wouldn't have noticed.' She probed her mind for something interesting to say. "Kim's going to *Eumeralla* for a holiday. She's keen on Fiona's brother."

"Really? When's she going?"

'Mention Fiona and he responds.' She picked up the teapot. "She's not sure yet. More tea?"

"No. I'm going to have a shower ... or do you want yours first?" he asked politely.

She suppressed a sigh. "No. Are we voting before we go to *Kingower*?"

"Yes."

"If the papers are right, this time tomorrow we'll have a Labor government."

Stefan smiled. "Let's hope so."

After her shower Catriona dressed in jodhpurs and a white shirt. She tied her hair back and put on make-up and Dior perfume. 'But I'm still plain,' she thought as she looked in the mirror. 'I wish I was beautiful. If I was, Stefan would never have fallen for Fiona."

When they arrived at *Kingower* Fiona and Ruth had just pulled up in front of the homestead. David was helping Fiona take the cases out of the boot.

"Hello, Stefan," said David. "You're just in time to help carry the cases."

Stefan didn't know whether to smile or not. He found it unnerving being in the presence of a woman with terminal cancer. Ruth solved his dilemma. She acknowledged him cheerfully, as if her visit was the same as any other, enabling him to return her smile without feeling callous. He saw Margot walking over the lawn. She went straight up to Ruth and hugged her. When she turned away her eyes were full of tears. To his surprise Fiona put out her hand and touched her shoulder. The sympathetic gesture undid Margot completely. She spluttered and burst into tears. Catriona left his side and went to her. Ruth, the centre of the drama, remained unaffected by emotion. He picked up two of her cases and followed David down the track to Catriona's old cottage.

Kim had just finished stocking up the refrigerator. The scent of the lilac blossoms in the front garden drifted through the open windows. Vases of wildflowers stood on the mantelpiece and bookcase.

Ruth kissed her. "It looks very cosy. Thank you."

"I'll make the tea," said Kim. "Aunty Margot's baked a ginger and lemon cake."

"I'll help you," said Fiona, following her into the kitchen.

Stefan looked round the lounge. It looked the same, but felt different. Catriona had left the sofa and armchairs and curtains, but had taken her stereo and lamps. The bookcases in the alcoves beside the fireplace were empty and he was surprised how much this altered the atmosphere. Kim's dog put his head on Ruth's lap.

'A stranger would think this is an intimate gathering,' thought Stefan. 'Aunt moves into cottage and family surround her. Favourite niece helps other niece make the tea and cut the cake. Newlyweds watch while aunt takes over the cottage where much of their own history took place. We made love on the rug by the fire. I proposed to her in the same place. We planned our future here. But the stranger wouldn't know that the aunt is going to die soon, niece's new husband is besotted with her cousin and the other niece is a psychic who's had two premonitions, and one's come true.' His scalp tightened. 'She's even got the time of Ruth's death right.'

So far he had avoided looking at Fiona. When she came into the lounge, carrying a tray bearing a teapot and cups, he feigned interest in a pair of blackbirds on the lawn. He heard the background talk and the clinking of china.

"Stefan." She was behind him.

He turned. She was holding out a cup of tea. 'She's haunted again,' he thought. He knew Catriona was watching, but the compulsion to gaze at Fiona was too strong to resist. When he took the cup Fiona went to the coffee table and began handing out the cake. Catriona's expression was agonized. He hated himself. The arrival of Alex and Virginia caused the distraction he needed. 'The family are all here now. One of them is dying and it changes things,' he thought as Virginia went over to Margot and kissed her.

Margot returned her kiss with gratitude.

'If Kim's right this new family unity won't last,' he thought.

"We're going for a ride, Fiona," he heard Kim say. "Would you like to come?"

Fiona looked at her gratefully. "No, I'll help Aunty Ruth unpack. Thanks for asking me."

When they had finished their tea, Catriona left the cottage first and hurtled down the track towards the stables. Before Kim had time to join them, Stefan ran after her. He caught her arm and pulled her to a stop. "Tree."

"I knew that's how it would be," she said flatly. "A good start to a marriage that's supposed to last a lifetime, isn't it? Three years' separation from me and you can marry Fiona ... if she wants you."

"I wouldn't do that to you, Tree."

"That's no consolation. None. I know you want her. When I saw you looking at her today I wished it was me who was dying."

He pulled her to him and held her tightly. "No, Tree, no."

"Yes, Stefan, yes."

Kim ran round the corner and almost collided with them. "Oops!" She laughed. "Sorry, young lovers."

Kingower
2nd December 1972

Aunty Ruth's illness has ended the family feud. Today I really felt for Aunty Margot. She responded to my sympathy and for once we shared something other than hostility. Catriona looks devastated. Kim's upset too. I feel guilty that Aunty Ruth is leaving everything to me. They love her too. And she's their real aunt. She's not related to me. I shouldn't think like this, but I can't help it. I've been an outsider for so long. When I found my real family I didn't care so much, but now I've lost them it hurts as much as it ever did. I wish I'd been born a Lancaster. It's like being a member of a select club. But I've been admitted on sufferance because the man who adopted me is one of them.

With all of us falling apart the person who's being the most brave is Aunty Ruth. Maybe it's because we're all upset. Sorrow when someone dies is the best tribute to their life they can have. Imagine if your death made everyone happy. What a waste of an existence that would be.

Labor won the election. Gough Whitlam has promised that all the draft evaders will be freed from jail unconditionally. Australia's part in the Vietnam War is over. Tree, Kim and Stefan will be discreetly celebrating with champagne. I wasn't invited to join them. I wish I had someone to share this with. The older generation are upset and say that it will be the end of Australia. Do they think it's going to sink into the sea or something?

Ω Ω Ω

Catriona dreaded the weekends. She had to be pleasant to Fiona when what she wanted to do was scream at her and tell her to stay away. When she and Stefan arrived at *Kingower* a week after Ruth had moved into the cottage, they parked in front of the homestead just as Fiona came onto the verandah. Dressed in a white shirt and jodhpurs, she looked bewitching.

"Hello, Fiona, ready for the ride?" she asked, knowing that her welcome sounded contrived.

"Yes. None of the visitors are here yet."

"They arrive at nine," said Catriona, hating to be informed by

Fiona.

"I'm going to the stables to help Aunty Margot."

'You'll be more of a hindrance,' Catriona thought, wishing she could slap Fiona's face. 'Men brawl over women. Why do we have to be ladylike? I want to yank out handfuls of her hair. I want to mar her beauty.' The ferocity of her emotions shamed her. 'What would Stefan do if he knew my thoughts?' To her relief Kim came outside and they walked over to the stables together. After she, Kim and Stefan got the horses into the enclosure, Fiona helped saddle them.

'She's not a useless ornament any more,' Catriona thought as she watched Fiona put on their bridles. 'Even the horses like her. Why can't one of them kick her?'

When the riders arrived she was infuriated to see several men surrounding Fiona. "Idiots," she muttered to Kim. "The air's bristling with rivalry."

Kim tethered her horse to the fence. "Maybe she'll fall for one of them. Preferably the Yank. He's going back to America next year. Hopefully he'll take her with him."

"We're leaving in ten minutes," called David.

Three men stuck close to Fiona all day. Catriona was unsure if that aggravated her more than the fact that Fiona treated them with indifference. She saw Alex and Virginia looking amused when they stopped for the barbecue and the men waited on Fiona, piling her plate with salad and bread, getting her chops and sausages and saving her a seat. Their chagrin was comical when Fiona sat between Ruth and Alex.

Stefan, noticed Catriona, had sat as far away from Fiona as he could, but she knew that his detachment was a pretence. It was when they were getting back on their horses after the barbecue that she saw his eyes stray to Fiona. Quickly he turned away, but not before Catriona had seen the longing on his face.

On Sunday morning Virginia, baffled by Fiona's defection from

Eumeralla, caught her alone as she walked to the paddock. "Where are all your admirers?" she asked, careful to keep her tone casual.

Fiona shrugged.

"Don't any of them interest you? They seem pleasant. One's a doctor, isn't he?"

She shrugged again.

"Darling, what's wrong? There's no joy in you any more, like there was when I saw you at *Eumeralla*. Your father and I are worried about you."

"It's Tom. I feel about him the way I shouldn't."

Virginia wanted to put her arm around Fiona. 'This is my fault,' she thought. "There's no comfort or advice I can offer. I'm so sorry. My actions have caused you a lot of sorrow. If I'd known the outcome I would have never taken you."

Fiona stopped walking and turned to her. "Where does *if* begin or end? How far back can we go? *If* I'd never been born? *If* you were able to have a baby? You and Dad taught me good values and I've never had any money worries. It's time I counted up the good things and stopped mulling over the bad. I've got to plan my future, but I don't know what I want to do. Well, I do, but it's difficult. I want to get married and have children, but finding the right person has proved impossible. Tom's the only man I've ever loved."

Virginia, who had braced herself for a bitter rejoinder, opened the gate to the paddock. "What about going to England again?"

"I could. I'll wait till the end comes for Aunty Ruth ... then I'll decide." She let the gate swing shut. "I'll be so envious when Tree gets pregnant."

To Virginia's surprise she felt Fiona touch her arm.

"I know how you felt when you couldn't have a baby. Sometimes I feel like getting pregnant and facing the ridicule of being an unmarried mother, but it wouldn't be fair to the baby and I don't want it hating me the way I've hated you."

Ω Ω Ω

As Catriona moved the last horse into the stables the following Saturday, she saw Fiona driving towards the cottages. Twenty minutes later she arrived at the paddock, just as three men were attempting to lead a squealing, kicking horse down the ramp of a horsebox.

"Okay," called Kim. "Get him back. Slack the ropes!"

The horse retreated into the horse box.

"What's happening?" asked Fiona.

"The owner's hoping Kim will be able to tame him. He attacks other horses and people too."

Fiona frowned. "How unusual is this?"

"What?"

"An animal not responding to Kim."

"It's never happened before. But he's calmer with her around. You should have seen him before she arrived."

"I'm glad I didn't." Fiona lowered her voice. "Have the owners ill-treated him?"

"No."

Kim looked at the three men. "Devil will come out eventually to drink and eat. We'll leave him and see what happens. I'll come down first thing in the morning."

"His name's Devil?" said Fiona.

"Yes."

"No wonder he's being difficult."

"It's a nickname," Catriona replied, unable to contain her malice. "His real name's Tasmania, because he's got a mark on his rump the shape of Tasmania. Tasmanian Devil – get it?"

"I was joking, Tree."

Seeing the confusion in Fiona's eyes Catriona forced herself to sound civil. "Sorry. We've been trying to get him out of the horsebox for two hours. We thought it would be easier to put him in a stable rather than evacuating all the others out of the paddock. We were wrong."

Dinner at the homestead that night was an ordeal for Catriona. Now that the schools had broken up for the holidays she sensed that Stefan dreaded spending time alone with her. Although he came to the door and kissed her when she left for work, his relief was palpable. She had hoped that he would spend some of his days at *Kingower* helping Margot with the accounts and coming into Whittlesea and taking her out to lunch, but he had already made two trips to Melbourne to visit his friends. Both had been on days when she was on late duty. 'Spending even a morning with me is too much for him,' she thought.

Throughout dinner she saw him striving not to look at Fiona, who was dressed in navy linen slacks and a pale-blue silk shirt. Her new haircut was gamine and made her eyes seem larger and her cheek bones even more prominent. Finally, when they were having coffee and liqueurs in the lounge, Catriona saw him succumb. She felt reckless. "Stefan and I are going Christmas shopping in Melbourne on Wednesday. Would you like to join us, Fiona? We could go to a restaurant for lunch afterwards."

Fiona smiled. "That'd be great, Tree. Thanks."

"What are you trying to do, Catriona?" Stefan demanded when they arrived home.

She went into the bathroom and squeezed toothpaste onto her brush. "Have an affair with her. It might purge her out of your system. You'll get to know her."

If he had been as contrite as he had been on their honeymoon, and told her that his feelings were an aberration that he would get over, she would have softened, but he said nothing while she cleaned her teeth. When she finished he was standing in the doorway looking at her with scorn.

She took off her shirt and camisole and flung them into the laundry basket. "Experience her conceit. Watch her preening in front of the mirror. Witness her tantrums. She looks frigid. See how you feel about that. If you decide you still want her then I'll give you a divorce on the condition that you tell everyone that I left you because I'm capricious and you couldn't satisfy me." She bared her teeth. "On any level – intellectually, spiritually or physically."

"And what if I don't want a divorce? What if she doesn't want an affair?"

She took her kimono from the hook on the door. "You'd divorce me if it frees you for her. And she's so unhappy at the moment she'll probably sleep with you if you do things right."

"I'm not going to seduce her. Fiona's not a puppet we can play with."

"Are you worried about hurting her?"

"Yes."

"Shame you don't worry about hurting me." She pushed past him and went into the bedroom. "I'd rather be alone than suffer the purgatory of knowing that you're thinking about her all the time. I mean it. I want a divorce."

He unbuttoned his shirt. "And I want to sleep. You're talking rot. I hate you like this."

"And I hate you and our life together," she shouted. "I want a man who's worthy of me. A proper man not a dag who falls for a half-witted blonde."

"I'm not the only man in your life to fall for Fiona, am I? Men find her irresistible and that's why you hate her. You made a blunder when you told me she was a dope. I was shocked when I saw her. Shocked by her looks and her class. And now she can ride she's more of a threat, isn't she? And her father's a hero and her mother's not an alcoholic, so you can't hold that over her. You want a proper man? I want a proper woman, not a malicious bitch. Fiona's going to tear this family apart, is she? The way you treat her you all deserve it."

"Sleep in the spare room tonight, Stefan. You know where the sheets and blankets are."

"No. You sleep in the spare room." He reached under her pillow, pulled out her nightdress and threw it at her. Then he saw the book on her bedside table. "Take this with you," he said, flinging it across the room. It struck her in the face and she yelped. He jumped up and went to her. "Tree, Tree, I'm sorry. Did I hurt you?"

She bent down and picked up the book.

He held her arm. "Tree."

With her free hand she slapped him across the face. Then she ran down the hall and slammed the door of the spare bedroom.

The sound of birdsong woke Catriona the next morning. She lay in bed trying to summon up the nerve to face Stefan. They were going to *Kingower* for a ride after lunch, but she didn't think she would be able to conceal her misery. She looked around the guest room. When they had decided how to decorate it, she had imagined their friends from Melbourne occupying it after stimulating dinner parties and games of cards afterwards. 'I never guessed I'd be sleeping here,' she thought.

"Tree," she heard Stefan say outside the door. She debated what to say and whether to sound nonchalant, frosty or normal. 'But I couldn't sound normal if I tried,' she thought as she saw the door open.

"Ah, you're awake," he said, looking as uncertain as she felt. He was dressed and had shaved and his hair was damp from the shower. She felt at a disadvantage.

"Last night was the first time we've had a real fight," she said quietly. "Did we mean all those things we said?"

He went to the bedside table where he picked up her engagement ring and looked at it as if he had never seen it before. "I don't know."

"I'd rather you hated me than pitied me."

"I don't hate you, Tree, but I hate what you're becoming."

Determined not to give in to the tears that threatened, she tried to think of a retort that would not sound bitter.

"I'm sorry I threw the book," he said, before she could devise one.

"I'm not sorry I slapped you."

"No. I deserved it." He put her ring back on the bedside table.

"But you're not entirely blameless."

She got out of bed. "I'm not the one who fell in love with someone else. You married me knowing how you felt about Fiona. Either it was because you were too cowardly to call off the wedding or you wanted both of us, but whatever the reason you're not much of a man."

"Pushing me at her won't solve our problems."

"It might. If you get to know her it might rid you of your fixation or you'll find that what you feel for her is the real thing. If it is, then I've lost you, but I'll take that gamble." She walked down the hall to the bathroom. "I'm going to have a shower."

"I bet she doesn't want anything to do with me," he said before she could close the door.

"Be subtle."

"No, Tree. It won't work."

"You'll think of something."

Stefan went out to the car on Wednesday morning and waited for Catriona. They were already running late. When she failed to appear he went inside. She was sitting in the kitchen reading the paper.

"What are you doing, Tree?"

She kept her eyes on the page. "Tell Fiona I've got the flu."

"So this is your plan."

"Yes. You'll have all day alone with her. You'll be able to ogle her without me watching you."

"You've got a poor opinion of me, haven't you?"

She looked at him. "Not you." Her expression softened. "You know how I feel about you. It's the biological pull of lust I have a poor opinion of. But it's a curse that especially afflicts men. You feel it and put everything at risk because of it. Henry the Eighth risked his crown and his immortal soul because of it. Edward the Eighth gave up his crown because of it. All you risk is a marriage that you don't value much."

"Don't, Tree."

She turned over the page. "Goodbye, Stefan."
He left.

They had arranged to meet Fiona at eleven o'clock in Myers, the largest department store in Melbourne. Stefan was thirty minutes late and he hurried through the crowds to the book department with a comforting feeling of anonymity. In Whittlesea the friendliness of everyone was becoming claustrophobic. Before the wedding he had found it refreshing. As soon as he had arrived in the district he had been welcomed as Catriona's fiancé and was overwhelmed by their interest in him. They knew where he lived, what he taught and which classes.

Now, surrounded by strangers, he felt he could be himself. He would be served by people he didn't know. No one would ask him about Catriona or Kim or their family. No one would care. He would buy what he wanted and walk away. Shopping trips in Whittlesea took longer than necessary because people stopped and chatted. Yesterday when someone in the newsagent asked about Catriona he had been tempted to tell them to mind their own business. His animosity had appalled him.

In spite of his guilt and his anger toward Catriona, he felt a pleasurable sense of anticipation. He saw Fiona looking at a book. She was wearing a simple pink linen dress, short enough to reveal a great deal of her slender legs. Normally Stefan detested pink and felt it should be worn by baby girls only, but on Fiona, who had teamed it with grey shoes and hosiery, it was stylish. He thrust his hands into the pockets of his jacket and strolled over. "Hi, Fiona."

"Hello, Stefan." She put the book back on the shelf. "Where's Tree?"

"She's got the flu. She'll see you at the weekend."

"We could have made it another day. I've done a lot of my shopping already. It helps working in the city, I can do bits at lunchtime and after work."

"When she checked her diary we realized there was no other day."

"Well you can help me with her present. What do you reckon about this?"

He followed her over to a display where she selected a book about the relationship between humans and horses. He flicked through the illustrated pages. "She'd love it."

"Good." She took it over to the cashier and paid for it with her account card. "Right, now what about you? Have you got a list?"

"Yes." He pulled it out of his pocket.

Stefan noticed that she shopped in the same efficient way as Catriona, consulting her list and going straight to the department she wanted without stopping to browse.

"I booked a table in a restaurant," she said when he had bought everything. "Shall we cancel it or are you hungry?"

Although gratified by her willingness to have lunch with him, he pondered the wisdom of accepting her offer. 'Now Tree and I are married, she believes I'm safe,' he thought. "Can you put up with my company for longer?"

She nodded.

"You're not just being polite, are you?"

She looked at him quizzically. "Polite? You know me better than that."

He laughed. "Okay."

The restaurant she had chosen was, he thought, her type of place. Elegant, with white tablecloths, it would have been fashionable eighty years ago, still was, and would be into the next century. There was a vase containing a red carnation and a wisp of maidenhair fern on every table. After the waiter had taken their orders he felt disconcerted. They were alone without the prop of a menu. Every time he saw her he loathed the way Catriona and Kim had depicted her. A marcasite pendant in the shape of a spider's web spangled with dew, hung round her neck, so delicately wrought that it looked like a miniature of the real thing. She wore pearl earrings and her watch was white gold with a bracelet strap.

"Happy about the election?" she asked.

He nodded. "Tree, Kim and I snuck back to our place and drank champagne."

"Uncle David said that university corrupted them politically."

"Did it?"

She smiled. "Depends what you mean by corruption. They did think like their parents until they went."

"What about you?" he asked, hoping that she would tell him she supported the Liberals. 'Come on,' he thought. 'Give me a reason to despise you. Tell me you agree with the genocide of the aboriginals or the White Australia policy.'

"To my parents' distress I was against conscription and the Vietnam War – and that was without a university education. They say that Labor will be bad for the economy, but I don't understand economics so I can't dispute that. Inflation, recession and depression, and how they're caused are a mystery to me. I hated arithmetic at school. The only subjects I was good at were English and History – that's what you teach, isn't it?"

Seeing that her interest was sincere he told her about the *Imagine If* essays he made his students write.

"Brilliant," she said. "How interesting to speculate how the world have been today if Hitler had become an architect."

Her knowledge surprised him, but he regretted his change of expression when she glared at him.

"Why are you flabbergasted?" Her tone was challenging.

"Well – it's just ... "

"That you think I'm stupid."

"Not many people know history that well. And I don't think you're stupid."

"Kim and Tree do." She frowned. "When I was in Europe they didn't answer my letters. When I came back they didn't ask me one single thing about my travels. I was invited to *Kingower* and I was so excited, but they put up with my presence and that was all. I had so much to tell them. I'd seen and experienced lots of fascinating things – Russia, the Berlin Wall, Anzac Beach – they didn't want to know." She sighed. "Ah well. How's Devil?"

"Obnoxious."

"I would have thought Kim could have tamed him. They should put him down."

"Kim and Tree want to give him more time. It's only been three days."

"She usually only needs three seconds."

He wanted to tell her that her loyalty was wasted on Kim, but he said, "He's not as aggressive toward her as he is to everyone else, but he's unpredictable. He lashed out at her yesterday and she had to jump out of the way. But she's confident she can master him." He wanted to get the conversation to a point where he could ask her why she had returned to Melbourne. "How's your job?"

"All right." Her apathetic shrug was unsurprising.

"Why did you leave Queensland?"

"I was almost bitten by a snake." She blushed.

"You wouldn't run away from something like that."

The pink in her cheeks intensified. "It was extremely venomous."

"Why did you really leave?"

She looked down at the tablecloth. "Don't, Stefan. Let's talk about something safe."

"There are no safe topics. And I need to talk to you. Unfortunately, it's far from safe."

"Go on."

"You know Kim's psychic?"

She nodded. "Do you take it seriously? Men usually scoff at that sort of thing."

"I did at first, most of me still does. But in April Kim had a premonition that Ruth was going to die soon. It was more precise than that. She said it would be within the year or in a year."

Her eyes widened and she stared at him. Right into his eyes. He stared back unable to look away. When she looked down he studied her, noticing her thick dark lashes and the curve of her dark eyebrows against her fair skin and silver-blonde hair. He saw that her nose was slightly crooked. "She had another one at the same time," he continued. "About you. You're going to tear the family apart."

"No. The one about Aunty Ruth was right, but she dreamt this one or made it up. We're coming together now. I feel sad for Aunty Margot and so does Mum. We're not divided any more."

"I was there," he said. "She couldn't understand it. In her premonition the person who was going to tear the family apart was May."

Fiona shut her eyes. "No."

"She didn't know who May was, but when she told her parents and Margot they reacted drastically. I thought it might have been the month. Then David told me who May was. That's why I came to see you."

Fiona, whose earlier blush had just faded, went red again.

'She's mortified because she thinks she misunderstood me,' he thought.

"I was so rude to you," she said. "You must have thought I was off my rocker."

The waiter arrived with their food and Fiona concentrated on eating her fillet steak. He was pleased that his disclosure had not spoilt her appetite. They ate in silence and Stefan let his mind roam. He imagined being married to Fiona.

'What does she wear in bed?' He pictured her in black silk pyjamas, then a white Victorian nightdress. He was sure that, like Catriona, Fiona was not the type to sit in front of the television all night. 'We'd go out once a week to candle-lit restaurants. What would we talk about? Politics. History. She can ride so we'd go horse-riding at weekends. And play tennis. She skis too. We would ski in winter. And go to Europe in January ... Austria and Switzerland.'

"Stefan." Her eyes were wide with consternation. "I've just remembered something Eleanor – she's my real mother, told me. When Juju and I were a year old she couldn't tell us apart. She wanted us to have our own identity so she cut my hair in a fringe.

The one with the fringe was May. The one without the fringe was June. That would be all right if our names had been Sue and Mary or something. But it was different with Juju and me. The one born first was May – because she was born in May. The one who was born second was June because she was born in June."

"So what?"

She put down her knife and fork. "Don't you understand? I might be June and she might be May. And Kim's going out with our brother. When she goes to *Eumeralla* she sees June who might really be May."

He shook his head. "It doesn't matter who was born first. You were known to be May, not your sister. No one knows so it can't matter."

"It does, Stefan. Because the fates know which of us was born first."

CHAPTER 23

Catriona was still up when Stefan arrived home at nine. Once she would have gone to the door when she heard his car, but now she stayed on the sofa and continued to read.

"Still up?" he asked coldly. "Waiting for a detailed account?" Faced with his enmity her neutral expression crumpled. He put the bags on the floor. "We did our Christmas shopping, then we went to a restaurant for lunch. I feel the same about her as I did. No, I feel more strongly."

With a cry Catriona leapt off the sofa.

Stefan caught her before she could leave the room. "You instigated it so you're going to listen to the outcome. While I'm at it, I got a confession to make. Today's not the first time I've visited her. I went once before – the Monday after Kim had her premonition. You know what she did? She was aggressive and told me to get out. I was there when her twin turned up. So I knew all about it before you did. Today she was nice to me. Probably because I'm married to you. Hilarious, isn't it? Ha, ha, ha. I don't know what we can do about this mess that's our marriage. I'll sleep in the guest room tonight."

Ignoring the agony on Catriona's face he stalked out of the lounge. He collected his dressing gown from their bedroom and went and had a shower. He stood under the stream of water wondering what Catriona had expected when he returned from Melbourne. 'A kiss? Affection? A denial of my feelings for Fiona? A new beginning for our marriage? Had she imagined her strategy had worked?' He dried himself and cleaned his teeth.

On his way to the guest room he heard Catriona sobbing. He paused. The light was still on in the lounge. He pushed open the door. She was curled up on the sofa with her face buried in a cushion. Shame hit him like a tidal wave. It was his fault that the once strong, humorous and independent woman had become an insecure wreck. As it was out of character for Catriona to cry, it was out of character for him to hurt people. Feeling drained, he sat beside her. "Oh, Tree. What are we going to do?"

Catriona arrived at work the following morning pale and exhausted. She had bathed her eyes in cold water, but they were still bloodshot. Until lunchtime, when she went to the chemist and bought some eye drops which worked within minutes, she parried Kim's questions. In the afternoon Kim was manifestly pleased by the improvement in Catriona's appearance and her expression of disquiet changed to comprehension.

When they were settling the animals down for the night, Kim took her arm. "You're pregnant aren't you?" she asked gleefully.

Catriona shook her head as she checked the plaster on a cat's leg.

"Come on, Tree, tell me – am I going to be an aunty?"

She put him back in the cage and closed it. "No."

"Then what's wrong?"

Catriona turned away.

"Tree, tell me – I might be able to help."

"I doubt it. Stefan's in love with Fiona." Seeing Kim's lack of surprise, she said, "You knew, didn't you?"

Kim put her hand on Catriona's shoulder. "I suspected. How did you find out?"

Catriona went to the desk and put her head in her arms. Tears made her voice choke as she told Kim everything, beginning with the honeymoon and ending with last night.

The following evening Kim took advantage of Catriona's late duty at the surgery to visit Stefan. Struck by the normality of their attractive house, which had been painted white with a red front door and was surrounded by trees, shrubs and flowers, she went up the path and lifted the horseshoe-shaped knocker. 'It looks so cheerful,' she thought. To Kim everything about their house suggested it was occupied by people who anticipated the future with pleasure, not a couple locked in a conflict they did not deserve and had not caused.

"Tree doesn't know I'm here," she said the moment Stefan opened the door.

"Hello, Kim, come in."

"You're a swine."

He did not react, but turned and walked down the carpeted hallway into the kitchen where the scent of mown grass wafted through the open windows.

She saw that he looked as unhappy as Catriona, and tried to sound less accusing. "She hasn't been telling me tales about you – I got it out of her. It wasn't hard."

He poured boiling water from a saucepan containing two eggs and turned on the cold tap.

Riled by his silence, she hovered beside him. "I've suspected for a long time that you're infatuated with Fiona. You lack the subtlety to conceal it."

"And I've suspected for a long time that you're a fake. You're no more psychic than I am, but you make thing up so you'll have power over people." He walked to the other side of the kitchen.

To look at him she had to shade her eyes from the reflection of the sun which struck the glass front of the cabinets. "I've never threatened anyone, I've only used ... whatever it is I've got ... for the good," she said, stunned by his accusation. "I swear to you that Oliver told me Aunty Ruth was going to die. How do you account for that?"

"Yes, that's buffeted even my scepticism," he conceded, rolling an egg on the worktop to crack the shell. "But I bet you knew what Fiona's name was before she was adopted and you used it to blacken her. Maybe the thing about Ruth was an accurate guess – she's a heavy smoker. You're trained to look for the cause of illness in animals, that would make you more astute when it comes to humans. You might have seen symptoms that no one else did."

"Then how come Tree didn't see them too?"

He shrugged. "I don't know."

Instinct told her that Stefan was determined not to face her and when he shelled the egg his concentration was so intense he could have been performing surgery.

"Fiona's manipulated you, Stefan. She knows men. Did she tell you about our boyfriends lusting after her – while she stood innocently doing nothing to invite their attentions? Did she hypnotize you with those beguiling turquoise eyes, and declare her puzzlement? Did it never occur to you that she came to *Kingower* just after you and Tree got engaged? She didn't flirt with you, but she caused a memorable scene. Since then she's been on your mind, hasn't she?" Her voice rose. "Hasn't she?"

"Yes. Which gives you plenty of reasons to make out that she's going to tear your family apart. If there's a malign influence among the Lancasters it's you – not her."

"How can an intelligent man like you be such a moron? You don't know Fiona's cunning ways. At school she was a dunce and she was jealous that Tree and I did so well – jealous because we went to uni while she had a monotonous office job. She couldn't ride, and we could and she was jealous about that too."

"And were you never jealous of her?"

"Yes, Stefan, we were. But only when she took our boyfriends. What would you have done if you'd found Tree and your best man kissing before the wedding, and Tree's shirt was pulled up and if they hadn't been interrupted it would have gone further?"

"I don't know. I've never thought about it."

"Think about it now."

He looked at the clock on the wall. "I'm trying to get dinner ready so that when Tree gets home she'll have something to eat. I'm too busy to hypothesize. And if you're going to stay here pestering me, do something useful." He gave her a knife.

"You want me to stab you? That'd be useful."

His smile was grim. "While Catriona would probably rather be a widow at the moment, she'd be upset that her sister was going to spend the rest of her life in jail."

"I might get away with it. The way I feel now I wouldn't have you on my conscience."

"She'll be home soon so hurry up and either stab me and make your escape or slice up the tomatoes and cucumber."

She picked up the tomatoes and washed them. "Would you remain friends with him?"

"Back to that again are we? No."

"Would you still have married Tree?"

He opened the refrigerator and took out a jar of mayonnaise. "Of course not."

"Exactly. But that happened to me and you expect us to feel kindly towards Fiona who was going to be one of my bridesmaids. She did it out of spite. For years she'd resented us – we had brains, we could ride. When we grew up we were plain and she was beautiful. Finally she had a weapon. She's wielding it now. Tree's miserable because you've got a crush – "

"Fiona doesn't know," he said, mixing the yokes with a dollop of mayonnaise.

"Don't be ridiculous! Of course she does – it's what she's been wanting ever since she met you. She might not find you attractive, but it would suit her twisted mentality to know how much she's causing you to suffer. I feel sorry for you, Stefan, because if Tree divorces you, you'll lose the best wife you could ever have."

"I know," he said in a voice that was deep with regret.

"And you used to love her – before you met Fiona." Tears filled her eyes and ran down her face. "I thought we were all going to be so happy."

"So did I, Kim. So did I."

$$\Omega \quad \Omega \quad \Omega$$

The strain between Stefan and Catriona ruined Kim's enjoyment of the ride on Saturday. Fiona had stayed behind to be with Ruth, and her absence would had been a relief if the men had not bombarded

Kim with questions about her. Their disappointment that she was not on the ride had been annoying, but their exaltation when she joined everyone for dinner at the homestead was farcical.

As soon as Kim got back to her cottage she had a shower and got into her pyjamas. She was just about to make some cocoa when there was a knock on the door. Toby walked out of the kitchen, but did not growl.

It was Fiona. "Kim, can I talk to you?"

"I was just about to go to bed." Instantly she regretted her curt reply. "Sorry. I'm tired," she said in a more friendly tone, knowing it would be foolish to antagonize Tom's sister.

"It's important."

"Okay. I'm making some cocoa; would you like some?"

"Thanks."

They went into the kitchen. While Kim heated the milk they talked about *Eumeralla*.

"What's so urgent?" Kim asked, putting a mug in front of Fiona.

"Stefan told me about your premonitions. After Aunty Ruth dies I'm going to England permanently. I don't want to cause this family any harm. I've never wanted that."

Kim knew she had to hide her delight. 'If I show how happy I am, she'll stay,' she thought. "Are QANTAS transferring you?"

"No, I haven't been there long enough, but they'll give me a reference."

"What will you do? Where will you live?" Kim asked, putting a tin of Margot's homemade biscuits on the table.

"Buy a flat somewhere in London and join a tennis club. And a ski club. Ski-ing in Europe's fabulous. And now I can ride I can join a riding club. I'd go on lots of holidays. I still keep in touch with the friends I made there."

Kim wondered at Fiona's lack of enthusiasm. She might have been telling someone how she was going to endure a long jail sentence. "Isn't going to England a bit drastic?" she said. "You could just not come here any more. And stay away from *Eumeralla* when I'm there."

Fiona dunked a biscuit in her cocoa. "It's not as simple as that. We were called May and June because – "

"You were born in May and June was born in June," Kim finished impatiently.

"Exactly. We're identical twins and our mother couldn't tell us apart. Then when we were a year old she cut me a fringe. It was only then she could tell which twin was which. Do you know what I'm saying?"

"You might be June?" Kim felt a prickle of dread. "And June might be May?"

Fiona nodded. "And you're going out with Tom. So to be sure there's no danger you'll have to stop seeing him. June and Tom are close. If I go to England and never come back and the family are torn apart, it'll be by June. Not me. And if you don't see Tom – "

"June's not like you."

Fiona drank the last of the cocoa and banged her mug on the table. "You mean she's much nicer, don't you? I know you hate me. It used to hurt, but recently I thought you'd warmed towards me. But now I can feel your hostility – your face hardened when you saw me at the door. What have I done now?" She shoved back her chair. "Ah, don't bother," she said wearily. "I wanted to warn you. Even though it's suited you, Tree and your father to castigate me for years, I don't want anything to happen to any of you." She left the cottage and slammed the door after her.

Toby barked.

Kim patted him. "It's only Fiona in a temper."

Kingower
December 1972

My motives for telling Kim that June might be May were devious. If her premonition is real she'll stop seeing Tom. With Kim off the scene he might fall for Gabby. I hope he won't be too upset if Kim decides not to see him again, but he's pragmatic. Her decision won't blight his life. He'll be a bit miserable for a while and then he'll go on to the next one. And I hope that'll be Gabby.

Kim's gone back to hating me again. She must have found out that Aunty Ruth is leaving me everything. I never thought she was mercenary.

Ω Ω Ω

"What am I going to do?" Kim asked, praying that Margot agree with her theory that Fiona was May because her character was darker than June's.

Instead Margot looked dubious as she poured the coffee. "You'll get over Tom," she said finally. "It's not as if you see him much, is it?"

"But I want to see him again. He's great."

"You've felt like this before. Tom's nice, but so are lots of men."

Kim put a spoonful of sugar in her cup. "He's different. I've never felt like this before."

Margot chuckled. "The number of times I've heard you say that."

"But I'm more sensible now. I want to settle down and have a family."

"You've only known each other since September," Margot said, handing her a cup of coffee and a lamington.

"I know what I want, and Tom is it. He's sensitive, great with animals and he admires me. He won't expect me to be a housewife."

"If you and Tom get married, would you be prepared to go and live on *Eumeralla*?"

"I would have been, but now ... I don't know." She put her thumb in her mouth and nibbled at the nail. "*Eumeralla* has astronomical vet bills. If I lived in the Darling Downs I'd be in demand all over the place. There'd be things to discuss and we'd have to compromise. I'd have to tell him about my premonition."

"Which he probably wouldn't believe. In any case, he's too closely related to Fiona and June. You've got commitments here. You and Catriona want to start your own surgery."

"She can start her own surgery without me."

"She's got too many problems. She needs you. Break it off with Tom."

"I can't."

"Then why come asking me for advice?" snapped Margot. "Stop being selfish. What Fiona said is true. If June was born in May then *Eumeralla*'s not safe and neither is Tom. You've got to think of your family. You must see that. Even Fiona's making a sacrifice. You must too. Because if your premonition comes true ... it won't be Fiona's fault – it'll be yours."

Only once had Kim been on the receiving end of Margot's anger. She had been six and had kicked Catriona during a quarrel. Margot hadn't smacked her or told her father. Her expression and a lecture delivered in chilling tones had made Kim quail. Tears stinging her eyes, she said, "I'll write and tell him."

Margot put her arm around her. "Don't tell him why or he'll try and talk you out of it."

Kingower
Christmas Day 1972

This morning we all went to Church. Every time we sang a hymn I had to bite my lip to stop myself from bawling. Kim looked unhappy, so she must have decided not to see Tom any more. Our determination to make Aunty Ruth's last Christmas the best ever was a failure. I thought about *Eumeralla* all day, and imagined them having a jolly Christmas lunch on the verandah. Tree's pale. She might be pregnant. Neither she nor Stefan look happy about it, if she is.

Ω Ω Ω

On the second of January Kim arrived back at her cottage at four in the morning, swaying with exhaustion but satisfied that she had saved the horse. Too tired to do anything other than scrub her hands and arms she put on her oldest pair of pyjamas and crawled into bed.

When she heard knocking at the front door she groaned and got up, looking at the clock as she did. All the curtains were closed and in her befuddled state she was unsure whether it was nine o'clock in the morning or night. She opened the door and screwed up her eyes against the sun.

"Got another man in your bed?" asked Tom. He looked and sounded sardonic.

"No!" Ashamed of her scruffy pyjamas and stale breath she said, "Come in. Do you want some coffee?"

He sauntered into the lounge. "I want some answers."

"Did you get my letter?" she asked, rubbing her eyes.

"Sure did." He pulled it out of his pocket and waved it at her. "I want to know why you can't see me again. Don't bother lying. I can take the truth – there are lots more females around. I'll get over you, but I don't like being cut off without a reason. Whenever I broke it off with a girl I'd tell her to her face and I'd tell her why. I expect the same."

"How did you get here?"

"Plane. I hired the car at the airport. I can only stay a few days. Dad's cross that I left at such short notice. So?"

"It's complicated, Tom."

"It's not complicated, everything's simple. People make complications. What is it – another bloke?"

She shook her head.

"*Eumeralla* not posh enough for you? Couldn't take the dunny?"

She smiled. "Come off it. I spend a lot of time with my arm stuck up the rear end of cows and horses. It'd take more than that to put me off you."

"You don't look pleased to see me."

"I'm not. I've been up most of the night with a sick horse, I stink of sweat and I've got bad breath. The night before I didn't get home from a New Year's Eve party until six in the morning. My eyes feel as if I've got a cactus bush in them. Let me go and have a shower and clean my teeth."

"And give you time to think up an excuse for not seeing me again? No, tell me now." He folded his arms. "Are you pregnant with another bloke's baby?"

"Your guesses are getting wilder."

"Okay. I've covered the worst things I can think of." He sat on the sofa. "I'm not leaving till you tell me."

"All right."

When she had finished he laughed. "You silly galah. I thought it was something serious." He jumped up and knelt beside her armchair. "There's no such thing as premonitions."

"What about the snake and the foal and Aunty Ruth?"

"Something subconscious. The first thing Fiona said when she saw June was 'Juju'. They hadn't seen each other since they were toddlers. You must have heard your mum and dad talking about Oliver when you were little." He picked up her hand and kissed it.

"I was three when I had the premonition about the snake," Kim said, resenting his reference to Fiona.

He pushed up her sleeve and stroked her forearm. "Do you remember it?"

Her skin tingled at his touch. "No."

"So you've only got other people's versions," he said kissing her wrist. "They exaggerated things."

"Why would they do that?"

"It made a good yarn."

"Then why did I say Oliver told me?"

"Maybe you didn't. Maybe you were babbling and you said something that sounded like 'Oliver', but wasn't. You saw the snake in the bush and said something like 'horrible', which you pronounced 'obble'. Anyway, what makes them think you didn't see the snake?"

"I was nowhere near the bush. Tree was about to go into it. She would have been bitten. We can't just say this is all coincidence. You saw how I was with the animals."

"That's different. Animals like you because they can sense something humans can't. I said it was magic, but it's probably something to do with the way you smell."

"Thanks." She pulled a face. "I'll have to change my perfume."

He stood up and pulled her into his arms.

"Tom, let me have a shower."

"We can have one together after." He kissed her. "You smell okay to me."

"At least let me clean my teeth."

He pushed up her top and stroked her breasts. Kim put her arms round him and kissed him. They sank to the floor.

Tom pulled down her pyjama pants. "Magic, I've missed you."

During lunch at the homestead that afternoon Kim ignored the bleak looks Margot was giving her. Basking in Tom's affection and content from lovemaking she had convinced herself that he was right. 'I must have heard people talking about Oliver,' she thought. 'I don't remember it, but there are photos of him around the house, so I made friends with him. He was more than just an imaginary friend, he'd once lived at *Kingower* and he was my brother. It's natural that I'd build up some sort of relationship with him. Why didn't Tree? Because we're different and my imagination is more vivid than hers. No one knew I was around when they talked about Oliver ... children are small and hide behind and under things. That explains it.'

"Would you like to go for a ride later?" she asked Tom.

"Sure would."

"I'll come with you," said Fiona.

Kim hid her annoyance. "Good," she said graciously.

"Come back to *Eumeralla*, Sis, we miss you. If you come in the winter all the snakes will be hibernating. Don't go to England. Why do you want to go there anyway? Is it this absurd thing about Kim's premonition?"

She nodded. "The safest place for me to be is England."

"I agree," said Margot.

Tom laughed. "Women and their crazy visions. Don't go to England – come back to *Eumeralla* with me. You can ride really well now."

Kim felt a familiar stab of jealousy. 'But not as well as I can,' she thought. 'I'll ride Devil today. I'm a hundred times better than Fiona – I'll show him.'

"Is joining them on the ride wise?" asked Ruth as she and Fiona walked back to the cottage.

Fiona opened the front door. "I want to be with him."

"You're torturing yourself."

"At least I can see what they're doing," she said, going into her bedroom. "If I stay here I'll torture myself more by imagining them being all romantic. Why couldn't he stay away? I didn't seek him out. He came."

"To see Kim."

"Yes. I know how jealousy feels now," Fiona said as she opened her wardrobe and pulled her jodhpurs off the hanger. "I've always envied Tree and Kim, but jealousy's different. I understand how they felt when their boyfriends looked at me. I can understand how people can murder because of it."

"Don't give into it. I didn't," Ruth said.

"You've been jealous?"

"Of course. I just didn't let it dominate me."

"Who were you jealous of?"

"It doesn't matter," replied Ruth.

"Yes it does. I'm interested."

"Everyone feels jealous at some point in their life. Hiding such a powerful emotion is hard, but you must do it. Stay here with me. We can play chess."

Fiona shook her head. "I can't let them go off alone. I'll be in torment all afternoon."

"Better to suffer for one afternoon than suffer for the rest of your life. Tom likes and respects you; don't do anything to earn his derision."

Fiona picked up her riding hat. "I'm being pulled – I must go."

Tom and Kim were already at the paddock when Fiona arrived. Three horses were tethered to the fence. Fiona stared in alarm at the chestnut that was straining to be free. "Who's riding Devil?"

"I am," said Kim, untying his reins.

'Show-off,' thought Fiona, relieved it wasn't Tom.

"Don't ride him," said Tom, as Devil's eyes rolled.

Kim stroked Devil and he became still. She mounted him gently and swiftly, but as soon as she was on his back he pranced, tearing up clods of earth. She leaned over his neck and stroked his ears. "Come on, boy, you can do it. We're going for a ride. You'll see lots of new things." She smiled at Tom. "See, he's calmer."

"He is," said Tom. "But Snowy's terrified of him. Trojan's okay – he's big and can defend himself. Have you ridden him before?"

Kim smiled confidently. "No. I'm trying him out today."

Tom put his foot in the stirrup. "Maybe he'll settle with some exercise. Where are we going?"

"Not too far. An hour there and an hour back. We'll stay away from the mountains. I want to keep him on the flat. Don't let Snowy too close," she said to Fiona, as she lead the way out of the paddock.

"That won't be difficult," said Fiona, urging the reluctant horse forward.

During the first hour of the ride Fiona watched Kim and understood why she had chosen to ride Devil. 'It's not so she can show off to Tom,' she thought. 'It's because she still thinks of me as a rival. This is her way of showing her superiority. She knows, I know and Tom knows I'd never be able to control Devil. Tom might just be able to, and she can, so that puts me on the outside. Where I belong,' she reminded herself. 'Aunty Ruth was right, I shouldn't have come.'

"You're handling him brilliantly, Kim," said Tom. "I couldn't do as well as you."

Recalling Ruth's words, Fiona said, "I wouldn't even be able to mount him. Tom's right. You're fantastic, Kim. I'll never be that accomplished."

Kim smiled. "Thanks."

"I could get used to this," said Tom as they headed towards the forest. "At *Eumeralla* riding's part of the work. You know, riding out to check the sheep and water tanks – rounding up the sheep for dipping, and droving them to the shearing sheds. We never ride for fun. It feels different."

Fiona saw them look at each other. 'Bet they wish I wasn't here. They would have made love in the forest.'

Kim relaxed her grip on the reins, and Devil tossed his head so violently, they whipped through her fingers. While she was grabbing them back, he lunged at Snowy who shied away, almost unseating Fiona. Before anyone had time to regain control, he had bitten Snowy on the rump. Snowy neighed and bolted into the forest. Fiona struggled to recover her balance in the saddle. One of her feet had lost its stirrup. She heard the thunder of hooves behind her.

"Keep your head down, Fiona!" yelled Kim.

She lowered her head and clung to the pommel. Snowy swerved to the right and Fiona fell off. Devil galloped towards her. Kim jerked on the reins and he reared. Fiona rolled out of the way and struggled to her feet. His front hooves hit the ground and he bucked. Kim stayed on his back, but she had lost the reins and was clinging to his mane, trying to kick her feet out of the stirrups. Her riding hat had fallen sideways. Fiona saw something on Kim's face she had never seen before. Fear. Avoiding his hooves, she dashed forward, but before she could get Kim's foot out of the stirrup so she could jump off, he galloped away, knocking her aside and sending her crashing into a tree. The rough bark shredded the sleeve of her shirt and sliced into her upper arm. With relief she heard Trojan approaching.

"Tom!" she called.

"Are you okay?"

She pointed. "They went that way – go after them!"

"No. It will make things worse. If something's chasing him he'll be madder than ever, that's why I held back." He dismounted and looked at her ragged shirt. "You're hurt."

"Devil reared and bucked!"

"She's a brilliant rider – the best I've ever seen. It's a miracle she stayed on his back."

"She couldn't get her feet out of the stirrups."

"You're bleeding all over the place."

"It only looks bad because my shirt's white."

"Hell," he said running forward. "She's lost her hat. Quick. Get on the horse. I'll lead you."

He helped her mount Trojan and led them through the forest.

Ten minutes later they found Kim lying on her back. A trickle of blood ran from her nose. Tom threw himself down beside her and picked up her hand. His face turned white. "Can't find a pulse." He put his ear to her mouth. "She's not breathing. Can you do resuscitation, Sis, mouth to mouth?"

Fiona fell to her knees. "Yes."

Tom ran to his horse. "I'll go for help!"

CHAPTER 24

'Better to suffer for one day than suffer for the rest of your life. That's what Aunty Ruth said,' Fiona thought as the doctor sprayed her arm with local anaesthetic. 'If I hadn't gone riding with Kim and Tom she wouldn't have ridden Devil. He wouldn't have bitten Snowy and Snowy wouldn't have bolted and Devil wouldn't have chased him.'

The doctor ran his finger around the wounded area. "Can you feel that?"

Fiona shook her head. The nurse handed him a pair of tweezers. Fiona had never been in the small local hospital, and the distress of the staff when the ambulance had arrived with Kim, brought home to her how intimate country communities were. The receptionist had burst into tears. The doctors and nurses, trained to control their emotions, had put their energy into comforting the family.

"Let me know if I hurt you," he said as he pulled out the first sliver of bark. "Good girl, you're being very brave."

'Because I can't feel anything,' thought Fiona. 'If my arm wasn't numb I'd be howling.'

"I think that's the worst one," said the doctor.

'If I hadn't brought Tom to the wedding would Kim be alive? Or was she destined to die when she was twenty-three? She heeded Oliver's warning, but Tom came to her. And I introduced them. I am May. I am May. I am May.'

"Are you all right, Fiona?" asked the nurse.

Realizing she had almost been in a trance, she nodded.

"It won't be too long now ... just got to remove a bit more of the forest from your arm," said the doctor. "Are your tetanus injections up to date?"

"Yes."

"Right, that's most of them out. We'll start you on antibiotics as a precaution. Normally I'd stitch the deepest laceration, but there're still some bits in there so I'll apply a poultice and they'll work their way out. You'll need painkillers once the anaesthetic wears off." When her arm was bandaged, the doctor put his hand on her shoulder. "A nurse will come tomorrow afternoon and change the dressing. Is there anything you'd like me to do?"

"Bring Kim back to life," she whispered.

He sat down and took her hand. "She had a severe head injury. Her temple was smashed – probably by the horse going under a low branch. She also had a broken neck. If by some miracle she had survived, she would have been confined to a wheelchair for the rest of her life. She would have hated that, wouldn't she?"

"Yes," she agreed, hearing the emotion in his voice.

"Come along. Your family are waiting to take you back to *Kingower*."

An hour after Catriona was supposed to have arrived home from work, Stefan rang the surgery. There was no reply. She was rarely late and always rang if an emergency had delayed her. After checking her schedule to make sure he had not confused the times, he phoned *Kingower*. There was no reply. There was no reply from Kim's cottage or Margot's house. He was reluctant to ring Ruth in case she was asleep. Thinking that the phone in the surgery, which should be open for another two hours, might be out of order he walked down the road, but the door was locked. He tried to think what sort of a crisis would need all the vets, nurses and the receptionist. It was almost six and the shops were closed.

He drove to *Kingower*. As he drove through the gates the sight of an abandoned motor mower on the lawn increased his unease. The door of the homestead was open and he went inside, but it was deserted. In the kitchen he found signs that it had been left in a hurry. There were half-shelled peas and the kitchen bin was open and had attracted flies. His heart thumped. Had they been kidnapped? Margot and his mother-in-law would have been preparing dinner. He ran outside intending to go to Kim's cottage. To his relief he saw David's car coming down the drive, but he was not at the wheel, he was in the passenger seat. The driver, who owned the hardware shop, got out. His expression temporarily paralysed Stefan. Margot's face when she emerged from the back seat with his mother-in-law made his throat constrict with terror.

'Tree,' he thought. He went down the steps, and put his arm around Margot to steady her. "David," he managed to croak. "What's happened?"

"Kim," was all David could say.

Hours later Stefan, who had not thought of Fiona until he saw her, pondered, 'My panic was for Tree. My only concern was for her.' He understood the significance. 'Infatuation. I've wrecked my marriage for a pathetic infatuation.' Recalling his cruelty to Catriona and the way he had tried to blame her equally for their problems, he was desperate to atone.

The family were so dazed by grief they hardly noticed him. When they did, they looked at him as if he was a casual acquaintance whose name they could not remember. Shock had rendered them unable to communicate properly with anyone they had not known for most of their lives. Catriona accepted his solicitude with a remote air, but he was gratified that she did not spurn him. Deciding that it would be best for him and Catriona to stay at *Kingower* until after the funeral he went home and packed their bags. She had no black summer dresses so he took her to Melbourne and helped her choose one. At night, when they went to bed, he handed her the glass of water and a sleeping tablet the doctor had given her. Then he put his arm around her and held her till she slept. Now that she no longer tried, he discovered that her false jollity had jarred his nerves. She was being herself again and his love for her re-ignited.

Stefan made the funeral arrangements and went through Kim's address book and contacted her friends in Melbourne. When the local paper did a piece on the tragedy, he was the one who gave them photographs. On behalf of the family he accepted condolences and gifts. The headmistress of her old school arrived with a white rose bush to be planted in memory of Kim. Tom, who had kept himself busy exercising the horses, helped the gardener plant it. Weeping children from the riding school arrived with posies they had picked and tied with ribbons. These moved Stefan more than magnificent bouquets would have done. The vicar suggested planting a horseshoe-shaped garden of remembrance in the church grounds and asked Tom and Stefan if they would help the gardeners mark it out and dig it.

The homestead was so hushed that, until Virginia and Alex arrived from Sydney two days later, he had the illusion that he was living with ghosts. He knew they were coming, and when he heard their Jaguar he went outside to meet them. Both were shocked, but in command of their emotions. He helped carry their cases inside.

Virginia spoke quietly. "Where is everyone?"

"Tree's in her old room, I think her parents are in the lounge, Margot's in her house – "

"Let's go and see her."

"Do you want to unpack first?" Stefan asked.

She was already out in the hallway. "No."

He followed them to Margot's house. When she answered the door, Alex held out his arms and she almost fell into them. "Alex. Alex."

Stefan saw that Virginia was concerned by Margot's appearance. "When was the last time you had something to eat?"

Margot looked vague.

"Come to the homestead. I'll make lunch." She interrupted Margot's protests. "Catriona needs you ... you've still got a niece, her parents have still got a daughter, but she's lost her sister. We've all got to help her survive this." Her voice blended compassion with authority.

Margot nodded. Before going to the homestead Virginia went to the cottage to check on Fiona and Ruth. "They won't come to lunch. Ruth's weak and Fiona's looking after her," she reported.

To Stefan's surprise everyone else not only arrived at the dining table at the time Virginia had stipulated, they ate the salad she had prepared and the ice cream with chocolate sauce that followed.

"Alex and I were discussing things on the drive down," she said when they were having coffee. "We thought that a charity could be set up in Kim's name. It would be a permanent commemoration to her."

"Virginia and I would donate a substantial amount," said Alex.

Finally the family began to talk. As they discussed the idea it occurred to Stefan that Virginia must have been a formidable nurse.

"Donations instead of flowers," said Margot.

They all agreed.

"What about a foundation?" said Catriona. "To award veterinary scholarships in Kim's name."

"That's an excellent idea," said Virginia.

After lunch Catriona and Margot composed the eulogy and when they had finished Virginia typed it. Stefan promised to administer the fund until he returned to school, but knew that nothing he did would eliminate his guilt.

The night before Kim's funeral, Fiona went to close the curtains in the lounge. It was midnight. Through the trees she saw that a light was on in Margot's house. Making sure Ruth was asleep, she picked up a torch and left the cottage. As she neared the house she heard music and through the window she saw Margot playing the piano. Her face was haggard and her iron-grey hair, usually neatly twisted in a bun, hung untidily around her face. Biting her lip, Fiona tapped on the fly-screen door. Kim's dog scampered down the hall. His disappointment when he saw her was so poignant that her emotions, frozen by the shock of Kim's death, dissolved. Tears poured down her face. She saw Margot walking slowly down the hall.

"Fiona," she said, unlocking the door. "Is it Ruth?"

"No." She wiped her eyes. "I saw your light. Can't you sleep? I heard you playing."

Margot nodded. "When I'm unhappy I play Brahms Piano

Concerto. Your grandfather used to call it my melancholy music. I played it when he died."

"I'll make you some Ovaltine."

"The real Fiona's emerging," Margot said when Fiona came back with the mugs.

"How do you mean?"

Margot fondled Toby's ears. "You used to love me when you were little. In those days I was one of the few people who could make you smile. You were a solemn little thing. When Virginia and Alex came to *Kingower* for the holidays this was the first place Alex brought you. He'd walk through the door with you and say, 'She can't wait to see her Aunty Margot.' And you'd hold your arms out to me. Then Virginia poisoned your mind against me."

"She told me about *Acacia*."

Margot sipped her Ovaltine. "And the wicked stepmother who stole it. You've heard that story so many times that you believe it. You've never heard my side of things."

"What are they?"

Margot sighed. "It's not relevant now."

"Yes, it is. I know my mother's capable of telling terrible lies."

"She wouldn't see them as lies ... not the ones about *Acacia*. I doubt she even knows the truth."

"What is it? Tell me. Please, Aunty Margot."

"You're beautiful, Fiona. You were a beautiful baby, a beautiful child and now you're a beautiful young woman. Like all the Clarksons you've got an intriguing nature. I've been ugly all my life ... an ugly child, an ugly young woman and now I'm an ugly old woman." She put up her hand to silence Fiona's denial. "My hair's coarse and frizzy – when I was young it was mousy, my eyes are too small and my nose is too big and my face is too long and square. The First World War wiped out so many young men that I didn't have a hope of finding a husband, even though I was only eighteen when it ended. The men who survived had the pick of the women – none of them were interested in me. I accepted that I'd be an old maid so I pushed aside my longing for marriage and children and threw myself into teaching. My pupils liked me – that was my reward. In my free time I rode and played the piano. When our mother died I brought up Francesca and Ruth. Unmarried friends said I was lucky because I had an outlet for my maternal urges.

"In 1932 David wanted to buy new stallions. There was a horse sale in the Northern Territory and he asked me to go with him. I'd never left Victoria before, so it was an adventure for me. We were staying in the same guest-house as your grandfather – he was there to buy horses too. Every night for a week we had dinner together and discussed farming methods and horses. William was surprised I knew so much. David invited him to *Kingower*. Three weeks later he came. My family liked him and accepted him as a friend of David's. We didn't know then that he was forty-seven, he looked fifteen years younger. He helped with the horses and in our leisure time we rode and picnicked. At night we sang round the piano.

But incredibly, he'd come to *Kingower* because he was interested in me. He fell in love with me – my mind, my horse-riding skills and the way I played the piano. I was overwhelmed at the unexpectedness of it all. He was fifteen years older than I was, but so handsome and intelligent. Suddenly my life was perfect. He was a widower and had three children for me to mother, and who would love me in return. Well, that's what I thought. I didn't for one moment doubt that these three motherless teenagers would love me. When I first went to *Acacia* they were waiting on the verandah with the housekeeper. Virginia was the most exquisite girl I'd ever seen and Laurence and Jonathan the most good-looking boys.

"William introduced us. 'This is Miss Lancaster. We're getting married and she's going to be your stepmother.' I'll never forget their horrified expressions."

Fiona could see that Margot was reliving the moment. Having experienced the repertoire of Virginia's expressions she knew exactly which one she would have used on that occasion and understood the effect it would have had on Margot. She wanted to say something, but Margot was still talking.

"After a tense dinner that night I heard Virginia saying to her brothers, 'She's the most grotesque woman I've ever met.' Johnny said, 'She looks like a hawk,' but Laurence said, 'That's being horrible ... to hawks.' Until then I'd considered myself plain. Then I knew I was ugly. Virginia started crying. It was their despair that hurt me most."

Fiona burst out, "You're not ugly. You dress well and you've got a good figure even though you're old. You looked like Tree when you were young and she's not ugly."

"I wasn't meant to hear them," Margot continued. "The doors and windows of the homestead were open most of the time and if the wind was in the right direction even whispers were audible. I heard lots of things I shouldn't ... most of them hurtful. When I had a miscarriage they wondered how their father could possibly have given me a baby. Laurence said to Johnny, 'How could he have done *that* with *her*?'"

Fiona was startled. "I didn't know you'd had a miscarriage."

Margot stood up and went to the window. Guessing that she was trying to curb her tears Fiona stayed silent.

"I had two."

When Margot turned round, Fiona asked gently, "Is that why you lied about Johnny being a coward?"

Margot shook her head. "One of the boys had to stay on the land. Johnny and Laurence tossed a coin to decide who would go and who would stay. They did it on the verandah and I heard. I was looking for a book to read. This time I did eavesdrop. I hoped it would be Johnny who went. He hated me even though Eleanor liked me. Laurence, being married to Francesca, tried to control his feelings and I hoped that with Johnny gone and Virginia in Sydney Laurence might come round to liking me. So I listened. Johnny picked and Laurence threw. It landed heads. Johnny had chosen tails which meant he had to go. But he told Laurence that he was frightened. So Laurence said he'd go. Johnny was ashamed. He called himself a coward. They told their father that the coin had decided that Laurence had to go. I used Johnny's fears to convince myself that he was worthless. Being hated by a coward is not as bad as being hated by someone brave.

"I didn't tell William, but I wrote and told David. When I heard about the way Johnny died I didn't tell David. I just said he died in a fire. Virginia was too distressed to ever talk about it so it went on for years till you found out. When Kim and Catriona were upset about the effect you were having on their boyfriends I told them your real father was a coward because he wouldn't enlist when the war was declared. I didn't know they'd told you, but I don't suppose I would have cared if they had. I'll never forget your rejection. Being loathed by a child who once loved me was painful, but I should have weighed things up."

Fiona was silent for a while. She wondered why she had disregarded the fact that Alex, Kim and Catriona had adored Margot. 'I should have listened to Eleanor,' she thought. Finally she said, "I'm sorry I hurt you. Actually, in many ways Johnny was despicable. He left Eleanor because he thought she couldn't have children. And he was unfaithful."

"Unfaithful? Who told you that?"

"Eleanor. Didn't you know?"

"No."

Fiona looked thoughtful. "You seem surprised."

"I am."

"Funny. So was Mum. Still, Eleanor must be right. Why didn't you go and visit her when Johnny left?"

"I did – several times, but she wasn't there. I searched for her, but I couldn't find her. William and I were worried. The first time I went over to *Eumeralla* someone was with her."

"Who?"

"I don't know ... I didn't see them, but there were two places laid for breakfast on the verandah. The next couple of times I went the place was deserted. I left a note on the table, but she never replied, so I thought I must have said or done something to upset her. A month later she arrived at *Acacia* with you and June."

"She didn't get your note. She told me she was too ill to go to

Acacia and I asked her why no one from *Acacia* had visited her. It must have blown away."

"It shouldn't have – I put it under a jar of honey. I remember doing it. There was nothing on the table so I went into the kitchen and took a jar out of the cupboard. She must have forgotten about it." Margot looked at the clock. "And now we'd better go to bed – tomorrow is going to be a very distressing day."

Fiona stood up. "I understand now ... about how you felt. I'm sorry, Aunty Margot."

"So am I. Sorry for a lot of things. Good night, my dear."

Ω Ω Ω

On the morning of Kim's funeral Stefan stood by the windows in the lounge watching for the cars to arrive and take them to the church. Toby sat at Margot's feet. He jumped up expectantly when he heard someone arriving and whimpered when he saw they were not Kim. When she had gone to Queensland Stefan had been amused how profoundly Toby had missed her. He had been fussed over, comforted and told that she was coming back soon. Now Margot just stroked his head.

When they arrived at the church he saw that the ground had been prepared for the memorial garden. People's donations of rose bushes, azaleas and other small shrubs were on trestle tables in the shade ready to be planted. As they entered the porch Stefan thought they were too early before realizing that the church was so packed people were standing at the back. Kim's friends from school and university, her colleagues and people from the district crowded into the pews. On the coffin, devoid of flowers, was her riding hat. During the hymns and eulogy most of the congregation sobbed broken-heartedly. Even the choir from Kim's old school faltered during the anthem.

When the service ended they all went over to the memorial

garden. The first card that the vicar read out was attached to Tom's yellow rose bush.

Magic, I'll remember you always. You were magic. Love, Tom.

Catriona's self control broke and she began to weep. Stefan put his arm around her praying that she found some solace from his presence.

Melbourne
January 1973

All I can think about are the good times Kim, Tree and I had when we were children. I know that Kim rode Devil because I went on the ride, but no one is blaming me. I got blamed when I was innocent and exonerated when the guilt was mine. Uncle David is blaming himself for suggesting that Kim could conquer Devil and for not insisting that he be destroyed when it became plain that he was not responding to her. Devil has been put down. Catriona did it. She said it's the only time she's felt pleased to be killing an animal.

Aunty Ruth is getting worse. It's the shock. She's on morphine and keeps begging me to ring her solicitors as soon as she dies. She's so agitated about it that I looked in her address book and found their phone number. I rang them just to make sure they were the right ones. They are. They put me onto the senior partner and he knew what I was talking about. He has something to give me as soon as she dies. She keeps talking about old sins and long dark shadows.

Today I resigned from QANTAS. It's not fair that I'm away so much and I want to spend as much time with Aunty Ruth as I can. They were very good about it and said that they can arrange for me to take unpaid leave, but I said no. As I'm going to England soon anyway I've got a lot of preparation to do.

Before the school term began in February, Stefan took Catriona away on a holiday to Ballarat, which was famous for its goldfields a century ago. They visited the old Kingower diggings where her ancestor had made his fortune. The hotel in which they were staying packed them a picnic basket every morning. During the day they walked beside creeks and gullies. In the evening they dined at the hotel. Catriona seldom spoke, but her silence was not hostile.

On the third day of their holiday, as he was spreading the rug on the grass by a stream, Catriona said, "You're being very kind to me, Stefan."

He was pleased that she had initiated a conversation. "You deserve my kindness. I've caused you a lot of unhappiness." He sat beside her.

She opened the lid of the picnic basket. "We have to talk."

"Yes." Unable to look at her he stared at the water. He had planned what he wanted to say, but found himself unprepared. "Tree, I'll understand if you want a divorce," he began, dreading that she would tell him that she did. "If you do, I'll make it easy for you. You can keep everything." He dared to look at her. "But I don't want a divorce and if you'll give me another chance, I'd be very happy." He wondered if he could touch her, but decided against it. If she pulled away it would render him incapable of pleading his case coherently. He would say mawkish things and she would decide that he was not worth the effort. 'Which I'm not,' he thought.

"What about Fiona?" she asked in a detached voice.

"My infatuation for her died when I knew something dreadful had happened. I didn't think about her ... only you. My fear was for you." He was compelled by her silence to add. "It was infatuation ... my judgement was addled." His hope that she would understand was dashed by the way her eyes coolly scrutinized his face.

"That night you came home from Christmas shopping – did you mean what you said?" She sounded like a lawyer cross-examining a witness.

He was tempted to lie, but knew that the result of their discussion had to be based on the truth. He nodded. "At the time.

I'm sorry I said it. I was angry with you for trying to throw me at Fiona. I was trying so hard to get her out of my mind."

"She's going to England." Catriona looked in the box and picked out an egg and tomato sandwich. "You could follow her."

"I don't want to."

"Why not? Is it because if she turns you down you've lost both of us? I'm not convinced that you are over her. You just feel sorry for me, but the worst thing that could have happened to me has happened. Kim's dead. Divorcing you would be nothing compared to this. I think we should separate, because if you go to England and meet up with Fiona, you might be happy."

But he knew that the likelihood of her considering him as a love interest was negligible. Fiona had a puritanical streak that would forbid her having a relationship with the divorced husband of her cousin. Her loyalty to Catriona was ironic. "Tree, the major reason I fell for Fiona was because when I first saw her she was so different to what you and Kim had led me to believe." He touched her hand to silence her protest. "Darling, I'm not blaming you, I'm just telling you how it was from my point of view. And that lunch – it wasn't just an ordinary family Sunday lunch, was it? I don't think watching a play could have been more dramatic. And in a lot of ways that's what I was doing ... watching a play."

Catriona smiled wryly. "And the leading lady gave you a part when she asked you to read out that newspaper article about her real father." She threw crusts to a couple of sparrows. Her indifference was daunting.

"I don't want to lose you, Tree." He knew he sounded desperate, but no longer cared. "Before I met you I'd been out with lots of girls and not one of them touched me the way you did. Compared to you the others were trite. After I met you I felt excited for the first time since I'd left university. Often on a first date I'd be reduced to talking about the weather. With you everything was easy – you fascinated me. You were clever and unique. You still are. I want us to start again – if you can forgive me. I know it'll be more than I deserve, but ... "

Catriona picked up a stick and idly drew figures in a bare patch of earth. "Are you sure? You're being kind to me because I've lost Kim. What happens when your compassion dilutes and we're back to having to live with each other in normality? Think hard, Stefan. But if you do go to England and it doesn't work out, I won't be like the heroine in a romance. I'll never want to see you again and I'll change my name back to Lancaster. With Fiona on the other side of the world I won't have any competition from her. She's cast a pall over our marriage and I'm not sure it can be dispelled." She hurled the stick into the stream. "I'm not making it easy for you, but why should I?"

"Oh, Tree," he said despairingly.

She covered her face with her hands. He only knew she was crying because her shoulders were heaving. He held her and felt her tears splashing onto his arm.

"I've never felt so wretched," she spluttered. "I miss Kim so much it's agony. I want her to come and talk to me the way Oliver talked to her. At night I wait for her to speak to me, but she won't. She's gone."

He cuddled her till she stopped crying. "And you're married to a spineless bastard," he said, giving her a handkerchief.

She wiped her eyes. "No. Whatever happens to us – I'll never think of you like that."

"Dare I hope that you have some love left for me?"

"Yes. Not just some ... lots."

He gently kissed her lips. "I love you. I always have. My feelings went awry, but they never died ... they got tangled." He stroked her face. "They're untangled now. I promise."

Catriona put her head on his shoulder. "You got mixed up in something you couldn't fathom. And I can't blame Fiona for everything. Perhaps I can't blame her for anything."

Ω Ω Ω

"You're doing great, Gabby," said Tom as they rode toward the creek.

Although he was conscientious about supervising her riding, she knew his mind was elsewhere. They dismounted to let the horses drink.

Gabriella, remembering her own grief and the way she had rebuffed the gestures of support and comfort after Brett's death decided she should try and get him to talk about it. "Kim meant a lot to you, didn't she?"

He nodded. "An animal caused her death and she was magic with animals – all except that one. Even when he bolted I wasn't all that worried – I thought she was invincible. When they told us she was dead it was like watching a film where Superman gets killed." He stopped stroking the horse and looked at her. "You've been through it all, haven't you? Worse than this ... you were married."

She hoped their mutual feeling of loss might be a bond. "I know how you feel."

"It's not as if I'd known her for long, but, you know what? I wanted to marry her. I've never wanted that before. If a girl so much as mentioned marriage I'd have a fit. I wanted to settle down eventually, but not till I was thirty. Kim was different. She was Magic."

After Brett's death Gabriella had been disgusted when people had said, 'You'll find someone else. You're young.' 'But just now I nearly said that to Tom,' she thought.

CHAPTER 25

As soon as Ruth died Margot rang her solicitor. Three hours later he arrived at *Kingower* with a large envelope.

"Your sister's instructions were to hand this to Fiona Lancaster," he told Margot when she answered the door.

Thinking it was Ruth's will and uncomfortable because she was the only beneficiary, Fiona took it down to the cottage so she could read it in private. She sat on the floor and tore open the flap. It wasn't her will, but a letter dated October 1972.

Darling Fiona,

Most people think life is too short, but it's not – it's too long – much too long. I have six months at the most to live, but I hope I die before that.

My happy childhood did not prepare me for misery. I did exceptionally well at school, was popular and rode well. Only my unfulfilled wish to be a doctor marred my existence. Then the war came and my torment began. No. It began before that, but if it hadn't been for the war I would have got over it. There were lots of men my age so I probably would have married and been a wife and mother. At the end of the war there was a shortage of men. Some women had to go without and I was one of them – otherwise I might have been able to quell my desire for the man I really loved.

We first met at *Acacia*. But he only saw my ethereal sister Francesca. Laurence. Proud, impetuous, unpredictable, idealistic, Laurence. It wasn't just that he was handsome. It was his passion and the smile that started slowly and spread across his face. He never smiled just to be polite and that was what made his smiles special. His thoughts were transparent. He looked at Francesca like a man who is seeing heaven. At their wedding I behaved like a gracious sister and sister-in-law.

But I was confident. Soon I'd meet a man and we would marry and my fervour for Laurence would wane, and we would be affectionate in-laws. I would not compete with Cheska because it was immoral and I was a good person. I never competed with her. Never by a look or a gesture did I expose how I felt.

When she died in October 1945 I was heartbroken, but at the back of my mind was the hope that when Laurence came home he would turn to me. I knew I was betraying Cheska's memory and felt guilty about these feelings, but it didn't stop me having them.

Virginia had to write to him because communications were down and we couldn't send a telegram. But he didn't get her letter. When he arrived in Melbourne on 1st November he was excited about seeing Francesca. She'd been dead for two weeks and I had to tell him. Our exchange of two words each, his ... 'Where's Cheska?' And mine ... 'She's dead,' were stabbed into my consciousness like a rusty knife. They've festered ever since. I was a nurse used to dealing with bereaved people. I should have made Laurence sit down, and broken the news gently, but I was so astounded that he hadn't received the letter.

You don't know this. No one does. Everyone thinks he left the flat as soon as I'd told him, and disappeared. He did leave. That was true. But I ran after him. He walked fast and I had to run to keep up. I had no shoes on and as he strode down the pavement there was broken glass ahead. He stopped and told me to go home, but I was crying and that's why he came back. Even in his own distraught state he couldn't stand to see me crying. I poured him a brandy and I had one too. We got drunk. He had a lot more than I did and was much drunker than I was.

That night the inevitable happened. How prudish that sounds now. We went to bed together? In 1945 that would have sounded crude. It still sounds crude to me. We made love?

Well, he was drunk and called me Cheska. Yes, I suppose we did make love. I made love to him and he made love to Cheska.

In the morning I woke first and left the bed. Cheska's bed. Laurence woke later. He had a hangover and was sick all day. He wanted to think that me telling him Cheska had died was a nightmare. He had no idea what we'd done and I was too humiliated to say anything.

He stayed for three days. We remained sober and I slept in my own room. When he said he was leaving I didn't stop him. I asked if he was going to *Acacia* and he nodded. I offered to come to the station with him and told him he might not be able to get a ticket straightaway. He said that he was going to walk. I told him he couldn't walk all the way to Spencer Street Station – it was too far.

He looked at me as if I'd gone a bit queer, but when he spoke he sounded patient and told me he was going to walk to *Acacia*. I knew he meant it even though *Acacia* was a thousand miles away. Laurence always did what he said, but I tried to talk him out of it. I can still remember our dialogue.

He said, 'I want to walk away all the pain. Do you think I'll succeed?'

'No. Laurence, this is madness.'

'Yes. It was madness to think that now the war was over I could come home and settle down with Cheska, have children and be happy.'

His expectation of happiness with Cheska had not been mad – it had been reasonable. But my fantasy that I could replace her had been a chimera. I'd thought in years not days. I'd imagined that we'd begin by comforting each other, talking about Cheska and the past, and gradually Laurence would fall in love with me.

I gave him an atlas. He asked me if I minded if he tore out the maps of Victoria, New South Wales and Queensland. I told him I didn't. We were so courteous to one another. Like strangers. He tore them out, put them in his kit bag and left.

He did walk all the way. When he got to Brisbane he wrote to me. I enclose his letter with this. I didn't tell anyone his intentions, mainly because I didn't think he could walk all the way to Queensland and I didn't want them to worry about him. And the story I told them left no room for discussions about where he was going or how he was going to get there. I just said that I told him about Francesca and he left. Liars have to keep their stories simple so they can remember them.

When I became ill my family thought I was suffering from grief. Nowadays they'd have guessed I was pregnant. Fate was on my side. For the first sixteen weeks I was sick all day, so I lost weight instead of putting it on. No one knew – not even the nurses I worked with. As soon as the sickness stopped I gained weight. I had to get away. I left two weeks later.

Eleanor and Johnny were desperate for children. In the early days of their marriage he had turned one of the rooms into a nursery and had bought a pram and cot. I remember Margot saying that it was tempting providence. I bought a car and drove to *Eumeralla* with the idea of hiding there and giving them the baby when it was born. But when I arrived Johnny had gone and the time for Eleanor to pretend the baby was conceived before he left was wrong. My expected date of delivery was 26th July 1946 and he had left *Eumeralla* at the beginning of September 1945. Eleanor knew the exact date. She told me that deaths are so traumatic we never forget them and Johnny's leaving was the death of her marriage and her hopes of pregnancy. Cruelly, he left her the day after her period started.

But we wondered if we could get away with it. I had done midwifery and knew three vital facts. Women can bleed but still be pregnant. And babies sometimes arrive early. And the gestation of a normal pregnancy is 38 weeks not 40, because the time is calculated from the first day of the last period not in the middle of the cycle. Few men realize that.

Nevertheless, it was risky – with Margot, Laurence and

William so close. We had a couple of frights. Margot visited several times so we hid. Luckily she rode so we heard her. If she'd walked we would have been caught. Knowing that she had seen the car the first time she came Eleanor drove it far away from the house and parked it behind some trees as soon as Margot left.

We were right to be optimistic. I went into labour eight weeks early and Eleanor became the mother of twins. You were small, but healthy. Instead of leaving as soon as you were born, as I had planned, we decided I would breastfeed you because you were so premature. I was anxious to reappear as I knew everyone would be worried about me. Your early arrival made deception easier if we could work something out. I could have just turned up at *Acacia*, but if Margot remembered the car with its Victorian number plates parked at *Eumeralla* it would have been easy for her to work things out.

It was Eleanor's idea to forge the Melbourne postmark and date on an envelope containing a letter to Margot. She had letters from me that we copied, but it took six attempts before the postmark looked genuine. I wrote a letter telling Margot I was arriving in Brisbane and asking if she would meet me. We dropped it in *Acacia*'s post box one night. Because it was possible that she would see me at the station before the train arrived, I took the precaution of taking my cases, driving to the station before Brisbane and boarding the train there. When Margot met me she had no reason to think that I'd only travelled one stop.

After hugging me and telling me she was pleased to see me, she told me that Eleanor had arrived at *Acacia* with twins. She was so excited. My midwifery training gave me a reason to stay on. Twelve weeks later, when I was sure that you were both thriving, I left. If I stayed any longer I'd never have been able to tear myself away.

Deceit was easy because you strongly resembled the Clarksons. But as you grew up I saw things that no one else did.

How true it is that people see what they think is there – not what really is. Your expressions and mannerisms were Francesca's. It amazed me that David, Alex and Margot didn't notice. Sometimes, when we were all together, you'd do or say something and I'd hold my breath, sure that they must see and realize the truth, but they never did. I've often asked myself if Laurence ever saw Francesca in you. Did he really know nothing of what happened that night or did he sometimes look at you and wonder?

Eleanor and I vowed never to reveal our secret. But I have to break it because June and Keith want to get married. They are half-brother and sister. You told me the day after the wedding that they were in love. That's why I fainted.

I'm selfish enough to want everyone to think kindly of me. I'll tell you all that I've got cancer and you will fuss over me and do your best to ensure my final days are pleasant. It doesn't matter what you'll say about me when I'm dead. I don't believe in God or an afterlife. I hope there is nothing after death. I might have to pay for my sins. Instead others have to pay. Fiona, you've always paid for them. From the moment Virginia and Alex adopted you you've paid. June has to pay now. And so does Keith.

Old sins cast long shadows. But did they have to be this long and this dark?

Fiona let the last page drift to the floor. With trembling hands she picked up the enclosed letter with its faded writing and took it out of the envelope.

Dear Ruth,

I'm in Brisbane. It took me 50 days. I set myself a target of twenty miles a day and stuck to it. It was easy to find my way. I just followed the train line. Lots of people stopped to offer me a lift along the way, but I only accepted one because I was low on water. He took me twenty miles and dropped me at the next station so that saved me a day. You were right though, it didn't take away the pain.

*Love,
Laurence.*

Fiona imagined the man in uniform tramping one thousand miles trying to walk away his anguish. "My father," she whispered. "Juju's and mine. And Keith and Gabby's. How am I going to tell them? God, help me." She put her head in her hands and cried.

The light was fading when she opened her journal and turned on the lamp. She had just written, *How could Eleanor let Juju and Keith get married?* when she heard a knock on the door.

"Darling," said Alex. "Dinner's ready. We're waiting for you." He handed her a handkerchief. "Dry your eyes. Ruth wouldn't have wanted you to suffer like this."

"She was my mother."

"Yes, she was like a mother to you, wasn't she? Come up to the homestead. They're waiting to serve dinner."

She found it difficult to speak. "Dad, you don't understand."

Alex went inside and looked worriedly at Fiona.

"Ruth gave birth to me and Juju at *Eumeralla*. That's where she went when she disappeared. She wasn't having a breakdown, she was pregnant."

Alex shook his head. "She was only away three months and she wasn't pregnant when she left." He stared in bewilderment at the pile of paper on the floor. "Is that what was in the envelope?"

Fiona nodded.

"Darling, it wasn't possible."

"It was. It is. We were born eight weeks early." Fiona saw that he was doing mental calculations.

"It's still not possible. I saw her a week before she disappeared. She wasn't pregnant."

She picked up Ruth's letter and put the pages in order. "Read it."

Alex sat down and put on his glasses. Fiona watched his changing expressions.

"God," he said when he had finished. "Poor Ruth." He looked at Fiona's tear-stained face. "This has been a terrible shock for you. Your life seems to have been a series of shocks."

"Alex?" called Margot. Kim's dog preceded her into the room. "We rang from the house. Is the phone out of order?"

Alex picked it up. "No dial tone."

"Aunty Ruth's my mother," said Fiona. She smiled. "Dad, you're my uncle ... my real uncle. I'm happy about that."

Margot frowned. "She can't be."

"You'd better sit down, Margot," said Alex giving her the letter.

When Margot finished reading she took off her glasses. "Ruth was wrong," she said slowly. "When I heard that she was sick all the time, at first I did think it was grief. She looked ghastly at Cheska's funeral. But when it went on and on I wondered if she was pregnant. I wanted a baby, but William and I were too old to adopt. We talked about Ruth and decided that if she was pregnant she could come to *Acacia* and we'd adopt the baby. It was too delicate a subject to write in a letter. I might have been wrong and Ruth would have been furious, so I went down to Melbourne to see her. But when I got there she'd disappeared. I spoke to the matron, and asked if Ruth was 'in trouble', but she said she doubted it. Apart from the fact that I wanted to find her before she had the baby and gave it up for adoption, I was terrified she might have killed herself."

"Why were you so sure she was pregnant?" asked Fiona.

"To crack up wasn't in Ruth's nature. She wasn't a nervous-breakdown sort."

"But you thought she might have killed herself," said Alex. "Surely that wasn't in her nature either?"

"Grief over Cheska's death wasn't enough to make her unstable – being pregnant and unmarried on top of everything else was." Margot smiled grimly. "I know all about fluctuating hormones. The first time I was pregnant I was so grumpy William called me his snapdragon." She looked at the letter. "And I was right. I never guessed she was as far gone as sixteen weeks. When she appeared again after three months I thought she must have had a miscarriage. I never said anything, of course. She and Eleanor were ingenious. As soon as Ruth drove away Eleanor must have put you and June in a pram and walked to *Acacia*. I was just about to go to Brisbane and meet Ruth. We were so distracted that we didn't ask her many questions. As soon as we saw she was all right we asked her where she'd been. She wouldn't tell us so we didn't pursue it."

"Who did you think was the man?" asked Fiona.

Margot shook her head. "I never suspected it was Laurence. When he arrived back at *Acacia*, William was at the bank in Dalby. Laurence just walked in the front door as if he'd never been away. I said, 'Where on earth have you been?' and he said, 'I've walked all the way from Melbourne.' I told him to stop talking nonsense and get himself cleaned up before his father got back. He told me, but I didn't believe him. I should have – his clothes were a mess and his boots were falling apart. I didn't even tell him I was sorry about Cheska or give him any comfort. He'd been away for years and I didn't welcome him home or tell him how worried we'd all been. I thought he was mocking me."

"It takes an average person twenty minutes to walk a mile," said Alex. "One hour to walk three miles. He walked twenty miles a day so that means he walked for about seven hours each day. Yes, I can imagine Laurence doing that."

"So can I," agreed Margot.

"Where would he sleep?" asked Fiona.

"Probably at railway stations," said Alex.

David stood in the doorway. "What's going on down here? We've been ringing."

"The phone's out of order," said Margot. "We'd better go to the homestead."

"Yes," said Fiona. "Before everyone ends up here, coming down to find out what happened to the last person who didn't come back."

"We've got some news. We'll tell you all at the same time," said Alex.

Kingower
February 1973

Last night at the homestead I became a real Lancaster. Everyone is stunned. How would they have reacted twenty-six years ago when virginity in a bride was prized, and to be pregnant and unmarried was a sin? If Ruth thought she would get any sympathy from any of her family would she have gone away?

I am trying to be honest with myself. Years ago, if I'd discovered that she was my real mother, would I have been kind? Would I have understood? Probably not. Aunty Ruth knew I might have condemned her. What did she once say about Laurence, Johnny and Virginia? Something about them being the most unreasonable trio she had ever met. I have inherited their traits. But Juju hasn't. What am I going to do about her and Keith?

Something good has happened at last. Catriona is pregnant. Stefan is fussing over her. He's worse than her mother. I'm happy for her ... for both of them. The baby is due in August. If it's a girl they are going to call her Kim.

CHAPTER 26

The large envelope arrived at *Eumeralla* with the name of a Melbourne firm of solicitors stamped on the back. **Private and Confidential** was written in red across the front. Tom collected it from the box at the gate, rode back to the house and gave it to Eleanor who looked at it suspiciously.

"Quick, open it. Some distant relation might have died and left you all their money."

"Unlikely, Tom." With a knife she slit the flap open and took out the contents.

"If it's a will it's a long one," said Tom. "Is it?"

After reading the covering letter from the solicitor Eleanor went into the bedroom and shut the door. More curious than ever, Tom dried the breakfast dishes and emptied the buckets on the compost heap. When he had hung out a load of washing and cleaned the kitchen and bathroom, his mother was still in the bedroom. He knocked on her door. There was no reply so he pushed it open. Eleanor was lying face down on the bed.

"Mum?" he asked in alarm.

She rolled over and looked at him. "Their eyes," she whispered. "They were turquoise like Laurence's."

"Mum, what's the matter?"

"Go and find your father."

Greg was on the boundary chopping down a dead tree. Leaving his saw and axe he got into the car with Tom. Eleanor was still in the bedroom. He sat on the bed and put his arm around her. "What's happened?"

"Ruth Lancaster's dead. She wrote this before she died." She gave him the photocopied letter.

As he read it rain began to pound on the roof. When he got to the end he threw the pages down. "You lied to me."

"I had to. Don't be angry, Greg."

"You ask me not to be angry for twenty-six years of deceit?"

"Ruth and I made a vow."

He stood up. "It was an excuse for lies. When you married me you thought you couldn't have children. If you'd told me the truth I'd still have married you, but you never gave me a choice. You needed a husband to help with all the hard work and I was available. I bet you couldn't believe your luck."

His anger shocked her. She had expected him to console her. "It wasn't like that. How could I break a vow? It was sacred."

"What about the vows you made to me in church on our wedding day? They were more sacred."

A gust of wind blew through the window lifting the pages and whirling them round the room.

Greg banged the window shut with such force that the glass cracked. "I know I was only ever a poor substitute for Johnny. And now I know why you never loved Juju."

She stood up and faced him. "I did."

"For God's sake, you were willing to let her marry her half-brother to preserve your lies!"

"No. I didn't know Laurence was their father. I thought it was Johnny. For the rest of my life I'll have to live with the fact that I vilified Ruth. No wonder my coldness bewildered her."

Greg laughed bitterly. "So that's why you wouldn't have him back. For all these years that's stumped me. Sometimes I've even kidded myself that it was because of me. But it wasn't. It was because you thought he'd had an affair with Ruth."

"No. I didn't know then. She refused to tell me who the man was. It was only when the twins started to look like Clarksons that I thought Johnny was their father. It was when they were eighteen months old and Virginia kept going on about how much they looked like Johnny that I realized she was right."

"And that was why you were so willing to give one of them away?"

"Partly. And I knew that Virginia and Alex were their Aunt and Uncle and I was no relation to them. By that time you and I had Tom and Hazel. Please understand," she pleaded, putting her hand on his arm.

He pulled away. "And I suppose I've got to tell Juju? Just like I had to tell her that pack of lies about her birth. Or had you forgotten about her? Over the years I've put up with a lot from you, Eleanor. I've lived with the fact that you never felt for me the way you felt about Johnny. I've put up with your ways of letting me know who's the boss round here. But I can't live with this."

"You can't leave me."

"No, I can't. And I'm not going to. My children need me and I need them and this place, even though it's not mine. I don't need you. My feelings for you are dead."

She burst into tears.

He seized her arms. "Spare your tears for the girl you used as a hoax to get Johnny back!"

"I married you, Greg. When he came back I had a choice. But I married you."

"If I hadn't been here when he came back, would you have let him stay?"

"Yes."

"So why did you send him away? Why did you marry me when he died?"

"Because I loved you. And I'd promised."

"Eleanor, you talk in your sleep. After all these years, it's still his name you say, never mine. And if you'd had a scrap of affection for me you would have told me the truth. You didn't have to tell me who the real mother was. You let me marry you thinking that we could have children of our own when you thought we couldn't." He pulled the door open. "I'm going to find Keith and Juju and tell them they can't get married." He went onto the front verandah. It was raining steadily. He could see two riders in the distance cantering towards the paddock. 'Juju and Keith. Their last moments of happiness,' he thought.

"Dad?" Tom was behind him. "What's up with you and Mum? I heard you shouting."

Greg stared at Tom, regretting that he was witnessing the disintegration of their marriage. "Everything." Then he looked at the sheet of paper in his hand.

Dear Eleanor,

I have to break our secret. The enclosed copies will explain. Fiona has the original. If you had told me why you were angry with me I would have written to you personally or come to see you, but you will have to make do with a copy.

Ruth.

He looked at Tom. "She's telling the truth. This proves she didn't know," he said absently.

"Didn't know what? What's going on, Dad?"

"Someone died. And something died."

"What? Who's died?"

"I'll tell you the whole thing later, Son. But first I've got to tell Juju and Keith."

Ω Ω Ω

Fiona glanced at the clock on the dashboard. "Bloody rain, we'll never get to *Eumeralla* at this rate." She slowed down to drive through the water spread across the road. The gears on the car they had hired at Brisbane airport were unfamiliar and crunched every time she changed them. "Knowing our luck we'll get stuck by floods."

"Don't panic," said Virginia. "Keith and June will be trapped too."

Neither Virginia nor Fiona had had time to change after Ruth's funeral and both wore black dresses, tights and shoes. Gabriella's frantic phone call had come just as they had returned to *Kingower* from the church.

"What's Juju going to do? *Eumeralla* is the only place she's ever lived."

"You could take her to England with you. Buy a farm and start a riding school and organize trekking holidays like at *Kingower*."

Fiona felt cheered. For the rest of the journey she dreamed of a new start and imagined living in the country with June. Remembering her trips around Britain and Ireland she tried to think of the best location. She decided that Cornwall would have the most suitable climate, but that Scotland and the north of England had the most beautiful winters. She wondered if June would be as enchanted by snow as she was. 'I'm being selfish, but I'd be happy if Juju was with me. Rather than me being lonely in London and working for QANTAS we can be together in a farmhouse,' she thought as she took the turning to *Eumeralla*.

Virginia got drenched as she opened the gate. As they walked up the steps, slippery with rain, Fiona's hopes that Tom would be absent from the gathering were dashed when he came onto the verandah to greet them. Memories of the first time she had come to *Eumeralla* invaded her mind. The contrast between the occasions could not have been more marked. Gone was Tom's grin and his cheerful greeting when he had called her Sis. Kim's death and the revelations and grave decisions that had to be made had scarred him.

"You look as if you've jumped in the creek," he said, turning away before her blush became noticeable. "Come to the bathroom and dry yourself off a bit." As they went down the hall her colour subsided.

"Mum's not here. Dad refused to speak to her so she's gone to stay with Hazel," he told them as they rubbed towels over their faces and hair. "She told lies and all that, but she's still my mum."

"I'm sure Greg will understand once he's had time to think," said Virginia.

They took off their shoes and followed him into the lounge. Greg, looking shattered, was sitting on the only part of the sofa where springs were not protruding.

Keith looked sullenly at Gabriella. "You sent for the troops to back you up. I thought that you of all people would understand."

"I'm sorry we told you," said June. She took Keith's hand and led him to the opposite side of the room. The division gave the illusion that they were two armies ready for battle. "We should have just gone and done it. We'd be married by now."

"It would have been invalid," said Greg.

Fiona, feeling scorched by their anger, admired Virginia's composure as she asked them each in turn if they wanted children.

When they both nodded, she put up the first barrier. "You do realize, don't you, that they might be deformed, insane – maybe worse?"

"But we've got different mothers," countered Keith. "The risk can't be that high."

Virginia nodded. "Even marriages between cousins can result in problems. A friend of mine married her cousin. Their daughter is healthy, but both sons are so short-sighted they're almost blind and one is deaf."

"We can adopt," argued June.

"The pill's stopped a lot of unwanted pregnancies," said Virginia. "The waiting lists are long. And what if you got pregnant accidentally? This is harrowing for both of you, but you must think of your children."

"I'll have a hysterectomy," said June.

"Don't be ridiculous," said Fiona. "Keith might die or be killed."

He glowered at her. "Are you trying to make us even more miserable?"

"She's being realistic," Virginia said. "Premature deaths happen a lot in this family."

"Stop trying to wreck our lives!" June cried.

Virginia walked over and held June's arms. "We're trying to

stop you wrecking your own lives. You think you're suffering now – how will you feel if you give birth to a deformed baby? You must split up. This is a tragedy, and not your fault, but if you don't separate future tragedies will be."

"I'll make sure I don't get pregnant."

Virginia's expression became more implacable. "And how many women have said that? Even with the pill accidents happen."

"We'll both take precautions," said Keith. "Tom agrees with us."

"Well, sure, if they're both careful," he said. "And they will be."

"On my birth certificate Jonathan Clarkson was my father. If you all keep quiet no one will ever know any different," June pleaded, trying to pull herself away from Virginia.

"Too many people know already... us and everyone at *Kingower*," said Virginia, resisting June's attempt to free her arms. "They've all been talking about you – "

"Why should any of them care what we do?" asked June. "It's nothing to do with them."

"You're a Lancaster. You've got an Aunty, two uncles and a cousin," said Fiona. "You could go to *Kingower* if you want or – "

"I want to stay here!"

"Then Keith will have to leave," said Virginia.

"There must be another solution," pleaded Tom.

"Can you think of one?" Virginia waited. "No? Neither can I. There are only two choices. Keith leaves or June leaves. Because apart from the genetic problem, there is the matter of incest."

"Which we've already committed," said Keith.

"Unknowingly," said Virginia. "Both of you have good morals. If you get married the knowledge that you are committing incest will prey on your mind and taint your love."

Keith looked at her defiantly. "Nothing could – "

"It will happen insidiously," Virginia cut in. "You won't notice at first. But it'll happen."

Gabriella, looking as if she was too nervous to move, spoke. "I've suffered worse than this. Please believe me when I say that things will get better."

Fiona had a moment of panic. 'Don't tell Tom you've fallen for him yet,' she thought. 'It's too soon after Kim.' To her relief Gabriella simply said that hope had replaced her anguish.

Virginia smiled. "If Gabriella can find hope after the death of her husband, you will too."

June finally pulled her arms free. "It's your fault!"

Keith looked appalled. "No, Juju."

"It is! If you hadn't taken Fiona away none of this would have happened, so shut up you sanctimonious – "

Greg stood up. "June! Don't you dare speak to Virginia like that. This is nothing to do with her. Ruth was the only person who knew who your real father was. You and Keith can't get married, so stop this crazy talk and decide which one of you is staying."

June ran from the room. Keith and Fiona followed her. Out in the hall Fiona seized Keith by the arm. "Stay here – let me." As she ran onto the verandah she saw June heading for the paddock. The wind was driving the rain through the railings and the table and chairs were soaked. The straight skirt of her dress hampered her progress. As she tore off her tights to ease the friction she heard a whimper. It was Toddles. "Go after Juju, quick!"

Burrs pricked her feet as she ran. By the time she reached the paddocks June was with the horses who were gathered under the shelters. Even from the fence Fiona could hear her sobbing. The horses gathered protectively around June who fell to her knees and hugged Toddles. As Fiona climbed over the fence her dress got caught on a splinter of wood. When she failed to free it she tugged it so hard the linen tore. As she headed for the shelters she saw Digger lower his head and nudge June's arm. As soon as she reached them, Fiona knelt in the mud and put her arms around June, relieved that she did not resist. For a few moments she stayed silent.

When she dared to speak she swallowed and said, "I feel the same way about Tom as you feel about Keith. That's why I left *Eumeralla*."

"Oh." For an instant June's expression was sympathetic. Then she laughed bitterly. "Now you know he's not your brother you can stay here while I go into exile alone."

"For Tom it will feel like incest, because he grew up with you. And my presence will remind Keith of you. It'll be a torture for him."

"Anyway, he was never yours, was he? Right from the start you had no hope. But Keith and I were going to get married."

"I'm not trying to belittle your loss, I just wanted to tell you. We can help each other start a new life."

June shook her head. "Doing what?"

"Come to England with me."

"No, I hate cities!"

Startled by the vehemence of June's voice, Toddles jumped up and put his paw on her leg. The rain stopped and Fiona looked at the patches of sky as the clouds scudded away.

"Not London, Juju. There are lots of beautiful places in England – the Lake District, Norfolk, Cornwall and Yorkshire where the Brontës lived. There's Scotland and Wales or we could go to Ireland. Aunty Ruth's left me her house and all her money. You were her daughter too so half of it's yours. We can buy a farm and start a riding school."

June glared at her with scorn. "And live in one of those cute houses with hay on the roof?"

"No." Fiona recalled the bed-and-breakfast places in which she had stayed. "A big farmhouse hundreds of years old with an open fire and an oak staircase and – "

"I want to see trees!"

Fiona smiled. "Trees. There are more trees in England than here ... millions more. It's green and there's plenty of rain – we'll never have to worry about droughts or bush fires. It'll be like *Eumeralla* without the problems. Come with me and give it a try." Desperate to conjure up a seductive picture, she continued, "You'll meet lots of people. The neighbours are close, but not too close. There's so much history. You'll see where your favourite writers and poets came from and the landscape that inspired them. Please, Juju, please."

June sprang to her feet and went over to Digger. "I can't leave everything I love," she wept, putting her head on his neck.

"If you don't leave then Keith will have to. He's got less choices than you. He can't go to *Kingower* – you can if you don't want to leave Australia. He can't come to England with me because if he had to see me every day he'll never be able to get over you and that'll be unfair to him and any girl he has a relationship with. You and I have got each other. If Keith leaves here he's got nothing. Do it for his sake."

To Fiona's profound relief, June nodded.

"We'll buy horses and dogs. I know you feel you're being severed from *Eumeralla*, but, Juju, you'll find other things to love – I promise."

While June packed, Fiona, not wanting to see Tom, stayed outside. Most of the clouds had disappeared and the sun glinted on the drops of water clinging to the bushes and trees. Steam rose from her soaked dress. She was leaning against the trunk of a eucalyptus tree picking burrs out of her feet when she heard someone coming down the steps. It was Tom. His bare feet squelched as he walked over the grass towards her.

"Ah, Sis. I've come to say good-bye."

She wanted to say something memorable, but her mind blanked. "Good-bye," she whispered.

"It's all ... so ... I don't know. Kick me so I'll wake up and Kim will be alive and things back to normal." Suddenly he put his arms around her and hugged her fiercely.

With a jolt of compassion Fiona realized he was crying. She stroked his dark curls and inhaled his smell of soap and the clean cotton shirt still scented with the pure air in which it had dried on the clothes line.

"Kim would have been ace for *Eumeralla*. We all liked her ... Mum, Dad. On that last ride I thought about us living here and raising a family." He pulled away and thrust his hands in the pocket of his jeans and pulled out a handkerchief. "Sorry, Sis, I'm being a sissy."

"You're not."

"I haven't cried since I was ten when my horse died. Well, not in front of anyone," he admitted.

Knowing this would be the last time she saw him she gazed at his tanned face and brown eyes, wishing she could fling herself into his arms and tell him she loved him. The urge to kiss him was so powerful she took a step backwards.

He blew his nose and put the handkerchief back in his pocket. "You're a trooper, Sis."

She blushed. "I'm used to it. As my father said, my life has been a series of shocks and upheavals. This is just one more. I've built up a lot of scar tissue over the years. Juju's a mess because she's never experienced real pain."

"It's the best thing to do ... taking her to England, but I'll miss her a lot. Christ, I'll miss you both."

"You could visit us." She bit her lip and looked at the ground. She thought, 'When I've settled down and met someone else and no longer have romantic thoughts about you.'

"Do you want to get married?"

She nodded. "And have lots of children."

"You and Juju will write, won't you?"

"Yes – and we'll send photos too."

He reached out and touched her cheek.

Desperate not to break down she whispered. "We don't want to both be howling our eyes out ... there's been enough rain already."

"I won't see you again for a long time. By then I hope we'll all be married with children. Keith too." He held out his hand. "Bye, Sis. Good luck."

She shook his hand, but was unable to speak. Her throat ached as she watched him walk away. When she was alone she allowed herself to cry. Gabriella came from round the front of the house. Unable to stop the flow of tears she stared mutely at the ground.

"Aunty Virginia and Juju are nearly ready to leave." She took Fiona's hand. "My sister. It's just beginning to sink in. I wish you could both stay, but I know you can't. And it's time for me to take stock of my life. I'm going to sell my house."

"Do you want to come to England with us?" Fiona asked.

"No. Keith needs me. I'm thinking of buying into *Eumeralla*. What do you reckon?"

"Because of Tom?"

"Yes. I want to be near Keith too, but I love this place and the life. What do you think?"

Fiona considered how Gabriella would feel if Tom never became interested in her and how desolate she would be if he fell in love with someone else. She was about to try and persuade her to come to England when the memory of Keith's haunted face struck her and she knew it would be unfair for him to lose Gabriella too.

"If you buy into *Eumeralla*, and Tom's not interested in you romantically, you'll be stuck here. Eleanor's the only other female." She saw Gabriella's expression of disappointment. "But there's another option. Rent your house out, come to *Eumeralla* for a few months and see how things work out – that way you've got nothing to lose."

"Do you reckon I've got a chance ... with Tom?"

"I hope so, Gabby. I really do. But don't let him know too soon. He's still broken up over Kim. But the Darling Downs isn't swarming with women, so yes, I reckon your chances are good."

Dalby
February 1973

For Juju and me the truth is the same, but for her the consequences have been much more traumatic. We are staying at Gabby's till we fly to Melbourne – I've got to put as much distance between her and Keith as I can. The sale of Aunty Ruth's house will take about eight weeks, but Dad said we should leave sooner than that and he'll send us the money. If we arrive in England in the spring its beauty might lift Juju's spirits.

I've known three mothers. Virginia who adopted me. Eleanor, the woman I thought was my natural mother and Ruth who really is. Actually there are four. Eleanor had two personas, the real one and the fictitious one I had believed for years before Juju's advent enlightened me.

Four mothers and three fathers. Alex will always be Dad to me. Johnny the coward and Johnny the hero. And Laurence. Grief stricken Laurence.

Last night I swore to the fates that Juju and I will find happiness. We will buy a farm in England. We will start a riding school. We will fall in love and get married. We will have children. We will. We will.

Ω Ω Ω

Greg was preparing a plot for the winter vegetables when he heard a car. Shading his eyes he saw it was Hazel's, but the only occupant was Eleanor. As soon as she began to walk towards him, he was aware that she looked ten years younger. The grey streaks in her hair had gone. It was shorter and the gleaming dark curls were the same colour as they had been thirty years ago. The navy trousers and white cotton shirt were new. He wondered, with a sense of panic, how much her transformation had cost.

"Greg, I've got something important to tell you."

Hardening his voice he said, "More lies? The most useful thing you can do is change out of those posh clothes and get to work." He thrust his shovel into the wheelbarrow and lifted out a pile of manure.

"I've made a decision about *Eumeralla*."

He saw her satisfied expression, and was furious with himself for displaying his fear. He tried and failed to sound calm. "What about it?"

"Let's go inside and sit down."

"I haven't got time."

"If that's the way you want it I'll get a solicitor to notify you." She began to walk away.

"Wait, Eleanor. Please."

She went onto the verandah and sat down, leaving him no choice but to follow.

"Okay. What are you going to do?"

She rested her elbows on the table and linked her fingers. He saw that she had even had a manicure and wore clear nail polish. As he caught a whiff of perfume he realized she was wearing make-up. Barely discernible, he only knew because her lips gleamed, her cheeks were pink and she had plucked her eyebrows. Signalling his indifference by not bothering to wash his hands, he sat opposite her.

"Greg, a long time ago I made two mistakes. The first one was sending Johnny away and the second was marrying you. I refuse to apologize that I didn't tell you about Ruth."

"You've got a cheek. You knew how I felt about having children."

"I was giving you children – twin girls that would grow up thinking you were their father. I'd suffered because of Johnny's obsession – I wasn't going to endure all that again with another man."

"That's all I was to you, wasn't it? Another man. It could have been any man, but I was around at the time and you knew me. Saved you a lot of trouble, didn't it? I don't want to listen to your excuses. Get to the point. What about *Eumeralla*?"

"No. I'll tell you this my way in my time. I'm not giving you excuses – I'm giving you reasons. The time for charades is over. You accused me of never loving you and I denied it. For years I denied it to myself. But you were right. I didn't love you and I never have. I wanted to and I tried, but I couldn't. I was grateful to you and sorry I couldn't feel more."

Hiding his pain, he scowled.

"And I've ceased to be grateful to you," she continued. "Because if you revile me for one lie I don't think that you ever loved me either."

Her accusation infuriated him. "Are you trying to soothe your conscience, or what? I wanted to marry you for ages, but Johnny got there first. You're the one who killed my feelings for you so don't try and make it my fault."

"Greg, you never listened to what I wanted. *Eumeralla* was mine and you took over the running of it. Anything you wanted we got and anything I wanted we didn't. The children were so completely yours ... except Hazel. The thing I wanted most was a flushing toilet – and we still haven't got it."

"Because they cost a fortune."

"We've got thousands stashed away in the bank. I didn't know how much till I went to Brisbane and checked. You immediately took over the money and left me out."

"If I hadn't we'd have been bankrupt with all your fancy schemes."

"One flushing toilet would have bankrupted us? Was *Eumeralla* bankrupt when you arrived on the scene? I'm capable of managing money – I did all right when Johnny left. You're a miser."

"I did what I did for the family. For you ... for all of us. Your accusations are unfair."

"And so is your judgement of me. I can't live like this any more. I'm moving to Brisbane. I've rented a flat near Hazel."

"What?" He felt sick. "You can't sell *Eumeralla*."

"I could. It's mine." She said nothing further.

"Get on with it, Eleanor."

"When I'm ready. I want you to suffer the same unhappiness that I've had."

He didn't care any more that his misery was transparent. "I never thought we'd come to this ... deliberately hurting each other."

"Neither did I," she said more gently. "I'm not selling *Eumeralla*. I'm going to give it to Tom and Neil and Keith if he wants it. He's already a part owner."

His face regained some of its colour. "Thanks." He reached over and took her hands. "Stay here. We need you. How are you going to pay the rent for this stupid flat in Brisbane? The money in the bank's our insurance against disaster."

"It's not a stupid flat. It's clean and modern. It's got – "

"But how are you going to pay the rent?"

"Don't panic about money. I had an interview yesterday and I start work on Monday."

"You've got a job?"

His astonishment made her laugh. "Yes. With an insurance company. I start at nine, finish at five, an hour for lunch and four weeks' holiday a year. The pay's good too. So I'll be independent. You won't miss me – you'll just miss the extra person to share the work."

"I'm sorry you think like that. It's not true." He stood up and went over to the verandah rails. "You never loved *Eumeralla* the way I did. Even though it was yours."

"When I was young I did." She sounded wistful. "And when I was here with Johnny. It's when you took over that I began to dislike it. Johnny and I had fun in the early days ... before the urge for children became desperate, and the months were not just the passing of time, but if I was pregnant or not. Marriage to you was a chore."

Greg turned and looked at her. "I'm sorry I made things difficult for you. I was frightened about losing all our money. If things don't work out in the city, I'll welcome you back here and when you go I'll miss you. Tom and Neil will too – and not just because of the work. It won't be much good here now – all coves together. The last few days have been dismal. Keith's broken up about Juju, Tom's still sad about Kim and I'm cut up about you. I'll have to encourage the lads to get married."

"When we get divorced maybe you'll find someone else."

He snorted. "Divorce. Is that what you want?"

She nodded.

"My feelings for you were true, Eleanor. I don't want any other woman – I never have. Would it have made a difference if I'd got a flushing toilet?"

She smiled wryly. "The success of a marriage depending on something so mundane ... sounds mad, doesn't it? But yes, I would have known that what I wanted was important."

"If you hadn't told me the truth just now about not loving me – I would have gone into town and got one right now. Is it too late?"

"Yes."

He sighed. "What did Hazel say?"

"She had no idea I'd harboured such secrets. She thought it was dramatic and thrilling."

"She would." He shook his head in disgust. "She's superficial."

"Just because she doesn't like *Eumeralla*?"

"No. The only things that interest her are boys and clothes, going to the pictures and having a good time. Her reaction disappoints me, but I expected it."

"Did you want her to condemn me?"

"No, Eleanor. She should have had some pity. It doesn't upset her that our marriage is over or that Juju can't marry Keith. And it bothers me that you're going to live in Brisbane near her. She'll be to busy going out to keep you company."

"Hazel's normal. She believes life is fun and people should be happy. You're the superficial one. And you've made Tom, Juju and Neil just like you. Your passion for *Eumeralla*'s stunted you all. You're contemptuous about anyone who lives in a city. I won't be lonely. Contrary to your opinion of city people, the ones I've met so far are friendly. I can walk to the shops and I'm going to buy some more decent clothes."

He envisaged going to the bank and finding there was no money in the account. "Make sure it's your own money you spend."

"Stop being dictatorial or I'll demand my share," she retorted. "I've been to the hairdresser and Hazel's bought me perfume and make-up."

"I had noticed."

"I was sick of looking older than I am. I want to be smart like

Virginia. I'll go down to Sydney and ask her to help me choose more new clothes. I'll buy a car too – a new one."

"Oh, Eleanor, I don't know you any more."

"You never knew me." She stood up. "Well, it's time to go and tell Tom and Neil."

As she walked to the steps, he put his hand out and touched her arm. "Hang on. Last week you told me you married me because you loved me. Now you tell me you didn't – so when Johnny came back, why did you send him away? Were you punishing him at my expense?"

"No. You'd proposed to me and I'd said yes. I didn't want to hurt you, Greg. We'd had such fun together when we were children. I keep my promises. I almost broke it though. Sending Johnny away was the hardest thing I ever did. I knew I'd made the wrong decision. I intended to tell you I wanted Johnny back, but I couldn't bring myself to hurt you. Besides I wouldn't have been free to marry you for another two and a half years. I thought I had plenty of time. But I didn't. One week ... that's all I had. It was so hard. I felt that my promise to marry you was the same as my vow to Ruth. The promise you made to me in church didn't mean the same though, did it? As soon as you found out I'd deceived you, you stopped loving me. It's all been for nothing," she said bitterly. "I could have broken our engagement and let Johnny come back. He'd still be alive ... nowhere near that fire. We would have been happy."

"How? Your happiness would have been based on the lie that Juju and Fiona were his."

"I wouldn't have had to lie for long – after all I'd thought for years that they were his daughters."

"Exactly. Surely it would have killed your trust?"

"I blamed Ruth."

"Would you ever have tackled him about it?"

"No."

"And the continuation of your marriage to him would have been based on a lie – just as ours was. Johnny only came back because of the twins – not because of you. You must have loved him a lot more than he loved you."

She turned her back on him, but not before he had seen how his words had wounded her.

"I'll go and find Neil and Tom and tell them what I've decided."

Greg stood on the verandah and watched her walk to the car. Long after she'd driven away he gazed at the spot where she had vanished from view. When he went into the bedroom he saw that she had left her wedding ring on the chest of drawers. Beside it was the leather box that had contained the wedding ring Jonathan had given her. It was empty.

Tom and Neil came back to the house. Keith was setting the table and had almost convinced Greg that Eleanor would never leave once she had talked to her sons. Greg saw from their dazed expressions that he had been foolish to hope.

"She's gone. She's not coming back," said Tom.

"We tried to persuade her to stay." Neil shook his head.

"I'm sorry," said Greg. "I was too harsh and unforgiving." He put their plates of salad and bread and butter on the table. Keith had set a place for Eleanor, but unable to stand the sight of the empty chair he took it and the cutlery into the kitchen. The events of the past few months had been so cataclysmic that he found it difficult to believe that he had looked forward to anything. The prospect of Kim and Tom getting married and living on *Eumeralla* and having children had compensated for the decline in his agility and the ache in his bones when he got up in the morning. Although he had been concerned about any children Keith and June might have, he had reassured himself that if the risk was too great cousins would not be permitted to marry. He had seen himself and Eleanor teaching their grandchildren to ride and nurture the land. In their old age they would know that when they died *Eumeralla* would be safe for another generation. Instead, four sorrowing men were left and he wondered how it would survive.

Toddles circled the table whimpering in distress. Neil bent down to stroke her. Red lay near the steps with his head on his front legs, looking doleful.

"They can sense everything's gone wrong in paradise," said Tom.

Keith pushed his plate away. "Heaven. It was heaven for me ... the few months it lasted. The land and Juju."

"You've still got the land," said Greg.

Keith nodded. "Thanks."

Greg wished that he had hidden his anger from Eleanor. The knowledge that she had never loved him pierced his heart and although he had never believed in living a lie, that was what he now wanted. The truth was too painful.

"It's gone upside down," said Neil. "Tom and I've lost two sisters and you've got two sisters, but they're going to England and we'll never see them again."

Greg saw Neil's bewilderment and wished he could comfort him. He tried to laugh. It came out like a cough. "We're a miserable lot of coves. I can hear a car!" His face lit up.

They jumped up, ran to the rails and looked down. It was Gabriella.

She ran up the steps and stood uncertainly. "I just saw Eleanor ... she told me ... I'm sorry," she said.

Tom set a place for her. "You're just in time for dinner."

She hovered by the chair. "I was wondering if I could stay here for a few months and – "

"You can stay forever if you like," said Tom.

"I was going to give it a try," she said with a smile. "And if things work out I can sell my house and buy in, if that's okay."

"You sure can!" said Greg.

"Beaut," said Neil. "As long as you don't mind being the only woman."

Tom, looking happier than he had since Kim's death, stood up and hugged her. "Welcome to *Eumeralla*, Gabby."

Ω   Ω   Ω

The urn containing Ruth's ashes was heavy. Fiona cradled it in her arms as she walked through the cemetery. She got lost several times before she found the grave she was looking for. Standing in the sun in front of Laurence's headstone she took the top off the urn and stared at the ashes inside. They were pale and coarse. She had expected them to be dark-grey and powdery. Holding the urn with both hands she turned it upside down. When it was empty she placed it on the grave and walked away.

Thank you for buying this publication.

POPHAM GARDENS PUBLISHING

If you would like to find out more about

Popham Gardens Publishing

please visit our web site at:

www.publishingforyou.com

or e-mail us on:

enquiries@publishingforyou.com

If you have enjoyed this novel and would like to recommend it to a friend it is available from Amazon.com as a paperback or as a Kindle download.

Printed in Great Britain
by Amazon.co.uk, Ltd.,
Marston Gate.